MAIGRET'S
CHRISTMAS

SIMENON

MAIGRET'S CHRISTMAS

NINE STORIES

Translated from the French by
JEAN STEWART

A HARVEST BOOK
A HELEN AND KURT WOLFF BOOK
HARCOURT, INC.
Orlando   Austin   New York   San Diego   Toronto   London

"Maigret's Christmas" and "Seven Little Crosses in a Notebook" first
published in France 1951 under the titles *Un Noël de Maigret* and
Sept Petites Croix dans un carnet, copyright © 1951 by Georges Simenon;
"Maigret and the Surly Inspector," "The Evidence of the Altar-boy,"
"The Most Obstinate Customer in the World," and "Death of a Nobody"
first published in France 1947 under the titles *Maigret et l'inspecteur
malgracieux, Le Témoignage de l'enfant de choeur, Le Client le plus obstiné du
monde,* and *On ne tue pas les pauvres types,* copyright © 1947 by Georges
Simenon; "Sale by Auction" and "The Man in the Street" first published
in France 1950 under the titles *Vente à bougie* and *L'Homme dans la rue*
(from *Maigret et les petits cochons sans queue*), copyright © 1950 by Georges
Simenon; "Maigret in Retirement" first published in France 1949 under
the title *Maigret se fâche,* copyright © 1949 by Georges Simenon.

Library of Congress Cataloging-in-Publication Data
Simenon, Georges, 1903–1989
Maigret's Christmas.
A Harvest book
"A Helen and Kurt Wolff book."
Contents: Maigret's Christmas.—Seven little crosses in a notebook.
—Maigret and the surly inspector. [etc.]
1. Detective and mystery stories, French—Translations into English.
2. Detective and mystery stories, English—Translations from French.
I. Title.
PZ3.S5892Maih5 [PQ2637.I53] 843'.9'12 77-1724
ISBN 0-15-602853-0

Text set in Ehrhardt

Printed in the United States of America
A C E G I K J H F D B

Contents

Maigret's Christmas   1

Seven Little Crosses in a Notebook   62

Maigret and the Surly Inspector   126

The Evidence of the Altar Boy   163

The Most Obstinate Customer in the World   196

Death of a Nobody   233

Sale by Auction   267

The Man in the Street   282

Maigret in Retirement   297

MAIGRET'S
CHRISTMAS

Maigret's Christmas

I

It always happened like that. Presumably he had said with a sigh as he went to bed: 'Tomorrow I shall have a long lie-in.'

And Madame Maigret had taken him at his word, as if the years had taught her nothing, as if she did not know better than to pay attention to such casual remarks. She could quite well have slept late herself. She had no reason to get up early.

And yet, even before it was quite light, he had heard her moving cautiously about in the bedclothes. He had not stirred. He had forced himself to go on breathing deeply and regularly, as if he were asleep. It was a kind of game. There was something touching about the way she edged across the bed, pausing after every movement to make sure that he had not woken up. He invariably waited in suspense for the moment when the springs of the bed, relieved of his wife's weight, would relax with a slight sound like a sigh.

Then she would pick up her clothes from the chair, take an inordinate time turning the handle of the bathroom door, and at last, in the distant kitchen, allow herself to move about in a normal way.

He had fallen asleep again, not deeply and not for long; just long enough to have a confused and uneasy dream. He could not remember it afterwards, but he knew it had been disturbing and it left him feeling unusually sensitive.

A streak of pale, bleak daylight was visible between the curtains, which never quite met. He waited a little longer, lying on his back with his eyes open. He could smell coffee, and when he heard the door of the flat open and close again, he knew that Madame Maigret had hurried down to go and buy him some hot croissants.

Usually he took nothing for breakfast but a cup of black coffee. But this was another ritual, one of his wife's notions. On Sundays and holidays he was supposed to lie in bed till late in the morning, while she went to fetch croissants for him from the corner of the Rue Amelot.

He got up, put on his dressing gown and slippers and drew the curtains. He knew that he was doing the wrong thing and that she'd be distressed. He was prepared to make great sacrifices to give her pleasure, but not to stay in bed when he no longer wanted to.

It was not snowing. When one was past fifty it was absurd to be disappointed because there was no snow on Christmas morning, but elderly people are never quite as sensible as the young imagine.

The low, dense, off-white sky seemed to lie heavily on the roofs. The Boulevard Richard-Lenoir was completely deserted, and across the street, above the main gate of the warehouse, the words *Entrepôt Légal, Fils et Cie* stood out in pitch-black letters. The *E,* heaven knows why, looked particularly gloomy.

He heard his wife going about the kitchen again, tiptoeing into the dining room, still moving gingerly because she did not realize that he was up, standing by the window. When he looked at his watch on the bedside table he realized that it was only ten minutes past eight.

They had been to the theatre the night before. They would have liked to go to a restaurant afterwards for something to eat, like everybody else, but everywhere tables had been reserved for midnight suppers, and so they had walked home arm in arm. They had got in just before midnight and had not had long to wait before giving each other their presents.

His was a pipe, as usual. Hers was an electric coffeepot of the latest model, which she had wanted, and for the sake of tradition a dozen finely embroidered handkerchiefs.

He filled his new pipe automatically. In some of the houses on the other side of the boulevard the windows had Venetian blinds; in others, not. Few people seemed to be up. Only here and there a light was on, probably because somebody's children had got up early to rush and look at the toys round the Christmas tree.

Maigret and his wife would spend a peaceful morning together in their cosy flat. He would sit about late in his dressing gown, without shaving, and chat with his wife in the kitchen while she prepared lunch.

He was not feeling sad. It was just that his dream—which he could still not remember—had left him feeling peculiarly sensitive. And perhaps after all it was not his dream, but just Christmas. He'd have to be very careful today, weighing his words, as careful as Madame Maigret had been getting out of bed, because she, too, would be in a rather more emotional state than usual.

Hush! He must not think of that. He must say nothing that could suggest such thoughts. He must not look into the street too often, presently, when the youngsters began showing off their toys on the pavements.

There were children in most, if not all, of the houses. Soon there would be heard the sound of shrill trumpets, drums and popguns. Little girls were already cradling their dolls.

Once, many years ago, he had remarked casually:

'Why don't we take advantage of Christmas to go off for a trip somewhere?'

'Go off where?' she had asked with her unassailable common sense.

Go and see whom? They hadn't even any relatives to visit, apart from her sister, who lived too far away. To stay in a hotel in a strange town, or an inn in some country place?

Hush! It was time to drink his coffee, and afterwards he would feel steadier. He was never at his best before that first cup of coffee and his first pipe.

Just as he was reaching out towards the handle of the door it opened noiselessly, and Madame Maigret appeared, carrying a tray; she looked at the empty bed and then at him, disappointed, almost on the verge of tears.

'You've got up!'

She was looking fresh and spruce already, with her hair neatly done and wearing a light-coloured apron.

'And I was looking forward to bringing you breakfast in bed!'

He had so often tried, tactfully, to make her realize that this was no treat for him, that it didn't agree with him, that it made him feel like an invalid or a cripple, but breakfast in bed still remained her ideal for Sundays and holidays.

'Won't you go back to bed?'

No! He couldn't face that.

'Come along then . . . Happy Christmas!'

'Happy Christmas! You're not vexed with me?'

They were in the dining room, with the silver tray on one corner of the table, the steaming cups of coffee, the golden-brown croissants in a napkin.

Laying down his pipe, he ate a croissant to please her, but he remained standing up, and commented as he looked out of the window:

'It's snow-dust.'

It was not true snow. A kind of fine white dust was falling from the sky and it reminded him how, when he was small, he used to put out his tongue to catch a few tiny particles.

His gaze settled on the door of the house opposite, to the left of the warehouse. Two women had just come out, bareheaded. One of them, a blonde of about thirty, had flung a coat loosely over her shoulders; the other, an older woman, was huddled in a shawl.

The fair woman seemed to hesitate, as though ready to beat a retreat. The dark one, a thin little creature, was being insistent, and Maigret had the impression that she was indicating his own windows. Then the concierge appeared in the doorway behind them, as though coming to the rescue of the thin woman, and the blonde finally made up her mind to cross the street, casting an anxious glance behind her.

'What are you looking at?'

'Nothing . . . Some women . . .'

'What are they doing?'

'They seem to be coming here.'

For the pair of them, in the middle of the boulevard, were looking up in his direction.

'I hope they're not going to disturb you on Christmas day. I haven't even done my housework.'

Nobody would have noticed that, for apart from the tray there was nothing lying about and no speck of dust on the polished furniture.

'Are you certain they're coming here?'

'We shall see.'

He took the precaution of going to comb his hair, brush his teeth and splash some water on his face. He was still in the bedroom, re-lighting his pipe, when he heard a ring at the door. Madame Maigret must have put up some resistance, for it was a little time before she came to fetch him.

'They insist on speaking to you,' she whispered. 'They say it may be important, that they need advice. I know one of them.'

'Which one?'

'The little skinny one, Mademoiselle Doncoeur. She lives across the street on the same floor as ours, and she spends all day working beside her window. She's a very respectable person, who does fine embroidery for a shop in the Faubourg Saint-Honoré. I've sometimes wondered whether she might not be in love with you.'

'Why?'

'Because when you leave the house she frequently gets up to watch you go off.'

'How old is she?'

'Forty-five or fifty. Aren't you going to get dressed?'

Surely, when people came and disturbed him at home, at half-past eight on a Christmas morning, he was entitled to appear in his dressing gown? He pulled on a pair of trousers under it, however, then he opened the door of the dining room, where the two women were standing.

'Forgive me, ladies . . .'

Perhaps Madame Maigret had been right after all, for Mademoiselle Doncoeur did not blush but turned pale, lost her smile for a moment and then recovered it, and opened her mouth without finding anything to say right away.

As for the blonde, who was in perfect control of herself, she remarked somewhat petulantly:

'It wasn't me that wanted to come.'

'Won't you sit down?'

He observed that the blonde was only partly dressed under her coat and wore no stockings, whereas Mademoiselle Doncoeur was in her Sunday best.

'You may wonder at our being bold enough to come to you,' the latter began, choosing her words with care. 'Of course, like everyone else in the neighbourhood, we know whom we're privileged to have living among us...'

By now she was blushing a little and staring at the ceiling.

'We're preventing you from finishing your breakfast.'

'I had finished. Go on.'

'This morning, or rather last night, something happened in our building, something so disturbing that I immediately thought it was our duty to speak to you about it. Madame Martin didn't want to bother you. I told her...'

'Do you live across the street too, Madame Martin?'

'Yes, Monsieur.'

She was clearly annoyed at having been forced to take this step. As for Mademoiselle Doncoeur, she had started off again.

'We live on the same floor, just opposite your windows' (and she blushed again, as if this constituted a confession). 'Monsieur Martin is often away on business, which is quite understandable since he's a commercial traveller. For the past two months their little girl has been in bed, as the result of a silly accident.'

Maigret turned politely to the blonde.

'You have a daughter, Madame Martin?'

'That's to say she's not our daughter but our niece. Her mother died a little over two years ago, and since then the child has been living with us. She broke her leg in the stairway, and she would have recovered after six weeks if there hadn't been complications.'

'Is your husband out of town at the moment?'

'He's probably in the Dordogne.'

'Go on, please, Mademoiselle Doncoeur.'

Madame Maigret had gone back to the kitchen by way of the bathroom, and the clatter of pans could be heard. From time to time Maigret glanced out at the livid sky.

'This morning I got up early as usual, to go to the first Mass.'

'You went to it?'

'Yes. I got back about half-past seven, for I heard three Masses. I prepared my breakfast. You may have seen a light in my window.'

He indicated that he had not noticed.

'I was eager to take Colette a few little presents, because this is such a wretched Christmas for her. Colette is Madame Martin's niece.'

'How old is she?'

'Seven. That's right, isn't it, Madame Martin?'

'She'll be seven in January.'

'At eight o'clock I knocked at the door of Madame Martin's flat.'

'I wasn't up,' said the blonde woman. 'I sometimes sleep late.'

'As I was saying, I knocked and Madame Martin kept me waiting a few minutes, while she put on her dressing gown. I was carrying my presents for Colette and I asked if I could take them to her.'

He was aware that the blonde had had time to scrutinize everything in the room, and was meanwhile casting an occasional sharp, suspicious glance at him.

'We opened the door of the child's room together.'

'She has a bedroom to herself?'

'Yes. The flat consists of two bedrooms, a *cabinet de toilette*, a dining room and a kitchen. But I must tell you . . . No! that comes later. I'd got to where we opened the door. As it was dark in the room, Madame Martin switched on the electric light.'

'Was Colette awake?'

'Yes. You could see that she'd been lying awake for a long time, waiting. You know what children are like on Christmas morning. If she'd been able to use her legs she'd certainly have got up to see what

Father Christmas had brought her. Maybe another child would have called out. But Colette is a very mature little girl. You feel that she thinks a lot, that she's much older than her age.'

Madame Martin now glanced out of the window, and Maigret tried to guess which her flat was. Probably the one on the right, at the far end of the block, where two windows were lighted.

Mademoiselle Doncoeur went on:

'I wished her a Merry Christmas. I said to her, and these were my very words: "Look, darling, what Father Christmas has left in my room for you."'

Madame Martin's fingers were twitching uneasily.

'And do you know what she answered me, without looking to see what I'd brought her—they were only trifles, anyway.

'"I saw him."

'"Who did you see?"

'"Father Christmas."

'"When did you see him? Where?"

'"Here, last night. He came into my room."

'That's what she told us, wasn't it, Madame Martin? Coming from any other child it would just have made you smile, but as I told you, Colette is a very mature little girl. She wasn't joking.

'"How could you have seen him in the dark?"

'"He had a light."

'"Did he switch on the electric light?"

'"No. He had a torch. Look, maman Loraine..."

'Because I must tell you that the child calls Madame Martin maman, which is quite natural since she's lost her own mother and Madame Martin looks after her...'

It had all begun to sound like a confused buzzing in Maigret's ears. He hadn't drunk his second cup of coffee, and his pipe had gone out.

'Did she really see somebody?' he queried without conviction.

'Yes, Superintendent. And that's why I insisted on Madame Martin coming to speak to you. We have a proof of it. The little girl gave a knowing smile and lifted the sheet to show us, lying beside her in the bed, a magnificent doll which hadn't been in the house the day before.'

'You hadn't given her a doll, Madame Martin?'

'I was going to give her one, not nearly such a fine one, which I had bought yesterday afternoon at the Galeries. I was holding it behind my back when we went into the room.'

'So that means that somebody came into your flat during the night?'

'And that's not everything,' hastily broke in Mademoiselle Doncoeur, who was now well under way. 'Colette's not the sort of child who would tell a lie or make a mistake. We questioned her, Madame Martin and I. She's certain she saw someone dressed as Father Christmas, with a white beard and a big red coat.'

'What time was it when she woke up?'

'She doesn't know. It was during the night. She opened her eyes because she thought she saw a light, and there actually was a light in the room, shining on part of the floor in front of the fireplace.'

'I can't understand what it all means,' sighed Madame Martin. 'Unless my husband knows more about it than I do...'

Mademoiselle Doncoeur was determined to keep control of the conversation. It was obviously she who had questioned the child without sparing her a single detail, just as it was she who had thought of consulting Maigret.

'Colette told us that Father Christmas had been crouching down, doing something on the floor.'

'Wasn't she frightened?'

'No. She watched him, and this morning she told us he had been making a hole in the floor. She thought he wanted to go down through it to the Delormes' flat below, where there's a little boy of three, and she added that the chimney was probably too narrow.

'The man must have felt that he was being watched. Apparently he got up, came over to the bed and deposited a big doll on it, laying a finger to his lips.'

'Did she see him go out?'

'Yes.'

'Through the floor?'

'No. By the door.'

'Into which room in the flat does this door lead?'

'It opens directly on to the passage. This is a room which used to be let out separately. It communicates both with the passage and with the rest of the flat.'

'It wasn't locked?'

'It was locked,' broke in Madame Martin. 'I wouldn't have left the child in a room that wasn't properly shut.'

'Had the door been forced?'

'Probably. I don't know. Mademoiselle Doncoeur immediately suggested coming to see you.'

'Did you discover a hole in the floor?'

Madame Martin shrugged her shoulders as though in exasperation, but the older woman answered for her.

'Not a hole strictly speaking, but you can see that some boards have been lifted up.'

'Tell me, Madame Martin, have you any idea what there might have been under that floor?'

'No, Monsieur.'

'Have you been living in this flat a long time?'

'Since I got married five years ago.'

'Did this room already form part of the flat?'

'Yes.'

'Do you know who lived there before you?'

'My husband did. He's thirty-eight. When I married him he was thirty-three already and he had a place of his own; he liked to have a home to come back to after his business trips.'

'Don't you think he might have wanted to give Colette a surprise?'

'He's six or seven hundred kilometres away from here.'

'Do you know where?'

'Most likely in Bergerac. His trips are organized beforehand and it's unusual for him not to keep to the timetable.'

'What is his line?'

'He's the representative of Zenith watches for the central and southwestern region. It's a very big firm, as you probably know, and he has an excellent job.'

'He's the best man in the world!' exclaimed Mademoiselle Doncoeur, and then corrected herself, blushing, 'Next to yourself!'

'In short, if I've understood aright, somebody broke into your flat last night disguised as Father Christmas?'

'So the child declares.'

'Did you hear nothing? Is your bedroom far from the child's?'

'There's the dining room between them.'

'Don't you leave the communicating doors open at night?'

'It isn't necessary. Colette is not a timid child, and she doesn't usually wake up. If she needs me she has a little brass bell on the bedside table beside her.'

'Did you go out last night?'

'No, Superintendent,' she replied curtly, sounding annoyed.

'You received no visitors?'

'I'm not in the habit of receiving visitors in my husband's absence.'

Maigret glanced at Mademoiselle Doncoeur, who remained unmoved, which implied that this must be the truth.

'Did you go to bed late?'

'As soon as the radio had played "Midnight, Christians". I had been reading until then.'

'Did you hear anything unusual?'

'Nothing.'

'Did you ask the concierge if she pulled the cord to let in any stranger?'

Mademoiselle Doncoeur interrupted again: 'I spoke to her about it. She says she didn't.'

'And this morning, you found nothing missing, Madame Martin? You didn't get the impression that anyone had been into the dining room?'

'No.'

'Who is with the child just now?'

'Nobody. She's used to being alone. I can't stop at home all day. There's the shopping to be done ...'

'I understand. Colette is an orphan, you told me?'

'Her mother's dead.'

'Then her father is still living? Where is he? Who is he?'

'He's my husband's brother, Paul Martin. As for saying where he is...' She waved her arms vaguely.

'When did you last see him?'

'At least a month ago. More than that. About All Saints' Day. He was just finishing one of his bouts.'

'What did you say?'

She replied with a touch of ill-humour:

'I may as well tell you at once, since now we're deep in family problems.'

She was obviously feeling resentful towards Mademoiselle Doncoeur, whom she held responsible for the situation.

'My brother-in-law, particularly since he lost his wife, is no longer a respectable person.'

'What exactly do you mean?'

'He drinks. He used to drink before, but not to excess, and he never got himself into trouble. He was in a regular job, quite a good job in a furniture store in the Faubourg Saint-Antoine. Since the accident...'

'The accident to his daughter?'

'I mean the one that caused his wife's death. One Sunday he took it into his head to borrow a friend's car and take his wife and child into the country. Colette was quite small then.'

'When did this happen?'

'About three years ago. They went for lunch to a riverside inn near Mantes-la-Jolie. Paul couldn't resist drinking too much white wine, and it went to his head. On the way back to Paris he was singing at the top of his voice, and the accident occurred near Bougival bridge. His wife was killed on the spot. He himself had his skull fractured, and only escaped death by a miracle. Colette was unhurt. Since then he's been only half a man. We took in the little girl, we practically adopted her. He comes to see her from time to time, but only when he's more or less sober. Then he relapses immediately afterwards...'

'Do you know where he lives?'

A vague gesture. 'Anywhere. We've met him slouching about in the Bastille area, like a beggar. Sometimes he sells newspapers in the street. I'm telling you this in front of Mademoiselle Doncoeur because unfortunately the whole house knows about it.'

'Don't you think he might have had the idea of dressing up as Father Christmas to pay his daughter a visit?'

'That's what I said to Mademoiselle Doncoeur right away. She insisted on our coming to consult you all the same.'

'Because he'd have had no reason to raise the floorboards,' Mademoiselle Doncoeur retorted rather tartly.

'Who knows if your husband might not have returned to Paris sooner than he expected and . . .'

'It must be something of the sort. I'm not worried. If it hadn't been for Mademoiselle Doncoeur . . .'

Again! Decidedly, she had not crossed the boulevard of her own free will.

'Can you tell me where your husband is likely to be staying?'

'At the Hôtel de Bordeaux in Bergerac.'

'Didn't you think of telephoning him?'

'There's no telephone in the house, except in the first floor flat, and the people there don't like being bothered.'

'Have you any objection to my ringing up the Hôtel de Bordeaux?'

She consented at first, then demurred: 'He'll wonder what's going on.'

'You can speak to him.'

'He's not used to my telephoning him.'

'Would you rather be left in uncertainty?'

'No. Just as you like. I'll speak to him.'

He lifted the receiver and asked for the call. Ten minutes later the Hôtel de Bordeaux was on the line; he handed the receiver to Madame Martin.

'Hello! I would like to speak to Monsieur Martin, please. Monsieur Jean Martin, yes . . . That doesn't matter . . . Wake him up . . .'

She explained with her hand over the mouthpiece:

'He's still asleep. They've gone to fetch him.'

She was evidently wondering what to say.

'Hello, is that you?... What?... Yes, happy Christmas!... Yes, everything's all right... Colette's fine... No, that's not the only reason I'm calling you... No, no, nothing dreadful, don't worry...'

She repeated, stressing each syllable: 'I tell you not to worry... Only, something peculiar happened last night... Somebody dressed as Father Christmas came into Colette's room... No, no! He didn't hurt her... He gave her a big doll... Yes, a *doll*... And he did something to the floor... He lifted up two boards and then put them back hurriedly... Mademoiselle Doncoeur insisted on my speaking about it to the police superintendent who lives across the street... It's from his place that I'm ringing you... You don't understand? Neither do I... You'd like a word with him?... I'll ask him...'

And to Maigret: 'He'd like to speak to you.'

Maigret heard the voice of a decent, anxious man, evidently bewildered.

'You're quite sure no harm's been done to my wife or the little girl? It's so extraordinary! If it had just been the doll, I'd have thought it was my brother... Loraine will tell you about him... Loraine is my wife... Ask her for details... But he'd not have played about with the floorboards... Do you think I'd better come back right away? There's a train about three this afternoon... What did you say? I can count on you to look after them?'

Loraine took back the receiver.

'You see! The Superintendent isn't worried. I'm sure there's no danger. It's not worth interrupting your round just when you've got the chance of being appointed to Paris...'

Mademoiselle Doncoeur was staring at her, and there was little fondness in her gaze.

'I promise to ring you up or send you a wire if there should be any fresh news. She's quite happy. She's playing with her doll. I haven't had time yet to give her what you sent for her. I'm going to do so right away...'

She hung up, remarking: 'You see!'

Then, after a pause: 'I apologize for having bothered you. It wasn't my fault. I'm sure the whole thing was just a bad joke, or else some whim of my brother-in-law's. When he's been drinking you can't foretell what he'll think of...'

'Are you not expecting to see him today? Don't you think he'll want to come and visit his daughter?'

'It depends. Not if he's been drinking. He takes care not to let her see him like that. When he comes he manages to be as decent as possible.'

'Will you allow me to go and have a chat with Colette presently?'

'I can't prevent you. If you think it's any use...'

'Thank you, Monsieur Maigret,' exclaimed Mademoiselle Doncoeur with a look that combined complicity and gratitude. 'She's such an interesting child! You'll see!'

She backed towards the door. A few minutes later Maigret watched them crossing the boulevard, one behind the other, the spinster lady following close on Madame Martin's heels and turning back to cast a glance up at the Superintendent's windows.

Madame Maigret looked in from the kitchen, where onions were sizzling crisply. She said gently:

'Are you happy?'

Hush! He mustn't even appear to understand. That Christmas morning he was not being given an opportunity to remember that they were an elderly couple with nobody to spoil.

It was time to shave before going to see Colette.

2

It was while he was in the middle of dressing, just about to wet his shaving brush, that he had decided to telephone. He had not bothered to put on his dressing gown; he was sitting in pyjamas in his special armchair next to the dining room window, waiting for the call to be put through and watching the smoke rising slowly from many chimneys.

The ringing of the telephone bell over in the Quai des Orfèvres had quite a different sound, in his ears, from the ringing of any other bell, and he could picture the wide empty passages, the doors open on to deserted offices, and the switchboard operator calling Lucas to say: 'It's the Chief!'

He felt rather like one of his wife's friends, whose greatest pleasure—in which she indulged almost every day—was to spend the morning in bed with the windows closed and the curtains drawn, by the dim light of a bedside lamp, calling up one or other of her friends at random.

'What, is it really ten o'clock? What's the weather like outside? It's raining? And you've been out already? You've done your shopping?'

Thus she sought to make contact with the troubled world outside, while sinking ever more voluptuously into the soft warmth of her bed.

'Is that you, Chief?'

Maigret, too, longed to ask Lucas who was on duty with him, what they were both doing, what the place was like that morning.

'Nothing new? Not too much work?'

'Hardly anything. Just routine...'

'I'd like you to make a few enquiries for me. I think you can get the information by telephone. First, a list of all prisoners who have been released during the last two, or let's say three, months.'

'From which prison?'

'From all prisons. Only bother with those who have served at least a five-year sentence. Try to find out if there's one of them who at some period of his life has lived in the Boulevard Richard-Lenoir. Do you follow?'

'I've made a note of it.'

Lucas must have been completely puzzled, but did not betray it.

'Another thing. I'd like you to trace a certain Paul Martin, an alcoholic, no fixed address, who often hangs about the Bastille district. He's not to be arrested or bothered. Just find out where he spent the night on Christmas Eve. The local stations may be able to help you.'

Actually, unlike his wife's friend, he felt uneasy at being at home in his armchair, unshaven and in pyjamas, looking out at a familiar landscape where there was no sign of life but the smoke from the chimneys, while at the other end of the line good old Lucas had been on duty since six in the morning and must already have unpacked his sandwiches.

'That's not all, old fellow. Ring up Bergerac. At the Hôtel de Bordeaux there's a commercial traveller called Jean Martin. No, Jean! It's not the same man, it's his brother. I'd like to know whether at any time yesterday or during the night he received a call or a wire from Paris. And while you're at it, find out where he spent the evening. I think that's all.'

'Shall I call you back?'

'Not immediately. I have to go out. I'll call you.'

'Has something been happening in your neighbourhood?'

'I don't know yet. Maybe.'

Madame Maigret came to talk to him in the bathroom while he finished dressing. And because of those chimney pots, he did not put on his overcoat. Seeing them with the smoke slowly rising and dissolving in the sky, one could imagine overheated rooms behind those windows, and he would be spending some time in poky flats where he would not be asked to make himself at home. He decided to cross the boulevard as though to make a neighbourly call, merely putting on his hat.

The block of flats, like his own, was old but decent, somewhat gloomy, particularly on this grey December morning. He avoided the concierge, who watched him go past somewhat resentfully, and as he went up the stairs, doors opened noiselessly and he could hear muffled footsteps and whispering voices.

On the third floor Mademoiselle Doncoeur, who must have been keeping watch through the window, was waiting for him in the passage, in a state of mingled shyness and excitement, as though for a rendezvous with a lover.

'This way, Monsieur Maigret. She went out quite a while ago.'

He frowned, and she noticed this.

'I told her she shouldn't, that you were coming and that she'd better stay at home. She answered that she hadn't done her shopping yesterday, that she was short of all sorts of things and that later the shops would all be shut. Come in.'

She was standing by the far door, which led into a dining room that was rather small and dark, but clean and tidy.

'I'm looking after the little girl till she comes back. Colette is looking forward to seeing you, for I've told her about you, and her only fear is that you might take away her doll.'

'When did Madame Martin decide to go out?'

'Immediately we got back from seeing you. She began dressing.'

'How fully did she dress?'

'I don't know what you mean.'

'I suppose that for shopping in the neighbourhood she doesn't dress quite in the same way as when she's going to town?'

'She's very nicely dressed, she's wearing her hat and gloves. She took her shopping bag with her.'

Before visiting Colette, Maigret went into the kitchen, where the remains of someone's breakfast were lying.

'Had she eaten before she came to see me?'

'No. I didn't give her time to.'

'Did she eat afterwards?'

'No, she just made herself a cup of black coffee. It was I who gave Colette her breakfast while Madame Martin was dressing.'

On the window ledge overlooking the courtyard there was a meat-safe, at which Maigret had a careful look; it contained cold meat, butter, eggs and vegetables. In the kitchen cupboard he found two fresh, untouched loaves of bread. Colette had eaten croissants with her cup of chocolate.

'Do you know Madame Martin well?'

'She's my neighbour, isn't she? I've seen more of her since Colette has been laid up, because she often asks me to keep an eye on the child when she goes out.'

'Does she go out a great deal?'

'Not much. Just for her shopping.'

Something had struck him on coming in, which he tried to define, something about the atmosphere, the arrangement of the furniture, the kind of order that prevailed there and even the smell of the place. It was while he looked at Mademoiselle Doncoeur that he found, or thought he had found, the answer.

He had been told, a little earlier, that Martin had lived in the flat before his marriage. Now in spite of the fact that Madame Martin had also lived there for five years, it still looked like a bachelor's flat. For instance, in the dining room, he pointed to two enlarged photographs on either side of the mantelpiece.

'Who are these two?'

'Monsieur Martin's father and mother.'

'Are there no photographs of Madame Martin's parents?'

'I've never heard them mentioned. I suppose she must be an orphan.'

Even the bedroom lacked any sort of feminine prettiness. He opened a hanging cupboard and beside a neat row of men's clothes he saw some women's garments, chiefly tailor-made suits and very plain dresses. He did not venture to open the drawers, but he was convinced that they contained no trinkets, none of those little trifles that women tend to collect.

'Mademoiselle Doncoeur!' called a quiet little voice.

'Let's go and see Colette,' he decided.

The child's room, too, was austere, almost bare, and in a bed that was too big for her there lay a little girl with a grave face and questioning but trustful eyes.

'Are you the Superintendent, Monsieur?'

'I am, my dear. Don't be frightened.'

'I'm not frightened. Hasn't maman Loraine come back?'

The phrase struck him. Hadn't the Martins more or less adopted their niece? But the child did not just say *maman*; she said *maman Loraine*.

'Do *you* believe it was Father Christmas who came to see me last night?'

'I'm sure it was.'

'Maman Loraine doesn't think so. She never believes me.'

She had a funny little face with very bright eyes and a piercing look, and the plaster which encased one of her legs half way up the thigh formed a little mountain under the blanket.

Mademoiselle Doncoeur was standing in the doorway, and tactfully, in order to leave them alone together, she announced:

'I'm going to run back and make sure there's nothing burning on my stove.'

Maigret, who had sat down beside the bed, did not know quite how to set about it. In fact, he did not know what question to ask.

'Are you very fond of maman Loraine?'

'Yes, Monsieur.'

She answered quietly, without enthusiasm but without hesitation.

'And your daddy?'

'Which one? Because I've got two, you know, papa Paul and papa Jean.'

'Is it a long time since you saw papa Paul?'

'I don't know. Some weeks, maybe. He promised to bring me a toy for Christmas and he hasn't come yet. He must have been ill.'

'Is he often ill?'

'Yes, often. When he's ill he doesn't come to see me.'

'And what about papa Jean?'

'He's away now, but he'll be back for New Year. Perhaps then he'll get the job in Paris and then he won't have to go away any more. He'll be glad and so will I.'

'Have you had a lot of friends to visit you since you've been laid up?'

'What friends? The girls at school don't know where I live. Or if they do know, they're not allowed to come by themselves.'

'Friends of maman Loraine, or your daddy's?'

'Nobody ever comes.'

'Never? Are you sure?'

'Only the gas man or the electricity man. I hear them, because the door's nearly always open. I know them. There was just twice that somebody else came.'

'A long time ago?'

'The first time was the day after my accident. I remember, because the doctor had only just left.'

'Who was it?'

'I didn't see him. I heard him knocking at the other door, and then maman Loraine shut the door of my room. They talked in low voices for quite a long time. Afterwards she told me he'd come bothering her about an insurance. I don't know what that is.'

'And he came back?'

'Five or six days ago. This time it was in the evening, after my light had been turned out. I was still awake. I heard the knocking and the quiet talking, just like the first time. I knew it wasn't Mademoiselle Doncoeur, who sometimes comes in the evening to keep maman Loraine company. Later on I thought they were quarrelling and I was frightened. I called out, then maman Loraine came in to tell me it was about the insurance again and I must go to sleep.'

'Did he stay a long time?'

'I don't know. I think I fell asleep.'

'Didn't you see him either time?'

'No, but I should recognize his voice.'

'Even when he speaks low?'

'Yes. Just because he speaks low and it makes a noise like a big bumble bee. I may keep the doll, mayn't I? Maman Loraine bought me two boxes of sweets and a little work-basket. She had bought me a doll too, much smaller than Father Christmas's, because she isn't very rich. She showed it me this morning before she went out, then she put it back in the box because I don't need it now I've got this one. The shop will take it back.'

The flat was overheated, the rooms were airless, and yet Maigret felt chilly. The house was like his own, over the way. Why did everything here seem smaller and meaner?

He bent over the floor, at the place where the boards had been lifted, and he saw only a dusty cavity, slightly damp, as under any other floor. A few scratches in the wood suggested that a chisel or some similar tool had been used.

He went to examine the door, and there too saw signs that force had been used. It had been an easy amateurish job, actually.

'Was Father Christmas cross when he saw you were watching him?'

'No, Monsieur. He was busy making a hole in the floor to go and see the little boy who lives underneath.'

'Did he say anything to you?'

'I think he smiled. I'm not quite sure because of his beard. It was rather dark. I'm sure he put his finger to his lips so that I shouldn't call out, because grown-up people aren't allowed to see him. Have you ever seen him?'

'A very long time ago.'

'When you were little?'

He heard steps in the passage. The door opened. It was Madame Martin, in a grey suit and little beige hat. She was carrying a shopping bag full of provisions. She looked very cold; the skin of her face was taut and pale, but she must have hurried up the stairs, because there were two red patches on her cheeks and she was panting for breath.

Without a smile, she asked Maigret:

'Has she been good?'

Then, taking off her jacket: 'I'm sorry to have kept you waiting. I had to go out to buy various things, and later on I'd have found all the shops shut.'

'Did you meet anyone?'

'What do you mean?'

'Nothing. I wondered if anybody had tried to talk to you.'

She had had time to go much further than the Rue Amelot or the Rue du Chemin-Vert, where most of the local shops were. She could even have taken a taxi or the métro, and gone almost anywhere in Paris.

All the tenants in the house must have been on the alert, and Mademoiselle Doncoeur now came in to ask if she was needed. Madame Martin was certainly going to say no, but Maigret replied for her:

'I'd like you to stay with Colette while I go into the next room.'

She realized that he wanted her to distract the child's attention while he interviewed Madame Martin. The latter must have understood it too, but she betrayed no sign of it.

'Please come in. Do you mind if I get rid of these things?'

She went into the kitchen to put down her provisions, then took off her hat and ran her fingers through her blonde hair, puffing it out a little. When the bedroom door was closed she said:

'Mademoiselle Doncoeur is very excited. What a treat for an old maid, isn't it? Especially for an old maid who collects newspaper articles about a certain police superintendent and who at last gets the chance to have him in her own house! Do you mind if I smoke?'

She took a cigarette from a silver case, tapped the end of it and lit it with a lighter. It might have been this gesture which prompted Maigret to put a question to her.

'You don't go out to work, Madame Martin?'

'It would be difficult for me to do a job as well as look after the flat and the little girl into the bargain, even when she goes to school. In any case, my husband doesn't want me to work.'

'But you had a job before you knew him?'

'Of course. I had to earn my living. Won't you take a seat?'

He sat down in a rustic straw-bottomed armchair, while she perched on the edge of the table.

'You were a typist?'

'I was.'

'For a long time?'

'Fairly long.'

'You were still working as a typist when you met Martin? Forgive me for asking you these questions.'

'It's your job.'

'You were married five years ago. Where were you working at that time? One minute. May I ask your age?'

'I'm thirty-three. So I was twenty-eight then and I was working for Monsieur Lorilleux in the Palais-Royal.'

'As a secretary?'

'Monsieur Lorilleux had a jeweller's shop, or rather he was a dealer in souvenirs and old coins. You know those old shops in the Palais-Royal? I was saleswoman, secretary and bookkeeper all at once. I ran the shop when he was away.'

'Was he married?'

'Yes, with three children.'

'Did you leave him when you married Martin?'

'Not exactly. Jean didn't like my going on working, but he wasn't earning much and I had a good job. I stayed on in it for the first few months.'

'And then?'

'Then something happened which was simple and yet unexpected. One morning I turned up at nine o'clock as usual at the door of the shop and I found it shut. I waited, supposing that Monsieur Lorilleux had been delayed.'

'He didn't live at the shop?'

'He lived with his family in the Rue Mazarine. At half-past nine I began to worry.'

'Had he died?'

'No. I rang up his wife, who told me he had left the flat at eight o'clock as usual.'

'Where did you telephone from?'

'From the glove shop next door. I waited all morning. His wife came along too. We went together to the police station, where, incidentally, they didn't treat the matter very seriously. They merely asked his wife whether he was subject to heart trouble, whether he had any liaison, and so forth. He's never been seen or heard of again. The business was taken over by some Poles, and my husband insisted on my not going back to work.'

'How long was this after your marriage?'

'Four months.'

'Was your husband already travelling in the southwest?'

'He did the same round that he does now.'

'Was he in Paris when your employer disappeared?'

'No, I don't think so.'

'Didn't the police visit the premises?'

'Everything was in order, just as it had been the night before. Nothing was missing.'

'Do you know what has become of Madame Lorilleux?'

'She lived for a while on the money she'd withdrawn from the business. Her children must be grown-up by now, maybe married. She runs a little haberdashery not far off in the Rue du Pas-de-la-Mule.'

'Have you kept in touch with her?'

'I've gone into her shop occasionally; in fact that's how I found out that she was in the haberdashery business. At first I didn't recognize her.'

'How long ago was that?'

'I don't know. About six months.'

'Has she got a telephone?'

'I couldn't say. Why?'

'What sort of man was Lorilleux?'

'Do you mean physically?'

'Physically, to begin with.'

'He was tall, taller than you and even broader. He was a big fellow, but flabby, if you see what I mean, and rather slovenly.'

'How old?'

'Fiftyish. I don't know for sure. He had a little pepper-and-salt moustache and his clothes were always too loose.'

'Were you familiar with his habits?'

'He used to walk to the shop every morning and get there about a quarter of an hour before me, so that he had gone through the mail by the time I came in. He never talked much. He was rather a depressed sort of man. He spent most of the day in the little office at the back of the shop.'

'Any affairs with women?'

'Not as far as I know.'

'He never made advances to you?'

She spat out curtly:

'No!'

'Did he depend on you a good deal?'

'I think I was a great help to him.'

'Did your husband meet him?'

'They never spoke to one another. Jean used occasionally to come and wait for me when I left the shop, but he always stood some way off. Is that all you wanted to know?'

There was impatience in her voice, and perhaps a touch of anger.

'I must point out to you, Madame Martin, that you yourself came over to fetch me.'

'Because that old fool seized the opportunity to see you at close quarters and dragged me along almost by force.'

'You're not fond of Mademoiselle Doncoeur?'

'I dislike people who don't mind their own business.'

'Is that the case with her?'

'We took in my brother-in-law's daughter, as you know. You may or may not believe me, but I do all that I can for her, I treat her as I'd treat my own daughter...'

Maigret had another vague, indefinable intuition; as he looked at the woman before him, who was lighting a fresh cigarette, he could not envisage her in a mother's role.

'Well, on the pretext of helping me, she keeps coming round here. If I go out for a few moments I find her in the passage, saying with her sugary smile: "You're not going to leave Colette all alone, Madame Martin? Do let me go and keep her company."

'And I wonder if when I'm not there she doesn't go through my drawers.'

'And yet you put up with her.'

'Because I've got to. Colette keeps asking for her, particularly since she's been laid up. My husband is fond of her too, because in his bachelor days he once had an attack of pleurisy and she came and looked after him.'

'Did you take back the doll you bought Colette as a Christmas present?'

She frowned, with a glance at the communicating door.

'I see you've been questioning her. No, I haven't taken it back, for the very good reason that it came from one of the big stores and they are closed today. Do you want to see it?'

She said this defiantly, and somewhat to her surprise he accepted her offer, and examined the cardboard box on which the price, a very low one, was still marked.

'May I ask you where you went this morning?'

'To do my shopping.'

'In the Rue du Chemin-Vert or the Rue Amelot?'

'In the Rue du Chemin-Vert and in the Rue Amelot.'

'If it's not indiscreet, what did you buy?'

Angrily, she went into the kitchen and picked up the shopping bag, which she flung on to the dining room table.

'See for yourself.'

There were three tins of sardines, some ham, some butter, potatoes and a lettuce.

She was staring at him with a hard, unflinching look in which there was more resentment than distress.

'Have you anything else to ask me?'

'I'd like to know the name of your insurance agent.'

She did not immediately understand, that was obvious. She searched her memory.

'My insurance agent . . .'

'Yes, the one who came to see you.'

'Sorry, I'd forgotten. It's because you spoke of *my* insurance agent, as though I was really doing business with him. I suppose it was Colette who told you about that. Yes, somebody did come, on two occasions, one of those people who knock on everybody's door and whom one has the utmost difficulty in getting rid of. I thought at first that he was selling vacuum cleaners, but it turned out to be life insurance.'

'Did he spend a long time with you?'

'He stayed until I could get rid of him and make him understand that I had no desire to sign a policy on my own life or my husband's.'

'What company did he represent?'

'He told me, but I've forgotten. The name had the word *mutual* in it.'

'He renewed the attempt?'

'That's right.'

'At what time is Colette supposed to go to sleep?'

'I turn out the light at half-past seven, but she sometimes goes on telling herself stories for quite a while.'

'On the second occasion, then, the insurance agent must have come to see you after half-past seven in the evening?'

She sensed the trap.

'It may have been. In fact I was just washing up.'

'And you let him come in?'

'He'd got his foot in the doorway.'

'Did he call on any other tenants in the house?'

'I've no idea. I suppose you'll go and find out. Because a little girl saw or fancied she saw Father Christmas you've been questioning me for half an hour as though I'd committed a crime. If my husband was here...'

'In fact, is your husband's life insured?'

'I believe so. Yes, of course.'

And as he made his way to the door, after picking up his hat from a chair, she exclaimed in some surprise: 'Is that all?'

'That's all. In the event of your brother-in-law's coming to see you, as he seems to have promised his daughter, I'd be obliged if you would let me know or send him to me. And now I'd like a few words with Mademoiselle Doncoeur.'

The older woman followed him into the passage and hurried forward to open the door of her flat, which had a sort of convent smell about it.

'Come in, Superintendent. I hope it's not too untidy.'

There was no cat to be seen, no small dog; there were no antimacassars on the furniture, no ornaments on the mantelpiece.

'How long have you lived in the house, Mademoiselle Doncoeur?'

'Twenty-five years, Superintendent. I'm one of the oldest tenants, and I remember that when I settled here you were already living across the street, and you wore a long moustache.'

'Who lived in the next door flat before Martin took it?'

'An engineer from the Highways and Bridges Department. I don't remember his name, but I could find it out. He lived with his wife and a deaf-and-dumb daughter. It was very sad. They left Paris and went to live in the country, in Poitou if I'm not mistaken. The old gentleman must be dead by now, because he was already of retirement age.'

'Have you been bothered recently by visits from an insurance agent?'

'Not lately. The last time that one called here was at least two years ago.'

'You don't like Madame Martin, I think?'

'Why?'

"I'm asking you if you do or don't like Madame Martin?'

'That's to say, if I had a son...'

'Go on!'

'If I had a son, I shouldn't want to have her for a daughter-in-law. Particularly as Monsieur Martin is so kind and gentle!'

'Do you think he's not happy with her?'

'I don't say that. I've no special criticism to make of her. She's got her own ways, you see, as she's quite entitled to.'

'What sort of ways?'

'I don't know. You've seen her. You're a better judge than I am. She's not really like a woman. For instance, I'm sure she's never cried in her life. She brings up the little girl quite properly, it's true. But she'll never say a loving word to her, and when I try to tell the child fairy tales I can feel it irritates her. I'm sure she's told Colette that Father Christmas doesn't exist. Luckily Colette doesn't believe her.'

'And does she love her?'

'She obeys her, she tries to please her. I think she's just as happy when she's left alone.'

'Does Madame Martin go out much?'

'Not a great deal. There's really nothing one can criticize her for. I don't know how to put it. You feel she leads her own life, don't you see? She pays no attention to other people. She never talks about herself either. She behaves correctly, always correctly, too correctly. She should have spent her life in an office, writing out figures or keeping an eye on the staff.'

'Is that what the other tenants think?'

'She doesn't really belong to the house at all! She barely says good-morning to people when she meets them on the stairs. Really, if we've got to know her at all it's only since Colette came, because one is always more interested in a child.'

'Have you ever met her brother-in-law?'

'In the passage. I've never spoken to him. He goes past you with his head bent, as though he was ashamed, and in spite of the care he must take to brush his clothes before coming here he always looks as if he'd slept in them. I don't think it was him, Monsieur Maigret. He's not the sort of man who'd do that. Unless he was very drunk indeed.'

Maigret stopped once more at the concierge's lodge, where it was so dark that the lights were kept on all day, and it was nearly twelve o'clock when he crossed the boulevard again. The curtains were being twitched at every window in the house he had left; and at his own window, too, he saw the curtain move. Madame Maigret was watching, to know whether she might put her chicken in the oven. He waved to her from down below, and he nearly put out his tongue to catch one of those tiny frozen flakes that were floating in the air and the faint taste of which he could still remember.

3

'I wonder if that child's happy,' sighed Madame Maigret as she got up from table to fetch the coffee from the kitchen.

She could see that he was not listening to her. He had pushed back his chair and was filling his pipe as he stared at the stove, which was purring gently with small regular flames licking the mica.

He gave her the vague smile that meant he didn't know what she had been saying, and turned back to contemplate the stove. There were at least ten like it in the house, making the same purring sound, ten dining rooms with the same Sunday smell, and probably just as many in the house across the street. In every cell of the honeycomb the same muted, leisurely life was going on, with wine and cakes on the table, the bottle of liqueur ready to hand in the sideboard, and all the windows letting in the bleak grey light of a sunless day.

It may have been this that had been baffling him without his realizing it ever since the morning. Nine times out of ten an investigation, a real one, would fling him at a moment's notice into an unfamiliar setting, confronting him with people of a set about which he knew little or nothing, and everything had to be learnt, down to the most trivial habits and mannerisms of a social class with which he was unacquainted.

In the present case, which was not really a case since he was not officially in charge of anything, the situation was quite different. For the first time, things were happening in a world that was close to his own, in a house which might have been his own house.

The Martins might have been living on his own landing, instead of in the house opposite, and probably Madame Maigret would have gone to look after Colette in her aunt's absence. On the floor above his there was an old lady who was a slightly fatter and paler version of Mademoiselle Doncoeur. The frames of the photographs of the Martin parents were exactly the same as those of the Maigret parents, and the enlargements had no doubt been done by the same firm.

Was this what put him off? He felt that he was too close to it all and that he couldn't see people and things with enough clarity and detachment.

He had described his morning's doings to his wife over lunch— a pleasantly festive little meal that left him feeling rather drowsy— and all the while she had been looking at the windows of the house opposite with a troubled air.

'Is the concierge certain that nobody could have come in from outside?'

'She's no longer quite so certain. She had friends visiting her until half-past twelve. Then she went to bed, and there was a good deal of coming and going, as you'd expect when people are celebrating.'

'Do you expect something further to happen?'

It was this remark that went on worrying him. In the first place, there was the fact that Madame Martin had not come to fetch him of her own accord, but under pressure from Mademoiselle Doncoeur.

If she had got up earlier, if she had been the first to discover the doll and hear the story of Father Christmas, might she not perhaps have kept quiet about it and ordered the little girl to say nothing?

Next, she had taken advantage of the first opportunity to go out, although there were enough provisions in the house for the whole day. She had even absentmindedly bought butter, when there was still a whole pound of it in the meat-safe.

He got up and moved over to his armchair by the window, lifted the receiver and called Police Headquarters.

'Lucas?'

'I did what you asked me, Chief, and I have the list of all the prisoners released in the last four months. There aren't as many of them as you'd expect, and I can't find one who ever lived in the Boulevard Richard-Lenoir.'

It no longer mattered. Maigret had practically given up that hypothesis. In any case it had only been a conjecture: somebody who lived in the flat across the street might have hidden the spoils of a theft or a crime before getting caught.

Once released, his first concern would naturally have been to recover the swag. Now, on account of Colette's accident, which confined her to bed, the room was never unoccupied at any time of day or night. Acting Father Christmas would have been an ingenious way of getting into it practically without risk.

But in that case, Madame Martin would have had no hesitation in coming to see him. Nor would she subsequently have gone out on an unconvincing pretext.

'Do you want me to go into each case separately?'

'No. Have you any news of Paul Martin?'

'That didn't take long. They know him in at least four or five police stations between the Bastille, the Hôtel de Ville and the Boulevard Saint-Michel.'

'Do you know how he spent last night?'

'First he went to eat on the Salvation Army barge; he goes there once a week on a particular day, like the other regulars, and on those evenings he's sober. They were given a special Christmas dinner. He had to wait in a longish queue.'

'And then?'

'About 11 p.m. he went along to the Latin Quarter and acted as doorkeeper at some night club. He must have earned enough to go out and drink, because at four in the morning he was picked up dead drunk some hundred yards from the Place Maubert. They took him to the station. He was still there at eleven o'clock this morning. He had just been let out when I obtained this information, and they've promised to bring him along as soon as they can lay hands on him. He still had a few francs in his pocket.'

'And Bergerac?'

'Jean Martin is taking the first train this afternoon. He seemed very surprised and worried about the telephone call he got this morning.'

'Did he only get one?'

'Only one this morning. But he'd been rung up yesterday evening when he was dining in the restaurant.'

'Do you know who called him?'

'The hotel cashier, who answered the call, says it was a man's voice, asking for Monsieur Jean Martin. She sent a waitress to fetch him, but when he got there the caller had rung off. It quite spoilt his evening. A party of them, all commercial travellers, had arranged a visit to some night club in the town. I was given the hint that there had been some pretty girls with them. Martin had a few drinks so as to be like everyone else, but apparently he spent the whole time talking about his wife and daughter, for he refers to the child as his daughter. However, he stayed out until three in the morning with his friends. Is that all you wanted to know, Chief?'

Lucas, whose curiosity had been aroused, could not resist adding:

'Has there been a crime in your neighbourhood? Are you still at home?'

'So far, it's only a matter of Father Christmas and a doll.'

'Oh!'

'One minute. I'd like you to try and get hold of the address of the managing director of Zenith Watches, in the Avenue de l'Opéra. Even during a holiday that should be possible, and the chances are that he'll be at home. Will you call me back?'

'As soon as I've got the information.'

His wife had just handed him a glass of Alsatian plum brandy, of which her sister sent her a bottle from time to time; he smiled at her and for a moment was tempted to give up thinking of this preposterous business and to suggest a peaceful afternoon at the cinema.

'What colour are her eyes?'

He had to make an effort to realize that Madame Maigret was referring to the little girl, who alone interested her in the case.

'Goodness, I really couldn't say. They're certainly not brown.
She's got fair hair.'

'Then they must be blue.'

'Maybe. At any rate they're very light. And particularly calm.'

'That's because she doesn't look at things as a child would. Did
she laugh at all?'

'She had nothing to laugh about.'

'A real child always finds something to laugh about, if she's allowed to feel at her ease and to think childish thoughts. I don't like
that woman!'

'You prefer Mademoiselle Doncoeur?'

'She may be an old maid, but I'm sure she knows how to get on
with the little girl better than that Madame Martin. I've met that
woman out shopping. She's one of those who keep a sharp eye on
the scales and pull their money out one coin at a time from the
depths of their purses, with a suspicious look as if everyone was
trying to cheat them.'

The ringing of the telephone interrupted her, but she found
time to repeat: 'I don't like that woman.'

Lucas was calling to give the address of Monsieur Arthur Gode-
froy, general representative in France of Zenith watches. He lived
in a big private house at Saint-Cloud and Lucas had made sure that
he was at home.

'Paul Martin is here, Chief.'

'Did they bring him along?'

'Yes. He's wondering why. Wait till I close the door. Okay, now
he can't hear me. At first he thought something had happened to his
daughter and he began to cry. Now he's calm and relaxed, with a
terrible hangover. What shall I do with him? Send him to you?'

'Have you anyone to bring him here?'

'Torrence has just turned up and he'd be glad of the outing, for
I think he made a night of it too. Anything else I can do?'

'Yes. Get in touch with the Palais-Royal central station. About five years ago, a certain Lorilleux, a dealer in jewellery and old coins, disappeared leaving no trace, and I'd like to have all possible details about that business.'

He smiled when he saw his wife sit down opposite him and take up her knitting. There was something decidedly domestic about the atmosphere of this enquiry.

'Shall I call you back?'

'I shan't stir from here.'

Five minutes later Maigret was on the line to Monsieur Gode-froy, who spoke with a very strong Swiss accent. When he heard the name of Jean Martin he assumed at first that if he had been disturbed on Christmas day, some accident must have happened to his representative, whom he proceeded to praise enthusiastically.

'He's such a loyal and able fellow that I intend next year, that's to say in a fortnight's time, to keep him here in Paris as assistant manager. Do you know him? Is there some grave reason for your interest in him?'

He silenced some children in the background.

'Excuse me. The whole family is here and . . .'

'Tell me, Monsieur Godefroy, do you know whether anyone, within the last few days, has contacted your office to find out where Monsieur Martin is at present?'

'Yes, someone did so.'

'Would you give me details?'

'Yesterday morning, somebody rang the office and asked to speak to me personally. I was very busy on account of the holidays. The caller must have given a name, but I've forgotten it. He wanted to know where he could get hold of Monsieur Martin with an urgent message, and I saw no reason not to reply that he was in Bergerac, probably at the Hôtel de Bordeaux.'

'You weren't asked anything further?'

'No. The caller rang off immediately.'

'Many thanks.'

'You're sure there's nothing unpleasant about this business?'

The children must have seized hold of him, and Maigret took the opportunity to bring the conversation to an end.

'Did you hear?' he asked his wife.

'I heard what you said, of course, but not what he answered.'

'Yesterday morning a man rang up his office to find out where Jean Martin was. The same man, probably, rang up Bergerac that evening to make sure that Martin was still there and so could not be at home in the Boulevard Richard-Lenoir on the night of Christmas Eve.'

'And that was the man who got into the house?'

'More than likely. It proves, in any case, that it could not have been Paul Martin, who would not have needed those two telephone calls. He could have found out from his sister-in-law without arousing suspicion.'

'You're beginning to get excited. Admit that you're glad this has happened.'

And as he was trying to justify himself, she went on:

'It's quite natural, you know! I'm interested too. How much longer do you suppose the little girl will have to keep her leg in plaster?'

'I didn't ask.'

'I wonder what the complication can have been?'

Once again, involuntarily, she had suggested a fresh train of thought to Maigret.

'There's some point in what you've said.'

'What have I said?'

'After all, since she's been in bed two months, it's quite likely that unless there are really serious complications she won't be laid up much longer.'

'At first she'll probably have to walk with crutches.'

'That's not the point. In a few days, or a few weeks, then, she'll be able to leave her room. She'll go out with Madame Martin sometimes. The coast will be clear and it will be easy for anybody to get into the flat without dressing up as Father Christmas.'

Madame Maigret's lips were moving, because while she listened, with her untroubled gaze fixed on her husband, she was counting the stitches in her knitting.

'In the first place, it was Colette's presence in the bedroom that obliged the man to resort to a stratagem. Now she's been in bed for two months. So he may have been waiting for two months. But for the complication that delayed her recovery, the floorboards might have been lifted some three weeks ago.'

'What are you getting at?'

'Nothing. Or rather I'm concluding that the man could not wait any longer, that he had some urgent reason to act without delay.'

'In a few days, Martin will be back from his round.'

'That's so.'

'What can have been found under the floorboards?'

'Was anything found there, in fact? If the visitor found nothing, the problem will remain as pressing for him as it was yesterday. So he'll take action again.'

'How?'

'That I don't know.'

'Tell me, Maigret, you're not worried about the child? Do you think she's all right with that woman?'

'I should know that if I knew where Madame Martin went this morning on the pretext of doing her shopping.'

He lifted the receiver and called Police Headquarters once more.

'It's me again, Lucas. This time I'd like you to enquire about taxis. I want to know if this morning, between nine and ten, a taxi picked up a woman somewhere near the Boulevard Richard-Lenoir, and where he took her. Wait a minute. Here we are. She's blonde, looks a little over thirty, fairly slender but well built. She was wearing a grey suit and a small beige hat. She was carrying a shopping bag. There can't have been all that many cabs out in the streets this morning.'

'Has Martin reached you?'

'Not yet.'

'He won't be long. As for the other fellow, Lorilleux, they're busy searching the files at the Palais-Royal station. You'll have the information in a short while.'

Just now, Jean Martin must be catching his train at Bergerac. Little Colette was no doubt having a nap. Mademoiselle Doncoeur's figure could be glimpsed behind her curtains, and she was probably wondering what Maigret was up to.

People were beginning to emerge from their houses, mostly families with children trailing their new toys along the pavements.

Queues must be forming outside cinemas. A taxi stopped; then footsteps were heard in the stairway. Madame Maigret went to open the door before the visitor had time to ring the bell. Torrence's deep voice asked:

'Are you there, Chief?'

And he ushered into the room a man of indeterminate age, who stood with lowered eyes, humbly shrinking back against the wall.

Maigret went to fetch a couple of glasses from the sideboard and filled them with plum brandy.

'Your good health,' he said.

Hesitantly, the man held out a trembling hand, and lifted puzzled, anxious eyes.

'Your health too, Monsieur Martin. I apologize for having brought you all this way, but you'll be all the nearer for visiting your daughter.'

'Nothing's happened to her?'

'No, no. I saw her this morning and she was playing happily with her new doll. You can go off now, Torrence. Lucas must have some jobs for you.'

Madame Maigret had vanished with her knitting into the bedroom, where she had settled down on the edge of the bed, still counting stitches.

'Sit down, Monsieur Martin.'

The man had merely dipped his lips in his glass and then set it on the table, but from time to time he cast an anxious glance towards it.

'Now don't worry, above all, and remember that I know your story.'

'I wanted to go and see her this morning,' the man sighed. 'I'd vowed to myself that I'd go to bed and get up early to come and wish her a happy Christmas.'

'I know that too.'

'It always happens the same way. I swear only to take one glass, just to buck me up . . .'

'You've only the one brother, Monsieur Martin?'

'Yes, Jean, who's six years younger than me. Next to my wife and daughter, he is the only person I love in the world.'

'You don't love your sister-in-law?'

He gave a start, surprised and embarrassed.

'I've no criticisms to make of Loraine.'

'You entrusted your child to her, didn't you?'

'That's to say that when my wife died and I began to lose my grip...'

'I understand. Is your daughter happy?'

'Yes, I believe so. She never complains.'

'Have you ever tried to turn over a new leaf?'

'Every night I promise myself I'll have done with that sort of life, and next day it begins all over again. I even went to see a doctor who gave me some advice.'

'Did you follow it?'

'For a few days. When I went back to see him he was very busy. He told me he hadn't time to attend to me, that I'd better go to a special clinic...'

He reached out towards his glass, then hesitated, and in order to allow him to drink Maigret tossed off a glassful.

'Have you ever happened to meet a man at your sister-in-law's?'

'No. I don't think she goes in for that sort of thing.'

'Do you know where your brother met her?'

'In a little restaurant in the Rue de Beaujolais, where he used to eat when he was in Paris between two trips. It was close to his office and close to the shop where Loraine worked.'

'Were they engaged for a long time?'

'I don't know exactly. Jean went off for two months and when he came back he told me he was getting married.'

'Were you your brother's witness at his wedding?'

'Yes. Loraine's witness was the landlady of the lodging-house where she was living. She has no relatives in Paris. Her parents were dead by then. Is there anything wrong...?'

'I don't know yet. A man got into Colette's room last night, disguised as Father Christmas.'

'He didn't do anything to her?'

'He gave her a doll. When she woke up he was lifting up a couple of floorboards.'

'Do you think I look decent enough to go and see her?'

'You shall go in a moment. If you feel like it, you can have a shave and brush-up here. Is your brother the sort of man who would hide anything under the floorboards?'

'Jean? Absolutely not!'

'Even if he had something to hide from his wife?'

'He hides nothing from her. You don't know him. When he comes home he shows her his accounts as though she were his boss, and she knows exactly how much spare cash he has.'

'Is she jealous?'

The man gave no answer.

'You'd better tell me what you think. You see, your daughter is involved.'

'I don't think Loraine is particularly jealous, but she's self-seeking. At least so my wife declared. My wife didn't like her.'

'Why?'

'She said Loraine's lips were too thin, that she was too cold, too polite, always on the defensive. According to my wife, she had run after Jean on account of his position, his home, his prospects.'

'Was she poor?'

'She never talks about her family. We learnt, however, that her father died when she was very young and that her mother went out to work as a charwoman.'

'In Paris?'

'Somewhere in the Glacière district. That's why she never talks about that part of the city. As my wife used to say, she's a woman who knows what she wants.'

'Do you believe she was the mistress of her former boss?'

Maigret poured him out a thimbleful of brandy, and the man looked at him gratefully, though uneasily, probably worrying about his breath and the forthcoming visit to his daughter.

'I'll make you a cup of coffee. Your wife must have had an opinion on that question too, didn't she?'

'How do you know? She never spoke ill of people, you know. But her dislike of Loraine was almost a physical matter. When we were to meet Loraine I used to beg my wife not to betray her mistrust or her aversion. It's odd that I should be telling you all this, considering the way things are with me. Maybe I was wrong to leave Colette with her? I blame myself for it sometimes. But what else could I do?'

'You've not answered my question about Loraine's employer.'

'Yes. My wife used to say that they seemed on pretty intimate terms, and that it was convenient for Loraine to marry a man who was away most of the time.'

'Do you know where she lived before her marriage?'

'In a street off the Boulevard Sébastopol, the first on the right when you're coming from the Rue de Rivoli towards the boulevards. I remember because we fetched her from there in the car on the wedding day.'

'The Rue Pernelle?'

'That's it. The fourth or fifth house on the left is a lodging-house that looks quiet and respectable, and is mainly lived in by people working locally. I remember for instance that there were some girls from the Châtelet theatre.'

'Would you like to shave, Monsieur Martin?'

'I'm really ashamed. And yet, now that I'm so close to where my daughter lives . . .'

'Come with me.'

He took him through the kitchen so as to avoid the bedroom, where Madame Maigret was sitting, and gave him all that was necessary, including a clothes-brush.

When Maigret returned to the dining room his wife peeped through the door to whisper: 'What's he doing?'

'He's shaving.'

He lifted the telephone receiver again; there was another job for good old Lucas on his Christmas day.

'Are you needed in the office?'

'Not if Torrence stays here. I've got the information you asked for.'

'In a minute. Hurry along to the Rue Pernelle, where you'll find a lodging-house which must surely still exist; I fancy I've noticed it among the houses nearest to the Boulevard Sébastopol. I don't know whether it's changed hands in the last five years. You may discover somebody who was working there at that period. I'd like to have all possible information about a certain Loraine...'

'Loraine what?'

'One minute. I hadn't thought of that.'

He went to ask Martin, through the bathroom door, for his sister-in-law's maiden name.

'Boitel!' the man called back.

'Lucas? The woman was called Loraine Boitel. The landlady of the house was a witness to her marriage with Martin. Loraine Boitel was then working for Lorilleux.'

'The Palais-Royal fellow?'

'Yes. I'm wondering whether they may have had another relationship, and whether he used to visit her in her room. That's all. Make haste. It may be more urgent than we think. What were you going to tell me?'

'About Lorilleux. He was a queer customer. Enquiries were made when he disappeared. In the Rue Mazarine, where he lived with his family, he passed for a respectable business man who brought up his three children irreproachably. But funny things went on in his shop in the Palais-Royal. He sold not only souvenirs of Paris and old coins, but obscene books and prints.'

'That's a specialty of the place.'

'Yes. In fact, they're not sure that something else didn't go on there too. There was some mention of a big divan covered in red rep that stood in the back room. But the matter was dropped for lack of evidence and to avoid embarrassing the shop's customers, who were mainly people more or less in the public eye.'

'Loraine Boitel?'

'She's barely mentioned in the report. She was already married at the time of Lorilleux's disappearance. She waited all morning at the door of the shop. She doesn't seem to have seen him the previous evening after closing time. I was on the phone about it when Langlois, from the Fraud Squad, came into my office. He jumped when he heard the name Lorilleux, told me it rang a bell and went to look through his files. Are you with me? Nothing very precise, only the fact that about this period Lorilleux had been observed frequently crossing the Swiss border, just when the gold smuggling wave was at its height. He was watched, and searched two or three times at the frontier, but nothing incriminating was ever found.'

'Rush off to the Rue Pernelle, Lucas old fellow. I'm more than ever convinced that it's urgent.'

Paul Martin, his close-shaven cheeks pale, stood in the doorway. 'I'm so embarrassed. I don't know how to thank you.'

'You're going to see your daughter, aren't you? I don't know how long you usually stay with her, nor how you're going to manage this. But I should like you not to leave her until I come and fetch you.'

'I can hardly spend the night there.'

'Spend the night there if necessary. Manage as best you can.'

'Is she in danger?'

'I don't know, but your place is beside Colette.'

The man drank his cup of black coffee avidly, and made his way to the stairs. The door had closed again when Madame Maigret came into the dining room.

'He can't go to see his daughter empty-handed on Christmas day.'

'But...'

Maigret was probably about to reply that there were no dolls in the house when she held out to him a small bright object, a golden thimble, which she'd had for years in her workbox and never used.

'Give him that. Little girls always like them. Hurry up...'

He shouted from the top of the stairs:

'Monsieur Martin!... Monsieur Martin!... Wait a moment, please!'

He thrust the thimble into the man's hand.

'Mind you don't tell her where it comes from.'

Standing on the threshold of the dining room, he protested with a sigh:

'When you've quite finished making me play Father Christmas!'

'I bet you she'll be just as pleased with it as with the doll. Because it's something grown-up, don't you see?'

They watched the man crossing the boulevard, pausing for a moment in front of the house and turning back to look up at Maigret's windows as though seeking encouragement.

'Do you think he can be cured?'

'I doubt it.'

'If anything happened to that woman, Madame Martin...'

'Well?'

'Nothing. I'm thinking of the child. I'm wondering what will become of her.'

Ten minutes at least went by. Maigret opened a newspaper. His wife had resumed her seat opposite him and was knitting, still counting her stitches, when he murmured, letting out a puff of smoke: 'And you've never even seen her!'

4

Later on, Maigret was to retrieve from the drawer in which Madame Maigret thrust any stray scraps of paper an old envelope on the back of which he had automatically summarized events during the course of that day. It was only then that something struck him about this enquiry, which was conducted almost from beginning to end from his own home, something which he was subsequently often to cite as an example.

Contrary to what so frequently happens, there was strictly speaking no element of the accidental, no really sensational surprise. That sort of chance did not come into play, but chance intervened nonetheless, indeed quite constantly, in so far as each piece of evidence turned up at the right time, obtained by the simplest and most natural means.

It sometimes happens that dozens of detectives work night and day to obtain a relatively unimportant piece of information. For instance, Monsieur Arthur Godefroy, the French representative of Zenith watches, might well have been spending Christmas in his hometown, Zurich. Or he might just not have been at home. Or again he might quite well have known nothing about the telephone call to his office the previous day concerning Jean Martin.

When Lucas arrived shortly after four o'clock, frozen and red-nosed, the same chance had played in his favour.

A dense yellowish fog had suddenly descended on Paris, which is unusual, and the lights were on in all the houses; on either side of the boulevard the windows looked like distant beacons; the details of real life were obliterated to such an extent that one expected to hear a foghorn blowing, as though one were by the sea.

For one reason or another—probably on account of some childhood recollection—Maigret enjoyed this, just as he enjoyed seeing Lucas come into his home, take off his overcoat, sit down and warm his frozen hands by the fire.

Lucas was almost a replica of himself, although a head shorter and with shoulders half as broad and a face which did not readily assume an expression of severity. Unostentatiously, perhaps unconsciously, through mimicry and through sheer admiration, he had come to copy his boss in his slightest habits, in his attitudes, in his expressions, and this was more striking here than in the office. Even his way of sniffing at the glass of plum brandy before putting his lips to it...

The landlady of the house in the Rue Pernelle had died two years previously in a metro accident, which could have complicated the enquiry. The staff of that sort of establishment changes frequently and there was little hope of finding in the house anyone who had known Loraine five years earlier.

Luck was on their side. Lucas had discovered that the present landlord had formerly acted as night watchman, and it so happened that he had once been in trouble with the police on a matter of public morality.

'It was easy to get him talking,' said Lucas, lighting a pipe that was too big for him. 'I was surprised that he'd had the wherewithal to buy the property on the spot, but he finally explained that he had acted as go-between for a man in the public eye who invests his money in that sort of concern but doesn't want his name to appear.'

'What sort of a joint?'

'Outwardly respectable. Pretty clean. An office on the mezzanine floor. Rooms let by the month, some by the week, and on the first floor some bedrooms let by the hour.'

'Does he remember the young woman?'

'Very well, for she lived in the house for over three years. I gathered, eventually, that he didn't like her because she was terribly stingy.'

'Did she have visits from Lorilleux?'

'On my way to the Rue Pernelle I had called in at the Palais-Royal station to pick up a photo of him that was in their files. I showed it to the landlord and he recognized it immediately.'

'Did Lorilleux often go to see her?'

'Two or three times a month on an average, and he always had luggage with him. He would arrive about half-past one in the morning and leave again at six. I wondered at first what this could signify. I checked with the railway timetable. His visits coincided with his trips to Switzerland. He used to come back by the train that arrives in the middle of the night, but let his wife believe that he'd taken one arriving at six.'

'Nothing further?'

'Nothing, except that the Loraine woman was mean about tipping and that she used to cook in her room at night on a spirit-lamp, which is against the rules.'

'No other men?'

'No. Apart from Lorilleux, she lived respectably. When she got married she asked the landlady to be her witness.'

Maigret had finally persuaded his wife to remain in the room, where she kept very quiet and seemed anxious to have her presence forgotten.

Torrence was outside in the fog, visiting taxi-ranks. The two men were waiting quite calmly, each sunk in an armchair, in identical attitudes with a glass of brandy within reach. Maigret was beginning to grow drowsy.

As it happened, they were as lucky about taxis as about everything else. Sometimes one happens immediately on the taxi one is looking for; at other times one spends several days without picking up a single clue, especially when the cab in question does not belong to a firm. Some drivers have no regular hours but prowl around at random, and they do not invariably read police notices in the newspaper.

But before five o'clock Torrence rang up from Saint-Ouen.

'I've found one of the cabs,' he announced.

'Why, were there more than one?'

'It looks like it. He took on the young lady this morning at the junction of Boulevard Richard-Lenoir and Boulevard Voltaire, and drove her to the Rue de Maubeuge, where it passes the Gare du Nord. She didn't keep him.'

'Did she go into the station?'

'No. She stopped in front of a shop selling travel goods, that stays open on Sundays and holidays. The driver didn't pay any further attention to her.'

'Where is he now?'

'Here. He's just come in.'

'Will you send him to me? He can come in his own car or in someone else's, it doesn't matter, but let him come as fast as possible. As for you, your next job is to find the driver who brought her back.'

'Okay, Chief. Just give me time to drink a laced coffee, because it's bloody cold.'

Maigret cast a glance across the street and noticed a shadow at Mademoiselle Doncoeur's window.

'Look in the telephone directory and find a shop selling travel goods, opposite the Gare du Nord.'

That took Lucas only a few minutes, and Maigret made another call.

'Hello! This is the police, Criminal Investigation Department. Did you have a customer this morning, shortly before ten o'clock, who must have bought something from you, probably a suitcase? A blonde young woman in a grey suit, carrying a shopping bag. Do you remember her?'

Did the fact of its being Christmas Day make things easier? There was less traffic, and trade was almost non-existent. Moreover, people tend to remember more clearly the things that happen on a day that is unlike others.

'I served her myself. She explained that she had to leave for Cambrai in a hurry to visit a sick sister, and hadn't time to go home first. She wanted a cheap fibre suitcase, such as we've got stacks of on either side of the door. She chose the medium-sized model, paid for it and went into the bar next door. I was standing in the entrance of the shop a little later when I saw her go towards the station, carrying the case.'

'Are you alone in your shop?'

'I've got an assistant with me.'

'Can you leave the shop for half an hour? Then jump into a taxi and come to see me at this address.'

'I suppose you'll pay my fare? Am I to keep the taxi?'

'Yes, keep it.'

According to the notes on the envelope, it was at 5.50 p.m. that the driver of the first taxi arrived, somewhat surprised that a call from the police should bring him to a private house. But he recognized Maigret, and glanced around with curiosity, obviously interested in the home setting of the famous Superintendent.

'Go immediately to the house across the street and up to the third floor. If the concierge stops you, say you're looking for Madame Martin.'

'Madame Martin, right.'

'Ring at the door at the end of the passage. If a blonde lady opens it and you recognize her, you must invent some pretext or other. Say you've come to the wrong floor, or something of the sort. If it's somebody else, ask to speak to Madame Martin in person.'

'And then?'

'Nothing else. Come back here and tell me whether it was in fact the person you took to the Rue de Maubeuge this morning.'

'Okay, Superintendent.'

As the door closed, Maigret involuntarily gave a little smile.

'At the first call, she'll begin to worry. At the second, if all goes according to plan, she'll be seized with panic. At the third, provided Torrence can lay hands on him...'

And everything seemed to be running smoothly today. Torrence rang up:

'I think I'm lucky, Chief. I've discovered a driver who took on a young woman answering your description at the Gare du Nord, but he did not take her back to the Boulevard Richard-Lenoir. She asked to be set down at the corner of the Boulevard Beaumarchais and the Rue du Chemin-Vert.'

'Send him along.'

'I'm afraid he's a bit sozzled.'

'Never mind. Where are you?'

'At the Barbès station.'

'It won't take you too much out of your way to come by the Gare du Nord. Go to the left luggage office. Unfortunately the man on duty won't be the same as this morning. See if they've got a small fibre suitcase there, brand new, probably lightweight, which must have been deposited between 9.30 and 10 this morning. Make a note of the number. You won't be allowed to take it out without the ticket. But ask for the name and address of the attendant who was on duty this morning.'

'What shall I do then?'

'Ring me up. I'll be expecting your second driver. If he's drunk, write my address on a bit of paper so that he doesn't lose his way.'

Madame Maigret had retreated into her kitchen, where she was preparing dinner without venturing to ask whether Lucas was to eat with them.

Was Paul Martin still there with his daughter, across the street? Had Madame Martin attempted to get rid of him?

When the doorbell rang, there were two men, not just one, standing on the landing, staring with surprise at each other's unfamiliar face.

The first taxi driver, having just returned from the house across the street, had arrived on Maigret's staircase at the same time as the man from the travel goods shop.

'Did you recognize her?'

'Not only did I recognize her, but she recognized me too. She turned quite pale. She hurried to shut a bedroom door and asked me what I wanted.'

'What did you tell her?'

'That I'd come to the wrong floor. I saw she was wondering whether to let me get away with that, and I didn't leave her time to think it over. From down below, I've seen her at her window. She probably knows I've come up here.'

The travel goods salesman was out of his depth. He was a middle-aged man, completely bald, with an unctuous manner. When the driver had left, Maigret explained to him what he was to do, and he raised objections, repeating obstinately:

'She's a customer, don't you see? It's not the thing to give away a customer.'

He eventually consented to go, but Maigret took the precaution of sending Lucas close on his heels, in case he changed his mind on the way.

Before ten minutes had elapsed they were back.

'I must point out to you that I only acted under your orders, under constraint and compulsion.'

'Did you recognize her?'

'Shall I be called upon to give evidence under oath?'

'That's highly probable.'

'It'll be bad for business. People who buy luggage at the last minute are sometimes people who would rather not have their movements talked about.'

'Perhaps, if the occasion arises, your statement to the examining magistrate will serve the purpose.'

'Well! It was her all right. She's dressed differently, but I recognized her.'

'Did she recognize you?'

'She immediately asked who had sent me.'

'What did you reply?'

'I don't really know. I was very embarrassed. I said I'd come to the wrong door . . .'

'Did she offer you anything?'

'What do you mean? She didn't even ask me to sit down. That would have been even more awkward.'

Whereas the taxi driver had not asked for anything, this man, who was probably well off, insisted on being compensated for the time he had wasted.

'Now we've got to wait for the third, Lucas old fellow.'

Madame Maigret, meanwhile, was growing fidgety. Standing in the doorway, she signalled to her husband, as discreetly as she could, that he should follow her into the kitchen. There she whispered:

'Are you sure the father is still over there?'

'Why?'

'I don't know. I don't exactly understand what you're hatching. I'm thinking about the little girl and I'm a bit frightened...'

Darkness had fallen long since. Families had gone home. There were lights in most of the windows opposite, and the shadowy figure of Mademoiselle Doncoeur was still visible behind hers.

Maigret, who was still collarless and tieless, finished dressing while waiting for the second taxi driver. He called out to Lucas:

'Help yourself. Don't you want something to eat?'

'I'm full of sandwiches, Chief. There's only one thing I'd like, when we go out: a glass of draught beer.'

The second driver arrived at 6.20. At 6.35 he was back from the other house, with a randy glint in his eye.

'She looks even better in a housecoat than in a suit,' he said thickly. 'She made me come in and asked me who'd sent me. As I couldn't think what to answer I said the Director of the Folies Bergère. She was livid. She's a dish, all the same. I don't know if you noticed her legs...'

It was not easy to get rid of him, and Maigret only managed to do so after giving him a glass of plum brandy, for he had been eyeing the bottle with obvious longing.

'What are you planning to do, Chief?'

Lucas had seldom seen Maigret take so many precautions, prepare his attack so carefully, as though he were tackling a powerful adversary instead of an apparently insignificant bourgeois housewife.

'Do you think she'll go on defending herself?'

'Fiercely, and what's more, coldly.'

'What are you waiting for?'

'A call from Torrence.'

It came as expected, as though in a well-prepared musical score.

'The suitcase is here. It must be practically empty. As we foresaw, they won't give it to me without a form. As for the attendant who was on duty this morning, he lives outside Paris, somewhere near La Varenne-Saint-Hilaire.'

This might have proved a hitch, or at any rate have caused a delay. But Torrence went on:

'Only it's not worth going all that way. After his day's work he plays the trumpet in a dance band in the Rue de Lappe.'

'Go and fetch him.'

'Shall I bring him to your house?'

After all, perhaps Maigret too felt like a glass of cool beer.

'No, to the house opposite, third floor, Madame Martin's. I'll be there.'

This time he took down his thick overcoat, filled a pipe and said to Lucas: 'Coming?'

Madame Maigret ran after him to ask when he'd be back for dinner, and he hesitated for a moment, then replied with a smile: 'Usual time!' which was scarcely reassuring.

'Take good care of the little girl.'

5

By ten o'clock that evening they had still obtained no tangible result. Nobody in the house was asleep save Colette, who had finally dropped off and by whose bedside her father was still keeping watch in the darkness.

At half-past eleven Torrence had arrived with the railway clerk who was a spare-time musician, and the man, as unhesitatingly as the others, had declared:

'That's her, right enough. I can still see her slipping the receipt not into a handbag but into her brown canvas shopping bag.'

The bag was brought from the kitchen to show him.

'That's the one. At any rate it's the same sort and the same colour.'

It was very warm in the flat. They were speaking in lowered voices, as though by mutual consent, so as not to wake the sleeping child in the next room. Nobody had eaten or thought of eating. Before going up Maigret and Lucas had drunk a couple of beers each in a small café in the Boulevard Voltaire.

As for Torrence, after the musician had left, Maigret took him into the passage and gave him his instructions in a low voice.

There seemed to be no nook or cranny of the apartment which had not been searched. Even the framed photographs of Martin's parents had been taken down, to make sure the left-luggage receipt had not been slipped under the cardboard. The crockery had been taken out of the cupboard and stacked on the table, and even the meat-safe had been emptied.

Madame Martin was still wearing the pale blue housecoat in which the two men had seen her. She was chain-smoking cigarettes, and the smoke, mingling with that of the men's pipes, formed a heavy cloud that drifted round the lamps.

'You are entitled to say nothing, to refuse to answer any questions. Your husband will arrive at 11.17 and perhaps you'll be more talkative in his presence.'

'He knows no more than I do.'

'Does he know as much as you do?'

'There's nothing to know. I've told you everything.'

She had denied everything, from beginning to end. On one point only had she been shaken. When she had been questioned about the house in the Rue Pernelle she had admitted that her former employer had happened to visit her at night on two or three occasions. She maintained nonetheless that there had never been any intimate relations between them.

'In other words, he visited you on business at one in the morning?'

'He'd just got off the train, and often had large sums of money with him. I've already told you he was sometimes involved in gold smuggling. That's nothing to do with me. You can't prosecute me for that.'

'Had he a large sum in his possession when he disappeared?'

'I don't know. He didn't always keep me informed about such matters.'

'And yet he came to your room at night to talk about them?'

As to her movements that morning, she once again denied everything, in the teeth of the evidence, declared that she had never before seen the people who had been sent to call on her, the two taxi drivers, the travel goods salesman and the clerk from the left-luggage office.

'If I really deposited a parcel at the Gare du Nord you must be able to find the receipt.'

It was practically certain that it would not be found in the flat, not even in Colette's room, which Maigret had searched before the little girl went to sleep. He had even thought of the plaster round the child's leg, but it had not been renewed lately.

'Tomorrow I shall lodge a complaint,' she said fiercely. 'It's all a plot hatched by a spiteful neighbour. I was quite right to be suspicious of her this morning when she insisted on taking me to see you.'

She kept glancing anxiously at the alarm clock on the mantelpiece, evidently thinking of her husband's return, but in spite of her impatience, she was not to be caught off guard by any question.

'Admit that the man who came last night found nothing under the floor because you'd changed the hiding-place.'

'I don't even know if there ever was anything under the floor.'

'When you learnt that he had come, that he was determined to regain possession of what you were hiding, you thought of the left-luggage office, where your treasure would be safe.'

'I didn't go to the Gare du Nord and there are thousands of blonde women in Paris who answer to the same description as myself.'

'What did you do with the receipt? It isn't here. I am convinced it isn't in the flat, but I think I know where we shall discover it.'

'You're very clever.'

'Sit down at this table.'

He handed her a piece of paper and a pen.

'Write!'

'What do you want me to write?'

'Your name and address.'

She did so, after a little hesitation.

'Tonight all the letters posted in the nearest letter-box will be examined and I'm willing to bet there'll be one on which your writing will be recognized. You've probably addressed it to yourself.'

He instructed Lucas to ring up a police officer and have such an investigation put in hand. In fact he did not expect it to produce any results, but the thrust had gone home.

'You hate me, don't you?'

'I admit that I don't feel particularly fond of you.'

They were alone together in the dining room now, Maigret prowling slowly round the room while she sat at the table.

'And in case you're interested, I'll add that what shocks me most is not what you may have done but your coolness. I've had to cope with many people, both men and women. For the past three hours we've been sitting opposite one another and it's clear that since this morning you've been on tenterhooks. You've not flinched yet. Your husband will be back soon, and you'll try to make yourself out a victim. Now you know that inevitably, sooner or later, we're going to learn the truth.'

'What good will that do you? I've done nothing.'

'Then why try to hide something? Why tell lies?'

She did not reply, but she was thinking. It was not her nerves that were giving way, as usually happens. It was her mind working to find a way out, weighing the pros and cons.

'I shan't say anything,' she declared at last, sitting down in an armchair and pulling her housecoat over her bare legs.

'Just as you please.'

He settled comfortably in another armchair opposite her.

'Do you intend to stay in my flat a long time?'

'At any rate until your husband gets here.'

'Are you going to tell him about Monsieur Lorilleux's visits to the lodging-house?'

'If it's necessary.'

'You're a cad! Jean knows nothing about the business, he has nothing to do with it.'

'He's your husband, unfortunately.'

When Lucas returned he found them face to face, both casting stealthy glances at each other.

'Janvier is seeing to the letter, Chief. I met Torrence down below and he told me the man is at the wine merchant's, two houses beyond your place.'

She sprang to her feet.

'What man?'

And Maigret, never moving, replied:

'The man who came here last night. I suppose you expected him to come back to see you, since he'd found nothing? Perhaps this time he'll be in different frame of mind?'

She was looking at the clock in terror. In another twenty minutes the train from Bergerac would be in. If her husband took a taxi she could not depend on more than forty minutes' respite.

'Do you know who he is?'

'I can guess. I only have to go downstairs to make certain. It's obviously Lorilleux, who is very anxious to retrieve his property.'

'It's not his property.'

'Let's say what he rightly or wrongly considers his property. He must be broke. He's visited you twice without getting hold of what he wanted. He came back disguised as Father Christmas and he'll be back again. He's going to be very surprised to find you in our company, and I'm sure he'll be more talkative than you are. Contrary to what people think, men talk more readily than women. Do you suppose he's armed?'

'I've no idea.'

'I think he will be. He's fed up with waiting. I don't know what you've told him, but he's not too pleased with it. He looks a nasty customer. There's nothing worse than those weak men when they get going.'

'Shut up!'

'Would you like us to go away so that you can receive him?'

Maigret's notes read: '10.38 p.m. She talks.'

But there was no police report of her first statement. It came in brief phrases, uttered with venom, and often Maigret spoke instead of her, proffering random assertions which she did not deny, or which she merely corrected.

'What do you want to know?'

'Was there money in the case you left at the station office?'

'Bank notes. Just under a million francs.'

'To whom did this sum belong? To Lorilleux?'

'It was no more his than mine.'

'Did it belong to one of his customers?'

'A man called Julien Boissy, who often visited the shop.'

'What happened to him?'

'He's dead.'

'How did he die?'

'He was killed.'

'By whom?'

'By Monsieur Lorilleux.'

'Why?'

'Because I had led him to believe that if he had enough money at his disposal I would go away with him.'

'Were you already married at that time?'

'Yes.'

'You don't love your husband?'

'I loathe being hard up. I've been poor all my life. All my life I've heard talk of nothing but money and having to do without things. All my life I've seen people scrimping and saving and I've had to scrimp and save myself.'

She spoke as though Maigret was responsible for her unhappiness.

'Would you have gone off with Lorilleux?'

'I don't know. For a while, maybe.'

'Long enough to get his money from him?'

'I hate you!'

'How was the murder committed?'

'Monsieur Boissy was one of our customers.'

'A connoisseur of erotic books?'

'He was as dirty-minded as all the rest, as Monsieur Lorilleux, as you yourself probably. He was a widower and lived alone in a hotel room, but he was very rich, very miserly too. The rich are always miserly.'

'You're not rich yourself, though.'

'I should have become rich.'

'If Monsieur Lorilleux had not turned up again. How did Boissy die?'

'He was afraid of devaluation and he wanted gold, like everybody else at that time. Monsieur Lorilleux was involved in the gold traffic; he used to go to Switzerland regularly to get it. He was always paid in advance. One afternoon, Monsieur Boissy brought the big money along to the shop. I wasn't there. I'd gone out on an errand.'

'On purpose?'

'No.'

'You didn't suspect what was going to happen?'

'No. Don't try to make me say that. You'd be wasting your time. Only, when I got back, Monsieur Lorilleux was packing up the body in a big trunk he'd bought specially for the job.'

'Did you blackmail him?'

'No.'

'How do you account for his disappearance after handing over the money to you?'

'It was because I frightened him.'

'By threatening to give him away?'

'No. I just told him that some neighbours had been giving me a funny look and that it might be wiser to put the money away in safety for some time. I told him about a floorboard in my flat that could easily be lifted and then replaced. He thought it was only going to be for a few days. A couple of days later he suggested my crossing the Belgian frontier with him.'

'You refused?'

'I made him believe that a man who looked like a detective had stopped me in the street and asked me questions. He took fright. I gave him a little of the money and promised to join him in Brussels as soon as we were out of danger.'

'What did he do with Boissy's body?'

'He took it to a little house he had in the country, on the banks of the Marne, and there I suppose he buried it or threw it into the river. He took a taxi. Nobody ever spoke of Boissy again, nobody wondered about his disappearance.'

'You managed to send Lorilleux into Belgium by himself?'

'That was easy.'

'And for five years you were able to keep him at bay?'

'I used to write to him, *poste restante*, that the police were looking for him, that if nothing was said about it in the papers it was because a trap was being laid for him. I told him the police were constantly questioning me. I even sent him off to South America ...'

'And he came back two months ago?'

'About then. He was broke.'

'Didn't you send him any money?'

'Very little.'

'Why?'

She made no reply, but glanced at the clock.

'Are you going to take me off? What are you going to charge me with? I've done nothing. I didn't kill Boissy. I wasn't there when he died. I didn't help to hide the corpse.'

'Don't worry about your fate. You kept the money because all your life you've wanted to have money, not in order to spend it but to feel yourself rich and safe from want.'

'That's my own business.'

'When Lorilleux came to ask you to help him, or to keep your promise to run away with him, you took advantage of Colette's accident to pretend that you couldn't get at the hiding-place. Isn't that how it happened? You tried to get him to cross the frontier once again.'

'He stayed in Paris, in hiding.'

Her lips curled in a curious involuntary smile, and she could not resist muttering:

'The idiot! He could have told everybody his name without getting into any trouble.'

'All the same he thought of the Father Christmas plan.'

'Only the money was no longer under the floor. It was here, under his nose, in my workbox. He only had to lift the lid.'

'In ten or fifteen minutes, your husband will be here. Lorilleux, who is across the street, is probably aware of it; he knows that Martin was in Bergerac and he must have consulted the railway timetable.

He's no doubt plucking up his courage. I should be much surprised if he isn't armed. Do you want to wait for the pair of them?'

'Take me away. Just give me time to slip on a dress . . .'

'The left-luggage receipt?'

'At the *poste restante* in the Boulevard Beaumarchais.'

She had gone into the bedroom, leaving the door ajar, and without the least concern for modesty she took off her housecoat, sat down on the edge of the bed to pull on her stockings and took a woollen dress out of the wardrobe.

At the last minute she grabbed a travelling bag and thrust into it a confusion of toilet articles and underclothes.

'Let's leave at once.'

'Your husband?'

'To hell with that idiot.'

'Colette?'

She shrugged her shoulders in silence. The door of Mademoiselle Doncocur's flat moved slightly as they passed. Down below, as they stepped out on to the pavement, she took fright and shrank back between the two men, peering into the surrounding fog.

'Take her to Headquarters, Lucas. I'll stay here.'

There was no car in sight and she was evidently scared at the thought of walking through the darkness escorted only by little Lucas.

'You needn't be afraid. Lorilleux is not in the neighbourhood.'

'You've lied to me!'

Maigret went back into the house.

The conversation with Jean Martin took a good two hours, and most of it took place in his brother's presence.

When Maigret left the building at about half-past one in the morning, he left the two men alone together. A light was showing under Mademoiselle Doncoeur's door, but she tactfully refrained from opening it, and merely listened to the Superintendent's footsteps.

He crossed the boulevard and went home. He found his wife asleep in her armchair in front of the dining room table, where his place was laid. She gave a start.

'You're all alone?'

And as he stared at her in amused surprise:

'You've not brought the child back?'

'Not tonight. She's asleep. Tomorrow morning you can go and fetch her, and make sure you're nice to Mademoiselle Doncoeur.'

'Really?'

'I'll have a couple of nurses sent, with a stretcher.'

'But then . . . Can we . . .'

'Sh! . . . Not for good, you understand? Maybe Jean Martin will find somebody else . . . and maybe his brother will get back into normal life and marry again someday . . .'

'In short, she won't be our own?'

'Not our own, no. Only lent to us. I thought that would be better than nothing and that you'd be pleased.'

'Of course I'm pleased . . . Only . . . only . . .'

She sniffed, hunted for a handkerchief, failed to find one and hid her face in her apron.

30 May 1950
Carmel-by-the-Sea, California

Seven Little Crosses in a Notebook

'At home,' said Sommer, who was making coffee on a hot plate, 'we used to go to midnight Mass all together, and the village was half an hour from the farm. There were five of us boys. Winters were colder in those days, for I remember going to church in a sleigh.'

Lecoeur, sitting at his switchboard with its hundreds of plugs, had pushed back the headphones from his ears in order to follow the conversation.

'In what part of the country?'

'In Lorraine.'

'Winters weren't any colder in Lorraine forty years ago, but the peasants had no cars. How many times did you go to midnight Mass in a sleigh?'

'I don't know ...'

'Twice? Three times? Perhaps only once? But it impressed you because you were only a kid.'

'In any case when we got home we had a splendid blood sausage, the like of which I've never tasted since. And that's not fancy. We never discovered how my mother made it, nor what she put into it, to make it different from all other blood sausages. My wife has tried. She asked my elder sister, who claimed to have mother's recipe.'

He went up to one of the great curtainless windows behind

which lay nothing but darkness, and scratched the glass with his fingernail.

'Why, it's all frosted up. And that again reminds me of when I was little. In the mornings when I wanted to wash I often had to break the ice in my jug, although it was standing in my bedroom.'

'Because they didn't have central heating then,' Lecoeur objected calmly.

There were three of them on night duty, and they had been shut up in the huge room since 11 p.m. the previous evening. Now they were limp with 6 a.m. fatigue. Remains of food lay about on the tables, with three or four empty bottles.

A light as big as an aspirin tablet appeared on one of the walls.

'Thirteenth arrondissement,' muttered Lecoeur, putting back his headphones. 'Croulebarbe district.'

He seized a plug and thrust it into one of the holes.

'Croulebarbe district? Your van's just gone out. What's up?'

'Officer calling, Boulevard Masséna. A scuffle between two drunks.'

Lecoeur carefully made a little cross in one of the columns in his notebook.

'What are you chaps doing?'

'There are only four of us in the station. Two of them are playing dominoes.'

'Have you been eating black pudding?'

'No. Why?'

'Oh, no reason. I must hang up; something's happening in the sixteenth.'

A gigantic map of Paris was painted on the wall in front of him, and the little lights that flashed on represented police stations. As soon as one of these received a warning for one reason or another, the light went on and Lecoeur pushed in the plug.

'Hello! Chaillot district? Your van's just gone out.'

In each of the twenty arrondissements in Paris, in front of the blue lamp of every police station, one or more vans stood ready to rush off at the first warning.

'What is it?'

'Veronal.'

A woman, obviously. It was the third that night, the second in the fashionable Passy district.

Lecoeur marked a cross in another column while Mambret, at his desk, filled in official forms.

'Hello! Odéon? What's happening your way? Stolen car?'

That concerned Mambret, who took notes, picked up another phone, dictated the description of the car to Piedboeuf the telegraphist, the drone of whose voice could be heard immediately overhead. It was the forty-eighth stolen car that Piedboeuf had reported since eleven o'clock.

For other people, Christmas Eve must have a special flavour. Hundreds of thousands of Parisians had flocked to cinemas and theatres. Thousands more had been shopping until a late hour in the big stores where weary-legged assistants were bustling about, as though in some nightmare, in front of their almost denuded shelves.

There were family gatherings behind drawn curtains, with turkeys roasting and blood sausages probably prepared, like Sommer's, from some private recipe carefully handed down from mother to daughter.

There were children sleeping restlessly, while their parents were quietly setting out presents round the Christmas tree.

There were restaurants and nightclubs where all the tables had been reserved days in advance. There was the Salvation Army's barge on the Seine, where dossers queued up, hungrily sniffing the good smells.

Sommer had a wife and children. Piedboeuf, the telegraphist on the floor above, had become a father a week ago.

Except for the ice on the windows, they would not have realized that it was cold outside. Christmas Eve, for them, wore the drab yellow colour of their big office facing the Palais de Justice, in the now deserted buildings of the Préfecture of Police, where in two days' time, and not before, crowds would pour in with requests for aliens' cards, driving licences, passport visas, demands of every sort.

Down below in the courtyard vans were waiting for urgent calls, with their drivers dozing on the seats.

But there had been no urgent calls. The little crosses in Lecoeur's notebook were eloquent. He did not trouble to count them. He knew that there were some two hundred in the drunks' column.

The police were being indulgent that night. They tried to persuade people to go home quietly, and only intervened when some drunks turned nasty and began to smash glasses or threaten peaceful fellow customers.

Two hundred individuals, some of them women, were sound asleep on the floor in various police stations, behind bars.

There had been five knifings, two at the Porte d'Italie and three at the summit of Montmartre, not the Montmartre of the nightclubs but the outer zone, among the shanties built of old wooden boxes and tarred felt, inhabited by over a hundred thousand North Africans.

A few children reported missing—they were found again soon after—in the throng attending Mass.

'Hello! Chaillot? How's your veronal case?'

She had not died. They seldom do. They usually manage things so as not to die. They've made their gesture.

'Talking of blood sausages,' began Randon, who was smoking a big meerschaum pipe, 'that reminds me . . .'

They never learnt what it reminded him of. They heard hesitant footsteps in the unlighted staircase, a hand fumbled at the door and they saw the knob turn. The three of them stared in surprise that anyone should come to visit them at six o'clock in the morning.

'*Salut!*' said the man, throwing his hat down on a chair.

'What are you doing here, Janvier?'

Janvier was a young detective from the Homicide Squad, who went first of all to warm his hands over the radiator.

'I was bored, all alone over there,' he said. 'If the killer gets going I'll get the information here soonest.'

He, too, had spent the night on the job, but across the street, in the offices of the Police Judiciaire.

'May I?' he asked, lifting the coffeepot. 'The wind's icy.'

He was blinking and scarlet-eared from the cold.

'We shan't know anything before 8 a.m. or later,' said Lecoeur.

For the past fifteen years he had spent all his nights here in front of the map with its little lights and the telephone switchboard. He knew most of the Parisian police by name, at any rate those on night duty, he was even knowledgeable about their private affairs, since on quiet nights, when long intervals elapsed between the flashing of the lights, they could gossip together across space.

'How are things going with you?'

In this way he knew most of the police stations, too, although not all of them. He could imagine the atmosphere, as the policemen sat around with loosened belts and open-necked shirts, making coffee, just as they were doing here. But he had never seen them. He would not have recognized them in the street, any more than he had set foot in the hospitals whose names he knew as well as other people know the names of their uncles and aunts.

'Hello! Bichat? How's the injured man they brought in twenty minutes ago? Dead?'

A little cross in his notebook. You could ask him difficult questions:

'How many crimes are committed for money each year in Paris?'

He would reply unhesitatingly: 'Sixty-seven.'

'How many murders committed by foreigners?'

'Forty-two.'

'How many . . .'

He did not pride himself on it; he was meticulous, that was all. It was his job. He was not obliged to inscribe the little crosses in his notebook, but it helped to pass the time and it gave him as much satisfaction as collecting stamps.

He was unmarried. Nobody knew where he lived or what he did once he had left that office where he spent every night. Actually, one could scarcely imagine him outside in the street, like anybody else.

'For important happenings, you have to wait till people get up, till the concierge brings up the mail and the maids prepare breakfast and wake up their employers.'

His knowledge did him no particular credit, since things always happened that way. Earlier in summer, later in winter. And today it would be even later than usual, because a large proportion of the population was still sleeping off the wine and champagne drunk at last night's *réveillon* suppers. There were still some people about in the streets, and restaurant doors opened to let out the last customers.

More stolen cars would be reported, and probably two or three drunks overcome by the cold.

'Hello! Saint-Gervais?'

His Paris was a peculiar Paris, whose monuments were not the Eiffel Tower, the Opéra or the Louvre, but sombre administrative buildings with a police van standing under the blue lamp and policemen's bicycles propped up against the wall.

'The Chief's convinced,' Janvier was saying, 'that the man will do something tonight. It's the sort of night for those people. Holidays get them excited.'

No name was mentioned, because no name was known. One couldn't even say 'the man in the brown overcoat' or 'the man in the grey hat', because nobody had seen him. Some newspapers had called him 'Monsieur Dimanche', because three of the murders had been committed on a Sunday, but since then there had been five more, committed on weekdays, one per week on an average, only there was no regular pattern about that either.

'Is it on his account you've been kept up?'

For the same reason, an extra close watch was being kept throughout Paris, which meant that constables and detectives had to work overtime.

'You'll see,' said Sommer, 'when we lay hands on him, he'll turn out to be a lunatic.'

'A lunatic, but a killer,' sighed Janvier, as he drank his coffee. 'Say, one of your lights has gone on.'

'Hello! Bercy? Your van's gone out? What's that? Half a minute. Drowned?'

They could see Lecoeur hesitating into which column he should put his cross. There was one for suicide by hanging, another for people who, for lack of a weapon, threw themselves out of windows. There were columns for drownings, for shootings, for ...

'Listen, you fellows! Do you know what a chap's just done on the Pont d'Austerlitz? Who was talking about lunatics just now? This man tied a stone to his ankles and a rope round his neck, climbed on to the parapet and shot himself through the head.'

Come to think of it, there was a column for that too: mentally disturbed.

It was the time now when people who had not been celebrating last night were going to early Mass, with damp noses, hands thrust deep into pockets, walking bent double against the cold wind that drove a sort of powdery rime along the pavements. It was the time, too, when children were beginning to wake up, switch on the light and rush, barefooted and nightgowned, towards the wonderful tree.

'If our chap were really a crackpot, according to the pathologist, he would always kill in the same way, whether with a knife or a revolver or whatever.'

'What weapon did he use last time?'

'A hammer.'

'And the time before?'

'A dagger.'

'What proof is there that it's always the same man?'

'In the first place, the fact that the eight crimes were committed almost immediately one after another. It would be surprising if eight new murderers suddenly went to work in Paris.'

Inspector Janvier had obviously heard the matter discussed at length at Police Headquarters.

'Moreover there's a sort of family resemblance about these murders. Each time the victim has been somebody living alone, whether old or young, somebody without friends or relations.'

Sommer looked at Lecoeur, whom he could not forgive for being a bachelor and above all for having no children. He himself had five and his wife was expecting a sixth.

'Like you, Lecoeur! Take care!'

'Another clue is the areas in which he operates. Not one of the murders has been committed in wealthy or even middle-class districts.'

'And yet he steals.'

'He steals, but never much at a time. Small sums. Hoards hidden in mattresses or old clothes. He doesn't go in for housebreaking, he doesn't seem to be specially well equipped for burglary, and yet he leaves no trace.'

A small light flashed on. A stolen car, at the door of a restaurant in the Place des Ternes, not far from the Etoile.

'What must particularly infuriate people who can't find their car is having to go home in the metro.'

Another hour, an hour and a half, and they would be relieved, all except Lecoeur; he had promised to replace a colleague who was spending Christmas with his family near Rouen.

This often happened. It had become so usual that people no longer hesitated to ask him.

'Say, Lecoeur, couldn't you take my place tomorrow?'

In the beginning they used to find some sentimental pretext, a sick mother, a funeral, a child's first communion. They used to bring him a cake, something from a delicatessen or a bottle of wine.

In fact, if he had been able to, Lecoeur would have spent twenty-four hours out of the twenty-four in that room, with an occasional rest on a camp bed, and his meals simmering on the hot plate. Oddly enough, although he was as well-groomed as the rest, more so than some, more than Sommer for instance, whose trousers seldom looked pressed, there was something drab about him which betrayed his bachelordom.

He wore glasses with heavy lenses which made his eyes look round and staring, and it came as a surprise, when he took off his spectacles to wipe them with the chamois leather he always carried in his pocket, to discover his evasive, almost timid glance.

'Hello! Javel?'

One of the lights of the fifteenth arrondissement, in the industrial zone near the Quai de Javel, had just flashed on.

'Your van's gone out?'

'We don't know what's happened yet. Someone's broken the glass of an emergency call box in the Rue Leblanc.'

'Did anybody speak?'

'Not a word. The van's gone to investigate. I'll call you back.'

All along the streets of Paris there are hundreds of these red call boxes, of which one has only to break the glass to be in telephonic communication with the nearest police station. Might a passerby have broken this one by accident?

'Hello! Central? Our van's just back. There was nobody there. All quiet in the neighbourhood. We're going to patrol the district.'

Not to miss out altogether Lecoeur inscribed a little cross in the last column, devoted to the unclassified.

'Any more coffee?' he asked.

'I'll make some more.'

The same light came on again on the board. It was not ten minutes since the last signal.

'Javel? What's up?'

'Another emergency call.'

'And nobody spoke?'

'Not a word. A practical joker. Somebody who thinks it's fun to disturb us. This time we're going to try and get hold of him.'

'Where was it?'

'Pont Mirabeau.'

'I say, your friend's a fast walker!'

It was in fact quite a distance between the two red alarm call boxes. But these calls were not yet being taken seriously. Three days earlier, somebody had broken the glass of a call box and shouted defiantly: 'Death to the pigs!'

Janvier, with his feet up on one of the radiators, was starting to doze off, and when once again he heard Lecoeur's voice at the telephone he opened his eyes, noticed that one of the little lights was on and asked sleepily:

'Is it him again?'

'A glass broken in the Versailles area.'

'How idiotic!' he muttered, sinking back into comfortable drowsiness.

Daylight would come late, not before half-past seven or eight. From time to time the church bells sounded dimly, as though from another world. The poor police officers down below in the standby cars must be frozen.

'Talking of blood sausages...'

'What blood sausages?' muttered Janvier, who, drowsy and rosy-cheeked, looked like a small boy.

'The sausages that my mother...'

'Hello! You're not going to tell me someone's broken the glass of one of your emergency call boxes?...What?...It's true?...He's just broken two in the fifteenth...No, they've not managed to get hold of him...I say, he can run, that chap...He crossed the Seine by the Pont Mirabeau...He seems to be making for the city centre...Yes, try...'

That made another little cross, and by half-past seven, half an hour before relief time, there were five of them in the same column.

Maniac or not, the fellow was going at a good pace. It's true that it was hardly the temperature for lounging about. At one point he had seemed to be keeping to the banks of the Seine. He did not follow a straight line; he had made a detour through the wealthy streets of Auteuil and broken a glass in the Rue Fontaine.

'He's only five minutes away from the Bois de Boulogne,' Lecoeur announced. 'If that's where he's going we shall lose track of him.'

But the unknown person had made a virtual about turn and come back towards the river, breaking a glass in the Rue Berton, close by the Quai de Passy.

The first calls had come from the poor, working-class districts of Grenelle. The stranger had only had to cross the Seine to be in a different setting, wandering through spacious streets that were certainly deserted at this time of day. Everything must be shut; his footsteps would echo on the hard, frozen pavement.

A sixth call: he had skirted the Trocadéro and was now in the Rue de Longchamp.

'He must think he's Hop o' my Thumb,' commented Mambret. 'Failing breadcrumbs and white pebbles, he marks his trail with broken glass.'

Other messages came through, at rapid intervals: more stolen cars, a shot fired in the Rue de Flandre region, where the injured man denied all knowledge of his assailant, although he'd been seen drinking all night with a companion.

'Well, well! It's Javel again! Hello, Javel! I assume it's your glass-breaker again; he's not had time to get back to his starting-point. What? Yes indeed, he's been carrying on. He must be somewhere near the Champs-Elysées by now. What's that?... Wait a minute... Tell us... What street? Michat?...*chat* like cat, yes... Between the Rue Lecourbe and the Boulevard Félix-Faure... Yes... There's a railway bridge near... Yes... I'm with you, No. 17... Who called?... The concierge?... She was up at this hour?... Shut up, you lot!

'No, I didn't mean you. I was talking to Sommer, who's boring us stiff with his blood sausage...

'So then the concierge... I can picture it... A big shabby block... seven floors... Okay...'

That district was full of buildings that were not old, but so badly built that they seemed decrepit as soon as they were lived in. They stood in the midst of waste ground, with their bare gloomy walls, their gable-ends bedizened with advertisements, towering above the suburban houses and bungalows.

'You say she heard someone running down the stairs and then slamming the door... It had been open?... The concierge didn't know why?... On which floor?... The mezzanine, overlooking the courtyard... Go on... I see the van of the eighth arrondissement has just gone out and I bet it's my pane-smasher... An old woman... What did you say?... Old Madame Fayet?... She used to go out charring... Dead?... A blunt instrument... Is the doctor there?... You're quite sure she's dead?... Have her savings been pinched?... I ask that because I presume she had savings... Yes... Call me back... Otherwise I'll ring you...'

He turned towards the sleeping detective.

'Janvier! Hey, Janvier! I think this is something for you.'

'Who? What is it?'

'The killer.'

'Where?'

'At Javel. I've written the name on this bit of paper. This time he's attacked an old charlady, Madame Fayet.'

Janvier was putting on his overcoat and hunting for his hat; he swallowed the remaining drop of coffee in his cup.

'Who's in charge of the fifteenth?'

'Gonesse.'

'Let them know at Headquarters that I'm down there.'

A moment later Lecoeur was able to inscribe another little cross, the seventh, in the last column in his notebook. Someone had broken the glass of an emergency call box in the Avenue d'Iéna, a hundred and fifty metres from the Arc de Triomphe.

'Among the fragments of glass they've found a bloodstained handkerchief. It's a child's handkerchief.'

'No initials?'

'No. It's a blue and white checked handkerchief, rather grubby. Whoever it was must have wrapped it round his fist when he broke the pane.'

Steps sounded in the stairway. It was their relief, the day shift. The men had shaved, and their cheeks had a raw pink look that came from washing in cold water and facing the icy wind.

'Had a good party, you chaps?'

Sommer was closing the little tin box in which he had brought his meal. Lecoeur alone did not bestir himself, since he was going to stay behind with the new team.

Godin, a big stout fellow, was pulling on the denim overall that he wore for working; as soon as he arrived he put some water on to boil for a hot toddy. His invariable cold dragged on all winter, and he dosed it, or coddled it, with copious toddies.

'Hello! Yes...No, I'm not leaving...I'm replacing Potier who's gone to visit his family...So what...Yes, I'm personally interested...Janvier has gone, but I'll pass on the message to Headquarters...A cripple?...What sort of cripple?'

It always takes patience to begin with, to get the hang of things, because people talk to you about the case they're dealing with as if the whole world knew all about it.

'The bungalow at the back, yes...So not in the Rue Michat... Which street?...Rue Vasco de Gama?...Yes, I know it...The little house with a garden and a railing...I didn't know he was a cripple...Right...So he doesn't sleep much...A small boy climbing up the drainpipe...How old?...He doesn't know?...True, of course it was dark...How does he know it was a small boy?... Listen, be kind enough to call me back...You're going off too?... Who's replacing you?...Big Jules?...The one who...Yes... Okay...Say hello to him from me and ask him to call me.'

'What's all that about?' asked one of the newcomers.

'An old woman who's got herself bumped off at Javel.'

'By whom?'

'A crippled fellow who lives in a house behind the block of flats says he saw a small boy climbing up the wall towards her window.'

'Could the boy have killed her?'

'At any rate it was a child's handkerchief that they picked up beside one of the alarm boxes.'

They were listening to him inattentively. The lights were still on, but bleak daylight was coming through the frost-patterned panes. Once again somebody went to scratch the crisp surface; an instinctive gesture, perhaps a childhood memory recalled, like Sommer's blood sausage?

The night shift had left. The others were getting organized, settling down for the day, leafing through reports.

A stolen car, Square La Bruyère.

Lecoeur looked at his seven little crosses with a preoccupied air, and got up with a sigh to stand in front of the huge mural map.

'Are you learning your map of Paris by heart?'

'I know it already. But there's one detail that's struck me. In about an hour and a half seven emergency call boxes have had their glass broken. Now I've noticed that the person who's been playing this game not only didn't go straight ahead, or take a definite route from one place to the next, but he zigzagged about to a considerable extent.'

'Perhaps he doesn't know Paris well?'

'Or else he knows it too well. He didn't once go past a police station, whereas if he'd taken the shortest way he would have passed several of them. And which are the crossroads where one is likely to meet a policeman?'

He pointed them out.

'He didn't go past these either. He skirted them. The only risk he ran was when he crossed over the Pont Mirabeau, but it would have been just the same if he'd crossed the Seine anywhere else.'

'He's probably tight,' said Godin jokingly, as he sipped his hot rum after cooling it with his breath.

'What I'm wondering is why he's stopped breaking panes of glass?'

'The chap's probably gone home by now.'

'A fellow who turns up in the Javel district at six in the morning isn't likely to be living near the Etoile.'

'Are you interested?'

'I'm frightened.'

'You don't mean it?'

Such signs of uneasiness were in fact surprising in the case of Lecoeur, for whom the most dramatic nocturnal happenings of Paris were usually summed up by a few little crosses in a notebook.

'Hello! Javel?...Big Jules?...Lecoeur here, yes...Tell me... Behind the block of flats in the Rue Michat, there's the cripple's house...Yes...But beside it there's another block, a red brick building with a grocer's shop on the ground floor...Yes...Has anything happened in that house?...The concierge didn't say?... I don't know...No, I know nothing...Perhaps it would be as well to go and ask her, yes...'

He suddenly felt very warm, and he stubbed out a half-smoked cigarette.

'Hello! Les Ternes? You've had no emergency calls in your district? Nothing? Only drunks? Thanks. By the way, has the cyclist patrol gone out?...They're just going out?...Ask them to look out in case they happen to see a small boy...A boy who's looking tired and whose right hand is bleeding...No, it's not a missing person...I'll explain another time...'

His eyes never left the mural map, where for at least ten minutes no light appeared; and then it was to report a case of accidental gassing in the eighteenth arrondissement, right at the top of Montmartre.

The cold streets of Paris were empty save for the dark figures of people returning from early Mass, shivering with cold.

2

Among the sharpest impressions that André Lecoeur retained from his childhood was one of stillness. His world, then, had been a large kitchen on the outskirts of Orléans. He must have spent winters there as well as summers, but he remembered it chiefly as flooded with sunlight, its door wide open, with a barred gate which his father had put up one Sunday to prevent him from wandering alone into the garden, where hens were clucking and rabbits nibbling all day behind their netting.

At half-past eight his father used to go off on his bicycle to the gas works where he was employed, at the other end of the town. His mother did the housework, always following the same routine, going up into the bedrooms and laying the mattresses on the windowsill.

And then almost at once the greengrocer's bell, as he pushed his barrow along the street, told that it was ten o'clock. At eleven, twice a week, the bearded doctor came to see his small brother, who was always ill and whose room he was not allowed to visit.

That was all. Nothing else ever happened. He barely had time to play and drink his glass of milk before his father was back for lunch.

Now his father had been round several districts collecting payments and had met lots of people, about whom he talked at table, while here time had scarcely moved. And the afternoon, maybe because he had to take a rest, passed even more quickly.

'No sooner have I got down to my housework than it's time to eat,' his mother used to sigh.

It was somewhat the same here, in the big room at the Central

Office where even the air never stirred, where the men on duty seemed to grow numb, until they heard voices and telephone calls as though through a thin layer of sleep.

A few little lights flashed on against the wall, a few little crosses were put down—a bus had run into a car in the Rue de Clignancourt—and then there came a call from the Javel police station.

It was not big Jules this time. It was Inspector Gonesse, the one who had gone to visit the spot. They had had time to contact him and tell him about the house in the Rue Vasco de Gama. He had been there, and had just got back, highly excited.

'Is that you, Lecoeur?'

There was a special note of annoyance or suspicion in his voice.

'Say, how did you come to think of that house? Did you know old Madame Fayet?'

'I never saw her, but I know who she is.'

What was happening this Christmas morning was something André Lecoeur had been anticipating for ten years at least. More precisely, when he let his eyes wander over the map of Paris where the electric lights flashed on, he sometimes said to himself:

'One of these days, inevitably, it'll be somebody I know.'

Occasionally something had happened in his own district, not far from his own street, but never actually in it, moving nearer or further away like a thunderstorm without ever striking the exact spot where he lived.

Now it had happened.

'Have you questioned the concierge?' he asked. 'Was she up?'

He could imagine the ambiguous expression of Inspector Gonesse at the other end of the line, and he went on:

'Is the boy at home?'

And Gonesse growled: 'You know him too?'

'He's my nephew. Didn't they tell you his name is Lecoeur, François Lecoeur?'

'They told me.'

'Well then?'

'He's not at home.'

'And his father?'

'He came back soon after seven this morning.'

'As usual, I know. He's a night worker too.'

'The concierge heard him go up to his flat, third floor at the back.'

'I know it.'

'He came down again almost immediately and knocked at the door of the concierge's lodge. He looked very upset, quite wild, she said.'

'Has the boy disappeared?'

'Yes. His father asked if anyone had seen him go out, and if so, when. The concierge didn't know. Then he asked if a telegram had been delivered during the evening, or early this morning.'

'Had there been a telegram?'

'No. Do you understand anything about it? Don't you think, since you're a relative and in the picture, you'd better come over here?'

'It wouldn't be any use. Where's Janvier?'

'In Mère Fayet's room. The fingerprints people have just come and have set to work. The first thing they found was a child's prints on the handle of the door. Why don't you come along?'

Lecoeur replied half-heartedly:

'There's nobody to take my place here.'

It was true: at a pinch, by telephoning here and there, he might have found a colleague prepared to spend an hour or two at the Central Office. The truth was that he had no desire to be on the spot, that it would have served no useful purpose.

'Listen, Gonesse, I've got to find that boy, do you understand? Half an hour ago he must have been wandering about near the Etoile. Tell Janvier I'm stopping here, and that Mère Fayet probably had a good sum of money hidden in her place.'

Somewhat hectically, he transferred his plug to another hole and rang up the various police stations of the eighth arrondissement.

'Look for a small boy, ten or eleven years old, rather poorly dressed, and keep a special watch on emergency call boxes.'

His two colleagues stared at him with some curiosity.

'Do you think it's the kid who did the job?'

He did not bother to reply. He was calling the telephone exchange overhead.

'Justin! Why, so it's you on duty? Will you ask the radio cars to look out for a ten-year-old boy wandering somewhere in the Etoile region? No, I don't know where he's making for. He seems to be avoiding the streets where there's a police station and the main crossroads where he might come across a traffic cop.'

He knew his brother's flat in the Rue Vasco de Gama, a couple of dark rooms and a minute kitchen, where the boy spent all his nights alone while his father was out at work. The windows looked on to the back of the Rue Michat, where there were lines of washing hanging out, pots of geraniums, and behind the windows, many of them curtainless, there lived a motley assortment of human beings.

Incidentally, there too the panes must be frosted over. This detail struck him. He put it away in a corner of his memory, for he felt it might be of some importance.

'Do you think it's a child who's been smashing the panes of the call boxes?'

'A child's handkerchief has been picked up,' he said briefly.

And he stayed there in suspense, wondering into which hole he should push his plug.

Outside, people seemed to be doing things at a breathless speed. No sooner had Lecoeur answered a call than the doctor was on the spot, then the Deputy Public Prosecutor and an examining magistrate who must have been torn from his slumbers.

What was the point of going to the spot, since from where he sat he could see the streets and houses as clearly as the men who were there, with the railway bridge cutting across the landscape in a great black line?

Only the poor lived in that district, young people who hoped to get out of it some day, others less young who were beginning to lose heart, and those, even less young, almost old or really old, who were trying to come to terms with their lot.

He called Javel once again.

'Is Inspector Gonesse still there?'

'He's writing up his report. Shall I get him?'

'Yes, please...Hello, Gonesse? Lecoeur here...I'm sorry to bother you...Did you go up into my brother's flat?...Good! Was the child's bed unmade? That reassures me a little...Wait a minute... Were there any parcels?... That's right... What? A chicken, a blood sausage, a cream cake and... I don't understand the rest... A radio set?... It hadn't been unwrapped?... Obviously!... Is Janvier with you?... He's already rung up Headquarters?... Thank you...'

He was quite surprised to see that it was already half-past nine. There was no longer any point in watching the Etoile district on the map of Paris. If the boy had gone on walking at the same pace, he'd have had time to reach one of the city suburbs by now.

'Hello! Police Judiciaire? Is Superintendent Saillard in his office?'

He, too, must have been dragged out of his warm home by Janvier's call. How many people were having their Christmas spoilt by this business?

'Excuse me for calling you, Superintendent. It's about the Lecoeur boy.'

'Do you know anything? Is he a relative of yours?'

'He's my brother's son. He's probably responsible for smashing the glass of seven emergency call boxes. I don't know if they've had time to inform you that after the Etoile we've lost track of him. I'd like to ask your permission to send out a general message.'

'Couldn't you come and see me?'

'I've nobody available to replace me here.'

'Send out the message. I'll come round.'

Lecoeur remained calm, but his hand shook a little as he manipulated the plug.

'Is that you, Justin? A general message. Give the boy's description. I don't know how he's dressed, but he's probably wearing his khaki jacket cut down from an American Windcheater. He's tall for his age, and thinnish. No, no cap, he's always bareheaded, with hair hanging over his forehead. Perhaps you'd better give his father's description too. That's rather harder for me. You know me, of course? Well, he's like me, only paler. He looks timid and rather sickly, the sort of man who dares not walk in the middle of the pavement but slinks along beside the walls of houses. He walks a bit awkwardly, because he was wounded in the foot during the last war. No, I haven't the least idea where they are going. I don't believe they are together. What's more than likely is that the kid's in danger. Why? That would take too long to explain. Send out your message. Let me know here if there's anything new.'

By the time that phone call was over Superintendent Saillard had appeared, having had time to leave the Quai des Orfèvres and walk across the street and through the empty buildings of the Préfecture of Police. He was an imposing figure in a huge overcoat. To greet the company he merely touched the rim of his hat, then he picked up a chair as if it were a straw and sat down astride it.

'The kid?' he asked at last, staring at Lecoeur.

'I wonder why he's stopped calling us.'

'Calling us?'

'Why should he break the glass of emergency call boxes if not to draw our attention to himself?'

'And why, having taken the trouble to break them, doesn't he speak into the telephone?'

'Suppose he's being followed? Or that he's following somebody?'

'I thought of that. Tell me, Lecoeur, isn't your brother in low water financially?'

'Yes, he's a poor man.'

'Only a poor man?'

'He lost his job three months ago.'

'What job?'

'He was a linotype operator at La Presse in the Rue du Croissant, where he worked nights. He always worked nights. It seems to run in the family.'

'Why did he lose his job?'

'He probably quarrelled with somebody.'

'Was that a habit of his?'

A call interrupted them. It came from the eighteenth arrondissement, where a small boy had just been picked up in the street, at the corner of the Rue Lepic. He was selling sprigs of holly. He was Polish and could not speak a word of French.

'You were asking me if quarrelling was a habit of his? I don't know quite how to answer that. My brother had been a sick person for most of his life. When we were young he lived almost entirely in his bedroom, all alone, reading. He's read tons of books. But he never had any regular schooling.'

'Is he married?'

'His wife died after two years of marriage, leaving him alone with a ten-month-old baby.'

'He brought up the child himself?'

'Yes. I can still see him bathing it, changing its nappies, preparing its bottles.'

'That doesn't explain why he was quarrelsome.'

Of course, words hadn't the same meaning in the Superintendent's big head as they had in Lecoeur's heart.

'Was he embittered?'

'Not particularly. He was used to it.'

'Used to what?'

'To not living like other people. Maybe Olivier (that's my brother's name) isn't very intelligent. Perhaps he knows too much about some subjects, owing to his reading, and not enough about others.'

'Do you think he'd have been capable of killing the old Fayet woman?'

The Superintendent was puffing at his pipe. Upstairs the telegraphist could be heard walking about, and the other two policemen in the room were pretending not to listen.

'She was his mother-in-law,' Lecoeur said with a sigh. 'You were bound to find out sooner or later.'

'He didn't get on with her?'

'She hated him.'

'Why?'

'Because she held him responsible for what happened to her daughter. There was some business about an operation that wasn't done in time. It was not my brother's fault but the hospital's; they refused to take her in because her papers were not in order. None the less the old woman has always held it against my brother.'

'Did they ever see one another?'

'They must have met in the street sometimes, since they lived in the same district.'

'Did the boy know?'

'That Mère Fayet was his grandmother? I don't think so.'

'Hadn't his father told him?'

Lecoeur's eyes remained fixed on the map with its little lights, but this was the slack time of day; they seldom came on, and almost always, now, for traffic accidents. Somebody's pocket had been picked in the metro, somebody's luggage had been stolen at the Gare de l'Est.

No news of the boy. And yet the streets of Paris were half empty. In the more densely populated districts a few children were trying out their new toys on the pavements, but most houses seemed shut up and most windows were clouded with steam from the warmth of the rooms. Shops were closed, and small bars deserted save for a few regular customers. Only the pealing bells rang out over the rooftops, while families in their Sunday best made their way to churches from which the boom of great organs flowed out in waves.

'Will you excuse me a moment, Superintendent? I'm still thinking about the boy. It's obviously harder for him now to smash panes of glass without attracting attention. But perhaps we could have a look in the churches? In a bar or a café he could not pass unnoticed. In a church, on the other hand...'

He rang up Justin again.

'The churches, old man! Get them to watch the churches. And the stations. I hadn't thought of the stations either.'

He took off his glasses and revealed reddened eyelids, possibly from lack of sleep.

'Hello! Yes, Central Office here. What? Yes, the Superintendent's here.'

He handed the receiver to Saillard.

'It's Janvier wanting to speak to you.'

The north wind was still blowing outside and the light was harsh and bleak, although behind the massed clouds a faint yellowness gave a promise of sunlight.

As the Superintendent hung up again, he commented gruffly:

'Dr. Paul says the crime must have been committed between five and six o'clock this morning. The old woman was not killed immediately. She must have been lying down when she heard a noise;

she got up to confront her attacker, and probably hit him with a shoe.'

'Was the weapon found?'

'No. It looks as if it was a piece of lead piping or a rounded instrument, such as a hammer.'

'Was her money taken?'

'Only her purse, containing notes of small amounts and her identity card. Tell me, Lecoeur, did you know that woman lent money at high rates of interest?'

'Yes, I knew.'

'Didn't you tell me just now that your brother lost his job about three months ago?'

'That's correct.'

'The concierge didn't know.'

'Nor did his son. It was on his son's account that he said nothing about it.'

The Superintendent sat uneasily crossing and uncrossing his legs, and glanced at the other two men, who could not help hearing. At last he stared at Lecoeur with a baffled air.

'Do you realize, old man, what . . .'

'Yes, I realize.'

'Have you thought of that?'

'No.'

'Because he's your brother?'

'No.'

'How long has the killer been at it? Nine weeks, isn't that so?'

Lecoeur deliberately consulted his little notebook and looked for a certain cross in a certain column.

'Nine and a half weeks. The first crime took place in the Epinettes district at the other end of Paris.'

'You've just told me that your brother did not admit to his son that he was out of a job. He therefore went on leaving home and coming back at the usual time. Why?'

'So as not to lose face.'

'What do you mean?'

'It's hard to explain. He's not an ordinary sort of father. He brought up the child entirely on his own. They live together, they're a sort of little household, don't you see? During the day my brother prepares the meals and does the housework. He puts his son to bed before going out, wakes him up when he gets back...'

'That doesn't explain...'

'Do you think such a man would consent to appear in his son's eyes as a poor sort of chap who finds every door shut against him because he's incapable of adapting himself?'

'And what's he been doing at night over the past few months?'

'For a couple of weeks he had a job as night watchman in a factory at Billancourt. It was only temporary. Most often he washed cars in garages. When he couldn't find any other work he carried vegetables in Les Halles. When he had one of his attacks...'

'Attacks of what?'

'Asthma...He got them from time to time...He'd go and lie down in a railway station waiting-room. Once he came to spend the night here, gossiping with me...'

'Suppose the boy had looked out early this morning and seen his father at old Madame Fayet's!'

'There was frost on the window panes.'

'Not if the window had been left ajar. Many people sleep with open windows, even in winter.'

'That's not the case with my brother. He feels the cold, and they are too poor to waste heat.'

'The child might have scratched the frost with his fingernails. When I was little I used to...'

'So did I. We'd have to find out whether the old woman's window was found open.'

'The window was open and the light was on.'

'I wonder where François can be.'

'The kid?'

It was surprising and somewhat embarrassing to find him thinking solely of the child. It was even more embarrassing to hear him calmly saying such devastating things about his brother.

'When he came back this morning his arms were full of parcels; have you thought about that?'

'It's Christmas.'

'He'd have needed money to buy a chicken, cakes, a radio set. Has he borrowed any from you lately?'

'Not for the past month. I wish he had, for I'd have told him not to buy a radio for François. I've got one here in the cloakroom which I was going to take him when I went off duty.'

'Would Mère Fayet have been willing to lend her son-in-law money?'

'It's not likely. She's a queer sort of woman. She must have enough savings to live on and she still goes out charring from morning till night. She often lends money at a high rate of interest to the people she works for. The whole district knows about it. People go to her when they're hard up at the end of the month.'

The Superintendent rose, still feeling ill at ease.

'I'm going round there,' he said.

'To the old woman's?'

'To the old woman's and to the Rue Vasco de Gama. If anything fresh turns up, give me a ring.'

'There's no telephone in either of the buildings. I'll send a message to the police station.'

The Superintendent was on his way down and the door had closed behind him when the telephone bell rang. No light had flashed on. The call came from the Gare d'Austerlitz.

'Lecoeur? Inspector on special duty speaking. We've got your chap.'

'Which chap?'

'The one whose description we were given. His name's Lecoeur, like yours. Olivier Lecoeur. I've checked his identity card.'

'One moment.'

He ran to the door and rushed downstairs into the courtyard, catching Saillard just as the latter was getting into a small police car.

'Gare d'Austerlitz on the line. They've found my brother.'

The Superintendent, who was a stout man, sighed as he climbed up the stairs again. He took up the receiver.

'Hello, yes ... Where was he? ... What was he doing? ... What does he say? ... What? ... No, it's not worth your questioning him now ... You're sure he doesn't know? ... Keep up your watch at the station... That may very well be... As for him, send him here right away...'

He hesitated, with an eye on Lecoeur.

'Yes, send somebody with him. It's safer.'

He took time to fill and light his pipe before explaining, as though he were addressing nobody in particular:

'When they picked him up he'd been prowling for over an hour about the waiting-rooms and platforms. He seems to be in a very excited state. He's talking about a message from his son; he was waiting for the boy there.'

'Has he been told of the old woman's death?'

'Yes. It seems to have terrified him. They're bringing him along.'

He added, hesitantly:

'I thought it was best to have him come here. Seeing you're his relative, I didn't want you to think...'

'I'm grateful to you.'

Lecoeur had been sitting on the same chair in the same office since 11 p.m. the previous evening, and he felt just as he used to as a child in his mother's kitchen. Nothing stirred around him. Little lights came on, he thrust plugs into holes, time flowed by smoothly without one's noticing it, and yet, outside, Paris had lived through another Christmas; thousands of people had attended midnight Mass, others had supped noisily in restaurants, drunks had spent the night in the police station and were waking up now in the presence of an inspector; later, children had rushed towards the bright lights on the tree.

What had his brother Olivier been doing all this while? An old woman had died, and before dawn a small boy had walked the empty streets of Paris to the point of exhaustion, and thrust his fist, wrapped in a handkerchief, through the glass panes of a number of emergency call boxes.

What had Olivier been waiting for, with such tense excitement, in the overheated waiting-rooms and on the draughty platforms of the Gare d'Austerlitz?

Less than ten minutes elapsed, just time enough for Godin, whose nose was really running by now, to brew himself another toddy.

'Would you like one, Superintendent?'

'No, thanks.'

Saillard whispered anxiously to Lecoeur: 'Would you rather we went into the other room to question him?'

But Lecoeur had no intention of leaving his little lights and his switchboard that connected him with every corner of Paris. Footsteps came up the stairs. Olivier was flanked by two policemen, but he had not been handcuffed.

He looked like a bad, faded photograph of André. His eyes turned to his brother immediately.

'François?'

'We don't know yet. They're looking for him.'

'Where?'

And Lecoeur could only point to the map and his switchboard with its innumerable holes.

'Everywhere.'

The two policemen had been dismissed, and the Superintendent said:

'Sit down. You've heard that the old Fayet woman is dead, haven't you?'

Olivier wore no spectacles, but he had the same pale, evasive eyes that his brother revealed when he took off his glasses, so that he always looked as if he had been weeping. He glanced briefly at the Superintendent, taking little notice of him.

'He left me a note,' he said, hunting in the pockets of his old raincoat. 'Can *you* understand it?'

He finally held out a scrap of paper torn from a schoolboy's exercise book. The writing was not very steady. The lad was probably not one of the best pupils in his class. He had used a purple pencil, moistening the tip, which had doubtless left a stain on his lip.

Uncle Gédéon arriving this morning Gare d'Austerlitz. Come quick meet us there. Love. Bib.

Without saying a word, André Lecoeur handed the paper to the Superintendent, who turned it round several times in his thick fingers.

'Why Bib?'

'It was my pet name for him. Not in front of people, because it would have embarrassed him. It goes back to the time when I used to feed him as a baby.'

He spoke in a neutral, unemphatic voice, probably seeing nothing around him but a sort of fog in which figures were moving.

'Who is Uncle Gédéon?'

'He doesn't exist.'

Did he even realize that he was speaking to the chief of the Homicide Squad, in charge of a criminal investigation?

His brother explained:

'Or rather he no longer exists. A brother of our mother's, whose name was Gédéon, left for America when he was very young.'

Olivier was looking at him as though to say: 'What's the good of telling them all that?'

'It had become a family joke; we used to say: "Some day we shall inherit from Uncle Gédéon."'

'Was he a rich man?'

'We didn't know. He never sent us news of himself. Just a New Year's card signed Gédéon.'

'Is he dead?'

'He died when Bib was four years old.'

'Do you think there's any point, André?'

'We're trying to find out. Leave it to me. My brother carried on the family tradition by talking to his son about Uncle Gédéon. He'd become a sort of legendary figure. Every night before going to sleep the boy demanded a story about Uncle Gédéon, and we made up all sorts of adventures about him. Of course he was fabulously wealthy, and when he came back ...'

'I think I understand. And he died?'

'In hospital. At Cleveland, where he washed dishes in a restaurant. We never told the boy. We kept up the story.'

'Did he believe it?'

The father put in a timid word, almost raising his hand like a schoolboy.

'My brother says he didn't, that he had guessed, that it was just a game for him. But I'm practically sure, myself, that he still believed it. When his friends told him Father Christmas didn't exist he went on contradicting them for two whole years.'

When he spoke of his son he came to life again; he was transformed.

'I can't understand why he wrote me that note. I asked the concierge if there had been a telegram. For one moment I thought André had played a trick on us. Why did François leave home at six in the morning, telling me to meet him at the Gare d'Austerlitz? I rushed there like a madman. I looked everywhere, I kept expecting him to appear. Look here, André, are you sure that...'

He was looking at the map on the wall and the telephone switchboard. He knew that all the disasters, all the accidents in Paris were inevitably recorded here in the end.

'He hasn't been found,' said Lecoeur. 'They're still looking. At eight o'clock or thereabouts he was in the Etoile district.'

'How do you know? Did anyone see him?'

'It's hard to explain. All along the way from your house to the Arc de Triomphe someone has broken the panes of glass in the emergency call boxes. A child's blue and white checked handkerchief was picked up beside the last of them.'

'He had handkerchiefs with blue checks.'

'Since eight o'clock there has been nothing.'

'But then I must go back to the station at once. That's where he's sure to go, since he told me to meet him there.'

Surprised at the silence that seemed suddenly to gather oppressively around him, he stared at each of them in turn, puzzled and then anxious.

'What...'

His brother lowered his head, while the Superintendent, after a slight cough, finally asked in a reluctant tone:

'Did you pay a visit to your mother-in-law last night?'

Perhaps, as his brother had implied, his intelligence was not quite normal. Words took a long time to reach his brain. And one could practically follow the slow progress of his thought by watching his face.

He stopped looking at the Superintendent and turned to his brother, suddenly flushed, his eyes glittering, and cried:

'André! You dared to . . .'

Without any transition his excitement lapsed, he leaned forward on his chair, buried his head in his hands and started weeping with great hoarse sobs.

3

Superintendent Saillard looked at André uneasily, surprised to find him so calm, and possibly a little shocked at what he must have taken for indifference. Perhaps Saillard had no brother. Lecoeur had been used to his since early childhood. He had seen Olivier subject to such attacks when he was quite small, and in the present circumstances he was almost relieved, for things might have been worse; instead of tears, of exhausted resignation, of this sort of numbness, Olivier might have embarrassed them by bursting forth in declamatory indignation, giving them all a piece of his mind.

Wasn't that how he had lost most of his jobs? For weeks, for months at a time he would be meek and subservient, brooding over his humiliation, nursing his pain; then suddenly, when it was least expected, almost invariably for some trivial reason, for a casual word, a smile, an unimportant contradiction, he would flare up.

'What shall I do?' the Superintendent's glance questioned.

And André Lecoeur's eyes replied:

'Wait.'

It did not take long. The sobs, like a child's, grew less violent, almost dying away, then broke out again for a moment with increased intensity. Then Olivier sniffed, ventured to glance around, but seemed to sulk a little longer, hiding his face.

At last he drew himself up in bitter resignation, and said with a certain pride:

'Ask your questions, I'll answer them.'

'At what time during the night did you go to Mère Fayet's? One minute. Tell me first at what time you left home.'

'At eight o'clock as usual, after putting my boy to bed.'

'And did nothing unusual happen?'

'No. We had supper together. He helped me wash the dishes.'

'Did you talk about Christmas?'

'Yes. I'd hinted that there'd be a surprise for him when he woke up.'

'Was he expecting a radio set?'

'He'd been wanting one for a long time. He doesn't play in the street, he's got no friends, he spends all his spare time at home.'

'Did you never think that your son might perhaps know that you'd lost your job at La Presse? Did he never ring you up there?'

'Never. He's always asleep when I'm at work.'

'Could nobody have told him?'

'Nobody knows about it in the neighbourhood.'

'Is he observant?'

'He misses nothing of what goes on around us.'

'You put him to bed and you went off. Didn't you take a snack with you?'

The Superintendent had just thought of that on seeing Godin unwrap a ham sandwich. Then Olivier Lecoeur suddenly looked at his empty hands and muttered:

'My tin!'

'The tin in which you carried something to eat?'

'Yes. I had it last night, I'm sure. There's only one place where I could have left it . . .'

'At Mère Fayet's?'

'Yes.'

'One minute . . . Lecoeur, pass me the phone . . . Hello! Who am I speaking to? Is Janvier there? . . . Call him, will you? . . . Is that you, Janvier? . . . Have you searched the old woman's lodging? Did you notice a tin containing some food? . . . Nothing of the sort? . . . You're sure? . . . Yes, I'd rather you did . . . Call me back as soon as you've checked . . . It's important . . .'

And turning to Olivier, he asked:

'Was your son asleep when you left?'

'He was just going to sleep. We kissed each other goodnight. I began by walking in the neighbourhood. I went as far as the Seine and sat down on the parapet to wait.'

'To wait for what?'

'For the boy to be sound asleep. From our flat we can see Madame Fayet's windows.'

'You'd decided to call on her?'

'It was the only way. I couldn't even afford to take the métro.'

'What about your brother?'

The two Lecoeurs looked at one another.

'I've asked him for so much money lately that he can't have any to spare.'

'You rang at the door of the block of flats? What time was it?'

'A little after nine o'clock. The concierge saw me go in. I wasn't hiding, except from my son.'

'Had your mother-in-law not gone to bed?'

'No. She opened the door to me and said: "So here you are, you bastard!"'

'Did you know that she would let you have some money nonetheless?'

'I was practically certain of it.'

'Why was that?'

'I only had to promise her that she'd make a big profit. She could never resist that. I signed a paper saying I owed her double the sum.'

'To be paid back when?'

'In a fortnight.'

'And when it fell due, how would you have paid it?'

'I don't know. I'd have managed somehow. I wanted my son to have his Christmas treat.'

André Lecoeur longed to interrupt his brother to tell the astonished Superintendent:

'He's always been like that!'

'Did you find it easy to get what you wanted?'

'No. We argued for a long time.'

'About how long?'

'Half an hour. She reminded me that I was a good-for-nothing, that I'd brought her daughter nothing but misery and that it was my fault she had died. I didn't say anything. I wanted the money.'

'Did you threaten her?'

He flushed and hung his head, mumbling: 'I told her that if I didn't get the money I would kill myself.'

'Would you have done so?'

'I don't think so. I don't know. I was very tired, very disheartened.'

'And once you'd got the money?'

'I went on foot as far as Beaugrenelle station, where I took the métro. I got out at the Palais-Royal and went into the Grands Magasins du Louvre. The place was very crowded. People were queuing up at the counters.'

'What time was it?'

'Maybe eleven o'clock. I was in no hurry. I knew the store would stay open all night. It was hot there. There was an electric train running.'

His brother looked at the Superintendent with a slight smile.

'Didn't you notice that you had mislaid the tin with your supper in it?'

'I was only thinking of Bib's Christmas.'

'In short, you were very much excited at having cash in your pocket?'

The Superintendent was beginning to understand, even though he had not known Olivier as a child. Whereas when his pockets were empty he was dim and depressed and would slink along timidly, crouching against the walls, when he had a little money on him he became self-confident and almost reckless.

'You've told me you signed a paper for your mother-in-law. What did she do with it?'

'She slipped it into an old wallet she always carried about with her, in a pocket she wore fastened to her belt, underneath her skirt.'

'You're familiar with that wallet?'

'Yes. Everybody is.'

The Superintendent turned to André Lecoeur.

'It hasn't been found.'

Then he said to Olivier: 'You bought the radio, then the chicken and the cake. Where?'

'In a shop I know in the Rue Montmartre, next to a shoe-shop.'

'What did you do the rest of the night? What time was it when you left the shop in the Rue Montmartre?'

'It was close on midnight. Crowds were leaving the theatres and cinemas and hurrying into the restaurants. There were some very lively gangs of people and a great many couples.'

His brother, at that time, had already been sitting here at his switchboard.

'I was on the Grands Boulevards, near the Crédit Lyonnais bank, carrying my parcels, when the bells began to ring. People were kissing one another in the street.'

Why did Saillard feel impelled to ask a preposterous, cruel question: 'Did anybody kiss you?'

'No.'

'Did you know where you were going?'

'Yes. At the corner of the Boulevard des Italiens there's a cinema that stays open all night.'

'Had you been there before?'

Somewhat embarrassed, and avoiding his brother's eye, he replied:

'Two or three times. It doesn't cost more than a cup of coffee in a bar, and you can stay there as long as you want to. It's warm there. Some people go there to sleep.'

'When did you decide to spend the rest of the night in the cinema?'

'As soon as I'd got the money.'

And the other Lecoeur, the calm, meticulous switchboard operator, longed to explain to the Superintendent:

'You see, these poor wretches aren't always as miserable as you think. Otherwise they wouldn't hold out. They have their own world, too, and in the corners of it they have a certain number of small joys.'

It was so typical of his brother that, having borrowed a few notes—and heaven knows how he'd ever repay them—he had forgotten his troubles and thought only of making his son happy next morning, and then, nonetheless, had given himself a little treat!

He had gone to the cinema all alone, while family parties were gathering round loaded tables, crowds were dancing in nightclubs and other people were finding spiritual exaltation in dark, candlelit churches.

In short he'd had his own Christmas, a Christmas cut down to size.

'What time did you leave the cinema?'

'Shortly before six o'clock, to take the métro.'

'What film did you see?'

'*Burning Hearts*. And there was a documentary about the Eskimos.'

'Did you see the programme only once?'

'Twice, except for the news, which was just being shown again when I left.'

André Lecoeur knew that this would be checked, if only as a matter of routine. But this proved unnecessary. His brother fumbled in his pockets and pulled out a scrap of torn cardboard, his cinema ticket, and at the same time another bit of pink cardboard.

'Here you are! Here's my métro ticket too.'

It bore the time and date and the stamp of the Opéra station where it had been issued.

Olivier had told the truth. He could not have been in the old woman's room between five and half-past six that morning.

Now there was a flash of slightly scornful defiance in his eye. He seemed to be saying to them all, including his brother:

'Because I'm a poor specimen, you suspected me. It's the rule. I don't bear you ill-will for it.'

And curiously enough a sudden chill seemed to fall over that great room where one of the clerks was having a telephone discussion with a suburban inspector about a stolen car.

It was probably due to the fact that, now Lecoeur had been cleared, everyone's thoughts were once more concentrated on the child. This was so true that all eyes now turned instinctively to the map of Paris; for quite a while now, the lights had stopped coming on.

It was the slack period. On any other day there would have been, from time to time, some traffic accident, some old lady run over at a busy crossroads in Montmartre or some other densely crowded area.

Today the streets remained almost empty, just as they are in August when most Parisians are in the country or at the seaside.

It was half-past eleven. For three hours now they had had no news of the little boy, had received no signal from him.

'Hello! Yes... Go on, Janvier... You say there's no sign of a tin in the flat?... Okay... You searched the dead woman's clothes yourself?... Gonesse had already done so?... You're sure she wasn't wearing an old wallet under her skirt? You'd heard about that?... The concierge saw somebody go up last night about half-past nine?... I know who that was... And then? There were comings and goings in the house all night... Of course... Will you go over to the other house, the one behind?... I'd like to know if anyone heard a noise during the night, particularly on the third floor... Call me back, that's right...'

He turned towards the father, who was sitting motionless on his chair, as meek again as though he were in a doctor's waiting-room.

'Do you see why I asked that question? Does your son often wake up during the night?'

'He sometimes calls out in his sleep.'

'Does he get up and walk about?'

'No. He sits up in bed and screams. It's always the same thing. He thinks the house is on fire. His eyes are open but he sees nothing. Then, gradually, he looks at you with a normal expression and he lies down again with a deep sigh. Next day he remembers nothing about it.'

'Is he always asleep when you get back in the morning?'

'Not always. But even if he's not asleep he pretends to be, so that I should go and wake him up by kissing him and tweaking his nose. It's a gesture of affection, don't you see?'

'The neighbours are likely to have been noisier than usual last night. Who lives on the same floor as you?'

'A Czech who works at the car factory.'

'Is he married?'

'I don't know. There are so many people in our block of flats and the tenants change so frequently that one scarcely knows them. On Saturdays the Czech usually gets together half a dozen of his friends to drink and sing their own popular songs.'

'Janvier is going to let us know if that was the case last night. If so, it may have woken up your son. In any case he was probably over-excited at the thought of the surprise you'd promised him. If he got up he may have automatically gone to the window and seen you with old Madame Fayet. Did he have any suspicion that she was your mother-in-law?'

'No. He didn't like her. He called her the bedbug. He often met her in the street and he used to say she smelt like a squashed bedbug.'

The child must have known what he was talking about, for there was probably no lack of such creatures in the great tenement where they lived.

'Would he have been surprised to see you in her room?'

'Certainly.'

'Did he know that she was a moneylender?'

'Everybody knew that.'

The Superintendent turned to the other Lecoeur.

'Do you think there'd be anyone at La Presse today?'

The former typographer replied for him:

'There's always someone there.'

'Ring them up then. Try to find out whether anyone has ever asked for Olivier Lecoeur.'

The latter, once again, averted his head. Before his brother had opened the telephone directory he gave them the number of the printing press.

While the call was going on, there was no alternative for them but to stare at one another and then to stare at the little lamps which obstinately refused to light up.

'It's very important, Mademoiselle. It may be a question of life or death . . . Yes, please take the trouble to put the question to anybody who's there at the moment . . . What did you say? I can't help that! It's Christmas for me too and yet I'm ringing you up . . .'

'Little bitch!' he muttered between his teeth.

And they waited again, while the clatter of the linotypes could be heard down the telephone.

'Hello! . . . What . . . three weeks ago? A child, yes . . .'

The father had turned very pale and was staring at his hands.

'He didn't ring up? He came himself? About what time? On a Thursday? And then? . . . He asked whether Olivier Lecoeur was working at the press . . . What? . . . What did they tell him? . . .'

His brother looked up and saw him flush and hang up the receiver with a furious gesture.

'Your son went there one Thursday afternoon . . . He must have suspected something . . . They told him you'd stopped working at La Presse some weeks before.'

What was the point of repeating the words he had just heard? What the boy had been told was: 'That fool was fired some time ago!'

It may not have been meant cruelly. They probably never imagined that the visitor might be his son.

'Are you beginning to understand, Olivier?'

Every evening the father went off, carrying his sandwiches and talking about his workplace in the Rue du Croissant, and the son knew that he was lying.

One might surely draw the conclusion that he knew the truth, too, about the mythical Uncle Gédéon.

He had played the game.

'And I'd promised him his radio . . .'

They scarcely dared speak to one another, because words might call up terrifying pictures.

Even those who had never been to the Rue Vasco de Gama could now visualize the shabby dwelling, the ten-year-old boy who spent long hours there alone, the strange household of father and son who told each other lies for fear of hurting one another.

One had to imagine things as they appeared to the child: his father leaving after a goodnight kiss, and Christmas everywhere around, neighbours drinking and singing at the tops of their voices.

'Tomorrow morning you shall have a surprise.'

It could only be the longed-for radio, and Bib knew how much that cost.

Did he know, that evening, that his father's wallet was empty?

The man went off as though he were going to his work, and that work did not exist.

Had the boy tried to go to sleep? Opposite his room, on the other side of the courtyard, rose a huge dark wall with lighted windows, behind which lived a motley crowd of people.

Had he leaned on the windowsill, in his nightshirt, to look out?

His father, who had no money, was going to buy him a radio.

The Superintendent gave a sigh as he knocked his pipe out against his heel and emptied it on to the floor:

'It's more than likely that he saw you in the old woman's room.'

'Yes.'

'I'll check up on one point presently. You live on the third floor and she lives on the mezzanine. It's probable that only part of the room is visible from your windows.'

'That's correct.'

'Could your son have seen you leave?'

'No! The door is at the back of the room.'

'Did you go up to the window?'

'I sat down on the windowsill.'

'One detail, which may be important. Was the window ajar?'

'Yes, it was. I remember it struck cold down my back. My mother-in-law always sleeps with her window open, winter and summer. She was a country woman. She lived with us for a while, when we were first married.'

The Superintendent turned to the switchboard operator.

'Did you think of that, Lecoeur?'

'The frost on the window? I've been thinking about it ever since this morning. If the window was partly open the difference between the temperature of the air outside and that of the room would not be great enough to produce frost.'

A call. The plug was thrust into one of the holes.

'Yes ... What did you say? ... A boy? ...'

They stood watching him, tensely.

'Yes ... Yes ... What? ... Yes, send all police cyclists to search the district ... I'll deal with the station ... How long ago was it? ... Half an hour? ... Couldn't he have informed us sooner?'

Without giving himself time to explain things to those around him, Lecoeur thrust his plug into another hole.

'Gare du Nord? ... Who am I speaking to? ... It's you, Lambert? ... Listen, this is very urgent ... Have the station thoroughly searched ... Keep an eye on all the premises and on the railway lines ... Ask the staff whether they've seen a boy of about ten years old wandering around the ticket offices or elsewhere ... What? ... Is there anybody with him? ... That doesn't matter ... There may well be ... Quickly! ... Keep me informed ... Of course, get hold of him ...'

'Somebody with him?' his brother repeated in bewilderment.

'Why not? Anything's possible. It may perhaps not be him, but if it is we've wasted half an hour ... It's a grocer in the Rue de Maubeuge, close by the station, who has an open-air stall ... He saw a kid take a couple of oranges from his display and run off ... He didn't chase him ... Some time later, however, as a policeman happened to pass he mentioned the fact.'

'Had your son any money in his pocket?' asked the Superintendent. 'No? None at all? Didn't he have a money-box?'

'He had one. But I'd taken the little it contained two days ago, on the pretext that I didn't want to change a big note.'

All these details seemed to have become so important now!

'Don't you think I'd better go to the Gare du Nord myself?'

'I think it would be pointless, and we may need you here.'

They felt imprisoned in this room, held captive by the great map with its lamps, the switchboard that connected them with every corner of Paris. Whatever happened, this was where they would get the first news of it. The Superintendent was so well aware of this that he did not return to his office, and had finally resigned himself to taking off his big overcoat, as though he now belonged to the Central Office.

'So he can't have taken the métro or a bus. Nor can he have gone into a café or a public call box to telephone. He's had nothing to eat since six o'clock this morning.'

'But what's he doing?' exclaimed the father, his agitation reviving. 'And why did he send me to the Gare d'Austerlitz?'

'Probably to help you to escape,' Saillard said in a low voice.

'To escape, me?'

'Listen, my lad...' The Superintendent had forgotten that this was the brother of Inspector Lecoeur and spoke to him as though to one of his 'clients'.

'The kid knows that you've lost your job, that you're broke and yet you've promised him a splendid Christmas...'

'My mother used to stint herself for months to give us Christmas treats...'

'I'm not blaming you. I'm just stating a fact. He leans at the window and sees you visiting an old harridan who lends money at high interest. What does he conclude from that?'

'I understand.'

'He says to himself that you've gone to borrow from her. All right. He may have been touched, or sorry, I don't know. He gets back into bed and goes to sleep.'

'D'you think so?'

'I'm practically certain. If he had discovered at half-past nine last night what he discovered at six o'clock this morning he'd not have stayed put quietly in his room.'

'I understand.'

'He goes back to sleep. Perhaps he's thinking more about his radio than about what you may have done to get the money for it. Didn't you yourself go to the cinema? He sleeps restlessly, as all children do on Christmas Eve. He wakes earlier than usual, while it's still dark, and the first thing he sees is that the windows are covered with frost-flowers. Don't forget that it's the first frost of the winter. He wants to look at it close, to touch it...'

The other Lecoeur, the man at the switchboard, the man who made little crosses in his notebook, gave a faint smile when he observed that the big Superintendent was not as remote from his childhood as one might have expected.

'He scratched it with his nails...'

'As I saw Biguet doing right here this morning,' broke in André Lecoeur.

'We shall have proof of that, if need be, through the fingerprints people, since the prints will show once the frost has thawed. What is the first thing that strikes the child? Whereas it's all dark in the neighbourhood, there's a light on in one single window, and it happens to be that of the room where he last saw his father. I shall get all these details checked. I'm willing to bet, however, that he caught sight of the body, at any rate of part of it. Even if he'd only seen the feet on the floor, this, combined with the fact that the light was on, would have been enough.'

'Did he believe?...' Olivier began, his eyes starting out of his head.

'He believed you had killed her, yes, as I was inclined to believe myself. Think, Lecoeur. The man who for a number of weeks now has been killing people in the outlying parts of the city is a night bird like yourself. It may be somebody who has suffered a grave shock, like yourself, since one doesn't become a killer overnight for no good reason. Does the child know what you've been doing every night since you lost your job?

'You told us just now that you sat down on the windowsill. Where did you put your sandwich tin?'

'On the ledge, I'm practically certain.'

'So he must have seen it... And he didn't know at what time you left your mother-in-law's... He didn't know if, after you'd gone, she was still alive... He must have imagined the light staying on all night... What would have struck you most, in his place?'

'The tin...'

'Exactly. The tin which would enable the police to identify you. Was your name on it?'

'I'd scratched it on with a penknife.'

'You see! Your son assumed that you'd be coming home at your usual time, that's to say between seven and eight. He did not know whether his venture would be successful. In any case he decided not to come home. He wanted to keep you out of danger.'

'Was that why he left me a note?'

'He remembered Uncle Gédéon, and wrote to tell you that his uncle was arriving at the Gare d'Austerlitz. He knew that you'd go, even though Uncle Gédéon didn't exist. The message couldn't possibly compromise you...'

'He's ten and a half!' the father protested.

'Do you think a lad of ten and a half doesn't know quite as much about such matters as yourself? Doesn't he read detective stories?'

'Yes...'

'If he's so keen on a radio, perhaps it's less for the sake of the music or broadcast plays than for the police thriller serials...'

'That's true.'

'Before anything else he had to get back the incriminating evidence, the tin. He knew the courtyard very well. He must have played there often.'

'He's spent days playing there with the concierge's daughter.'

'He knew, then, that he could use the drainpipe. He may have climbed up it before.'

'And now?' asked Olivier with striking quietness. 'He retrieved the tin, okay. He left my mother-in-law's house without difficulty, for the front door can be opened from inside without summoning the concierge. You say it must have been a little after six in the morning.'

The Superintendent grunted. 'I follow,' he said. 'Even without hurrying, he could have reached the Gare d'Austerlitz in under two hours. He'd told you to meet him there, but he didn't go there.'

Oblivious of these arguments, the other Lecoeur was thrusting in his plugs, saying with a sigh: 'Still nothing, old man?'

And the answer came from the Gare du Nord: 'We've questioned about twenty people accompanying children, but none of them answer to the description we've been given.'

Any child, obviously, might have stolen oranges from a stall. But not every child would have smashed in the glass of seven emergency call boxes in succession. Lecoeur kept reverting to his little crosses. He had never thought himself much cleverer than his brother, but he had patience and obstinacy in his favour.

'I'm sure,' he said, 'that we shall find the sandwich tin in the Seine, close to the Pont Mirabeau.'

Footsteps sounded on the stair. On ordinary days one would not have noticed them, but on a Christmas morning one listened involuntarily.

It was a police cyclist bringing the bloodstained handkerchief that had been picked up beside the seventh call box. This was shown to the boy's father.

'Yes, that's Bib's.'

'So he's being followed,' the Superintendent declared. 'If he were not being followed, if he'd had time, he wouldn't confine himself to breaking glass. He would speak.'

'Excuse me,' said Olivier, the only one who had not understood. 'Followed by whom? And why should he call the police?'

They were all reluctant to enlighten him. His brother took on the job.

'Because, if when he went into the old woman's room he believed you were the murderer, when he left her house he no longer believed it. *He knew.*'

'He knew what?'

'He knew *who*! D'you understand now? He had discovered something, we don't know what, and that's what we've been hunting for for hours. Only he's not being given a chance to tell us.'

'You mean...'

'I mean that your son is on the murderer's heels, or else the murderer is on his. One of them's following the other, I don't know which, and won't let go. Tell me, Superintendent, has a reward been offered?'

'A big reward, since the third murder. It was doubled last week. All the papers have talked about it.'

'Then,' said André Lecoeur, 'it's not necessarily Bib who is being followed. It may be he who is following. Only in that case...'

It was twelve o'clock, and it was four hours since the child had given any sign of life, unless it was he who had stolen the oranges in the Rue de Maubeuge.

4

Perhaps, after all, his day had dawned? André Lecoeur had read somewhere or other that any human being, however dim and unfortunate he may be, has at least one glorious hour in his life during which he is able to fulfil himself.

He had never had a high opinion of himself or of his potentialities. When he was asked why he had chosen a sedentary and monotonous job instead of putting his name down, for instance, for the Homicide Squad, he would reply: 'I'm so lazy!'

And sometimes he would add: 'And perhaps I'm scared of getting hurt!'

That was untrue. But he knew he was slow-witted.

Everything he had learned at school had cost him a lot of effort. The police examinations, which are child's play to some people, had given him great trouble.

Was it because of this self-knowledge that he had never married? It might well be so. It seemed to him that whatever wife he chose, he would feel himself her inferior and let himself be dominated by her.

He was not thinking of all that today. He did not know that his hour, if there were such a thing, was at hand.

The morning's team had now been replaced by another lot, looking spruce and smart, who had had time to celebrate Christmas with their families and whose breath was redolent of cake and liqueurs.

Old Bedeau had taken up his position at the switchboard, but Lecoeur had not gone away; he had simply remarked:

'I'm staying a bit longer.'

Superintendent Saillard had gone for a quick lunch at the nearby Brasserie Dauphine, asking to be called if anything fresh turned up. Janvier had returned to the Quai des Orfèvres, where he was writing up his report.

Lecoeur did not feel like going to bed. He was not sleepy. In the past, he had once spent thirty-six hours at his post, during the riots in the Place de la Concorde, and on another occasion, during the general strike, the men from the Central Office had camped out in their room for four days and four nights.

His brother was more impatient.

'I want to go and find Bib,' he had declared.

'Where?'

'I don't know. Somewhere near the Gare du Nord.'

'And suppose it wasn't he who stole the oranges? Suppose he's in a quite different district? Suppose we get news of him in a few minutes or in a couple of hours?'

'I want to do something.'

They had made him sit on a chair, in one corner, since he refused to lie down. His eyelids were red with fatigue and anguish and he had begun to twist his fingers as he used to when, as a child, he'd been put in the corner.

André Lecoeur had tried to rest, by way of self-discipline. Adjoining the main room there was a sort of closet with a washbasin, two camp beds and a coatrack, where the men on night duty sometimes took a nap when things were quiet.

Lecoeur had closed his eyes. Then he happened to lay his hand on the notebook which he always kept in his pocket, and lying on his back, he began to turn its pages.

It contained crosses, nothing but columns of minute crosses which for years he had persisted in inscribing of his own free will, without knowing exactly what purpose they might serve some day. Some people keep a journal, others note down their most trivial expenses or their losses at bridge.

Those crosses in their narrow columns represented years of the city's nightly existence.

'Coffee, Lecoeur?'

'Yes, please.'

But since he felt too remote, in that closet from which he could not see his illuminated board, he pulled the camp bed into the office, and after that spent his time alternately consulting the crosses in his notebook and shutting his eyes. Sometimes, between half closed lids, he watched his brother hunched up on his chair, his shoulders bent, his head drooping, the only sign of his inner tension being the occasional convulsive clenching of his long pale fingers.

Hundreds of policemen now, in the suburbs as well as in the city, had been given the child's description. From time to time a police call brought a ray of hope; but the child in question turned out to be a little girl, or if a boy was either too young or too old.

Lecoeur had closed his eyes again and then suddenly he re-opened them, as though he had just dozed off, looked at the time and glanced round in search of the Superintendent.

'Has Saillard not come back?'

'He's probably gone round by the Quai des Orfèvres.'

Olivier looked at his brother, surprised to see him striding up and down the great room; Lecoeur scarcely noticed that, outside, the sun had finally pierced through the white dome of clouds, and that Paris, on this Christmas afternoon, had a bright, almost spring-like air.

He was watching out for a step in the stairway.

'You should go and buy a few sandwiches,' he said to his brother.

'What sort?'

'Ham, or whatever you like. Whatever you can find.'

Olivier left the office after a glance at the map on the wall, re-lieved in spite of his anxiety to be getting a breath of fresh air.

The men who had replaced the morning team knew scarcely anything about the affair, except that it concerned the killer and that somewhere in Paris a small boy was in danger. For those who had not spent the night here, it wore a different complexion; it was, as it were, decanted, reduced to a few cold, precise data. Old Be-deau, sitting in Lecoeur's place and wearing his headphones, was doing a crossword, barely breaking off for the traditional: 'Hello! Austerlitz? Your van's gone out?'

A drowned woman had just been fished out of the Seine. This, too, formed part of the Christmas tradition.

'Could I speak to you a moment, Superintendent?'

The camp bed had been replaced in the closet, and this was where Lecoeur now took the head of the Homicide Squad. The Su-perintendent was smoking his pipe; he shed his overcoat, and looked at his companion in some surprise.

'Please forgive me for interfering in what's not my business, but it's about the killer...'

He had his little notebook in his hand, but he appeared to know it by heart and to consult it only so as to keep himself in countenance.

'Forgive me if I tell you rather confusedly what's in my mind, but I've been thinking about it so much since this morning that...'

A short while ago, while he was lying down, it had all seemed dazzlingly clear to him. Now he was searching for words, and his ideas had become less precise.

'It's like this. I noticed first of all that the eight crimes were committed after 2 a.m. and most of them after 3 a.m.'

From the Superintendent's expression he realized that this observation implied nothing particularly disturbing for other people.

'Out of curiosity, I investigated the time at which most crimes of this sort have been committed during the last three years. It was almost always between 10 p.m. and 2 a.m.'

He must be on the wrong track, for he got no reaction. Why not say openly how the idea had occurred to him? This was not the time to be held back by embarrassment.

'Just now, while looking at my brother, I thought that the man you're looking for must be somebody like him. For a moment I even wondered if it could be him. Wait a minute...'

He was on the right track after all. He had seen the Superintendent's eyes expressing something more than merely polite but bored attention.

'If I'd had time I'd have set my thoughts in order. But you'll see... A man who kills eight times, almost in quick succession, is a maniac, surely? A person whose brain has been disturbed suddenly, for some reason or another...

'My brother lost his job, and in order not to admit it to his son, not to lose face in his eyes, he went on for weeks leaving home at the same time, behaving exactly as if he were going to work...'

The idea, translated into words and phrases, lost some of its force. He was well aware that, in spite of an obvious effort, Saillard could not see light there.

'A man who finds himself suddenly deprived of everything he had, everything that made up his life...'

'And who goes off his head?'

'I don't know if he goes off his head. Perhaps you could call it that. Somebody who thinks he has reasons for hating the whole world, for needing to be revenged on all men...

'You know, of course, Superintendent, that the other sort, the real murderers, always kill in the same way.

'This one used a knife, then a hammer, then a spanner. He strangled one woman.

'And nowhere did he let himself be seen. Nowhere did he leave a single trace. Wherever he lives, he must have covered miles in Paris at a time of night when there are no taxis or underground trains. Now, although the police have been on the watch ever since the man's first crimes, although they scrutinize passersby and challenge all suspicious characters, he never attracted their attention on a single occasion.'

So sure did he feel that he was on the right track at last, so anxious was he that his hearer should not tire of his argument, that he felt like murmuring: 'Please listen to me to the end...'

The closet was a constricted place, and he was walking three steps forward and three back, in front of the Superintendent who sat on the edge of the camp bed.

'These are not logical arguments, believe me. I'm not capable of any remarkable arguments. But it's because of my little crosses, the little facts I've noted... This morning, for instance, he crossed half Paris without passing in front of a single police station or going over a crossing where there's an officer on duty.'

'Do you mean that he knows the fifteenth arrondissement well?'

'Not only the fifteenth, but two others at least, to judge by the earlier crimes: the twentieth and the twelfth. He did not choose his victims at random. In every case he knew that they were lonely people, living in circumstances where he could attack them without much risk.'

He almost lost heart when he heard his brother's melancholy voice.

'The sandwiches, André!'

'Yes, thanks. You have some. Go and sit down...'

He dared not close the door, out of a sort of humility. He was not a sufficiently important person to be closeted with the Superintendent!

'If he took a different weapon each time, it's because he knows that this will confuse people's minds, he knows that murderers generally stick to a single method.'

'Look here, Lecoeur...'

The Superintendent had stood up and was now staring at him abstractedly, as though following out his own thoughts.

'Do you mean that...'

'I don't know. But it occurred to me that it might be one of our own people. At any rate, somebody who had worked with us.'

He dropped his voice.

'Somebody to whom the same thing had happened as to my brother, don't you see? A fireman who's been sacked would readily think of arson. That happened twice in the last three years. Somebody from the police...'

'But why steal?'

'My brother needed money, too, to make his son believe he was still earning his living, that he'd still got his job at La Presse. If the man's a night worker and wants to make out that he's still employed, he's bound to stay out all night, and that explains why he commits his crimes after three in the morning. He can't go home till daybreak. The earlier hours of the night are easy. There are bars and cafés open. After that he's alone in the streets...'

Saillard grunted, as though talking to himself: 'There's no one in the Personnel office today.'

'Perhaps we could contact the Personnel manager himself? Perhaps he might remember?'

Lecoeur was still unsatisfied. There were many things he would have liked to say but which escaped him. Perhaps the whole thing was merely fantasy. At times he thought so, and at other times he felt that what he had discovered was as clear as daylight.

'Hello!... Can I speak to Monsieur Guillaume, please? He's not at home? Do you happen to know where I'm likely to find him? At his daughter's, at Auteuil? Do you know her telephone number?'

There, too, they'd been enjoying a pleasant family lunch party, and must now be sipping their coffee and liqueurs.

'Hello, Monsieur Guillaume? Saillard here, yes. I hope I'm not disturbing you too much? You weren't still at table? It's about the killer. There's something new. Nothing definite yet. I'd like to check a hypothesis and it's urgent. Don't be too surprised at my question. Has any member of the force, of whatever grade, been dismissed during these last months? What did you say? Not one this year?'

Lecoeur felt his heart sink as though a disaster were overtaking him and cast a despairing glance at the map of Paris. He'd lost the game. From now on he'd give up; but to his surprise his chief persisted.

'It might be earlier than that, I don't know. The person involved would have been a man on night duty, working in several arrondissements, including the fifteenth, the twentieth and the twelfth. Somebody who strongly resented his dismissal. What did you say?'

Saillard's voice as he uttered these last words renewed Lecoeur's hopes, while those around them were nonplussed by the conversation.

'Sergeant Loubet? Yes, I've heard speak of him, but I wasn't on the disciplinary committee at that time. Three years, yes. You don't know where he lived? Somewhere near Les Halles?'

Three years, however, was too big a gap, and Lecoeur lost heart once more. It was unlikely that a man should nurse his humiliation and his rancour for three years before taking action.

'You don't know what's become of him? Obviously. Yes. It won't be easy today . . .'

He hung up again, and looked at Lecoeur attentively, speaking to him as though to an equal.

'Did you hear? There was Sergeant Loubet, who was given a whole series of warnings and moved from one station to another three or four times before finally being dismissed. He took it very badly. He used to drink. Guillaume believes he joined some private detective agency. If you'd like to try . . .'

Lecoeur did so without conviction, but after all it meant taking action instead of waiting in front of that map of his. He began with the most dubious agencies, assuming that a man like Loubet would not have been taken on by a reliable firm. Most of the offices were closed. He called people at their homes.

Often he heard children's voices.

'Never heard of him. Try Tisserand in the Boulevard Saint-Martin. He collects all the riff-raff.'

But he drew a blank at Tisserand's, whose specialty was shadowing. For three quarters of an hour Lecoeur stayed glued to the telephone, and finally he heard an angry voice protesting:

'Don't talk to me about that swine. Over two months ago I fired him and he's threatened to blackmail me, though he hasn't lifted a finger yet. If I meet him I'll punch his nose.'

'What work did he do for you?'

'Watching blocks of flats by night.'

André Lecoeur was once again transfigured.

'Was he a heavy drinker?'

'The fact is he was always drunk after an hour on duty. I don't know how he set about it, but he always managed to be given free drinks.'

'Have you got his correct address?'

'27 bis Rue du Pas-de-la-Mule.'

'Does he have a telephone?'

'He may. I've no desire to ring him up. Is that all? Can I get back to my bridge?'

As he hung up, the man could be heard explaining things to his friends.

The Superintendent had already seized a telephone directory and found Loubet's name. He rang the number. There was now a tacit understanding between himself and André Lecoeur. They shared the same hope. Now that their goal was within sight they were both tremulous with excitement, while the other Lecoeur, Olivier, sensing that something important was happening, was standing up and looking at each of them in turn.

Without being asked to, André Lecoeur took a liberty which,

only that morning, he would never have dared allow himself: he seized the second receiver. The bell could be heard ringing down there in the Rue du Pas-de-la-Mule; it rang a long time, as though the place were empty, and Lecoeur's heart was beginning to sink again when someone lifted the receiver.

Thank heaven! It was a woman's voice, an elderly-sounding woman's voice, that replied:

'Is that you at last? Where are you?'

'Madame, this is not your husband speaking.'

'Has something happened to him?'

She sounded almost pleased at the idea, as though she had been expecting such news for a long time.

'Am I speaking to Madame Loubet?'

'Of course.'

'Is your husband not at home?'

'In the first place, who is speaking?'

'Superintendent Saillard...'

'What d'you want him for?'

The Superintendent briefly held his hand over the receiver and whispered to Lecoeur:

'Ring up Janvier and tell him to go there immediately.'

There was a call from a local station at the same time, so that three telephones were in use simultaneously in the room.

'Has your husband not come home this morning?'

'If you policemen did your job properly, you'd know.'

'Does this often happen?'

'That's his business, isn't it?'

She probably detested her drunken sot of a husband, but since he was being attacked she took his side.

'You know he's no longer in the Force?'

'I suppose he's not enough of a bastard for that!'

'When did he stop working for the Argus agency?'

'What's that?...One moment, please...What are you saying?...You're trying to worm things out of me, aren't you?'

'I'm sorry, Madame. It's over two months since your husband was fired from the agency.'

'You're lying!'

'In other words, for the past two months he's been going to work each evening?'

'Where else would he have gone? To the Folies Bergère?'

'Why hasn't he come back this morning? Hasn't he rung you up?'

She was probably afraid of being caught out, for she simply hung up.

When the Superintendent himself replaced the receiver and turned round, he found Lecoeur standing close behind him, averting his head as he said:

'Janvier has gone over there...'

And with his finger he wiped away a trace of moisture at the corner of his eye.

5

He was being treated as an equal. He knew that it would not last, that tomorrow he would be merely an insignificant clerk at his switchboard, obsessively putting down little crosses in a futile notebook.

The others did not count. Even his brother stood unnoticed, staring at them each in turn like a timid rabbit, listening to them without understanding, wondering why, when his son's life was at stake, they were talking so much instead of taking action.

Twice he had tugged André by the sleeve.

'Let me go and look...' he had begged.

Look where? Look for whom? The description of ex-Sergeant Loubet had already been circulated to all police stations, railway stations and patrols.

Now the search was on not only for a child but for a man of fifty-eight, who was probably drunk, who knew Paris and the Parisian police like the back of his hand, and who was wearing a black overcoat with a velvet collar and an old grey felt hat.

Janvier had returned, bringing in a breath of fresh air. An aura of freshness invariably lingered for a while round those who had just come in from outside; then, gradually, they became submerged in the drab atmosphere in which life seemed to be lived in slow motion.

'She tried to shut the door in my face, but I took care to put my foot in the doorway. She doesn't know anything. She claims that he's brought back his pay these last months as usual.'

'That's why he was obliged to steal. He didn't need large sums, he'd not have known what to do with them. What's she like?'

'Small, swarthy, with very bright eyes and dyed hair, almost blue. She must have eczema or some skin eruption, for she wears mittens.'

'Did you get a photo of him?'

'I took one practically by force, off the sideboard in the dining room. She didn't want me to.'

It showed a thickset, full-blooded man with protuberant eyes, who must have been a lady-killer in his youth and still wore a look of stupid arrogance. Moreover the photo was several years old, and today Loubet had probably gone to pieces, become flabbily fleshy, with a shifty look instead of one of self-confidence.

'Were you able to discover what places he frequents?'

'As far as I can see she keeps him on a tight rein, except at night when he's at work, or supposed to be. I questioned the concierge. He's very much afraid of his wife. In the mornings, the concierge often sees him come staggering along, but he pulls himself together as soon as he puts his hand on the stair rail. His wife takes him shopping with her, he never goes out in the daytime except with her. When he's asleep and she has to leave the house, she locks him in and takes away the key.'

'What d'you think about it, Lecoeur?'

'I'm wondering whether he and my nephew are together.'

'What do you mean?'

'They weren't together to begin with, at half-past six this morning, for Loubet would have prevented the boy from smashing the glass of the call boxes. They were some distance apart. One of them was following the other . . .'

'Which, do you think?'

It was disconcerting to be listened to thus, as though he had on the spur of the moment become a sort of oracle. Such was his fear of making a mistake that he had never felt so small in his life.

'When the boy climbed up the drainpipe he must have believed his father was guilty, since he used the note about the legendary Uncle Gédéon to send him to the Gare d'Austerlitz, where he probably planned to join him after getting rid of the sandwich tin.'

'That seems likely . . .'

'Bib can't have believed . . .' Olivier attempted to protest.

'Shut up! . . . At that point the crime had just been committed. The child wouldn't have ventured on his climb if he had not caught sight of the body . . .'

'He did see it,' Janvier asserted. 'From his window he could see the body from feet to mid-thigh.'

'What we don't know is whether the man was still in the room.'

'No,' put in the Superintendent. 'No, for if he had been, he'd have stayed hidden while the boy came in through the window, and then done away with such a dangerous witness, as he'd just done away with the old woman.'

It was essential, however, to get the whole thing clear, reconstructing it down to the slightest detail, if they were to find young Lecoeur, for whom a Christmas present of not one but two radios was waiting.

'Tell me, Olivier, when you got home this morning was the light on?'

'It was.'

'In the boy's room?'

'Yes. It gave me a shock. I thought he must be ill.'

'So the killer must have seen the light. He was afraid of having a witness. He certainly never expected anyone to get into the room by way of the drainpipe. He rushed out of the house.'

'And waited outside to see what would happen.'

That was all they could do: put forward hypotheses, trying to be as logical as possible. The rest was up to the police patrols and the hundreds of policemen scattered about Paris; in the last resort it was a matter of chance.

'Rather than go back the way he'd come, the child left the old woman's house by the front door ...'

'One minute, sir. By that time he probably knew that his father was not the murderer.'

'Why?'

'I heard someone say just now, I think it was Janvier, that the old woman had lost a great deal of blood. If the crime had just been committed, the blood would scarcely be dry and the body would still be warm. Now it was the previous evening, about nine o'clock, that Bib had seen his father in the room.'

Each fresh piece of evidence brought fresh hope. They felt they were getting somewhere; the rest looked easier. Sometimes the two men spoke at once, struck by an identical idea.

'It was when he went out that the boy must have discovered the man, Loubet or someone else, probably Loubet. And the man couldn't know whether his face had been seen. The child was frightened and rushed straight forward ...'

This time the boy's father interrupted to contradict them, explaining in a monotonous tone of voice:

'Not if Bib knew there was a big reward. Not if he knew I'd lost my job. Not if he'd seen me borrowing money from my mother-in-law ...'

The Superintendent and André looked at one another, and because they felt that the other Lecoeur was right, they both felt frightened.

It was a nightmare picture. An empty street in one of the loneliest parts of Paris, while it was still dark, two hours before dawn. And here was a man with an obsession, who had just committed his eighth murder in a few weeks, out of hatred and resentment as well as from need, possibly to prove heaven knows what to himself, a man who put his ultimate pride into defying the whole world through the police.

Was he drunk, as usual? No doubt, on Christmas Eve when the bars stay open all night, he had been drinking more than usual and saw the world through an alcoholic haze; there, in that street, in that wilderness of stone, behind the blind housefronts, he saw a child, a small boy who knew, and who was going to get him arrested, to put an end to his frantic adventures.

'I'd like to know if he had a revolver,' the Superintendent sighed.

He did not have to wait for an answer; it came promptly from Janvier.

'I put that question to his wife. He always carries an automatic, but it was unloaded.'

'Why?'

'His wife is afraid of him. When he was in a certain condition, instead of submitting meekly he sometimes threatened her. She had shut away the cartridges, on the grounds that in case of need the sight of the weapon would be enough to frighten anyone without his having to fire it.'

Had the pair of them, the old maniac and the child, really been playing cat and mouse in the streets of Paris? The ex-policeman could not hope to run faster than a ten-year-old boy; the child, on the other hand, could not hope to overcome a man of that bulk.

Now that man, for the child, represented wealth, the end of all their miseries. His father would no longer have to wander through the town at night, pretending that he was still working in the Rue du Croissant, nor to carry vegetables in the market, nor finally to go crawling to an old woman like Mère Fayet to obtain a loan which he could scarcely hope to repay.

Words were scarcely needed now. They stared at the map, at the names of streets. No doubt the child was keeping at a prudent distance from the murderer and no doubt, too, the man had shown his weapon to frighten the child.

The houses of the city were honeycombed with rooms where thousands of people were sleeping who could be no help to either of them.

Loubet could not stop forever in the street watching the child, who kept warily away from him, and he had begun walking, avoiding dangerous streets, the blue lamps of police stations and the crossroads where policemen were on duty.

In two or three hours there would be people on the pavements, and the boy would probably rush at the first he met, calling for help.

'Loubet was walking in front,' the Superintendent said slowly.

'And my nephew smashed the glass of the call boxes because I'd told him how they worked,' added André Lecoeur.

The little crosses were coming to life. What had seemed a mystery to begin with was now acquiring a kind of tragic simplicity.

The most tragic aspect of it was possibly the question of hard cash, the reward for the sake of which a child of ten was deliberately undergoing such terrors and risking his life.

The boy's father had begun to weep, quite gently, without sobbing or gasping, and he did not attempt to hide his tears. His nervous tension had dropped and he had ceased to react in any way. He was surrounded by strange objects and barbarous instruments, by men who talked about him as though he were someone else or were not there, and his brother was one of these men, a brother whom he scarcely recognized and at whom he looked with involuntary awe.

Their sentences were becoming briefer, for Lecoeur and the Superintendent understood one another's slightest word.

'Loubet couldn't go home.'

'Nor enter a bar with the child at his heels.'

André Lecoeur suddenly gave a sudden smile.

'It can't have occurred to the man that the boy hadn't a centime in his pockets and that he could have escaped by taking the métro.'

That would not have worked, though; Bib had seen him and would give an exact description of him.

The Trocadéro. The Etoile district. Time had elapsed. It was nearly daylight. People came out of houses; steps sounded on the pavements. It was no longer possible, for a man without a weapon, to kill a child in the street without attracting attention.

The Superintendent pulled himself together, as though awakening from a nightmare. 'Well, however it happened, they must have made contact with one another,' he decided.

At that moment a light came on. As though he knew that it concerned their problem, Lecoeur took the phone instead of his colleagues.

'Yes . . . I guessed as much . . . Thank you . . .'

He explained: 'It was about the two oranges. They've just found a North-African boy asleep in the third class waiting room at the

Gare du Nord. He still had one of the two oranges in his pocket. He had run away from his home in the eighteenth arrondissement this morning, because he'd been given a beating.'

'Do you think Bib's dead?'

Olivier Lecoeur was twisting his fingers as though to break them.

'If he were dead Loubet would have gone home, because, after all, he'd have nothing more to be afraid of.'

So the contest was still going on, in the Paris streets where the sun was shining at last and family parties with children in their Sunday best were out walking.

'Probably Bib was afraid of losing track of him in the crowd. He edged up closer...'

Loubet must have spoken to him and threatened him with his gun:

'If you call out, I shall shoot...'

And thus each of them pursued a separate aim: the man hoping to get rid of the child, by leading him on to some lonely spot where murder could be done; the child trying to give the alarm before his companion had time to shoot.

Each was wary of the other. For each of them, life was at stake.

'Loubet won't have made for the centre of the city, where there are too many policemen about. Particularly since most of them know him.'

From the Etoile they must have gone up towards Montmartre, not the Montmartre of the nightclubs but the working-class district, towards drab streets which on a day like this must be looking particularly provincial.

It was half-past two. Had they had anything to eat? Had Loubet, despite the threat hanging over him, been able to last out so long without a drink?

'Tell me, Superintendent...'

In spite of himself, André Lecoeur could not bring himself to speak self-confidently; he still felt as though he was usurping a function to which he was not entitled.

'There are hundreds of small bars in Paris, I know. But if we began by the most likely ones, and put a great many men on the job...'

Not only did those present settle down to it, but Saillard contacted the Quai des Orfèvres, where six detectives on duty each took up his post at a telephone.

'Hello! *Le Bar des Amis?* Has a middle-aged man in a black overcoat, accompanied by a ten-year-old boy, been in at any time since this morning?'

Lecoeur was once more marking crosses, not in his notebook now but in the telephone directory. Here there were ten pages of bars, with more or less fanciful names. Some were closed. In others the sound of music could be heard.

On a map which had been spread out on the table he ticked off the streets with a blue pencil one by one, and it was somewhere behind the Place Clichy, in a passage with a somewhat unsavoury reputation, that the first red mark was made.

'A chap like that came in about noon. He drank three calvadoses and ordered a glass of white wine for the boy. The kid didn't want to drink it but did so in the end, and ate a couple of hard-boiled eggs.'

Olivier Lecoeur looked as if he were hearing his son's voice.

'You don't know where they went?'

'Towards the Batignolles... The man was pretty well soused already...'

The boy's father would have liked to seize hold of a telephone himself, but there was none available and he walked about from one to another, with knitted brows.

'Hello! The *Zanzi Bar?* Has a middle-aged man...'

It had become a regular refrain, and when one of the men had ceased uttering it another took it up at the far end of the room.

Rue Damrémont. Right at the top of Montmartre. At half-past one; the man's movements were becoming uncertain and he had broken a glass. The boy had made as though to go to the lavatory and his companion had followed him. Then the kid had given up the attempt, as if he'd been frightened.

'A queer sort of chap. He kept on sniggering as though he were having a good joke.'

'You hear, Olivier? Bib was still there, an hour and forty minutes ago.'

André Lecoeur, by now, was afraid to say what he thought. The struggle was nearing its end. Since Loubet had started drinking he'd go on doing so. Would this be the boy's opportunity?

In a way, yes, if he had the patience to wait and did not embark on any futile venture.

But suppose he was mistaken, suppose he believed his companion to be more drunk than he really was, suppose...

André Lecoeur's eyes fell on his brother, and he had a sudden vision of what Olivier might have become if his asthma had not, by some miracle, prevented him from drinking.

'Yes... What did you say?... Boulevard Ney?'

That meant the outer limits of Paris, and implied that the ex-policeman was not as drunk as he appeared. He was making his way along quietly, leading the child out of the city gradually and almost imperceptibly, towards the waste ground on the outskirts.

Three police vans had already left for that district. All available police cyclists had been sent there, and Janvier himself rushed off in the Superintendent's little car; they had great difficulty in restraining the child's father from accompanying him.

'I've told you, this is where you'll have the first news of him...'

Nobody had time to make coffee. They could not help being overexcited; their words came in nervous jerks.

'Hello! The *Orient Bar?* Hello! Who's speaking?'

André Lecoeur, at the telephone, stood up as he listened, made peculiar signals and was practically dancing with excitement.

'What?... Not so close to the phone...'

Then the others caught the sound of a high-pitched voice like a woman's.

'Whoever you are, tell the police that... Hello! Tell the police that I've got him... the killer... Hello! What? Uncle André?'

The voice dropped a tone lower, took on an anguished note. 'I tell you I'm going to shoot... Uncle André!...'

Lecoeur had no idea to whom he handed the receiver. He rushed up the stair and nearly broke in the door of the telegraphist's room.

'Quick! The *Orient Bar,* Porte de Clignancourt... Every available man...'

He did not wait to hear the call put through, but leapt down the stairs four at a time, then halted on the threshold of the big room, where to his stupefaction everyone was standing motionless, with the tension relaxed.

Saillard was holding the receiver, listening to a hearty working-class voice saying:

'It's okay... Don't worry... I hit him on the head with a bottle... He's out now... I don't know what he was trying to do to the boy, but... What's that? You want to talk to him?... Come here, kid... Give me your popgun... I don't much like that sort of toy... But say, it isn't loaded...'

Another voice: 'Is that you, Uncle André?'

The Superintendent, holding the receiver, looked about him, and it was not to André Lecoeur but to Olivier that he handed it.

'Uncle André?... I've got him... The killer!... I've got the re...'

'Hello, Bib!'

'What?'

'Hello, Bib, it's...'

'What are you doing there, dad?'

'Nothing... I was waiting... I...'

'I'm happy, you know... Wait... Here are some police cyclists who want to talk to me... And a car's stopped...'

There were confused sounds, a buzz of voices, the clink of glasses. Olivier Lecoeur held the telephone receiver awkwardly and stared at the map, probably without seeing it. It was happening a long way off, right up in the northern part of the city, in a great windswept open square.

'I'm going off with them...'

Another voice. 'Is that you, Chief? Janvier here...'

Olivier Lecoeur looked as if he was the one who had been knocked on the head, the way he held out the receiver into empty space.

'He's completely sozzled, Chief. When the kid heard the phone ring, he realized it was his opportunity; he managed to snatch the gun from Loubet's pocket and took a leap... Thanks to the *patron*, a tough guy who knocked the man out on the spot...'

A little light flashed out on the board, up in the Clignancourt district. Stretching his hand over his colleague's shoulder, André Lecoeur thrust the plug into a hole.

'Hello! Your van's gone out?'

'Someone's broken the glass of the emergency call box in the Place Clignancourt to say there's trouble in a bar there...Hello!... Shall I call you back?'

There was no need to this time.

Nor was there any need to mark a little cross in his notebook.

A very proud small boy was being driven across Paris in a police car.

September 1950
Shadow Rock Farm, Lakeville, Connecticut

Maigret and the Surly Inspector

I

The young man lifted the headphones from his ears.

'What was I telling you, uncle? ... Oh yes ... When the kid came back from school and my wife saw the red patches on her body, she felt sure at first that it was scarlet fever...'

It was impossible to complete a sentence of any length; invariably one of the little lights came on in the huge map of Paris that stretched over half a wall. It was in the thirteenth arrondissement this time, and Daniel, Maigret's nephew, thrusting his plug into one of the holes in the switchboard, muttered: 'What's up?'

He listened without interest, repeating for the benefit of the Superintendent, who was perched on the edge of the table:

'A fight between two Arabs in a bistro in the Place d'Italie...'

He was about to resume his story about his daughter, when another of the white bulbs embedded in the wall-map lit up.

'Hello! ... What is it? ... A motor accident in the Boulevard de la Chapelle?'

Through the tall uncurtained windows they could see the rain falling in torrents, a fine persistent summer rain that patterned the darkness with long hatchings. It was pleasant but somewhat close in the big Emergencies room, where Maigret had come to take refuge.

A little while before he had been in his office in the Quai des Or-fèvres. He was expecting a phone call from London about an international crook whom one of his detectives had run to earth in a grand hotel in the Champs-Elysées. The call might come through at midnight or at 1 a.m., and Maigret had nothing to do while he waited; he was bored, all alone in his office.

So he had ordered the switchboard to put all calls for him through to Emergencies, on the other side of the street, and he had come over for a chat with his nephew, who was on duty that night.

Maigret had always liked this huge room, as quiet and bare as a laboratory, unknown to most Parisians although it is the very core of the city.

At every crossroads in Paris there is a telephone apparatus painted red. One simply has to break the glass to be connected automatically with the local police station and at the same time with the central emergency post.

Whenever somebody appeals for help for one reason or another, one of the lights goes on on the huge map. And the man on duty hears the call at the same time as the sergeant in the nearest police station.

Down below, in the dark quiet courtyard of the Préfecture, there are two vans full of policemen ready to dash out in serious emergencies. In sixty police stations, other vans are waiting, as well as policemen with bicycles.

Another light.

'Attempted suicide by barbiturate poisoning, in a block of flats in the Rue Blanche,' Daniel echoed.

All day and all night the dramatic life of the capital is thus reflected in little lights on a wall; whenever a van or a patrol goes out from a police station the reason for its movement is reported to the central office.

Maigret always argued that young detectives should be obliged to spend a year at least in this room so as to learn the geography of crime in the capital, and he himself, when he had time to spare, liked to spend an hour or two there.

One of the men on duty was eating bread and sausage. Daniel resumed his story:

'She immediately sent for Dr Lambert, and when he arrived, half an hour later, the red blotches had disappeared ... It was only nettlerash ... Hello! ...'

A light had just gone on in the eighteenth arrondissement. It was a direct call. Somebody had that instant broken the glass of the alarm box at the corner of the Rue Caulaincourt and the Rue Lamarck.

For a beginner, this is a tense moment ... One imagines the street-crossing, deserted in the rain-streaked darkness, the wet pavement, the patches of lamplight, lighted cafés in the distance, and a man or a woman hurrying, staggering perhaps, or being pursued, somebody in terror or in need of help, wrapping a handkerchief round their hand to break the pane of glass ...

Maigret, automatically glancing at his nephew, saw the young man frown; his face assumed an expression of bewilderment and then of alarm.

'Good Lord! ...' he stammered.

He listened for a moment longer, then shifted his plug.

'Hello! ... Is that the Rue Damrémont station? ... That you, Dambois? ... Did you hear the call? ... It *was* a shot, wasn't it? ... Yes, I thought so too ... What did you say? ... Your van's already left?'

That meant that in less than three minutes policemen would be on the spot, for the Rue Damrémont is quite close to the Rue Caulaincourt.

'Sorry, uncle ... But it was so unexpected! ... First I heard a voice shouting into the telephone "*Merde* to the cops!"'

'Then, immediately afterwards, the sound of a shot ...'

'Will you tell the sergeant on duty at the Rue Damrémont station that I'm coming along and that nothing is to be touched in the meantime.'

Maigret had already set off through the empty passages, gone down into the courtyard and jumped into the small fast car that was kept for police officers.

It was only a quarter past ten.

'Rue Caulaincourt ... top speed!'

Strictly speaking, it was not his job. The local police were on the spot, and not until their report had been received would it be decided whether this was a matter for the Police Judiciaire. Maigret was impelled by curiosity. Moreover he had remembered something while Daniel was speaking.

At the beginning of the previous winter—it had been in October, a rainy night like tonight—he had been in his office at about eleven o'clock when the telephone rang.

'Superintendent Maigret?'

'Yes.'

'Is that Superintendent Maigret himself speaking?'

'It is ...'

'In that case, *merde* to you!'

'What?'

'I say *merde* to you! I've just shot down, through the window, the two cops you posted on the pavement ... You needn't send any more ... You won't get me! ...'

A shot rang out.

The Polish accent had already told Maigret what he needed to know. The incident had inevitably occurred in a small hotel at the corner of the Rue de Birague and the Faubourg Saint-Antoine, where a dangerous Polish criminal, who had attacked a number of farms in the north of France, had taken refuge.

Two policemen had in fact been set to watch the hotel, for Maigret had decided to arrest the man himself at dawn.

One of the detectives had been killed outright; the other recovered after five weeks in hospital. As for the Pole, he really had blown his brains out after speaking to the Superintendent.

It was this coincidence which had just struck Maigret, in the big Emergencies room; in the course of over twenty years on the job he had only encountered one case of this kind—a suicide over the telephone, accompanied by abuse.

It was strange indeed that six months later almost the same incident was repeated!

The small car sped through Paris and reached the Boulevard Rochechouart, with its brilliantly lit cinemas and dance-halls. Then, from the corner of the steeply sloping Rue Caulaincourt, all was quiet and practically deserted; here and there a bus raced down the street, and a few pedestrians hurried along the rain-drenched pavements.

A small group of dark figures stood at the corner of the Rue Lamarck. The police van had stopped a few yards down the street. People were looking out of their windows and concierges were standing in doorways, but the pouring rain discouraged onlookers.

'Evening, Dambois...'

'Evening, Superintendent...'

And Dambois pointed to a body lying on the pavement, less than a yard from the emergency call box. A man was kneeling beside the corpse, a local doctor whom they had managed to contact, even though barely twelve minutes had elapsed since the firing of the shot.

The doctor looked up and recognized Maigret's well-known figure.

'Death was instantaneous,' he said, wiping his wet knees and then his rain-splashed spectacles. 'The shot was fired point-blank into the right ear.'

Maigret automatically raised his hand as though to shoot himself through the ear.

'Suicide?'

'Looks like it...'

And Sergeant Dambois pointed to a revolver which none of them had yet touched, and which was lying half a yard from the dead man's hand.

'Do you know the man, Dambois?'

'No, Superintendent...And yet I can't think why, he looks to me like a local chap.'

'Will you look carefully to see if he's got a wallet?'

Water was dripping on to Maigret's hat. The sergeant handed him a well-worn wallet which he had just taken out of the dead man's jacket pocket. One compartment contained six hundred-franc notes and a woman's photograph; in another there was an identity card made out in the name of Michel Goldfinger, thirty-eight years old, diamond broker, 66 bis Rue Lamarck.

The photograph on the identity card was indeed that of the man lying there on the pavement, with his legs strangely twisted.

In the innermost compartment of the wallet, which fastened with a tab, Maigret found a tightly-folded scrap of tissue paper.

'Will you shine your torch on this, Dambois?'

Carefully, he undid the packet, and a dozen tiny brilliant stones, unmounted diamonds, glittered in the light.

'Nobody can say that robbery was the motive for the crime, or that poverty was the motive for suicide,' the sergeant said gruffly. 'What d'you think, Chief?'

'Have you had the neighbours questioned?'

'Inspector Lognon is seeing to that...'

Every three minutes a bus clattered down the slope. Every three minutes another bus climbed up it, changing gear. Twice or thrice Maigret glanced up, because an engine had backfired.

'It's odd...' he muttered to himself.

'What's odd?'

'In any other street we'd surely have had some evidence of the shot... You'll see that Lognon will get nothing from the neighbours, because the steep incline of the street causes the cars to backfire.'

He was not mistaken. Lognon, whom his colleagues called the Grouser because he was always in a sour temper, came to speak to the sergeant.

'I questioned about twenty people. Either they heard nothing— most of them, at this time of night, are listening to the radio, particularly as there's a gala programme being broadcast on *Poste Parisien*—or else they tell me that sort of noise goes on all the time... They're used to it... There was only one old woman, on the sixth floor of the second house on the right, who declared that she had heard two reports... Only I had to repeat my question several times, for she's as deaf as a post... Her concierge confirms that...'

Maigret slipped the wallet into his pocket.

'Get the body photographed,' he told Dambois. 'When the photographers have finished with it, take it to the Forensic Institute and ask Dr. Paul to do a postmortem... As for the revolver, as soon as it's been checked for fingerprints, send it to the expert Gastinne-Renette.'

Inspector Lognon, who had possibly seen the case as a chance to make his mark, was staring savagely at the pavement, his hands in his pockets and his sullen face wet with rain.

'Will you come with me, Lognon? Seeing that it's happened on your beat...'

And they went off together. They took the right-hand pavement of the Rue Lamarck, which was deserted; only a couple of small cafés were lit up along the whole length of the street.

'I apologize, old fellow, for interfering with a case which doesn't concern me, but there's something that bothers me...I'm not quite sure as yet what it is...Something that doesn't fit, d'you understand?...Needless to say you're officially in charge of the investigation.'

But Lognon, true to his reputation for surliness, made no response to Maigret's advances.

'I don't know if you understand...A fellow like Stan the Killer, who knew that he'd be arrested before the night was out, and who moreover had realized for a month or more that I was on the heels...'

It was quite in character for Stan to defend himself to the end, like the wild beast that he was, and to put a bullet through his own head rather than face the guillotine. He had not wanted to die alone and in a final act of bravado, a last spasm of hatred against society, he had shot down the two detectives who were watching him.

All that was to be expected. Even the phone call to Maigret, who had become his personal enemy, as a final insult, a supreme act of defiance...

But the words shouted tonight into the emergency call box did not fit the little that was known as yet about the diamond broker.

As far as a rapid examination allowed one to judge, he had been an insignificant person, earning a mere pittance, and indeed, Maigret could have sworn, an unlucky man in poor health. For the diamond trade, like any other, has its princes and its paupers.

Maigret knew the centre of that trade, a big café in the Rue

Lafayette where the important brokers sat at a special table to receive the humble middlemen to whom they entrusted a few stones.

'This is the place,' said Lognon, stopping in front of a house just like all the other houses in the street, a six-storey building, no longer new, where a few windows showed lights.

They rang. The door was opened, and they saw that the light was still on in the concierge's lodge. Music from the radio issued from the room where, through the glazed door, they could see a bed, an elderly woman knitting and a man in carpet slippers and no collar, his shirt open on a hairy chest, reading his paper.

'Excuse me, Madame... Is Monsieur Goldfinger in?'

'Have you seen him come in, Désiré?... No... Besides, it's scarcely half an hour since he went out...'

'By himself?'

'Yes... I supposed he was going on some errand in the neighbourhood, possibly to buy cigarettes...'

'Does he often go out in the evenings?'

'Hardly ever... Only to go to the pictures with his wife and sister-in-law.'

'Are they upstairs?'

'Yes... They haven't gone out tonight... Do you want to see them? Third floor, right.'

The building had no lift. A dark carpet covered the stairs; the landing of each floor was lit by a single electric light bulb, with brown doors to right and left. The house was clean and comfortable, but not luxurious. The walls, painted to imitate marble, needed a good coat of fresh paint, for they were turning a dingy brown.

The radio again... The same tune that was being heard everywhere that night, the famous gala programme of *Poste Parisien*... It was audible once more on the third floor landing.

'Shall I ring?' asked Lognon.

They heard a bell ringing on the other side of the door and a chair being pushed back as somebody got up; a young voice called out:

'Coming...'

A swift, light step. The door knob turned, the door opened and the voice began:

'You haven't...'

Presumably the remark was going to be:

'You haven't been long.'

But the person who opened the door stopped short on seeing two unknown men, and she stammered:

'I'm sorry...I thought it was...'

She was young and pretty, dressed in black as though in mourning, with bright eyes and fair hair.

'Madame Goldfinger?'

'No, Monsieur...Monsieur Goldfinger is my brother-in-law...'

She stood there disconcerted, and it did not occur to her to invite the visitors in. There was anxiety in her gaze.

'May we?...' said Maigret, stepping forward.

And another voice, an older, somewhat weary voice called out from the depths of the flat:

'What is it, Eva?'

'I don't know...'

The two men were now standing in a tiny entrance hall. To the left, through a glazed door, could be seen in the semi-darkness a small drawing room which must seldom have been used, to judge by its impeccable tidiness and the upright piano covered with photographs and knickknacks.

The second room was lit up, and this was where low music was coming from the radio.

Before the Superintendent and the inspector could reach it the girl darted forward, saying:

'Do you mind if I close the bedroom door? My sister was unwell this evening and she's gone to bed already...'

Presumably the door between the living room and the bedroom was wide open. There was some whispering. Madame Goldfinger was probably asking:

'Who is it?'

And Eva answering in a low voice:

'I don't know... They've told me nothing...'

'Leave the door ajar so that I can hear...'

Quiet prevailed here, as in most of the flats in the neighbourhood, behind all those lighted windows that the two men had seen, a heavy, somewhat sickly quietness, that of homes where nothing happens, where one cannot imagine anything ever happening.

'I'm sorry... Please come in...'

The dining room furniture was of the mass-produced, pseudo-rustic sort; the inevitable brass flower bowl stood on the sideboard, the usual decorated plates were ranged on the dresser against a background of red-checked cretonne.

'Please sit down... Just a minute...'

Pieces of dress material lay on three chairs, with dress patterns of coarse brown paper, while on the table there were a pair of scissors, a fashion magazine and another piece of material which she had obviously been cutting out when the bell rang.

The girl turned the knob of the radio, and then complete silence fell.

Lognon, sulkier than ever, stared at the tips of his wet shoes, while Maigret fiddled with his pipe, which had gone out.

'Has your brother-in-law been gone long?'

There was a chiming clock on the wall, and the girl glanced at it automatically.

'He went out shortly before ten... Perhaps ten minutes to ten...? He had an appointment in the neighbourhood at ten o'clock.'

'You don't know where?'

Someone was moving about in the next room, which was in total darkness and the door of which had been left ajar.

'In a café, probably, but I don't know which... Quite close by, I'm sure, for he said he'd be back before eleven.'

'A business appointment?'

'Of course... What other sort could he have made?'

And it seemed to Maigret that a slight flush rose to the girl's cheeks. Moreover, for the last few minutes, while she watched the two men, she seemed overtaken by a growing unease. There was a mute question in her eyes. At the same time, she seemed to be frightened of what she might learn.

'Do you know my brother-in-law?'

'Well...a little...Did he often make appointments in the evening?'

'No...Very seldom...You might say never...'

'Did somebody ring him up?'

For Maigret had just noticed the telephone standing on a small table.

'No...It was while we were having dinner that he told us he had an appointment to keep at ten o'clock.'

Her voice was growing anxious. And a slight sound in the bedroom indicated that Madame Goldfinger had got out of bed and was standing barefoot behind the door to listen.

'Was your brother-in-law in good health?'

'Yes...That's to say he's never been very strong...Above all, he was a worrier...He had a stomach ulcer and the doctor was sure he could cure it; but my brother-in-law was convinced it was cancer.'

There was a noise, or rather a rustling; and Maigret looked up, certain that Madame Goldfinger was about to appear. He saw her standing in the doorway, wearing a blue flannel wrapper and looking at him with a cold, hostile stare.

'What has happened to my husband?' she asked. 'Who are you?'

The two men rose to their feet simultaneously.

'I apologize, Madame, for intruding in this way. Your sister tells me you are unwell this evening...'

'That doesn't matter...'

'Unfortunately I have bad news for you...'

'My husband?' she asked; her concern was unconvincing.

Maigret's eyes, however, were on the girl, and he saw her open her mouth for a cry that never came. She stood there, staring wild-eyed.

'Your husband, yes...He's met with an accident.'

'An accident?' the wife queried, hard and suspicious.

'Madame, I am very sorry to have to tell you that Monsieur Goldfinger is dead...'

She did not move. She stood there with her dark eyes fixed upon them. For whereas her sister was a blue-eyed blonde, Mathilde Goldfinger was a plump brunette with eyes so dark as to be almost black, and strongly marked eyebrows.

'How did he die?'

The girl, who had flung herself against the wall with her hands outstretched and her head buried in her arms, was sobbing silently.

'Before replying, it is my duty to ask you a question. Had your husband, to your knowledge, any reason to take his own life? Were his business affairs, for instance...'

Madame Goldfinger wiped her damp lips with a handkerchief, then passed her hands over her forehead, pushing back her hair with a mechanical gesture:

'I don't know... I don't understand... What you're telling me is so...'

Then the girl, unexpectedly, turned round abruptly, disclosing a flushed face smeared with tears, eyes in which there was anger, perhaps even fury, and cried out with surprising energy:

'Michel would never have committed suicide, if that's what you mean!'

'Keep calm, Eva... Will you allow me, gentlemen?'

And Madame Goldfinger sat down, leaning one elbow on the rustic table.

'Where is he?... Tell me... How did it happen?'

'Your husband died from a bullet in the head at exactly 10.15 p.m. in front of the emergency call box at the corner of the Rue Caulaincourt.'

There was a hoarse anguished sob from Eva. As for Madame Goldfinger, she was ashy pale, her features rigid, and she kept her unseeing gaze fixed on the Superintendent:

'Where is he now?'

'His body has been taken to the Forensic Institute, where you will be able to see it tomorrow morning.'

'Do you hear, Mathilde?' shrieked the girl.

The words called up a picture to her. Had she grasped the fact that an autopsy was about to be performed, after which the body would be put into one of the many compartments of that huge corpse refrigerator, the Forensic Institute?

'And you don't say anything? . . . You don't protest?'

The widow gave an imperceptible shrug of the shoulders, and repeated in a weary voice:

'I don't understand . . .'

'I must point out, Madame, that I do not assert that your husband took his own life . . .'

This time it was Lognon who gave a sudden start and looked at the Superintendent in astonishment. Madame Goldfinger merely murmured with a puzzled frown:

'I don't understand . . . Just now you said . . .'

'That it looked like suicide. But there are sometimes crimes that look like suicides . . . Had your husband any enemies?'

'No!'

An energetic denial. Why did the two women subsequently exchange a quick glance?

'Had he any reason to attempt suicide?'

'I don't know . . . I can't say . . . You must forgive me, gentlemen . . . I'm unwell myself today . . . My husband was a sick man, my sister will tell you. He thought himself more ill than he really was . . . He suffered great discomfort . . . The very strict diet he had to follow weakened him . . . Moreover he had been worried recently . . .'

'About his business?'

'You probably know that for almost two years now there has been a crisis in the diamond trade . . . Big business men can stand up to it . . . Those who have no capital and who live, so to speak, from hand to mouth . . .'

'Was your husband carrying diamonds on his person this evening?'

'Probably . . . He always had some . . .'

'In his wallet?'

'That's where he usually put them . . . They don't take up much room, you know.'

'Did these diamonds belong to him?'

'Probably not ... He seldom bought them on his own account, especially recently ... He had them given him on commission ...'

That was likely. Maigret was pretty familiar with the little world centred in the neighbourhood of the Rue Lafayette and which, like the underworld, has its own laws. Here you see stones each worth a fortune being passed from hand to hand round a table, without any receipt being asked for or given. These people all know one another; they know that within the fraternity no one would dare break his word.

'Were his diamonds stolen?'

'No, Madame ... Here they are ... Here is his wallet. I should like to ask you one further question. Did your husband keep you informed of all his business affairs?'

'All of them ...'

Eva gave a start; did that mean that her sister was not telling the truth?

'Had your husband any big bills due for payment in the near future?'

'A bill for thirty thousand francs was falling due tomorrow.'

'Had he the money?'

'I don't know ... That was why he went out this evening ... He had an appointment with a customer from whom he hoped to get that sum ...'

'And if he had not obtained it?'

'The bill would probably have been protested.'

'Has that already happened?'

'No ... He always found the money at the last minute ...'

Lognon sighed gloomily, as though he felt this was all a waste of time.

'So that if the person your husband was to meet this evening had not given him the money, Goldfinger would have been faced with a protest tomorrow ... Which means that he would automatically have been struck off the list of diamond brokers, wouldn't he? If I'm not mistaken, these gentlemen deal very harshly with that kind of misfortune.'

'Good heavens, what am I to say to you?'

Although Maigret was ostensibly looking at her, he had for the past few minutes been casting surreptitious glances at the little sister-in-law in her black dress.

She had stopped weeping. She had recovered her self-control. And the Superintendent was surprised at the keenness of her gaze, the strength and decision of her features. This was no longer a tearful little girl but, for all her youth, a woman listening, watching, and suspecting.

For there could be no mistake. Some detail must have struck her in the conversation and she was listening attentively, missing nothing of what was being said around her.

'You are in mourning?' he asked.

He had addressed Eva, but it was Mathilde who replied:

'We are both in mourning for my mother, who died six months ago. That was when my sister came to live with us.'

'Have you a job?' Maigret was speaking to Eva again, and again it was her sister who replied:

'She's a typist in an insurance agency in the Boulevard Haussmann.'

'One last question...I'm very sorry, believe me...Did your husband own a revolver?'

'Yes, he had one...But he hardly ever carried it...It must still be in the drawer of his bedside table.'

'Will you be good enough to make sure?'

She rose and went into the bedroom, where she switched on the light. They heard her opening a drawer and moving things about. When she came back she wore an anxious look.

'It isn't there,' she said, without sitting down.

'Is it a long time since you saw it?'

'Only a few days...I couldn't say exactly...Perhaps the day before yesterday, when I cleaned the flat thoroughly...'

Eva opened her mouth, but in spite of an encouraging glance from the Superintendent she said nothing.

'Yes. It must have been the day before yesterday...'

'Were you lying down when your husband came back for dinner this evening?'

'I went to bed at two in the afternoon, because I was feeling very tired.'

'If he had opened the drawer to take out the revolver, would you have noticed?'

'I think so . . .'

'Are there articles in that drawer which he might have needed?'

'No . . . A medicine which he only took at night, when he was in pain, some old pill boxes and a pair of glasses with one lens broken.'

'Were you in the bedroom this morning while he was dressing?'

'Yes, I was making the beds . . .'

'So that your husband must have taken the revolver last night or the night before last?'

Another movement of protest from Eva. She opened her lips, then closed them again in silence.

'Thank you, Madame. I've nothing else to add. By the way, do you know the mark of the revolver?'

'A Browning, 6 mm 38 calibre. You'll find the number of it in my husband's wallet, for he had an arms licence.'

This proved to be the case.

'Tomorrow morning, if it suits you, Inspector Lognon, who's in charge of the enquiry, will come and pick you up at whatever time you like to arrange to go and identify the body . . .'

'Anytime, after eight o'clock . . .'

'Agreed, Lognon?'

They left the flat and were back on the dimly lit landing, the staircase with its gloomy carpet and brownish walls. The door had closed and no sound came from the flat. The two women kept silent; not a word passed between them.

In the street, Maigret looked up towards the lighted window and muttered:

'Now that we're out of hearing I bet the sparks'll fly!'

A shadow was outlined against the curtain; although distorted, it was recognizable as the figure of the girl, hurrying across the dining room. Almost immediately the light went on in another window, and Maigret felt convinced that Eva had just locked herself into her bedroom and that her sister was trying in vain to make her open the door.

2

Life was a funny business. Maigret looked cross, but in fact he would not have exchanged his place, at such moments, for the best seat at the Opéra. He felt so perfectly at home in the great buildings of the Police Judiciaire, in the middle of the night, that he had removed his jacket and unbuttoned his collar. He had even, after a moment's hesitation, unlaced his shoes because they were hurting him a little.

In his absence, Scotland Yard had telephoned and the call had been put through to his nephew Daniel, who had just passed the information on to him.

The crook he was concerned with had not been seen in London for over two years, but according to the latest news he had been in Holland. Maigret had therefore contacted Amsterdam. He was waiting, now, for information from the Netherlands Police. From time to time he communicated by telephone with the detectives who were on the watch for the man at the door of his suite in Claridge's and in the lounge of the hotel.

Then, his pipe between his teeth and his hair ruffled, he would open the door of his office and look down the long empty passage where a couple of lamps were burning dimly; and at such moments he looked like some worthy suburban householder surveying his bit of garden on a Sunday morning.

At the far end of the corridor the old night watchman Jérôme, who had been in the place for over thirty years and whose hair was as white as snow, was sitting in front of his little table with its green-shaded lamp, reading, through his steel spectacles, the big medical treatise that he had been studying for years. He read as children do, moving his lips and spelling out the syllables.

Then the Superintendent would walk about a little, hands in pockets, paying a visit to the Inspectors' room where the two men on duty—who were in shirtsleeves like himself—were playing cards and smoking cigarettes.

He walked to and fro. At the back of his room, in a narrow closet, there was a camp bed on which he lay down two or three times without managing to doze off. It was hot, in spite of the torrential rain, because the sun had been beating down on the rooms all day.

Once Maigret went up to his telephone, but on the point of lifting the receiver his hand stopped short. He walked off again, paid another visit to the inspectors, watched the game of cards for a short while and then went back to the telephone.

He was like a child who cannot bring himself to give up something he longs for. If only Lognon hadn't been such an unlucky man! But Lognon or no Lognon, Maigret had the right, of course, to take in hand the Rue Lamarck case, as he was dying to do.

Not because he considered it particularly sensational. He would get far more kudos from catching the crook, but he could not work up any enthusiasm for that. Willy-nilly, he kept picturing the emergency call box in the rain, the thin, puny figure of the little diamond broker, and the two sisters in their flat together.

How could it be explained? It was one of those cases the smell of which attracted him; he would have liked to sniff it at his leisure till he was so deeply steeped in it that the truth would stand forth of its own accord.

And he had been landed with poor Lognon, the best of men basically, the most conscientious of detectives, quite unbearably conscientious, Lognon who was harried by such persistent bad luck that he had become as surly as a mangy dog.

Every time Lognon had taken up a case he had been unfortunate. Either, just as he was about to make an arrest it was discovered that the guilty man had friends in high places and must be left alone, or else he himself fell ill and had to pass his files on to a colleague, or else an ambitious examining magistrate took all the credit for a successful outcome.

How could Maigret cheat him of triumph yet again? Particularly as Lognon lived in Goldfinger's district—in the Place Constantin-Pecqueur, three hundred metres from the dead man's flat, one hundred and fifty from the call box beside which he had died.

'Is that Amsterdam?'

Maigret made a note of information received. Since the crook, on leaving Amsterdam, had taken the plane for Basel, he contacted the Swiss police; but his thoughts were still with the little broker and his womenfolk. And every time he lay down on his camp bed and tried to sleep, the three of them came into his mind's eye with ever greater vividness.

Then he went and drank a glass of beer in his office. On arriving there he had three pints of beer and a pile of sandwiches sent up from the *Brasserie Dauphine*. Watch out! The light was showing under the door of one of the rooms: that of the Superintendent of the Finance Squad. You couldn't disturb that gentleman; he was as stiff as a poker, always impeccably groomed, and he never gave his colleagues more than a formal greeting. If he was spending the night at Headquarters, that meant there'd be a rumpus in the Bourse tomorrow.

Come to think of it, there had been a gala performance, followed by a supper, at the Madeleine Theatre that evening, to celebrate the hundredth performance of some play; Dr. Paul, that Parisian to the core, who was friends with all the stars, was sure to have been there; he was not expected home before two o'clock. He'd just have had time to change—although he had been known to turn up at the morgue in evening dress—and he'd have got to the Forensic Institute about a quarter of an hour ago.

Maigret couldn't stand it any longer. He picked up the receiver.

'The Forensic Institute, please ... Hello! Maigret speaking. Will you ask Dr. Paul to come to the phone? ... What did you say? ... He's too busy? ... He's begun the autopsy? ... Who's that, his assistant? ... Good evening, Jean ... Will you take a message to the doctor for me—ask him if he'll kindly make an analysis of the dead man's stomach—yes, carefully ... I'd like to know, in particular, if the man swallowed anything, food or drink, after his evening meal, which he must have taken at about 7.30 ... Thanks ... Yes, let him call me back ... I shall be here all night ...'

He hung up and asked for the switchboard at the telephone exchange.

'This is Superintendent Maigret ... I should like you to note all calls made or received from the residence of a certain Goldfinger, 66 bis Rue Lamarck. Right away, yes ...'

Lognon might have thought of it too; that couldn't be helped. Anyhow, he rang up Lognon too, at home in the Place Constantin-Pecqueur. The inspector answered promptly, which showed that he had not gone to bed.

'Is that you, Lognon? Maigret here... Sorry to disturb you...'

How typical of the Grouser! Instead of sleeping he was already busy writing up his report. His voice was anxious and sullen:

'I suppose, sir, you're going to take me off the case?'

'No, no, old man!... You began it and you'll carry it through to the end... I shall only ask you to keep me in the picture, as a purely personal favour...'

'Am I to send you a copy of the reports?'

Just like Lognon!

'Don't bother.'

'Because I intended to send them to my superior, the local Superintendent.'

'Yes, yes, of course... By the way, I've thought of one or two little things... I'm sure they've occurred to you too... For instance, don't you think it would be useful to have the house watched by two detectives? Then if one of the women went out, or if both of them went out separately, we could keep an eye on their comings and goings.'

'I've already posted one man there... I'll get a second put on... I suppose, if I get blamed for mobilizing too many men...'

'Nobody will blame you... Have you heard anything from Records about the prints on the gun?'

The offices and labs of the Records department were immediately above Maigret's head, in the upper floors of the Palais de Justice, but the Superintendent was anxious to deal as tactfully as possible with the prickly inspector.

'They've just called me... There are a great many prints, but too confused to be of any use to us... It looks as if the gun was wiped, but it's hard to tell exactly because of the rain.'

'Have you had the gun sent to Gastinne-Renette?'

'Yes. He's promised to be in his lab by eight o'clock and to examine the weapon immediately.'

There were various other pieces of advice that Maigret would
have liked to give him. He was longing to be involved in the case up
to his neck. It was really agony. But when he heard the Grouser's
miserable voice at the end of the line he felt compassion.

'Well then . . . I'll let you get on with the job.'

'You really don't want to take over the case?'

'No, old fellow . . . Carry on, and good luck!'

'Thank you . . .'

The night passed slowly, in the warm privacy of the great buildings which the darkness seemed to make smaller, and where there
were only five of them working or wandering about. The phone
rang from time to time: Basel called back, then Claridge's.

'Listen, boys, if he's asleep let him sleep . . . When he rings for
his breakfast, and not before, you go quietly into his room and ask
him to pay us a little visit at the Quai des Orfèvres. Above all, no
fuss . . . The manager of Claridge's would hate that . . .'

He went home at eight o'clock, and all the way back he kept
thinking that at that very moment that blessed Lognon was putting
Mathilde and Eva into a taxi to take them to the Forensic Institute.

In the Boulevard Richard-Lenoir, the housework had already
been done, Madame Maigret was looking spick and span and breakfast was waiting on the table.

'Dr. Paul has just rung you.'

'He's taken his time . . .'

The stomach of the unfortunate Goldfinger contained only half-
digested foodstuffs: vegetable soup, ham and pasta. Since eight
o'clock in the evening the diamond broker had had nothing to eat or
drink.

'Not even a glass of mineral water?' Maigret persisted.

'At any rate not during the half-hour preceding death.'

'Did you notice a stomach ulcer?'

'A duodenal ulcer, to be accurate.'

'No cancer?'

'Certainly not . . .'

'So that he might have gone on living for a long while?'

'A very long while. And he might even have been cured.'

'Thank you, doctor... Be kind enough to send your report to Inspector Lognon... What?... Yes, the Grouser... Have a good day!...'

And Madame Maigret put in, as she saw her husband make his way to the bathroom:

'You're going to bed, I hope?'

'I don't know yet... I slept a bit last night...'

He had a bath, followed by a cold shower, and ate a substantial breakfast while watching the rain fall as continuously as on a November morning. At nine o'clock he had the ballistics expert on the line.

'Hello!... Tell me, Maigret, there's one point that worries me in this case... We're dealing with gangsters, aren't we?'

'Why do you say that?'

'I'll tell you... The gun I was sent to examine is the same that fired the bullet found in the dead man's skull, isn't it?'

Maigret quoted the registration number of the weapon, which corresponded to the one owned by Goldfinger. The expert was ignorant of the circumstances of the drama; he judged solely by the exhibits.

'What's worrying you?'

'When I examined the barrel of the gun I noticed some small shiny scratches on the outside, at the tip of the barrel. I experimented with other guns of the same calibre... And I got the identical result by fitting an American-type silencer to the barrel.'

'You're sure of that?'

'I can state categorically that not very long ago, two days at most and probably less, since the scratches would have been dulled, a silencer was fitted to the revolver I examined.'

'Would you be kind enough to send the written report to Inspector Lognon, who is in charge of the enquiry?'

And Gastinne-Renette exclaimed, just as Dr. Paul had done:

'The Grouser?'

Madame Maigret said with a sigh:

'You're going off?... Do at least take your umbrella.'

He was going off, yes, but he wasn't going where he wanted to, because of that wretched inspector and his bad luck. If he'd had his own way he'd have had himself driven in a taxi to the corner of the Rue Caulaincourt and the Rue Lamarck. For what purpose? Nothing very definite: to get back into the atmosphere of the street, to hunt about in corners, to go into local bistros and listen to people who, having bought their morning papers, would have heard the news.

Goldfinger, on leaving home, had said he had an appointment in the neighbourhood. If he had committed suicide, it might have been a fictitious appointment. But then, what was the point of the silencer? How could one reconcile the use of this device, which moreover was not in common use or easily available, with the sound that had resounded in the emergency call box?

If the broker really had an appointment... Generally, appointments are not made in the street, particularly at 10 p.m. in the pouring rain. More probably in a café or bar. But the diamond broker had swallowed nothing, not even a glass of water, after the moment when he left home. Maigret would have liked to go over the man's tracks, stopping in front of the emergency call box.

No! There was something that did not fit, he had been aware of that from the start. It might occur to a man like Stan the Killer to abuse the police, to defy them for one last time before blowing his brains out. Not to a timid little man like Goldfinger!

Maigret had taken the bus and was standing on the platform, vaguely watching the early-morning life of Paris, the dustbins in the slanting rain, the workers streaming like ants towards offices and shops.

... Two men, in the space of six months, couldn't have had the same inspiration... Particularly a notion as crazy as alerting the police in order to make them witnesses from a distance of one's own suicide...

In such a case one must assume *imitation* rather than *reinvention*... Just as, if for instance a man kills himself by jumping off the third storey of the Eiffel Tower and the newspapers are rash enough to speak of it, an epidemic of similar suicides will ensue: fifteen or twenty people, during the next few months, will throw themselves off the Tower...

Now nobody had ever talked about the last moments of Stan the Killer . . . except at Police Headquarters . . . That was what had been worrying Maigret from the start, ever since he had left Daniel to go to the Rue Caulaincourt.

'You've had a call from Claridge's, Superintendent.'

His two detectives . . . The crook, known as The Commodore, had just rung for his breakfast.

'Shall we go up, Chief?'

'Go up, boys . . .'

To hell with his international crook, and to hell with Lognon into the bargain.

'Hello! . . . Is that you, Superintendent? Lognon speaking.'

Of course! As though he had not recognized the lugubrious voice of the Grouser!

'I'm just back from the Forensic Institute . . . Madame Goldfinger couldn't come with us.'

'What's that?'

'She was in such a state of nervous tension this morning that she asked my permission to stay in bed . . . Her doctor was there when I arrived . . . a local doctor, Dr. Langevin . . . He confirmed that his patient had had a very bad night, in spite of taking a heavy dose of sleeping tablets.'

'Did the young sister go with you?'

'Yes . . . She identified the body . . . She didn't say a word the whole way . . . She's not quite the same person as she was yesterday . . . There's a certain hardness and resolution about her that struck me . . .'

'Did she shed any tears?'

'No . . . She stood quite still looking at the body . . .'

'Where is she now?'

'I took her home . . . She had a talk with her sister, then she went out again to Borniol's to see to the funeral arrangements.'

'Did you send an officer after her?'

'Yes . . . There's another by the door . . . Nobody went out during the night . . . There were no telephone calls . . .'

'Have you alerted the switchboard people?'

'Yes...'

Then Lognon added, with the hesitant gulp of someone who dislikes what he is going to say:

'A stenographer is taking down the report I am now making, I shall send you and my immediate superior a copy by special messenger before noon, to keep things correct.'

Maigret grumbled to himself:

'Go to the devil!'

Such administrative formality was typical of Lognon, who was so used to seeing his best efforts turned against him that he had made himself intolerable by dint of his absurd precautions.

'Where are you, old man?'

'At *Manière's*...'

This was a brasserie in the Rue Caulaincourt, not far from the spot where Goldfinger had been killed.

'I've just done all the bistros in the neighbourhood...I showed the photo of the broker, the one on his identity card...It's a recent one, for the card was renewed less than a year ago...Nobody saw Goldfinger at about ten o'clock last night...In any case he's not known, except in one small bar kept by an Auvergnat, about fifty yards from his home, where he often used to go and ring up before he had the telephone installed in his flat two years ago.'

'They've been married how long?'

'Eight years...Now I'm going to the Rue Lafayette...If there was an appointment that's where it would almost certainly have taken place...As these diamond brokers all know one another...'

Maigret was sick with vexation at not being able to do all that himself, at not being able to mingle with the people who had known Goldfinger and gradually fill in his picture of the man, touch by touch.

'Carry on, man...Keep me informed...'

'You shall receive the report...'

But the fine rain, which was falling as though it never meant to stop, made him long to be outside. And here he was, forced to concern himself with so commonplace a person as an international crook specializing in forging cheques and bearer bonds, a gentleman who was likely to ride his high horse for a certain length of time but who would talk in the end.

Now they were just bringing him in. He was a handsome fellow of about fifty, looking like a member of some very exclusive club and putting on an air of astonishment.

'Are you going to talk?'

'Excuse me?' the man said, fiddling with his monocle. 'I don't understand. It must be a case of mistaken identity...'

'Bosh!'

'I beg your pardon?'

'I said bosh!...Look here, I've not got the patience today to spend hours coddling you with a gentlemanly interview to get you to sing...You see this office, don't you?...Get it into your head that you won't leave it until you've talked...Janvier! Lucas!... Take off his tie and his shoelaces...Put the bracelets on him... Keep an eye on him and don't let him stir a limb...See you bye and bye, boys...'

Too bad about Lognon, who at any rate was lucky enough to be taking the air in the Rue Lafayette. He jumped into a taxi.

'Rue Caulaincourt. I'll tell you when to stop.'

He felt quite pleased already to be back in the street where Goldfinger had been killed, where he had died at any rate, in front of the red-painted post of the emergency call box.

He walked up the Rue Lamarck with his jacket collar turned up, since in spite of Madame Maigret's motherly solicitude he had left his umbrella at Headquarters.

A few steps away from no. 66 bis he recognized a detective whom he had met once before and who, although he knew the famous Superintendent, was tactful enough to pretend not to see him.

'Come over here...Has nobody gone out?...Nobody gone up to the third floor?'

'Nobody, Monsieur Maigret...I watched all the people who went up the stairs...there were very few of them, only tradesmen...'

'Is Madame Goldfinger still in bed?'

'Probably...As for the young sister, she's gone out and my colleague Marsac is on her heels.'

'Did she take a taxi?'

'She waited for the bus at the street corner.'

Maigret went into the house, passed the concierge's lodge without stopping, climbed up to the third floor and rang at the door on the right.

The bell sounded. He listened attentively, putting his ear close to the door, but heard no sound. He rang a second time, then a third. He said in a low voice:

'Police!'

He knew, to be sure, that Madame Goldfinger was in bed, but she was not so ill as not to be able to get up and answer, if only through the door.

He went downstairs quickly to the concierge's lodge.

'Madame Goldfinger hasn't gone out, has she?'

'No, Monsieur... She isn't well... The doctor came this morning... Her sister's gone out, though...'

'Do you have a telephone?'

'No... You'll find one at the Auvergnat's café just down the road.'

He hurried there, asked for the number of the flat, and heard the bell ring for a long time in the empty room. Maigret's face at this moment expressed utter bewilderment. He asked for the switchboard.

'You've had no call for the Goldfinger flat?'

'Not one... Not a single call since you contacted us this evening... By the way, Inspector Lognon has also...'

'I know...'

He was furious. This silence did not correspond in any way with what he had imagined. He went back to no. 66 bis.

'You're quite sure,' he asked the detective on duty there, 'that nobody has gone up to the third floor?'

'I'll take my oath on it... I followed everybody who went into the house... I even made a list of them, as Inspector Lognon told me to.'

Persnickety Lognon again!

'Come along ... If necessary you can go and fetch a locksmith ... There must be one in the neighbourhood ...'

They went up the three floors. Maigret rang again. At first there was silence. Then it seemed to him that he heard someone moving at the far end of the flat. He repeated:

'Police!'

A faraway voice said:

'One moment!'

That moment lasted more than three minutes. Did it take three minutes to slip on a wrapper and slippers, or at a pinch to touch up one's face?

'Is that you, Superintendent?'

'It's me, Maigret ...'

There was the click of a bolt being drawn and a key turned in the lock.

'I do apologize ... I made you wait a long time, didn't I?'

Suspicious and aggressive, he asked:

'What do you mean?'

Did she notice that she had blundered? She stammered in a drowsy voice—too drowsy for the Superintendent's liking:

'I don't know ... I was asleep ... I had taken a sleeping pill ... I thought I heard a bell ring in my sleep.'

'What sort of a bell?'

'I couldn't tell you ... It was mixed up with my dream ... Do come in. I wasn't in a fit state to go with your inspector this morning ... My doctor was here ...'

'I know.'

And Maigret, who had closed the door behind him, leaving the young detective on the landing, looked round him with a scowl. Mathilde was wearing the same blue wrapper as the night before. She said:

'May I go back to bed?'

'Please do.'

On the dining room table there was still a cup with a little *café au lait* in it, and some bread and butter, presumably the remains of

Eva's breakfast. In the untidy bedroom, Madame Goldfinger lay down again with a plaintive sigh.

What was odd about it all? He noticed that the young woman had kept on her wrapper; that might of course be a sign of modesty.

'Had you been on the landing along time?'

'No...'

'Did you telephone?'

'No...'

'That's odd... In my dream the telephone kept ringing and wouldn't stop...'

'Really?'

Good. He realized now what was wrong. The woman he was supposed to have roused from the depths of sleep, and of a drugged sleep at that, who only three hours previously, according to her doctor, had been suffering from nervous depression, had her hair as smoothly dressed as though she were paying a call.

There was something else, a silk stocking showing under the bed. Was it likely to have been there since the previous day? Maigret let his pipe fall and bent down to pick it up, which allowed him to ascertain that *there was no pair to it under the bed.*

'Have you brought me any news?'

'I've just come to ask you a few questions... One moment... Where is your powder?'

'What powder?'

'Your face powder.'

For her face was freshly powdered, and yet Maigret could see no signs of a powder box in the room.

'On the shelf in the *cabinet de toilette.* You say that because I kept you waiting? I automatically went to powder my face when I heard the bell...'

Maigret felt like contradicting her. Out loud, he said:

'Was your husband's life insured?'

'He took out an insurance for 300,000 francs the year we were married... Then later he took out another to make it up to a million.'

'Was that long ago?'

'You'll find the policies in the desk, just behind you . . . You can open it, it's not locked . . . They're in the left-hand drawer.'

Two policies from the same firm. The first was eight years old. Maigret promptly turned the page, looking for a clause which he was almost certain he would find.

In case of suicide . . .

Only a few companies cover the risk of suicide. It was the case here, with one restriction however: the premium was only payable, in such a case, if the suicide took place at least a year after the signing of the policy.

The second insurance, for 700,000 francs, included the same clause. Maigret turned to the last page right away, to see the date. The policy had been signed exactly thirteen months previously.

'And yet your husband's affairs were not going too well at that time?'

'I know . . . I didn't want him to take out such a large insurance, but he was convinced that he was seriously ill and he wanted to safeguard me . . .'

'I see that he was fully paid up, which can't have been easy . . .'

There was a ring at the door. Madame Goldfinger made as if to rise, but Maigret went to open the door and found himself face to face with Lognon, who turned white and stammered, taut-lipped like a child on the verge of tears:

'I'm sorry . . .'

'On the contrary; it's I who must apologize. Come in, old man . . .'

Maigret had the policies in his hand; the other man had seen them and was pointing to them.

'It's not worthwhile now . . . That was what I was coming for . . .'

'In that case let's go down together.'

'I think that since you're here there's nothing for me to do and I can just go home. My wife happens to be unwell . . .'

Because Lognon, to crown his misfortunes, was married to the most shrewish wife in the world, who was ill most of the time, so that the inspector had to do the housework when he got home.

'We'll go downstairs together, old man . . . Just let me get my hat . . .'

And Maigret was mortified, ready to stammer out excuses. He was vexed with himself for hurting the feelings of a poor well-meaning fellow. Someone was coming up the stairs. It was Eva; she cast a cold glance at the two men and her eye immediately fell on the insurance policies. She went past with a curt nod.

'Come on, Lognon. I think there's nothing for us to discover here this afternoon . . . Tell me, Mademoiselle, when is the funeral to be?'

'The day after tomorrow . . . They're bringing the body back this afternoon . . .'

'Thank you . . .'

A queer girl. She was the one whose nerves were so tense that she should have been put to bed with a good dose of barbiturate.

'Listen, Lognon old man . . .'

The two of them went down the stairs, one behind the other, and Lognon was sighing and shaking his head:

'I've understood . . . From the first moment . . .'

'What have you understood?'

'That this is not a case for me . . . I'm going to draw up my final report . . .'

'No, no, old man . . .'

They were passing in front of the concierge's lodge.

'Half a minute . . . Let's ask this good woman a question . . . Tell me, Madame, does Madame Goldfinger go out much?'

'In the morning to do her shopping . . . Sometimes in the afternoon to visit the big stores, but not often . . .'

'Have they lived a long time in this house?'

'Six years . . . If all tenants were like them . . .'

And Lognon, sunk in gloom, hanging his head, pretended to ignore a conversation which no longer concerned him, since a big chief from Police Headquarters had cut the ground from under his feet.

'Was there no time when she went out more frequently?'

'Well, really . . . This winter, there was a time when she used to spend almost every afternoon out of the house . . . She told me that she went to see a friend who was expecting a baby.'

'Did you ever see this friend?'

'No. Probably they've stopped seeing one another.'

'Thank you . . . It was before Mademoiselle Eva came, wasn't it?'

'It was about that time that Madame Goldfinger stopped going out, yes . . .'

'And nothing struck you? . . .'

The concierge must have thought of something. For a moment her gaze became more fixed, but almost immediately she shook her head.

'No . . . Nothing important . . .'

'Thank you . . .'

The two detectives in the street were pretending not to know each other.

'Come with me as far as *Manière's,* Lognon . . . I've got a phone call to make and then I'm all yours.'

'Just as you please,' sighed Lognon, gloomier than ever.

They took an apéritif in a corner of the café, and then Maigret went into the call box to telephone.

'Hello, Lucas? . . . How's our Commodore?'

'He's coming on nicely . . .'

'Still as proud?'

'He's beginning to feel thirsty, his mouth's watering . . . I think he'd give a lot for a pint or a cocktail.'

'He can have a drink after he's talked . . . See you.'

And he went back to join Lognon, who, sitting at the marble-topped table, had taken a sheet of the café's headed notepaper and in his best copperplate hand was writing his resignation.

3

The interrogation of the Commodore lasted for eighteen hours, punctuated by telephone calls to Scotland Yard, Amsterdam, Basel and even Vienna. Maigret's office, by the end, had come to look like a guardroom, with empty glasses and plates of sandwiches on the table, pipe-ash all over the floor and papers everywhere. And the

Superintendent, although he had taken off his jacket from the start, had great rings of sweat on his shirt, under his armpits.

He had begun by treating his impressive customer as a gentleman. By the end he was handling him as familiarly as any vulgar pickpocket or member of the underworld.

'Cut out that nonsense, my lad ... You know as well as I do ...'

He took no interest whatever in what he was doing. Perhaps that was what finally enabled him to get the better of this toughest of crooks. The fellow was bewildered when he saw the passionate interest with which the Superintendent made and received certain phone calls that did not always concern himself.

During this time it was Lognon who was looking after the case that meant so much to Maigret.

'You see, dear fellow,' he had told him at *Manière's*, 'only someone like you who knows the neighbourhood can really find his way about in this business ... You know the district and all the people concerned better than anyone ... And if I ventured ...'

Balm and ointment lavishly applied to soothe the wounded self-respect of the surly inspector.

'Somebody killed Goldfinger, didn't they?'

'If you say so ...'

'You think so, too ... And it's one of the finest crimes I've seen in the whole of my career ... With the Force itself to witness the suicide ... That's first-class, old man, and I noticed that you were struck by it from the start ... Our Emergency service called upon to witness a suicide ... Only there were those silencer marks ... You thought of that as soon as you got Gastinne-Renette's report ... Only a single bullet was fired from Goldfinger's revolver, and at the time that revolver had a silencer on it ... In other words, what we heard was *another* shot fired from a *second* gun ... You realize that as well as I do ...

'Goldfinger was a second-rater, doomed sooner or later to insolvency.'

A second-rater indeed. Lognon had had the proof of that in the Rue Lafayette, where they had spoken of the dead man with sympathy but also with a certain contempt.

For in those circles they spare no pity for people who let themselves be taken in. And he had been taken in! He had sold some stones, to be paid for in three months' time, to a jeweller from Bécon-les-Bruyères with a misleadingly respectable reputation, an elderly pater familias who, belatedly infatuated with a girl who was not even pretty, had fraudulently sold the gems and had eventually fled the country with his mistress.

A deficit of 100,000 francs in Goldfinger's account, which for the past year he had been struggling in vain to make up.

'A poor devil, you'll see, Lognon... A poor devil who did not commit suicide... The business of the silencer proves that... But who was foully murdered, shot down by a swine... That's your opinion, isn't it?... And his wife is going to get a million...

'I've no advice to give you, for you're as shrewd as I am...

'Suppose Madame Goldfinger was in league with the murderer, to whom somebody must have handed over the gun that was in the drawer... After the thing had been done they'd want to contact one another, wouldn't they, if only for mutual reassurance?...

'But she never left the building, and she received no phone calls...

'You get my meaning?... I'm sure you do, Lognon... Two detectives on the pavement... the switchboard permanently on the alert... It was smart of you to have thought of that...

'And the insurance policy?... And the fact that the suicide clause had only become operative one month previously?

'I'll leave you to cope, old man... I've another job on hand, and there's no one better qualified than yourself to bring this one to a successful conclusion...'

That was how he had won over Lognon.

But Lognon's reply was still melancholy:

'I shall go on sending my reports to you as well as to my immediate superior.'

Maigret was, so to speak, a prisoner in his office, almost as much as the Commodore. Only the telephone connected him with the Rue Lamarck case, which alone interested him. From time to time Lognon rang up, using the strictest official language:

'I have the honour to inform you that...'

There had been a scene between the two sisters, echoes of which had been heard outside their flat. That evening Eva had decided to go and sleep at the Hôtel Alsinia, at the corner of the Place Constantin-Pecqueur.

'It looks as though they hated one another...'

'I'll say they do!'

And Maigret added, keeping an eye on the astonished Commodore:

'Because the younger sister was the one who loved Goldfinger... You can be sure, Lognon, that she understood the whole thing... What remains to be learnt is how the murderer communicated with Madame Goldfinger...Not by telephone, we're sure of that, thanks to the switchboard...And she did not see him outside the house...'

Madame Maigret rang up:

'When are you coming home? You forget that you haven't slept in a bed for twenty-four hours.'

'Presently,' he replied.

Then he began again, for the twentieth or thirtieth time, questioning the Commodore, who finally weakened out of sheer weariness.

'Take him away, boys,' he said to Lucas and Janvier. 'One minute...Come into the Inspectors' room first.'

There were seven or eight of them there in front of Maigret, who was beginning to drop with fatigue.

'Listen, boys...You remember Stan's death in the Faubourg Saint-Antoine?...Well! There's something I can't put my finger on...a name I've got on the tip of my tongue...a recollection that I could bring back with a little effort...'

They all thought hard, somewhat awestruck, because at such moments, after hours of nervous tension, Maigret was always rather overpowering. Only Janvier raised a finger, schoolboy fashion.

'There was Mariani...' he said.

'Was he with us at the time of the Stan the Killer case?'

'It was the last case he was involved in...'

And Maigret went out, slamming the door. He had solved the

problem. Ten months previously he had been landed with a probationary detective who had the backing of some minister or other. The man was a dandy—a pimp, according to Maigret—whose presence in his department he had endured for a few weeks and whom he had been forced to get rid of.

The rest was up to Lognon. And Lognon did what had to be done, patiently, without genius but with his usual meticulousness.

For the space of ten or twelve days the Goldfingers' house was subjected to the closest surveillance. During the whole time nothing transpired except that the girl Eva was also spying on her sister.

On the thirteenth day the police knocked at the door of the flat where the diamond-broker's wife was supposed to be, and found it empty.

Madame Goldfinger had not gone out of the house, and she was discovered in the flat immediately above her own, rented in the name of a certain Mariani.

A gentleman who, since his expulsion from the police force, lived chiefly by his wits...A man of gross appetites and with a certain seductive power, at any rate for a woman like Madame Goldfinger, wife of a sick husband...

They had not needed to telephone one another nor to meet outside...

And there was a fine prize of a million francs in view if the wretched broker committed suicide more than a year after signing his insurance policy...

A shot fired with the silencer placed on the dead man's own revolver, provided by his wife.

Then a second shot with a different gun in front of the emergency call box, a shot which was to establish the fact of suicide unquestionably and prevent the police from looking for a murderer...

'You've done splendidly, Lognon.'

'Superintendent...'

'Which of us was it who caught them in their hideout on the fourth floor?...Wasn't it you who heard the signals they gave each other through the floor?'

'My report will say...'

'I couldn't care less about your report, Lognon...You've scored a victory...and against some damn clever people...Will you come and have dinner with me tonight at *Manière's*?'

'Well, it's just that...'

'That what?'

'My wife's unwell again and so...'

What can one do for people like that, who are forced to leave you in order to go home and wash the dishes, maybe polish the floor?

And yet it was on this man's account, it was to spare the sensitive feelings of the surly inspector, that Maigret had denied himself the delight of an enquiry on which he had particularly set his heart!

5 May 1946

The Evidence of the Altar Boy

A fine cold rain was falling. The night was very dark; only at the far end of the street, near the barracks from which, at half-past five, there had come the sound of bugle calls and the noise of horses being taken to be watered, was there a faint light shining in someone's window—an early riser, or an invalid who had lain awake all night.

The rest of the street was asleep. It was a broad, quiet, newish street, with almost identical one- or two-storied houses such as are to be seen in the suburbs of most big provincial towns.

The whole district was new, devoid of mystery, inhabited by quiet unassuming people, clerks and commercial travellers, retired men and peaceful widows.

Maigret, with his overcoat collar turned up, was huddling in the angle of a carriage gateway, that of the boys' school; he was waiting, watch in hand, and smoking his pipe.

At a quarter to six exactly, bells rang out from the parish church behind him, and he knew that, as the boy had said, it was the 'first stroke' for six o'clock Mass.

The sound of the bells was still vibrating in the damp air when he heard, or rather guessed at, the shrill clamour of an alarm clock. This lasted only a few seconds. The boy must already have stretched a hand out of his warm bed and groped in the darkness for the safety-catch that would silence the clock. A few minutes later, the attic window on the second floor lit up.

It all happened exactly as the boy had said. He must have risen noiselessly, before anyone else, in the sleeping house. Now he must be picking up his clothes, his socks, washing his face and hands and combing his hair. As for his shoes, he had declared:

'I carry them downstairs and put them on when I get to the last step, so as not to wake up my parents.'

This had happened every day, winter and summer, for nearly two years, ever since Justin had first begun to serve at Mass at the hospital.

He had asserted, furthermore:

'The hospital clock always strikes three or four minutes later than the parish church clock.'

And this had proved to be the case. The inspectors of the Flying Squad to which Maigret had been seconded for the past few months had shrugged their shoulders over these tiresome details about first bells and second bells.

Was it because Maigret had been an altar boy himself for a long time that he had not dismissed the story with a smile?

The bells of the parish church rang first, at a quarter to six. Then Justin's alarm clock went off, in the attic where the boy slept. Then a few moments later came the shriller, more silvery sound of the hospital chapel bells, like those of a convent.

He still had his watch in his hand. The boy took barely more than four minutes to dress. Then the light went out. He must be groping his way down the stairs, anxious not to waken his parents, then sitting down on the bottom step to put on his shoes, and taking down his coat and cap from the bamboo coatrack on the right in the passage.

The door opened. The boy closed it again without making a sound, looked up and down the street anxiously and then saw the Superintendent's burly figure coming up to him.

'I was afraid you might not be there.'

And he started walking fast. He was a thin, fair-haired little twelve-year-old with an obstinate look about him.

'You want me to do just what I usually do, don't you? I always walk fast, for one thing because I've worked out to the minute how long it takes, and for another, because in winter, when it's dark, I'm frightened. In a month it'll be getting light by this time in the morning.'

He took the first turning on the right into another quiet, some-what shorter street, which led on to an open square planted with elms and crossed diagonally by tramlines.

And Maigret noted tiny details that reminded him of his own childhood. He noticed, for one thing, that the boy did not walk close to the houses, probably because he was afraid of seeing some-one suddenly emerge from a dark doorway. Then, that when he crossed the square he avoided the trees in the same way, because a man might have been hiding behind them.

He was a brave boy, really, since for two whole winters, in all weathers, sometimes in thick fog or in the almost total darkness of a moonless night, he had made the same journey every morning all alone.

'When we get to the middle of the Rue Sainte-Catherine you'll hear the second bell for Mass from the parish church...'

'At what time does the first tram pass?'

'At six o'clock. I've only seen it two or three times, when I was late...once because my alarm clock hadn't rung, another time be-cause I'd fallen asleep again. That's why I jump out of bed as soon as it rings.'

A pale little face in the rainy night, with eyes that still retained something of the fixed stare of a sleepwalker, and a thoughtful ex-pression with just a slight tinge of anxiety.

'I shan't go on serving at Mass. It's because you insisted that I've come today...'

They turned left down the Rue Sainte-Catherine, where, as in all the streets in this district, there was a lamp every fifty metres, each of them shedding a pool of light; and the child unconsciously quick-ened his pace each time he left the reassuring zone of brightness.

The noises from the barracks could still be heard in the distance. A few windows lit up. Footsteps sounded in a side street; probably a workman going to his job.

'When you got to the corner of the street, did you see nothing?'

This was the trickiest point, for the Rue Sainte-Catherine was very straight and empty, with its rectilinear pavements and its street lamps at regular intervals, leaving so little shadow between them that one could not have failed to see a couple of men quarrelling even at a hundred metres' distance.

'Perhaps I wasn't looking in front of me ... I was talking to myself, I remember ... I often do talk to myself in a whisper, when I'm going along there in the morning ... I wanted to ask mother something when I got home and I was repeating to myself what I was going to say to her ...'

'What did you want to say to her?'

'I've wanted a bike for ever such a long time ... I've already saved up three hundred francs out of my church money.'

Was it just an impression? It seemed to Maigret that the boy was keeping further away from the houses. He even stepped off the pavement, and returned to it a little further on.

'It was here ... Look ... There's the second bell ringing for Mass at the parish church.'

And Maigret endeavoured, in all seriousness, to enter into the world which was the child's world every morning.

'I must have looked up suddenly ... You know, like when you're running without looking where you're going and find yourself in front of a wall ... It was just here.'

He pointed to the line on the pavement dividing the darkness from the lamplight, where the drizzle formed a luminous haze.

'First I saw that there was a man lying down and he looked so big that I could have sworn he took up the whole width of the pavement.'

That was impossible, for the pavement was at least two and a half metres across.

'I don't know what I did exactly ... I must have jumped aside ... I didn't run away immediately, for I saw the knife stuck in his chest, with a big handle made of brown horn. I noticed it because my Uncle Henri has a knife just like it and he told me it was made out of a stag's horn. I'm certain the man was dead ...'

'Why?'

'I don't know ... He looked like a corpse.'

'Were his eyes shut?'

'I didn't notice his eyes...I don't know...But I had the feeling he was dead...It all happened very quickly, as I told you yesterday in your office...They made me repeat the same thing so many times yesterday that I'm all muddled...Specially when I feel people don't believe me...'

'And the other man?'

'When I looked up I saw that there was somebody a little further on, five metres away maybe, a man with very pale eyes who looked at me for a moment and then started running. It was the murderer...'

'How do you know that?'

'Because he ran off as fast as he could.'

'In which direction?'

'Right over there...'

'Towards the barracks?'

'Yes...'

It was a fact that Justin had been interrogated at least ten times the previous day. Before Maigret appeared in the office the detectives had even made a sort of game of it. His story had never varied in a single detail.

'And what did you do?'

'I started running too...It's hard to explain...I think it was when I saw the man running away that I got frightened...And then I ran as hard as I could...'

'In the opposite direction?'

'Yes.'

'Did you not think of calling for help?'

'No...I was too frightened...I was specially afraid my legs might give way, for I could scarcely feel them...I turned right-about as far as the Place du Congrès...I took the other street, that leads to the hospital too after making a bend.'

'Let's go on.'

More bells, the shrill-toned bells of the chapel. After walking some fifty metres they reached a crossroads, on the left of which were the walls of the barracks, pierced with loopholes, and on the right a huge gateway dimly lit and surmounted by a clock-face of greenish glass.

It was three minutes to six.

'I'm a minute late... Yesterday I was on time in spite of it all, because I ran...'

There was a heavy knocker on the solid oak door; the child lifted it, and the noise reverberated through the porch. A porter in slippers opened the door, let Justin go in but barred the way to Maigret, looking at him suspiciously.

'What is it?'

'Police.'

'Let's see your card?'

Hospital smells were perceptible as soon as they entered the porch. They went on through a second door into a huge courtyard surrounded by various hospital buildings. In the distance could be glimpsed the white headdresses of nuns on their way to the chapel.

'Why didn't you say anything to the porter yesterday?'

'I don't know... I was in a hurry to get there...'

Maigret could understand that. The haven was not the official entrance with its crabbed, mistrustful porter, nor the unwelcoming courtyard through which stretchers were being carried in silence; it was the warm vestry near the chapel, where a nun was lighting candles on the altar.

'Are you coming in with me?'

'Yes.'

Justin looked vexed, or rather shocked, probably at the thought that this policeman, who might be an unbeliever, was going to enter into his hallowed world. And this, too, explained to Maigret why every morning the child had the courage to get up so early and overcome his fears.

The chapel had a warm and intimate atmosphere. Patients in the blue-grey hospital uniform, some with bandaged heads, some with crutches or with their arms in slings, were already sitting in the pews of the nave. Up in the gallery the nuns formed a flock of identical figures, and all their white comets bowed simultaneously in pious worship.

'Follow me.'

They went up a few steps, passing close to the altar where candles were already burning. To the right was a vestry panelled in dark wood, where a tall gaunt priest was putting on his vestments, while a surplice edged with fine lace lay ready for the altar boy. A nun was busy filling the holy vessels.

It was here that, on the previous day, Justin had come to a halt at last, panting and weak-kneed. It was here that he had shouted:

'A man's been killed in the Rue Sainte-Catherine!'

A small clock set in the wainscot pointed to six o'clock exactly. Bells were ringing again, sounding fainter here than outside. Justin told the nun who was helping him on with his surplice:

'This is the Police Superintendent...'

And Maigret stood waiting while the child went in, ahead of the chaplain, the skirts of his red cassock flapping as he hurried towards the altar steps.

The vestry nun had said:

'Justin is a good little boy, who's very devout and who's never lied to us... Occasionally he's failed to come and serve at Mass... He might have pretended he'd been ill... Well, he never did; he always admitted frankly that he'd not had the courage to get up because it was too cold, or because he'd had a nightmare during the night and was feeling too tired...'

And the chaplain, after saying Mass, had gazed at the Superintendent with the clear eyes of a saint in a stained glass window:

'Why should the child have invented such a tale?'

Maigret knew, now, what had gone on in the hospital chapel on the previous morning. Justin, his teeth chattering, at the end of his tether, had been in a state of hysterics. The service could not be delayed; the vestry nun had informed the Sister Superior and had herself served at Mass in place of the child, who was meanwhile being attended to in the vestry.

Ten minutes later, the Sister Superior had thought of informing the police. She had gone out through the chapel, and everyone had realized that something was happening.

At the local police station the sergeant on duty had failed to understand.

'What's that? ... The Sister Superior? ... Superior to what?'

And she had told him, in the hushed tone they use in convents, that there had been a crime in the Rue Sainte-Catherine; and the police had found nothing, no victim, and, needless to say, no murderer ...

Justin had gone to school at half-past eight, just as usual, as though nothing had happened; and it was in his classroom that Inspector Besson, a strapping little fellow who looked like a boxer and who liked to act tough, had picked him up at half-past nine as soon as the Flying Squad had got the report.

Poor kid! For two whole hours, in a dreary office that reeked of tobacco fumes and the smoke from a stove that wouldn't draw, he had been interrogated not as a witness but as a suspect.

Three inspectors in turn, Besson, Thiberge and Vallin, had tried to catch him out, to make him contradict himself.

To make matters worse his mother had come too. She sat in the waiting room, weeping and snivelling and telling everybody:

'We're decent people and we've never had anything to do with the police.'

Maigret, who had worked late the previous evening on a case of drug smuggling, had not reached his office until eleven o'clock.

'What's happening?' he had asked when he saw the child standing there, dry-eyed but as stiffly defiant as a little fighting cock.

'A kid who's been having us on ... He claims to have seen a dead body in the street and a murderer who ran away when he got near. But a tram passed along the same street four minutes later and the driver saw nothing ... It's a quiet street, and nobody heard anything ... And finally when the police were called, a quarter of an hour later, by some nun or other, there was absolutely nothing to be seen on the pavement, not the slightest trace of a bloodstain ...'

'Come along into my office, boy.'

And Maigret was the first of them, that day, not to address Justin by the familiar *tu*, the first to treat him not as a fanciful or malicious urchin but as a small man.

He had listened to the boy's story simply and quietly, without interrupting or taking any notes.

'Shall you go on serving at Mass in the hospital?'

'No. I don't want to go back. I'm too frightened.'

And yet it meant a great sacrifice for him. Not only was he a devout child, deeply responsive to the poetry of that early Mass in the warm and somewhat mysterious atmosphere of the chapel; but in addition, he was paid for his services—not much, but enough to enable him to get together a little nest egg. And he so badly wanted a bicycle which his parents could not afford to buy for him!

'I should like you to go just once more, tomorrow morning.'

'I shan't dare.'

'I'll go along with you . . . I'll wait for you in front of your home. You must behave exactly as you always do.'

This was what had been happening, and Maigret, at seven in the morning, was now standing alone outside the door of the hospital, in a district which, on the previous day, he had known only from having been through it by car or in a tram.

An icy drizzle was still falling from the sky which was now paler, and it clung to the Superintendent's shoulders; he sneezed twice. A few pedestrians hurried past, their coat collars turned up and their hands in their pockets; butchers and grocers had begun taking down the shutters of their shops.

It was the quietest, most ordinary district imaginable. At a pinch one might picture a quarrel between two men, two drunks for instance, at five minutes to six on the pavement of the Rue Sainte-Catherine. One might even conceive of an assault by some ruffian on an early passerby.

But the sequel was puzzling. According to the boy, the murderer had run off when he came near, and it was then five minutes to six. At six o'clock, however, the first tram had passed, and the driver had declared that he had seen nothing.

He might, of course, have been inattentive, or looking in the other direction. But at five minutes past six two policemen on their beat had walked along that very pavement. And they had seen nothing!

At seven or eight minutes past six a cavalry officer who lived three houses away from the spot indicated by Justin had left home, as he did every morning, to go to the barracks.

And he had seen nothing either!

Finally, at twenty-past six, the police cyclists dispatched from the local station had found no trace of the victim.

Had someone come in the meantime to remove the body in a car or van? Maigret had deliberately and calmly sought to consider every hypothesis, and this one had proved as unreliable as all the rest. At No. 42 in the same street, there was a sick woman whose husband had sat up with her all night. He had asserted categorically:

'We hear all the noises outside. I notice them all the more because my wife is in great pain, and the least noise makes her wince. The tram woke her when she'd only just dropped off... I can give you my word no car came past before seven o'clock. The dustcart was the earliest.'

'And you heard nothing else?'

'Somebody running, at one point...'

'Before the tram?'

'Yes, because my wife was asleep...I was making myself some coffee on the hot plate.'

'One person running?'

'More like two.'

'You don't know in which direction?'

'The blind was down...As it creaks when you lift it I didn't try to look out.'

This was the only piece of evidence in Justin's favour. There was a bridge two hundred metres further on. And the policeman on duty there had seen no car pass.

Could one assume that barely a few minutes after he'd run away the murderer had come back, picked up his victim's body and carried it off somewhere or other, without attracting attention?

Worse still, there was one piece of evidence which made people shrug their shoulders when they talked about the boy's story. The place he had indicated was just opposite No. 61. Inspector Thiberge had called at this house the day before, and Maigret, who left nothing to chance, now visited it himself.

It was a new house of pinkish brick; three steps led up to a shiny pitchpine door with a letter-box of gleaming brass.

Although it was only 7.30 in the morning, the Superintendent had been given to understand that he might call at that early hour.

A gaunt old woman with a moustache peered through a spy-hole and argued before letting him into the hall, where there was a pleasant smell of fresh coffee.

'I'll go and see if the Judge will see you.'

For the house belonged to a retired magistrate, who was reputed to have private means and who lived there alone with a housekeeper.

Some whispering went on in the front room, which should by rights have been a drawing room. Then the old woman returned and said sourly:

'Come in . . . Wipe your feet, please . . . You're not in a stable.'

The room was no drawing room; it bore no resemblance to what one usually thinks of as such. It was very large, and it was part bedroom, part study, part library and part junk-room, being cluttered with the most unexpected objects.

'Have you come to look for the corpse?' said a sneering voice that made the Superintendent jump.

Since there was a bed, he had naturally looked towards it, but it was empty. The voice came from the chimney corner, where a lean old man was huddled in the depths of an armchair, with a plaid over his legs.

'Take off your overcoat, for I adore heat and you'll not be able to stand it here.'

It was quite true. The old man, holding a pair of tongs, was doing his best to encourage the biggest possible blaze from a log fire.

'I had thought that the police had made some progress since my time and had learnt to mistrust evidence given by children. Children and girls are the most unreliable of witnesses, and when I was on the Bench . . .'

He was wearing a thick dressing gown, and in spite of the heat of the room, he had a scarf as broad as a shawl round his neck.

'So the crime is supposed to have been committed in front of my house? And if I'm not mistaken, you are the famous Superintendent Maigret, whom they have graciously sent to our town to reorganize our Flying Squad?'

His voice grated. It was that of a spiteful, aggressive, savagely sarcastic old man.

'Well, my dear Superintendent, unless you're going to accuse me of being in league with the murderer, I am sorry to tell you, as I told your young inspector yesterday, that you're on the wrong track.

'You've probably heard that old people need very little sleep. Moreover there are people who, all their life long, sleep very little. Erasmus was one such, for instance, as was also a gentleman known as Voltaire...'

He glanced smugly at the bookshelves where volumes were piled ceiling-high.

'This has been the case with many other people whom you're not likely to know either... It's the case with me, and I pride myself on not having slept more than three hours a night during the last fifteen years... Since for the past ten my legs have refused to carry me, and since furthermore I've no desire to visit any of the places to which they might take me, I spend my days and nights in this room which, as you can see for yourself, gives directly on to the street.

'By four in the morning I am sitting in this armchair, with all my wits about me, believe me... I could show you the book in which I was deep yesterday morning, only it was by a Greek philosopher and I can't imagine you'd be interested.

'The fact remains that if an incident of the sort described by your over-imaginative young friend had taken place under my window, I can promise you I should have noticed it... My legs are weak, as I've said, but my hearing is still good.

'Moreover, I have retained enough natural curiosity to take an interest in all that happens in the street, and if it amuses you I could tell you at what time every housewife in the neighbourhood goes past my window to do her shopping.'

He was looking at Maigret with a smile of triumph.

'So you usually hear young Justin passing in front of the house?' the Superintendent asked in the meekest and gentlest of tones.

'Naturally.'

'You both hear him and see him?'

'I don't follow.'

'For most of the year, for almost two-thirds of the year, it's broad daylight at six in the morning... Now the child served at six o'clock Mass both summer and winter.'

'I used to see him go past.'

'Considering that this happened every day with as much regularity as the passing of the first tram, you must have been attentively aware of it...'

'What do you mean?'

'I mean that, for instance, when a factory siren sounds every day at the same time in a certain district, when somebody passes your window with clockwork regularity, you naturally say to yourself: Hello, it must be such and such a time.

'And if one day the siren doesn't sound, you think: Why, it's Sunday. And if the person doesn't come past you wonder: What can have happened to him? Perhaps he's ill?'

The judge was looking at Maigret with sharp, sly little eyes. He seemed to resent being taught a lesson.

'I know all that...' he grumbled, cracking his bony finger-joints. 'I was a magistrate before you were a policeman.'

'When the altar boy went past...'

'I used to hear him, if that's what you're trying to make me admit.'

'And if he didn't go past?'

'I might have happened to notice it. But I might have happened not to notice it. As in the case of the factory siren you mentioned. One isn't struck every Sunday by the silence of the siren...'

'What about yesterday?'

Could Maigret be mistaken? He had the impression that the old magistrate was scowling, that there was something sullen and savagely secretive about his expression. Old people sometimes sulk, like children; they often display the same puerile stubbornness.

'Yesterday?'

'Yes...'

Why did he repeat the question, unless to give himself time to make a decision?

'I noticed nothing.'

'Not that he had passed?'

'No...'

'Nor that he hadn't passed?'

'No...'

One or the other answer was untrue, Maigret was convinced. He was anxious to continue the test, and he went on with his questions:

'Nobody ran past your windows?'

'No.'

This time the *no* was spoken frankly and the old man must have been telling the truth.

'You heard no unusual sound?'

'No' again, uttered with the same downrightness and almost with a note of triumph.

'No sound of trampling, of groaning, no sound of a body falling?'

'Nothing at all.'

'I'm much obliged to you.'

'Don't mention it.'

'Seeing that you've been a magistrate I need not of course ask you if you are willing to repeat your statement under oath?'

'Whenever you like.'

And the old man said that with a kind of delighted impatience.

'I apologize for disturbing you, Judge.'

'I wish you all success in your enquiry, Superintendent.'

The old housekeeper must have been hiding behind the door, for she was waiting on the threshold to show out the Superintendent and shut the front door behind him.

Maigret experienced a curious sensation as he re-emerged into everyday life in that quiet suburban street where housewives were beginning their shopping and children were on their way to school.

It seemed to him that he had been hoaxed, and yet he could have sworn that the judge had not withheld the truth except on one point. He had the impression, furthermore, that at a certain moment he had been about to discover something very odd, very elusive, very unexpected; that he would only have had to make a tiny effort but that he had been unable to do so.

Once again he pictured the boy, he pictured the old man; he tried to find a link between them.

Slowly he filled his pipe, standing on the curb. Then, since he had had no breakfast, not even a cup of coffee on rising, and since his wet overcoat was clinging to his shoulders, he went to wait at the corner of the Place du Congrès for the tram that would take him home.

2

Out of the heaving mass of sheets and blankets an arm emerged, and a red face glistening with sweat appeared on the pillow; finally a sulky voice growled:

'Pass me the thermometer.'

And Madame Maigret, who was sewing by the window—she had drawn aside the net curtain so as to see in the gathering dusk— rose with a sigh and switched on the electric light.

'I thought you were asleep. It's not half an hour since you last took your temperature.'

Resignedly, for she knew from long marital experience that it was useless to cross the big fellow, she shook the thermometer to bring down the mercury and slipped the tip of it between his lips.

He asked, meanwhile:

'Has anybody come?'

'You'd know if they had, since you've not been asleep.'

He must have dozed off though, if only for a few minutes. But he was continually being roused from his torpor by that blasted jingle from down below.

They were not in their own home. Since his mission in this provincial town was to last for six months at least, and since Madame Maigret could not bear the thought of letting her husband eat in restaurants for so long a period, she had followed him, and they had rented a furnished flat in the upper part of the town.

It was too bright, with flowery wallpaper, gimcrack furniture and a bed that groaned under the Superintendent's weight. They had, at any rate, chosen a quiet street, where, as the landlady Madame Danse had told them, not a soul passed.

What she had failed to add was that, the ground floor of the house being occupied by a dairy, the whole place was pervaded by a sickly smell of cheese. Another fact which she had not revealed but which Maigret had just discovered for himself, since this was the first time he had stayed in bed in the daytime, was that the door of the dairy was equipped not with a bell but with a strange contraption of metal tubes which, whenever a customer came in, clashed together with a prolonged jingling sound.

'How high?'

'38.5 . . .'

'A little while ago it was 38.8.'

'And by tonight it'll be over 39.'

He was furious. He was always bad-tempered when he was ill, and he glowered resentfully at Madame Maigret, who obstinately refused to go out when he was longing to fill himself a pipe.

It was still pouring with rain, the same fine rain that clung to the windows and fell in mournful silence, giving one the impression of living in an aquarium. A crude glare shone down from the electric light bulb which swung, unshaded, at the end of its cord. And one could imagine an endless succession of streets equally deserted, windows lighting up one after the other, people caged in their rooms, moving about like fishes in a bowl.

'You must have another cup of tisane.'

It was probably the tenth since twelve o'clock, and then all that lukewarm water had to be sweated away into his sheets, which ended up as damp as compresses.

He must have caught flu or tonsillitis while waiting for the boy in the cold early morning rain outside the school, or else afterwards while he was roaming the streets. By ten o'clock, when he was back in his room in the Flying Squad's offices, and while he was poking the stove with what had become almost a ritual gesture, he had been seized with the shivers. Then he had felt too hot. His eyelids were smarting and when he looked at himself in the bit of mirror in the cloakroom, he had seen round staring eyes that were glistening with fever.

Moreover his pipe no longer tasted the same, and that was a sure sign.

'Look here, Besson: if by any chance I shouldn't come back this afternoon, will you carry on investigating the altar boy problem?'

And Besson, who always thought himself cleverer than anybody else:

'Do you really think, Chief, that there *is* such a problem, and that a good spanking wouldn't put an end to it?'

'All the same, you must get one of your colleagues, Vallin for instance, to keep an eye on the Rue Sainte-Catherine.'

'In case the corpse comes back to lie down in front of the judge's house?'

Maigret was too dazed by his incipient fever to follow Besson on to that ground. He had just gone on deliberately giving instructions.

'Draw up a list of all the residents in the street. It won't be a big job, because it's a short street.'

'Shall I question the kid again?'

'No...'

And since then he had felt too hot; he was conscious of drops of sweat beading on his skin, he had a sour taste in his mouth, he kept hoping to sink into oblivion but was constantly disturbed by the ridiculous jingle of the brass tubes from the dairy.

He loathed being ill because it was humiliating and also because Madame Maigret kept a fierce watch to prevent him from smoking his pipe. If only she'd had to go out and buy something at the pharmacist's! But she was always careful to take a well-stocked medicine chest about with her.

He loathed being ill, and yet there were moments when he almost enjoyed it, moments when, closing his eyes, he felt ageless because he experienced once again the sensations of his childhood.

Then he remembered the boy Justin, whose pale face already showed such strength of character. All that morning's scenes recurred to his mind, not with the precision of everyday reality nor with the sharp outline of things seen, but with the peculiar intensity of things felt.

For instance he could have described almost in detail the attic room that he had never seen, the iron bedstead, the alarm clock on the bedside table, the boy stretching out his arm, dressing silently, the same gestures invariably repeated...

Invariably the same gestures! It seemed to him an important and obvious truth. When you've been serving at Mass for two years at a regular time, your gestures become almost completely automatic...

The first bell at a quarter to six...The alarm clock...The shriller sound of the chapel bells...Then the child would put on his shoes at the foot of the stairs, open the front door and meet the cold breath of early morning.

'You know, Madame Maigret, he's never read any detective stories.' For as long back as they could remember, possibly because it had begun as a joke, they had called one another Maigret and Madame Maigret, and they had almost forgotten that they had Christian names like other people...

'He doesn't read the papers either...'

'You'd better try to sleep.'

He closed his eyes, after a longing glance at his pipe, which lay on the black marble mantelpiece.

'I questioned his mother at great length; she's a decent woman, but she's mightily in awe of the police...'

'Go to sleep!'

He kept silence for a while. His breathing became deeper; it sounded as if he was really dozing off.

'She declares he's never seen a dead body...It's the sort of thing you try to keep from children.'

'Why is it important?'

'He told me the body was so big that it seemed to take up the whole pavement...Now that's the impression that a dead body lying on the ground makes on one...A dead person always looks bigger than a living one...D'you understand?'

'I can't think why you're worrying, since Besson's looking after the case.'

'Besson doesn't believe in it.'

'In what?'

'In the dead body.'

'Shall I put out the light?'

In spite of his protests, she climbed on to a chair and fastened a band of waxed paper round the bulb so as to dim its light.

'Now try to get an hour's sleep, then I'll make you another cup of tisane. You haven't been sweating enough...'

'Don't you think if I were to have just a tiny puff at my pipe...'

'Are you mad?'

She went into the kitchen to keep an eye on the vegetable broth, and he heard her tiptoeing back and forth. He kept picturing the same section of the Rue Sainte-Catherine, with street lamps every fifty metres.

'The judge declares he heard nothing...'

'What are you saying?'

'I bet they hate one another...'

And her voice reached him from the far end of the kitchen:

'Who are you talking about? You see I'm busy...'

'The judge and the altar boy. They've never spoken to one another, but I'll take my oath they hate each other. You know, very old people, particularly old people who live by themselves, end up by becoming like children...Justin went past every morning, and every morning the old judge was behind his window...He looks like an owl.'

'I don't know what you're trying to say...'

She stood framed in the doorway, a steaming ladle in her hand.

'Try to follow me. The judge declares that he heard nothing, and it's too serious a matter for me to suspect him of lying.'

'You see! Try to stop thinking about it.'

'Only he dared not assert that he had or had not heard Justin go past yesterday morning.'

'Perhaps he went back to sleep.'

'No...He daren't tell a lie, and so he's deliberately vague. And the husband at No. 42 who was sitting up with his sick wife heard somebody running in the street.'

He kept reverting to that. His thoughts, sharpened by fever, went round in a circle.

'What would have become of the corpse?' objected Madame Maigret with her womanly common sense. 'Don't think any more about it! Besson knows his job, you've often said so yourself...'

He slumped back under the blankets, discouraged, and tried hard to go to sleep, but was inevitably haunted before long by the image of the altar boy's face, and his pallid legs above black socks.

'There's something wrong...'

'What did you say? Something wrong? Are you feeling worse? Shall I ring the doctor?'

Not that. He started again from scratch, obstinately; he went back to the threshold of the boys' school and crossed the Place du Congrès.

'And this is where there's something amiss.'

For one thing, because the judge had heard nothing. Unless one was going to accuse him of perjury it was hard to believe that a fight could have gone on under his window, just a few metres away, that a man had started running off towards the barracks while the boy had rushed off in the opposite direction.

'Listen, Madame Maigret...'

'What is it now?'

'Suppose they had both started running in the same direction?'

With a sigh, Madame Maigret picked up her needlework and listened, dutifully, to her husband's monologue interspersed with wheezy gasps.

'For one thing, it's more logical...'

'What's more logical?'

'That they should both have run in the same direction... Only in that case it wouldn't have been towards the barracks.'

'Could the boy have been running after the murderer?'

'No. The murderer would have run after the boy...'

'What for, since he didn't kill him?'

'To make him hold his tongue, for instance.'

'He didn't succeed, since the child spoke...'

'Or to prevent him from telling something, from giving some particular detail . . . Look here, Madame Maigret.'

'What is it you want?'

'I know you'll start by saying no, but it's absolutely necessary . . . Pass me my pipe and my tobacco . . . Just a few puffs . . . I've got the feeling that I'm going to understand the whole thing in a few minutes—if I don't lose the thread.'

She went to fetch his pipe from the mantelpiece and handed it to him resignedly, sighing:

'I knew you'd think of some good excuse . . . In any case tonight I'm going to make you a poultice whether you like it or not.'

Luckily there was no telephone in the flat and one had to go down into the shop to ring up from behind the counter.

'Will you go downstairs, Madame Maigret, and call Besson for me? It's seven o'clock. He may still be at the office. Otherwise call the *Café du Centre,* where he'll be playing billiards with Thiberge.'

'Shall I ask him to come here?'

'To bring me as soon as possible a list, not of all the residents in the street but of the tenants of the houses on the left side of it, between the Place du Congrès and the Judge's house.'

'Do try to keep covered up . . .'

Barely had she set foot on the staircase when he thrust both legs out of bed and rushed, barefooted, to fetch his tobacco pouch and fill himself a fresh pipe; then he lay back innocently between the sheets.

Through the flimsy floorboards he could hear a hum of voices and Madame Maigret's, speaking on the telephone. He smoked his pipe in greedy little puffs, although his throat was very sore. He could see raindrops slowly sliding down the dark panes, and this again reminded him of his childhood, of childish illnesses when his mother used to bring him caramel custard in bed.

Madame Maigret returned, panting a little, glanced round the room as if to take note of anything unusual, but did not think of the pipe.

'He'll be here in about an hour.'

'I'm going to ask you one more favour, Madame Maigret... Will you put on your coat...'

She cast a suspicious glance at him.

'Will you go to young Justin's home and ask his parents to let you bring him to me... Be very kind to him... If I were to send a policeman he'd undoubtedly take fright, and he's liable enough to be prickly as it is... Just tell him I'd like a few minutes' chat with him.'

'And suppose his mother wants to come with him?'

'Work out your own plan, but I don't want the mother.'

Left to himself, he sank back into the hot, humid depths of the bed, the tip of his pipe emerging from the sheets and emitting a slight cloud of smoke. He closed his eyes, and he could keep picturing the corner of the Rue Sainte-Catherine; he was no longer Superintendent Maigret, he had become the altar boy who hurried along, covering the same ground every morning at the same time and talking to himself to keep up his courage.

As he turned into the Rue Sainte-Catherine:

'Maman, I wish you'd buy me a bike...'

For the kid had been rehearsing the scene he would play for his mother when he got back from the hospital. It would have to be more complicated; he must have thought up subtler approaches.

'You know, maman, if I had a bike, I could...' Or else, 'I've saved three hundred francs already... If you'd lend me the rest, which I promise to pay back with what I earn from the chapel, I could...'

The corner of the Rue Sainte-Catherine... a few seconds before the bells of the parish church rang out for the second time. And there were only a hundred and fifty metres of dark empty street to go through before reaching the safe haven of the hospital... A few jumps between the pools of brightness shed by the street lamps...

Later the child was to declare:

'I looked up and saw...'

That was the whole problem. The judge lived practically in the middle of the street, halfway between the Place du Congrès and the corner of the barracks, and he had seen nothing and heard nothing.

The husband of the sick woman, the man from No. 42, lived closer to the Place du Congrès, on the right side of the street, and he had heard the sound of running footsteps.

Yet, five minutes later, there had been no dead or injured body on the pavement. And no car or van had passed. The policeman on duty on the bridge, the others on the beat at various spots in the neighbourhood, had seen nothing unusual such as, for instance, a man carrying another man on his back.

Maigret's temperature was certainly going up but he no longer thought of consulting the thermometer. Things were fine as they were; words evoked images, and images assumed unexpected sharpness.

It was just like when he was a sick child and his mother, bending over him, seemed to have grown so big that she took up the whole house.

There was that body lying across the pavement, looking so long because it was a dead body, with a brown-handled knife sticking out of its chest.

And a few metres away a man, a pale-eyed man who had begun running... Running towards the barracks, whereas Justin ran for all he was worth in the opposite direction.

'That's it!'

That's what? Maigret had made the remark out loud, as though it contained the solution of the problem, as though it had actually been the solution of the problem, and he smiled contentedly as he drew on his pipe with ecstatic little puffs.

Drunks are like that. Things suddenly appear to them self-evidently true, which they are nevertheless incapable of explaining, and which dissolve into vagueness as soon as they are examined coolly.

Something was untrue, that was it! And Maigret, in his feverish imagining, felt sure that he had put his finger on the weak point in the story.

Justin had not made it up... His terror, his panic on arriving at the hospital had been genuine. Neither had he made up the picture of the long body sprawling across the pavement. Moreover there was at least one person in the street who had heard running footsteps.

What had the judge with the sneering smile remarked? 'You haven't yet learned to mistrust the evidence of children?' . . . or something of the sort.

However the judge was wrong. Children are incapable of inventing, because one cannot construct truths out of nothing. One needs materials. Children transpose maybe, they don't invent.

And that was that! At each stage, Maigret repeated that self-congratulatory *voilà*!

There had been a body on the pavement . . . And no doubt there had been a man close by. Had he had pale eyes? Quite possibly. And somebody had run.

And the old judge, Maigret could have sworn, was not the sort of man to tell a deliberate lie.

He felt hot. He was bathed in sweat, but nonetheless he left his bed to go and fill one last pipe before Madame Maigret's return. While he was up, he took the opportunity to open the cupboard and drink a big mouthful of rum from the bottle. What did it matter if his temperature was up that night? Everything would be finished by then!

And it would be quite an achievement; a difficult case solved from a sickbed! Madame Maigret was not likely to appreciate that, however.

The judge had not lied, and yet he must have tried to play a trick on the boy whom he hated as two children of the same age can hate one another.

Customers seemed to be getting fewer down below, for the ridiculous chimes over the door sounded less frequently. Probably the dairyman and his wife, with their daughter whose cheeks were as pink as ham, were dining together in the room at the back of the shop.

There were steps on the pavement; there were steps on the stair. Small feet were stumbling. Madame Maigret opened the door and ushered in young Justin, whose navy-blue duffel coat was glistening with rain. He smelt like a wet dog.

'Here, my boy, let me take off your coat.'

'I can take it off myself.'

Another mistrustful glance from Madame Maigret. Obviously, she could not believe he was still smoking the same pipe. Who knows, perhaps she even suspected the shot of rum?

'Sit down, Justin,' said the Superintendent, pointing to a chair.

'Thanks, I'm not tired.'

'I asked you to come so that we could have a friendly chat together for a few minutes. What were you busy with?'

'My arithmetic homework.'

'Because in spite of all you've been through you've gone back to school?'

'Why shouldn't I have gone?'

The boy was proud. He was on his high horse again. Did Maigret seem to him bigger and longer than usual, now that he was lying down?

'Madame Maigret, be an angel and go and look after the vegetable broth in the kitchen, and close the door.'

When that was done he gave the boy a knowing wink.

'Pass me my tobacco pouch, which is on the mantelpiece... And the pipe, which must be in my overcoat pocket... Yes, the one that's hanging behind the door... Thanks, my boy... Were you frightened when my wife came to fetch you?'

'No.' He said that with some pride.

'Were you annoyed?'

'Because everyone keeps saying that I've made it up.'

'And you haven't, have you?'

'There was a dead man on the pavement and another who...'

'Hush!'

'What?'

'Not so quick... Sit down...'

'I'm not tired.'

'So you've said, but I get tired of seeing you standing up...'

He sat down on the very edge of the chair, and his feet didn't touch the ground; his legs were dangling, his bare knobbly knees protruding between the short pants and the socks.

'What sort of trick did you play on the judge?'

A swift, instinctive reaction:

'I never did anything to him.'

'You know what judge I mean?'

'The one who's always peering out of his window and who looks like an owl?'

'Just how I'd describe him . . . What happened between you?'

'In winter I didn't see him because his curtains were drawn when I went past.'

'But in summer?'

'I put out my tongue at him.'

'Why?'

'Because he kept looking at me as if he was making fun of me; he sniggered to himself as he looked at me.'

'Did you often put out your tongue at him?'

'Every time I saw him . . .'

'And what did he do?'

'He laughed in a spiteful sort of way . . . I thought it was because I served at Mass and he's an unbeliever . . .'

'Has he told a lie, then?'

'What did he say?'

'That nothing happened yesterday morning in front of his house, because he would have noticed.'

The boy stared intently at Maigret, then lowered his head.

'He was lying, wasn't he?'

'There was a body on the pavement with a knife stuck in its chest.'

'I know . . .'

'How do you know?'

'I know because it's the truth . . .' repeated Maigret gently. 'Pass me the matches . . . I've let my pipe go out.'

'Are you too hot?'

'It's nothing . . . just the flu . . .'

'Did you catch it this morning?'

'Maybe . . . Sit down.'

He listened attentively and then called:

'Madame Maigret! Will you run downstairs? I think I heard Besson arriving and I don't want him to come up before I'm ready ... Will you keep him company downstairs? My friend Justin will call you ...'

Once more, he said to his young companion:

'Sit down ... It's true, too, that you both ran ...'

'I told you it was true ...'

'And I believe you ... Go and make sure there's nobody behind the door and that it's properly shut.'

The child obeyed without understanding, impressed by the importance that his actions had suddenly acquired.

'Listen, Justin, you're a brave little chap.'

'Why do you say that?'

'It was true about the corpse. It was true about the man running.'

The child raised his head once again, and Maigret saw his lip quivering.

'And the judge, who didn't lie, because a judge would not dare to lie, didn't tell the whole truth ...'

The room smelt of flu and rum and tobacco. A whiff of vegetable broth came in under the kitchen door, and raindrops were still falling like silver tears on the black window pane beyond which lay the empty street. Were the two now facing one another still a man and a small boy? Or two men, or two small boys?

Maigret's head felt heavy; his eyes were glistening. His pipe had a curious medical flavour that was not unpleasant, and he remembered the smells of the hospital, its chapel and its vestry.

'The judge didn't tell the whole truth because he wanted to rile you. And you didn't tell the whole truth either ... Now I forbid you to cry. We don't want everyone to know what we've been saying to each other ... You understand, Justin?'

The boy nodded.

'If what you described hadn't happened at all, the man in No. 42 wouldn't have heard running footsteps.'

'I didn't make it up.'

'Of course not! But if it had happened just as you said, the judge would not have been able to say that he had heard nothing ... And if the murderer had run away towards the barracks, the old man would not have sworn that nobody had run past his house.'

The child sat motionless, staring down at the tips of his dangling feet.

'The judge was being honest, on the whole, in not daring to assert that you had gone past his house yesterday morning. But he might perhaps have asserted that you had not gone past. That's the truth, since you ran off in the opposite direction...He was telling the truth, too, when he declared that no man had run past on the pavement under his window...For the man did not go in that direction.'

'How do you know?'

He had stiffened, and was staring wide-eyed at Maigret as he must have stared on the previous night at the murderer or his victim.

'Because the man inevitably rushed off in the same direction as yourself, which explains why the husband in No. 42 heard him go past...Because, knowing that you had seen him, that you had seen the body, that you could get him caught, he ran *after* you...'

'If you tell my mother, I...'

'Hush!...I don't wish to tell your mother or anyone else anything at all....You see, Justin my boy, I'm going to talk to you like a man...A murderer clever and cool enough to make a corpse disappear without trace in a few minutes would not have been foolish enough to let you escape after seeing what you had seen.'

'I don't know...'

'But I do...It's my job to know...The most difficult thing is not to kill a man, it's to make the body disappear afterwards, and this one disappeared magnificently...It disappeared, even though you had seen it and seen the murderer...In other words, the murderer's a really smart guy...And a really smart guy, with his life at stake, would never have let you get away like that.'

'I didn't know...'

'What didn't you know?'

'I didn't know it mattered so much...'

'It doesn't matter at all now, since everything has been put right.'

'Have you arrested him?'

There was immense hope in the tone in which these words were uttered.

'He'll be arrested before long... Sit still; stop swinging your legs...'

'I won't move.'

'For one thing, if it had all happened in front of the judge's house, that's to say in the middle of the street, you'd have been aware of it from further off, and you'd have had time to run away... That was the only mistake the murderer made, for all his cleverness...'

'How did you guess?'

'I didn't guess. But I was once an altar boy myself, and I served at six o'clock Mass like you... You wouldn't have gone a hundred metres along the street without looking in front of you... So the corpse must have been closer, much closer, just round the corner of the street.'

'Five houses past the corner.'

'You were thinking of something else, of your bike, and you may have gone twenty metres without seeing anything.'

'How can you possibly know?'

'And when you saw, you ran towards the Place du Congrès to get to the hospital by the other street. The man ran after you...'

'I thought I should die of fright.'

'Did he grab you by the shoulder?'

'He grabbed my shoulders with both hands. I thought he was going to strangle me...'

'He asked you to say...'

The child was crying, quietly. He was pale and the tears were rolling slowly down his cheeks.

'If you tell my mother she'll blame me all my life long. She's always nagging at me.'

'He ordered you to say that it had happened further on...'

'Yes.'

'In front of the judge's house?'

'It was me that thought of the judge's house, because of putting out my tongue at him... The man only said the other end of the street, and that he'd run off towards the barracks.'

'And so we very nearly had a perfect crime, because nobody believed you, since there was no murderer and no body, no traces of
any sort, and it all seemed impossible...'

'But what about you?'

'I don't count. It just so happens that I was once an altar boy, and
that today I'm in bed with flu... What did he promise you?'

'He told me that if I didn't say what he wanted me to, he would
always be after me, wherever I went, in spite of the police, and that
he would wring my neck like a chicken's.'

'And then?'

'He asked me what I wanted to have...'

'And you said a bike...?'

'How do you know?'

'I've told you, I was once an altar boy too.'

'And you wanted a bike?'

'That, and a great many other things that I've never had... Why
did you say he had pale eyes?'

'I don't know. I didn't see his eyes. He was wearing thick glasses.
But I didn't want him to be caught...'

'Because of the bike?'

'Maybe... You're going to tell my mother, aren't you?'

'Not your mother nor anyone else... Aren't we pals now?...
Look, you hand me my tobacco pouch and don't tell Madame Mai-
gret that I've smoked three pipes since we've been here together...
You see, grown-ups don't always tell the whole truth either...
Which door was it in front of, Justin?'

'The yellow house next door to the delicatessen.'

'Go and fetch my wife.'

'Where is she?'

'Downstairs... She's with Inspector Besson, the one who was so
beastly to you.'

'And who's going to arrest me?'

'Open the wardrobe...'

'Right...'

'There's a pair of trousers hanging there...'

'What am I to do with it?'

'In the left-hand pocket you'll find a wallet.'

'Here it is.'

'In the wallet there are some visiting cards.'

'Do you want them?'

'Hand me one ... And also the pen that's on the table ...'

With which, Maigret wrote on one of the cards that bore his name: *Supply bearer with one bicycle.*

3

'Come in, Besson.'

Madame Maigret glanced up at the dense cloud of smoke that hung round the lamp in its waxed-paper shade; then she hurried into the kitchen, because she could smell something burning there.

As for Besson, taking the chair just vacated by the boy, for whom he had only a disdainful glance, he announced:

'I've got the list you asked me to draw up. I must tell you right away ...'

'That it's useless ... Who lives in No. 14?'

'One moment ...' He consulted his notes. 'Let's see ... No. 14 ... There's only a single tenant there.'

'I suspected as much.'

'Oh?' An uneasy glance at the boy. 'It's a foreigner, name of Frankelstein, a dealer in jewellery.'

Maigret had slipped back among his pillows; he muttered, with an air of indifference:

'A fence.'

'What did you say, Chief?'

'A fence ... Possibly the boss of a gang.'

'I don't understand.'

'That doesn't matter ... Be a good fellow, Besson, pass me the bottle of rum that's in the cupboard. Quickly, before Madame Maigret comes back ... I bet my temperature's soaring and I'll need to have my sheets changed a couple of times tonight ... Frankelstein ... Get a search warrant from the examining magistrate ... No ... At this time of night, it'll take too long, for he's sure to be out playing bridge somewhere . . . Have you had dinner? . . . Me, I'm waiting for my vegetable broth . . . There are some blank warrants in my desk— left hand drawer. Fill one in. Search the house. You're sure to find the body, even if it means knocking down a cellar wall.'

Poor Besson stared at his Chief in some anxiety, then glanced at the boy, who was sitting waiting quietly in a corner.

'Act quickly, old man . . . If he knows that the kid's been here tonight, you won't find him in his lair . . . He's a tough guy, as you'll find out.'

He was indeed. When the police rang at his door, he tried to escape through backyards and over walls; it took them all night to catch him, which they finally did among the rooftops. Meanwhile other policemen searched the house for hours before discovering the corpse, decomposing in a bath of quicklime.

It had obviously been a settling of accounts. A disgruntled and frustrated member of the gang had called on the boss in the small hours; Frankelstein had done him in on the doorstep, unaware that an altar boy was at that very instant coming round the street corner.

'What does it say?' Maigret no longer had the heart to look at the thermometer himself.

'39.3 . . .'

'Aren't you cheating?'

He knew that she was cheating, that his temperature was higher than that, but he didn't care; it was good, it was delicious to sink into unconsciousness, to let himself glide at a dizzy speed into a misty, yet terribly real world where an altar boy bearing a strong resemblance to Maigret as he had once been was tearing wildly down the street, sure that he was either going to be strangled or to win a shiny new bicycle.

'What are you talking about?' asked Madame Maigret, whose plump fingers held a scalding hot poultice which she was proposing to apply to her husband's throat.

He was muttering nonsense like a feverish child, talking about the first bell and the second bell.

'I'm going to be late . . .'

'Late for what?'

'For Mass ... Sister ... Sister ...'

He meant the vestry-nun, the sacristine, but he could not find the word.

He fell asleep at last, with a huge compress round his neck, dreaming of Mass in his own village and of Marie Titin's inn, past which he used to run because he was afraid.

Afraid of what? ...

'I got him, all the same ...'

'Who?'

'The judge.'

'What judge?'

It was too complicated to explain. The judge reminded him of somebody in his village at whom he used to put out his tongue. The blacksmith? No ... It was the baker's wife's stepfather ... It didn't matter. Somebody he disliked. And it was the judge who had misled him the whole way through, in order to be revenged on the altar boy and to annoy people ... He had said he had heard no footsteps *in front of his house* ...

But he had not said that he had heard two people running off in the opposite direction ...

Old people become childish. And they quarrel with children. Like children.

Maigret was satisfied, in spite of everything. He had cheated by three whole pipes, even four ... He had a good taste of tobacco in his mouth and he could let himself drift away ...

And tomorrow, since he had flu, Madame Maigret would make him some caramel custard.

April 1956

The Most Obstinate Customer
in the World

The 'Café des Ministères', or Joseph's Domain

The records of the police knew nothing like it; nobody had ever shown as much obstinacy or vanity in displaying himself from every angle, in posing as it were for hours on end—sixteen successive hours, to be exact—and in attracting, whether deliberately or not, the attention of dozens of people, to such a degree that Inspector Janvier, who had been called in, had gone up for a closer look. And yet when it came to reconstructing his appearance, the image remembered was an utterly vague and hazy one.

So much so that to some people—who were not particularly fanciful—this self-display seemed like a particularly cunning and original ruse.

However, it is essential to go over that day, 3 May, hour by hour; it was a warm, sunny day with that special thrill in the air that belongs to Paris in the spring; and from morning till night the honeyed scent of the chestnut trees on the Boulevard Saint-Germain drifted into the cool café.

It was at 8 a.m. as usual that Joseph opened the café doors. He was in shirtsleeves and a waistcoat. The floor was covered with the sawdust he had sprinkled there at closing time on the previous evening, and chairs were piled high on the marble tables.

For the *Café des Ministères*, at the corner of the Boulevard Saint-Germain and the Rue des Saints-Pères, is one of the few old-fashioned cafés that still exist in Paris. It has not pandered to the vogue for bars serving quick drinks to casual customers, nor to the contemporary taste for gilt decorations, indirect lighting, pillars covered with looking glass and little tables of some plastic material.

It is the typical café where regular customers have their own tables, their favourite corners, their games of draughts or chess, and where Joseph the waiter knows everyone by name: mostly head clerks or civil servants from the nearby Government offices.

And Joseph himself is quite a character. He has been a waiter for thirty years, and one cannot imagine him wearing a business suit like other people; one might not recognize him in the street if one met him in the suburb where he has built himself a little house.

Eight in the morning is cleaning-up time; the double door on to the Boulevard Saint-Germain is wide open; part of the pavement is in broad sunlight, but a cool, blue-hazed shadow prevails inside.

Joseph smokes a cigarette. This is the only moment in the day when he allows himself to smoke on the premises. He lights the gas under the percolator, which he then polishes till it gleams like a mirror. There is a whole series of almost ritual acts which are performed in an unchanging order: bottles of spirits and apéritifs to be lined up on the shelf, the sawdust to be swept up, the chairs to be set out round the tables...

At eight ten exactly, the man came in. Joseph was bending over his percolator and did not see him enter, which he subsequently regretted. Did the man hurry in as though he were escaping from somebody? Why did he choose the *Café des Ministères*, when on the opposite side of the street there is a café with a bar where, at this time of day, you can buy croissants and rolls, and which is swarming with people?

Joseph said, later:

'I turned round and I saw somebody standing in the middle of the café, a man wearing a grey hat and carrying a small suitcase.'

Actually, although the café door was open, the place itself was not strictly speaking open yet; nobody ever came in so early, the coffee was not ready, the water was barely warm in the percolator and the chairs were still stacked on the tables.

'I can't serve you for another half-hour at least,' Joseph had said.

He thought that would settle it. But the man, still clutching his case, picked up a chair from one of the tables and sat down, quite calmly, like someone who is not going to change his mind, and muttered:

'Never mind.'

That in itself was enough to put Joseph in a bad temper. He's like those housewives who detest having someone in their way when they are turning out a room. Cleaning-up time is his own special time. And he grumbled between his teeth:

'I'm going to keep you waiting for your coffee!'

Until nine o'clock he carried on with his usual jobs, occasionally casting a furtive glance at his customer. A score of times he passed quite close to him, brushed up against him and even jostled him a little as he swept up the sawdust or removed chairs from tables.

Then, at two or three minutes past nine, he resigned himself to serving the man a cup of piping hot coffee with a small jug of milk and two lumps of sugar in a saucer.

'Have you any croissants?'

'You can get some across the street.'

'Never mind.'

Oddly enough, this stubborn customer, who must have been well aware that he was in the way, that this was not the moment to be settling down at the *Café des Ministères,* displayed a certain humility that was somehow endearing.

There was something else which Joseph was beginning to appreciate, used as he was to the various types of people who come to sit around in his café. Although he had been there for a whole hour, the man had not drawn a newspaper from his pocket nor asked for one, he had not found it necessary to consult the Bottin or the telephone directory, he had made no effort to enter into conversation with the waiter; he did not cross and uncross his legs, and he did not smoke.

It is excessively unusual to find anyone capable of sitting for an hour in a café without moving, without constantly checking the time, without displaying impatience in some way or another. If he was waiting for someone, he was waiting with remarkable placidity.

At ten o'clock, when the cleaning was finished, the man was still there. Another curious detail was that he had not chosen a seat by the windows, but at the far end of the room, close to the mahogany staircase that leads down to the lavatories. Joseph himself went down for a wash and brush-up. He had already turned the handle to let down the orange awning that shed a slight glow through the dark café.

Before going down he jingled some coins in his waistcoat pocket, hoping that his customer would take the hint, and make up his mind to pay and leave.

Nothing of the sort happened, and Joseph went down, changed his dickey and his collar, combed his hair and put on his short alpaca jacket.

When he came back the man was still sitting there in front of his empty cup. The cashier, Mademoiselle Berthe, appeared and settled down at her desk, took a few bits and pieces out of her bag and began to set out the telephone tokens in neat piles.

'I felt he was somebody very gentle, very respectable, and yet it seemed to me that his moustache was dyed like the Colonel's.'

For the man had short, upturned moustaches, probably twisted with curling-tongs, and of a bluish black that suggested dye.

Another regular morning ritual is the delivery of ice. A huge fellow with a canvas sack over his shoulder brings in the opalescent blocks from which a few limpid drops are trickling, and sets them in the icebox.

He, too, noticed the solitary customer, and later said of him:

'He reminded me of a seal.'

Why a seal? That the deliveryman was never able to specify.

As for Joseph, still following a changeless timetable, he took down yesterday's newspapers from the long handles to which they were attached and replaced them with today's.

'Would you mind giving me one?'

The customer had actually spoken, in a low, almost timid voice.

'Which would you like? *Le Temps? Figaro? Les Débats?*'

'I don't mind.'

This made Joseph think that the man was probably not a native Parisian. He couldn't have been a foreigner either, for he had no accent. More likely a visitor from the provinces. But there was no station near by. If he had got off a train before eight in the morning, why had he come halfway across Paris with his suitcase to settle down in a café he did not know? For Joseph, who has an excellent memory for faces, was sure he had never seen the man before. Strangers who drop into the *Café des Ministères* are immediately made aware that they are not at home, and go away again.

Eleven o'clock; the time when the proprietor, Monsieur Monnet, comes down from his flat, newly shaved, fresh-complexioned, his grey hair sleekly brushed, wearing a grey suit and his everlasting patent-leather shoes. He could have retired from business a long time ago. He has set up cafés in the provinces for each of his children. If he stays here, it is because this corner of the Boulevard Saint-Germain is the only place in the world where he can bear to live and because his customers are his friends.

'Everything all right, Joseph?'

He immediately spotted the customer and his cup of coffee. A questioning look came into his eye. And the waiter whispered, behind the bar:

'He's been here since eight o'clock.'

Monsieur Monnet walked to and fro past the stranger, rubbing his hands, which is a kind of invitation to open a conversation. Monsieur Monnet likes to chat with all his customers, to play cards or dominoes with them; he knows all their family problems and office gossip.

The man did not bat an eyelid.

'He looked to me very tired, like someone who has had a sleepless night on the train,' Monsieur Monnet was later to declare.

When Maigret asked all three of them—Joseph, Mademoiselle Berthe and Monsieur Monnet—whether the man seemed to be watching for someone in the street, their answers were very different.

'No,' said Monsieur Monnet.

'I got the impression he was expecting a lady,' said the cashier.

And Joseph declared:

'Several times I caught him looking across to the bar over the way, but he always dropped his eyes immediately.'

At eleven twenty he ordered a glass of Vichy. Some customers drink mineral waters; one knows them, one knows why: people like Monsieur Blanc from the War Ministry who are on a diet. Joseph noted automatically that this fellow neither smoked nor drank, which is pretty uncommon.

Then, for a couple of hours or so, they paid no more attention to him, because it was apéritif time; regular customers began to flock in, and the waiter knew beforehand what to serve each one of them, and which tables must be provided with cards.

'Waiter...'

One o'clock. The man was still there, having slipped his suitcase underneath the red velvet seat. Joseph pretended to think he was being asked for the bill, and after reckoning in an undertone, announced:

'Eight francs fifty.'

'Can you let me have a sandwich?'

'I'm sorry, we don't serve them.'

'You haven't any rolls either?'

'We don't serve any food.'

It was not strictly true. Occasionally in the evening a party of bridge players who have not had time for dinner are provided with ham sandwiches. This, however, is exceptional.

The man nodded, murmuring:

'It doesn't matter.'

This time Joseph was struck by the quivering of his lips, by the sad, resigned expression on his face.

'Can I bring you something else?'

'Another coffee, with plenty of milk.'

Because he was hungry, and milk would at any rate provide a little nourishment. He had not asked for any other newspaper. He had had time to read his from the first line to the last, including the small ads.

The Colonel turned up and was annoyed to find the stranger sitting in his place; for the Colonel, who hated the slightest draught and who maintained that spring draughts are always the most treacherous, always liked to sit at the far end of the room.

Jules, the second waiter, who had only been three years in the profession and who would never look like a real café waiter, came on duty at half-past one, while Joseph went through the glazed door to eat the lunch sent down for him from the first floor.

Why did Jules think the stranger looked like one of those men who sell rugs and peanuts?

'I didn't think he looked straight. I thought he'd got a shifty look, and something soft and smarmy about his expression. If it had been up to me I'd have sent him off to the nearest *crémerie.*'

Some customers noticed the man and were to notice him even more when they found him still there in the evening.

All this evidence came from amateur witnesses, so to speak. But it so happened that a professional observer also gave evidence, which proved as inconclusive as everyone else's.

For about ten years, at the start of his career, Joseph had been a waiter at the *Brasserie Dauphine,* a stone's throw from the Quai des Orfèvres, and a favourite haunt of most detectives of the Police Judiciaire. He had become a close friend of one of Maigret's best colleagues, Inspector Janvier, and he had married Janvier's sister-in-law, so that they were practically relatives.

At three o'clock in the afternoon, seeing his customer still in the same place, Joseph began to get really cross. He conjectured that if the fellow showed such obstinacy it must be not through love of the atmosphere of the *Café des Ministères,* but because he had some good reason not to leave it.

When he got off the train, Joseph argued, he must have felt himself being shadowed and come in for safety's sake to escape the police.

Joseph therefore rang up Police Headquarters and asked to speak to Janvier.

'I've got a queer sort of customer here who's been sitting in a corner since eight o'clock this morning and seems determined not to budge. He's had nothing to eat. Don't you think you'd better come over and have a look at him?'

Janvier, ever conscientious, collected the latest reports with photographs and descriptions of wanted persons, and came along to the Boulevard Saint-Germain.

By a strange chance, the café happened to be empty when he came in.

'Has he flown?' he asked Joseph.

But the waiter pointed to the basement. 'He's just asked for a telephone token and gone to make a call.'

This was a pity; a few minutes earlier it would have been possible, by contacting the switchboard, to find out to whom and about what he was telephoning. Janvier sat down and ordered a calvados. The man came upstairs again and went back to his place, as calm as ever, somewhat preoccupied but showing no signs of anxiety. It even seemed to Joseph, who was beginning to know him, that he was somewhat relaxed.

For twenty minutes Janvier scrutinized him from head to foot. He had plenty of time to compare that rather plump, flabby face with all the photographs of wanted persons. Finally he shrugged his shoulders.

'He's not on our lists,' he told Joseph. 'He looks to me like some poor devil who's been stood up by a woman. He must be an insurance agent or something of the sort.'

Janvier even went on to joke:

'I shouldn't be surprised if he's a traveller for a firm of undertakers... In any case I'm not entitled to ask him to show his papers. There's no regulation to prevent him from staying in the café as long as he likes and doing without lunch.'

Janvier stayed a little longer gossiping with Joseph and then went back to Police Headquarters, where he conferred with Maigret about an illegal gambling concern, but did not mention the man in the *Café des Ministères*.

In spite of the awning over the windows, rays of sunlight were now slanting into the café. By five o'clock, three tables were occupied by people playing *belote*. The proprietor himself was playing at one of them, just opposite the stranger, at whom he cast a glance from time to time.

By six o'clock the place was full. Joseph and Jules went from one table to another with their trays loaded with bottles and glasses, and the sharp odour of pernod conflicted with the oversweet scent of the boulevard chestnut trees.

At this point, each of the two waiters had his own sector. It so happened that the man's table was in Jules's sector, and Jules was less observant than his colleague. Moreover, he liked to slip behind the bar from time to time for a glass of white wine, so that from quite early on in the evening he tended to confuse things. All that he could say was that a woman had come.

'She was dark, nicely dressed, respectable-looking, not one of those women who come into a café in order to start a conversation with customers.'

On the whole, in Jules's view, the sort of woman who only goes into a public place because she has arranged to meet her husband there. There were three or four tables still unoccupied. She had sat down at the one next to the stranger's.

'I'm sure they didn't speak to one another. She ordered a port. I think I recollect that besides her handbag—it was a brown or black leather bag—she was carrying a little parcel. I saw it on the table to begin with. When I brought her drink it wasn't there; she'd probably laid it down on the seat.'

A pity! Joseph would have liked to have seen her. Mademoiselle Berthe, from the height of her pay-desk, had noticed the woman too.

'She looked quite a lady, hardly any make-up, in a blue suit with a white blouse, but I don't know why, I thought she wasn't a married woman.'

Until dinner time, around eight o'clock, there was a constant coming and going. Then the room began to empty. By nine o'clock only six tables were occupied, four of them by chess players, two by bridge players who came regularly every evening for a game.

'What's certain,' Joseph was later to assert, 'is that the chap knows how to play bridge and chess. I'd even bet he's a good player. I could see that from the way he watched his neighbours and followed the games.'

Had he been relatively carefree then, or was Joseph mistaken?

At ten o'clock, only three tables were occupied. Men from Ministries tend to go to bed early. At half-past ten Jules went home, for his wife was expecting a baby, and he had arranged with his colleague to get off early.

The man was still there. Since eight ten in the morning he had drunk three coffees, a bottle of Vichy and one lemonade. He had not smoked. He had drunk no spirits. In the morning he had read *Le Temps*. In the afternoon he had bought an evening paper from a newsboy who had come into the café.

At 11 p.m. as usual, although two card games were still going on, Joseph began stacking the chairs on the tables and spreading sawdust on the floor.

Shortly afterwards, having finished his game, Monsieur Monnet shook hands with his companions—including the Colonel—and went up to bed, carrying the day's takings in a canvas bag in which Mademoiselle Berthe had put away banknotes and change.

As he left he glanced at the persistent customer about whom most of the regulars had been talking during the evening, and he said to Joseph:

'If he's a nuisance, don't hesitate to ring...'

For behind the counter there is an electric bell connected with his private rooms.

That, in short, was all. When Maigret began his enquiry next day he could elicit no further information.

Mademoiselle Berthe left at ten minutes to eleven to catch the last bus to Epinay, where she lived. She, too, had cast a final curious glance at the man.

'I can't say he struck me as being nervous. But he wasn't calm, either. If I'd met him in the street, for instance, I'd have been afraid of him, if you see what I mean? And if he'd got off the bus at Epinay at the same time as me I shouldn't have dared go home alone.'

'Why?'

'He had a sort of inward look...'

'What do you mean by that?'

'He seemed to be indifferent to everything that was going on around him.'

'Were the shutters closed?'

'No, Joseph only closes them at the last minute.'

'From where you sit you could see the corner of the street and the café-bar over the way ... Did you notice any suspicious comings and goings? Did anybody seem to be keeping a lookout for your customer?'

'I shouldn't have noticed ... Although things are quiet enough on the Boulevard Saint-Germain side, people are on the go all the time along the Rue des Saints-Pères ... And in the café–bar they're constantly going in and out.'

'Did you see nobody as you left?'

'Nobody ... Yes, though; there was a policeman at the corner of the street.'

This was confirmed by the local police station. Unfortunately the officer on duty had been relieved shortly after.

Only two tables still occupied ... A couple had come in for a drink after the pictures, regular customers, a doctor and his wife who lived three doors further down and who often dropped in at the *Café des Ministères* on their way home. They quickly paid and left.

The doctor commented later:

'We were sitting just in front of him, and I noticed that he looked ill.'

'What sort of illness, in your opinion?'

'Liver trouble, undoubtedly.'

'How old do you think he was?'

'It's hard to say, for I didn't pay as much attention as I now wish I had. To my mind, he was one of those men who look older than they are ... You might say forty-five or more, because of those dyed moustaches.'

'They were dyed, then?'

'I suppose so ... But I've had patients of thirty-five who already had the same flabby colourless flesh, that lifeless air ...'

'Couldn't he have looked lifeless because he hadn't eaten all day?'

'Maybe ... But I stick to my diagnosis: a bad digestion, a bad liver, and I'd add bad bowels ...'

The game at the last table was interminable. Three times it looked like ending, and three times the declarer failed to fulfil his contract. A five of clubs doubled and unexpectedly successful, owing to the nervousness of a player who set free dummy's long suit, finally brought the game to a close at ten minutes to twelve.

'Closing time, gentlemen,' Joseph said politely, piling the last chairs on to the tables.

The cardplayers paid their bills, and the man still did not move. At that point, the waiter felt frightened, as he subsequently admitted. He almost asked the regulars to stay a few minutes longer, until he had got rid of the stranger.

He dared not do so, for the four cardplayers left together still discussing the game, and lingered for a moment's chat at the corner of the boulevard before finally separating.

'Eighteen francs seventy-five.'

The two of them were alone together in the café, where Joseph had already switched off half the lights.

As he later confessed to Maigret:

'I'd noticed a siphon at the corner of the bar and if he'd made a move, I'd have broken it over his head...'

'You'd put the siphon there on purpose, hadn't you?'

That was obvious. Sixteen hours in the company of this enigmatic customer had reduced Joseph's nerves to shreds. He had come to think of the man as a sort of personal enemy, who was only there to do him an injury, who was waiting till they were alone to attack him and rob him.

And yet Joseph had made a mistake. As the customer, without rising from his seat, hunted deliberately in his pockets for money, the waiter, afraid of missing his bus, went to turn the handle that lowered the shutters. It is true that the door was still wide open, letting in the cool night air, and that there were still a number of people passing on the pavement of the Boulevard Saint-Germain.

'Here you are, waiter...'

Twenty-one francs. A two franc twenty-five tip after a whole day! The waiter nearly flung the money down on the table in a fury, and only his well-trained professional conscience prevented him.

'Perhaps you were a bit afraid of him, too,' Maigret suggested.

'I don't know about that... At any rate I was in a hurry to get rid of him... Never in all my life has a customer made me as mad as that one did... If I could have foreseen, in the morning, that he was going to stay there all day!'

'Where were you, exactly, when he went out?'

'Let's see... For one thing, I had to remind him that he had a suitcase under the seat, for he was on the point of forgetting it.'

'Did he seem annoyed at being reminded?'

'No...'

'Relieved?'

'Not that either... Indifferent... Talk about keeping calm! I've had customers of all sorts, but fancy sitting still for sixteen hours in front of a marble table without getting pins and needles in your legs!'

'So where were you?'

'Beside the cash-desk. I was paying the eighteen francs seventy-five into the till... You'll have noticed that there are two doors, one big double door opening on to the boulevard, and a smaller one opening on to the Rue des Saints-Pères. I nearly told him he was making a mistake when I saw him going out by the little door, then I shrugged my shoulders because, after all, I didn't care... Now I could get changed and shut up the place.'

'In which hand was he holding his case?'

'I didn't notice.'

'And did you notice whether he had one hand in his pocket?'

'I don't know... He wasn't wearing an overcoat... I couldn't see because the tables stacked with chairs hid him from me... He went out...'

'You were still in the same place?'

'Yes... Here, exactly... I was taking the check out of the till... With my other hand I was pulling the last counters out of my pocket... I heard a bang... Not much louder than what goes on all day, when cars backfire... But I understood all the same that it was not a car... I said to myself: "Well, so he's got himself bumped off after all."

'One thinks very fast on such occasions... I've often had to witness some rather nasty fights; it's part of my job ... I've always been amazed how fast one's mind works ...

'I blamed myself for it ... For after all he was just a poor fellow who'd taken refuge here because he knew he'd get bumped off as soon as he stuck his nose outside the door ...

'I felt guilty ... He'd eaten nothing ... Perhaps he hadn't any money to get a taxi and jump into it before being shot at by the chap who was waiting for him ...'

'Did you rush out?'

'Well, to tell you the truth ...' Joseph looked embarrassed. 'I think I waited a few minutes to think it over ... I've a wife and three kids, you understand? ... First I pressed the electric bell that rings in the boss's room ... Outside I heard people hurrying, voices ... one woman was saying: "Don't you get mixed up in it, Gaston ..." Then a policeman's whistle.

'I went out. There were three people standing there in the Rue des Saints-Pères, a little way from the door.'

'Eight metres away,' Maigret specified after consulting the report.

'It's possible ... I didn't measure ... A man was crouching beside a figure lying on the ground ... I only learnt later that it was a doctor on his way back from the theatre, who happens to be one of our customers ... A good many doctors are customers of ours ...

'He got up saying: "He's had it ... The bullet went in at the back of his neck and came out through the left eye."

'The policeman arrived. I knew I was going to be questioned.

'Believe it or not, I dared not look on the ground ... The thought of that left eye made me feel particularly sick ... I didn't want to see my customer again in that state, with his eye out of his head ...

'I kept thinking that it was somehow my fault, that I ought to have ... But what exactly could I have done?

'I can still hear the voice of the policeman asking, with his note-book in his hand: "Does anyone know him?"

'And I said automatically: "I do ... At least I believe I ..."

'At last I did bend over him to have a look, and I swear to you, Monsieur Maigret, you who've known me such a long time, seeing how many thousands of glasses of beer and calvados I've served you with at the *Brasserie Dauphine,* I swear to you that I never had such a shock in my life.

'*It wasn't him*!

'It was a fellow I didn't know, that I'd never seen before, a tall thin chap, and on a lovely day like yesterday, on a night so mild you could sleep outside, he was wearing a fawn raincoat...

'It was a relief... Silly of me maybe, but I was glad not to have made that mistake... If my customer had been the victim instead of the murderer I'd have blamed myself for it all my life long...

'Since first thing that morning, you see, I'd felt there was something fishy about that fellow... I'd have sworn to it... That was why I rang up Janvier... Only Janvier, although he's practically my brother-in-law, he's a stickler for regulations... Suppose when I sent for him he'd asked to see the customer's papers... They surely weren't in order.

'An ordinary decent person doesn't spend a whole day in a café and end up shooting somebody on the pavement at midnight...

'He didn't take long to disappear, you'll notice. Nobody saw him after that shot.

'If it wasn't him who fired, he'd have stayed there... He'd not had time to go ten metres when I heard the shot...

'What I'm wondering is what the woman was up to, the one Jules served with a glass of port. For I've no doubt she came in on account of that fellow... We don't get many women on their own... We're not that sort of place.'

'I understood they hadn't spoken to one another,' Maigret objected.

'They wouldn't have needed to talk!... She had a small parcel when she came in; Jules noticed it, and Jules isn't a liar... He saw it on the table, then he didn't see it, and he assumed she'd laid it down on the seat... And Mademoiselle Berthe watched the lady going out, because she liked the look of her handbag and wished she had one like it. And Mademoiselle Berthe did not notice her carrying any parcel. That's the sort of thing that wouldn't escape a woman's eye, you'll admit.

'You can say what you like, I can't help feeling that I spent a whole day with a murderer and that I've probably had a narrow escape...'

2

The Man Who Drank White Wine
and the Lady Who Ate Snails

Paris was blessed, next day, with one of those days such as spring brings only three or four times each year, when it deigns to make an effort; one of those days which one ought to enjoy without doing anything else, as one savours a sorbet; the sort of day one remembers from one's childhood. Everything was pleasant, light, heady, having a very special quality: the blue of the sky, the floating softness of the few clouds, the caressing breeze that met one suddenly at a street corner and that set the chestnuts quivering just enough to make one raise one's head and look at their clusters of honeyed flowers. A cat on a windowsill, a dog lying on the pavement, a cobbler in his leather apron standing in his doorway, an ordinary green and yellow bus sailing past, everything was precious that day, everything made one's heart rejoice, and that was no doubt why Maigret retained all his life a delightful memory of the crossroads of the Boulevard Saint-Germain and the Rue des Saints-Pères, and why, later on, he would often pause at a certain café to sit in the shade and drink a glass of beer which, unfortunately, seemed to have lost its flavour.

As for the case, it had quite unexpectedly become famous, less on account of the inexplicable obstinacy of the man who sat in the *Café des Ministères* or the shot fired at midnight than because of the motive for the crime.

At eight o'clock next morning, the Superintendent was in his office with all its windows wide open on to the blue and golden panorama of the Seine, and he was studying reports while smoking his pipe in greedy little puffs. It was thus that he made his first contact with the man from the *Café des Ministères* and with the one who had been killed in the Rue des Saints-Pères.

The local police had done a good job during the night. The police surgeon, Dr. Paul, had performed a post mortem at six that morning. The bullet, which had been recovered on the pavement—the case had also been found, almost at the corner of the Boulevard Saint-Germain, close to the wall—had already been submitted to the ballistics expert, Gastinne-Renette.

And now on Maigret's desk there lay the dead man's clothes, the contents of his pockets and a number of photographs taken on the spot by the representatives of the Records Department.

'Come into my office, will you, Janvier? I see from the report that you're somewhat involved in the case.'

And so Maigret and Janvier were to be inseparable that day, as so often before.

The victim's clothes, in the first place: they were of good quality, less worn than appeared at first sight, but shockingly uncared for. The clothes of a man living alone, always wearing the same suit, which was never brushed and was even occasionally slept in. The shirt, which was new and had never been laundered, had been worn for a week at least, and the socks were as bad.

There were no identity papers in the pockets, no letters or documents making it possible to identify the stranger, but a collection of peculiar objects: a penknife with many blades, a corkscrew, a dirty handkerchief, a button off the man's coat, a key, an old pipe and a tobacco pouch; a wallet containing 2,350 francs and a photograph of a native hut in Africa, with half a dozen bare-bosomed black women staring at the camera; bits of string and a third class railway ticket from Juvisy to Paris, dated the previous day.

Finally, a child's printing set with an ink pad and rubber letters making up the words: I'LL GET YOU.

The pathologist's report included some interesting details. First, as regards the crime: the shot had been fired from behind, barely three metres away, and death had been instantaneous.

Secondly, the body bore a number of scars, including on the feet the marks left by 'jiggers', those ticks peculiar to Central Africa which burrow into a man's toes and have to be dug out with a knife.

The liver was in a deplorable state, a real alcoholic's liver, and furthermore it was established that the man suffered from malaria.

'So there we are!' said Maigret, looking for his hat. 'Off we go, Janvier old man.'

They walked together to the scene of the crime; through the windows of the café, they saw Joseph doing his morning clean-up.

The Superintendent's first visit, however, was to the café across the street. The two establishments which faced one another at the corner of the Rue des Saints-Pères could not have been more different. Whereas Joseph's domain was old-fashioned and quiet, the other, which bore the name *Chez Léon*, was aggressively and vulgarly modern.

Needless to say, it included a long bar where two waiters in shirt-sleeves were kept busy serving cups of coffee and glasses of white wine, to be followed later by draughts of red and aniseed-flavoured apéritifs.

There were pyramids of croissants, sandwiches, hardboiled eggs ... The *patron* and his wife took it in turns to preside over the tobacco-stall at the end of the counter; the room itself had pillars of red and gold mosaic, tables of some indeterminate substance with garish shimmering colours, and seats covered with embossed velvet of the crudest red.

Here, all doors open on to the street, there was a coming and going from morning till night. People came in and out, building workers in dusty overalls, deliverymen who left their carrier-tricycles by the curb for a moment, clerks and typists, people who were thirsty and others who wanted to use the telephone.

'One coffee! ... Two beaujolais! ... Three beers!'

The till never stopped working, and the waiters mopped their sweating brows with the cloths they used to wipe the counter. Glasses were plunged for an instant into the turbid water in the pewter bowls, then filled anew, without even being wiped dry, with red or white wine.

'Two dry white wines,' ordered Maigret, who enjoyed all this morning hubbub.

And the white wine had that particular coarse tang only to be savoured in bistros of this kind.

'Tell me, waiter . . . Do you remember this man's face?'

The Records Office had done a good job; a sordid task, but a necessary and extremely tricky one. The photograph of a dead man is always difficult to recognize, particularly if the face has suffered some injury. So the gentlemen from the Identité Judiciaire make up the corpse's face and touch up the print so that it looks like the portrait of a living man.

'That's him, isn't it, Louis?'

And the other waiter, dishcloth in hand, came to have a look over the shoulder of his mate.

'That's him! . . . He was such a bloody nuisance all day yesterday that we can't fail to recognize him.'

'Do you know what time he first came in here?'

'That's harder to say . . . You don't notice casual customers . . . But I remember that by ten o'clock in the morning this chap was all worked up . . . He couldn't keep still . . . He would come up to the bar, order a glass of the white, toss it off and pay . . . then he'd go outside. You thought you were rid of him and ten minutes later there he was again, sitting in the café and calling for another glass of white.'

'Did he spend the whole day like that?'

'I really believe he did . . . At any rate, I saw him at least ten or fifteen times . . . Getting more and more edgy, looking at you in a funny way, and his fingers shaking like an old woman's when he held out the money . . . Didn't he break one of your glasses, Louis?'

'Yes . . . And he insisted on picking up all the bits out of the sawdust, saying: "It was white wine . . . That's lucky, old man! And you see I need something to bring me luck today . . . Have you ever been to Gabon, young man?"'

'He talked about Gabon to me too,' the other waiter broke in, 'I can't remember in what connection . . . Oh yes, it was when he began eating hardboiled eggs. He ate twelve or thirteen, one after the other . . . I was afraid he'd choke, particularly as he'd already had a lot to drink . . .

'"Don't you worry kid," he said. "Once in Gabon I bet I'd eat thirty-six of them with as many glasses of beer, and I won the bet…"'

'Did he seem anxious?'

'Depends on what you mean by that. He kept going out and coming back. I thought at first he must be waiting for someone. He kept sniggering to himself as though he were telling himself funny stories. He got hold of an old chap who comes every afternoon for a couple of drinks, and he held him by his lapel for God knows how long…'

'Did you know he was armed?'

'How could I have guessed?'

'Because a man of that sort is quite capable of showing off his gun to everybody!'

He'd had one, in fact, a big revolver from which no shots had been fired and which had been found lying beside his body on the pavement.

'Another two glasses of white wine.'

And Maigret was in such a cheerful humour that he could not resist the pleas of a little barefoot flower seller, a thin grimy little girl with the loveliest eyes in the world. He bought a bunch of violets from her and then, not knowing what to do with it, stuck it into his jacket pocket.

A good deal of drinking went on that day, it must be confessed. For Maigret and Janvier now had to cross the street and enter the *Café des Ministères*, with its dim light and its special flavour, and Joseph hurried up to greet them.

Here they were concerned to establish the appearance of the man with the little suitcase and the dyed moustache; a picture increasingly hazy, or rather one which gave the impression of a blurred photograph, or one on which several snapshots have been superimposed.

None of their witnesses agreed. Everyone had a different picture of the customer, and now there was even a fresh witness, the Colonel, who swore that the man had looked like somebody who was up to no good.

To some people he had seemed excited, to others amazingly calm. Maigret listened, nodded, filled his pipe with a meticulous forefinger, and lit it with little puffs, screwing up his eyes with delight at the lovely day that heaven had graciously granted to mankind.

'The woman...'

'You mean the young lady?'

For to Joseph, who had scarcely seen her, she had been a pretty young girl from a comfortable background.

'I'm sure she's not a working girl.'

He could visualize her, rather, preparing dainty sweets and pastries in a bourgeois household. Mademoiselle Berthe, the cashier, on the other hand, expressed some doubts, saying:

'I shouldn't bank on her being an angel...But she's certainly worth two of him.'

There were moments when Maigret felt a longing to stretch, such as one feels in the country when one's whole being is soaked in sunshine, and everything delighted him about the Boulevard Saint-Germain that morning: the buses stopping and starting, the ritual gesture of the conductor reaching for his bell as soon as the passengers were all on, the grating sound of brakes and gears, the waving shadow of chestnut tree branches on the asphalt pavement.

'I bet she didn't go very far!' he muttered to Janvier, who was annoyed at not being able to give a more specific description of the man in spite of having looked so closely at him.

And they stood waiting for a while on the edge of the pavement. The two cafés, each at one corner of the street...A man in one of them, a man in the other...It seemed as though chance had set each of them in the appropriate atmosphere. Here, the little fellow with the moustache, who had not stirred all day except to make one telephone call, who had touched nothing but coffee, Vichy water and lemonade, and who had not even protested when Joseph had told him there was nothing to eat.

Across the street, amid the noisy throng of workmen, deliverymen, clerks, busy humble people, was a crazy fellow swilling white wine and devouring hardboiled eggs, restlessly coming and going, buttonholing all and sundry to talk to them about Gabon.

'I bet there's a third café,' said Maigret, looking across the boulevard.

He was wrong there. On the opposite pavement, just across from the Rue des Saints-Pères, at a place from which both corners of the street were visible, there was neither a café nor a bar but a restaurant with a narrow window and a long, low dining room two steps below street level.

It was called *À l'Escargot,* and it was a typical homely restaurant with a light wooden rack against the wall in which regular customers kept their table napkins. There was a good smell of garlicky cooking and, this being a slack time, the *patronne* herself came out of her kitchen to welcome Maigret and Janvier.

'What can I do for you, gentlemen?'

The Superintendent introduced himself.

'I would like to know whether yesterday evening you had a lady customer who stayed an unusually long time in the restaurant.'

The dining room was empty. The tables were already laid, and tiny carafes of red or white wine stood on each of them.

'My husband looks after the cash-desk, and he's gone out to buy fruit. As for Jean, our waiter, he'll be here in a few minutes, for he comes on duty at eleven o'clock. Can I get you something meanwhile? We've got a nice little Corsican wine that my husband gets sent over specially.'

Everybody was delightful that day. So was the little Corsican wine. And so was the low dining room where the two men waited for Jean, while watching the people pass on the pavement outside and keeping an eye on the two cafés across the boulevard.

'Have you got an idea, Chief?'

'I've got several. But only one of them can be right, can it?'

Jean appeared. He was an elderly white-haired fellow who could have been recognized anywhere as a restaurant waiter. He dived into a cupboard for a change of clothes.

'Tell me, do you remember having a lady customer yesterday evening who behaved in a rather unusual way? ... A girl with dark hair.'

'A married lady,' Jean corrected him. 'At any rate I'm sure she was wearing a wedding ring; I noticed it because it was made of gold and copper alloy, and my wife and I have rings like that too...'

'Was she young?'

'I'd say about thirty...A very respectable person, hardly made up at all, and she spoke to one very politely...'

'What time did she come in?'

'That's just it! She came in about a quarter past six, while I was finishing laying the tables for dinner. Our customers, who are nearly all regulars' (he glanced towards the rack that held their napkins) 'seldom come before seven o'clock...She seemed surprised when she came into the empty room and she seemed to draw back.

'"Is it for dinner?" I asked her. Because sometimes people make a mistake and think we're a café.

'"Come in," I said. "I can serve you in a quarter of an hour or so...Would you take something while you're waiting?"'

'She ordered a glass of port...'

Maigret and Janvier exchanged a glance of satisfaction.

'She sat down beside the window. I had to ask her to move, because she had taken the table where the gentlemen from the Registry Office usually sit; they've been coming here for the past ten years.

'Actually she had to wait almost half an hour, because the snails weren't ready...She didn't seem impatient. I brought her a paper, but she didn't read it; she just sat peacefully looking out of the window.'

Just like the gentleman with the dyed moustache! A quiet man, a quiet lady, and, at the other street corner, a crazy fellow in a state of nervous tension. Up till now, it was the crazy fellow who had been armed; it was he who had in his pocket a rubber stamp with the threatening words: *I'll get you.*

And it was he who had died, without having used his gun.

'She was a very nice lady. I thought she must be someone from the neighbourhood who had forgotten her key and was waiting for her husband to come so as to go home. That happens oftener than you'd think, you know.'

'Did she eat a good dinner?'

'Let's see . . . A dozen snails . . . Then sweetbreads, cheese, straw-berries and cream . . . I remember because there's an extra charge . . . She drank a small carafe of white wine and a coffee . . .

'She stayed very late. That's what made me think she must be ex-pecting somebody. She wasn't quite the last to leave, but there were only two people left when she asked for the bill . . . It must have been soon after ten o'clock. We usually close at half-past ten . . .'

'You don't know in which direction she went off?'

'I hope she's not in any trouble?' asked old Jean, who seemed to have taken a fancy to his unusual customer. 'Then I may as well tell you that when I left at a quarter to eleven and crossed the pave-ment, I was surprised to see her standing under one of the trees . . . It was the second tree on the left of the lamppost.'

'Did she still seem to be waiting for somebody?'

'I imagine so . . . She wasn't the sort of woman you might be thinking of . . . When she caught sight of me she looked away as if she was embarrassed.'

'Tell me, was she carrying a handbag?'

'Why yes, of course . . .'

'Was it large or small? Did she open it in your presence?'

'Let's see . . . No, she didn't open it in my presence . . . She had put it on the window ledge, because her table was close to the win-dow . . . It was a fairly large rectangular bag, of dark leather . . . There was an initial on it, made of silver or some other metal . . . I think it was an M.'

'Well, Janvier old man?'

'Well, Chief?'

If they went on having little drinks here, there and everywhere, they would end up by behaving like schoolboys on holiday, this wonderful spring day.

'Do you believe it was she who killed the chap?'

'We know that he was shot from behind, about three metres away.'

'But the fellow from the *Café des Ministères* might have...'

'One minute, Janvier... Which of the two men, as far as we know, was on the lookout for the other?'

'The dead man...'

'Who wasn't yet dead... He was the one who was keeping watch... who was *certainly* armed... who was threatening the other. In the circumstances, unless he was dead drunk by midnight, it's hardly likely that the other man, coming out of the *Café des Ministères*, could have taken him unawares and shot him from behind, particularly at such close range. Whereas the woman...'

'What shall we do?'

To tell the truth, if Maigret had followed his instincts he would have lingered a little longer in the neighbourhood, he had taken such a sudden fancy to the atmosphere of the crossroads. He would have liked to go back to Joseph's, then to the bar over the way; to sniff around, have a few more drinks, study the same subject from different angles: the man with the waxed moustache, the other, riddled with drink and disease, and the woman, so respectable that she had won the heart of old Jean, dining off snails, sweetbreads and strawberries.

'I bet she's used to very simple, homely food and that she seldom eats out in restaurants.'

'How can you tell that?'

'Because people who often eat out don't choose three dishes for which there's an extra charge, two of which one seldom cooks at home: snails and sweetbreads... Two dishes that don't go well together, and that suggest greediness.'

'And do you think that a woman who's going to kill somebody is likely to bother about what she eats?'

'For one thing, Janvier my boy, nothing proves that she *knew* she was going to kill somebody that evening...'

'If she was the one who fired, she must have been armed... I saw what you meant by your questions about the handbag... I was expecting you to ask the waiter if it looked heavy.'

'For another thing,' went on Maigret imperturbably, 'the most shocking dramas don't usually prevent people from minding what they eat ... You must have noticed that as I have ... There's been a death in a family, the house is topsy-turvy, everyone's weeping and groaning; you'd think life would never resume its normal course ... All the same, a neighbour, or an aunt, or an old servant prepares a meal ...

'"I couldn't eat a thing," the widow declares.

'The others encourage her, they force her to sit down to dinner. Eventually the whole family gets down to it, abandoning the deceased; very soon the whole family is enjoying the meal; and the widow is the one who demands salt and pepper because she finds the stew rather tasteless ...

'Off we go, Janvier ...'

'Where are we going?'

'To Juvisy ...'

They really should have gone to the Gare de Lyon and taken the train. But to face that crowd, to wait at the booking office and then on the platform, to travel standing, maybe, or in a non-smokers' compartment, would have spoilt such a beautiful day.

The cash clerk at Police Headquarters could grumble if he liked; Maigret picked an open taxi and settled down in comfort.

'Take us to Juvisy and stop in front of the station.'

And he spent the journey dozing luxuriously, with his eyes half closed and a thin thread of smoke issuing from the lips that held the stem of his pipe.

3
The Uncertain Identity of a Dead Woman

Many a time, when he was asked to talk about one of his cases, Maigret might have taken the opportunity to describe some enquiry in which he had played a brilliant role, literally forcing truth to emerge by dint of his obstinacy, his intuition and his understanding of human nature.

But the story that, in after time, he most enjoyed telling was that of the two cafés in the Boulevard Saint-Germain; true, it was not one of the cases that had earned him the most glory, but he could not help recalling it with a smile of pleasure.

And even so, when he was asked where the truth lay, he would add:

'It's up to you to choose which truth you prefer...'

For on one point at least, neither he nor anybody else ever discovered the whole truth.

It was half-past twelve when the taxi deposited Maigret and Janvier opposite Juvisy station, on the outskirts of Paris, and they first went into the *Restaurant du Triage*, a very ordinary sort of restaurant with a terrace surrounded by bay trees in green tubs.

One cannot enter a café without drinking something. They exchanged a glance; well, since they had been drinking white wine all morning, like the dead man in the Rue des Saints-Pères, they might as well go on.

'Tell me, *patron*, do you happen to know this fellow?'

The bruiser in shirtsleeves who was officiating behind the zinc counter examined the faked photograph of the dead man, held it out at some distance from his shortsighted eyes, and called out:

'Julie!...Come here a minute...It's the chap from next door, isn't it?'

His wife, wiping her hands on her blue linen apron, carefully picked up the photograph.

'Sure, it's him!...But he's got a funny sort of look on this photo...'

Turning to the Superintendent, she went on:

'Only yesterday he kept us up till eleven o'clock while he put away one glass after another.'

'Yesterday?' Maigret had a nasty shock.

'Wait, though...No, I mean the day before yesterday...Yesterday I was doing the washing and in the evening I went to the pictures.'

'Can we eat here?'

'Of course you can eat...What would you like? *Fricandeau* of veal? Roast pork with lentils?...There's some nice *pâté de campagne* to start off with.'

They lunched on the terrace, side by side with the taxi driver, whom they had kept. From time to time the *patron* came to have a chat with them.

'They'll tell you more at the place next door, where they take lodgers. We don't have rooms . . . It must be a month or two since your man came to stay there . . . When it comes to drinking, though, you'll find him all over the place . . . Only yesterday morning . . .'

'You're sure it was yesterday?'

'Positive . . . He came in at half-past six, just as I was opening the shutters, and he treated himself to two or three glasses of white wine for a pick-me-up . . . Then suddenly, as the Paris train was about to leave, he rushed off to the station.'

The *patron* knew nothing about him except that he drank from morning till night, that he was always talking about Gabon, that he had the utmost contempt for anyone who had not lived in Africa and that he bore a grudge against somebody.

'Some people think themselves clever,' he used to say. 'But I'm going to get them in the end. Sure, there are plenty of swine about. Only some of them go too far.'

Half an hour later, Maigret, still accompanied by Janvier, entered the *Hôtel du Chemin de Fer*, which boasted a restaurant exactly like the one they had just left except that the terrace was not surrounded by bay trees and the iron chairs were painted red instead of green.

The proprietor, at his bar, was reading a newspaper article aloud to his wife and the waiter. Maigret understood at once, when he saw the picture of the dead man splashed on the front page: the mid-morning papers had just reached Juvisy, and it was he himself who had sent the photographs to the press.

'Is that your lodger?'

A suspicious glance. 'Yes . . . And what about it?'

'Nothing . . . I just wanted to know if it was your lodger.'

'Good riddance, in any case!'

They had to order something, yet again, and you couldn't go on drinking white wine after lunch.

'Two calvados.'

'You're from the police?'

'Yes...'

'I thought as much...I seem to know your face...Well?'

'I'd like to know your opinion.'

'My opinion is that he's more likely to have bumped off someone else...Or to have got himself knocked out in a fight...Because when he was tight, and he was tight every evening, there was no holding him.'

'Have you his registration?'

With great dignity, to show that he had nothing to conceal, the proprietor went to fetch his register and held it out to the Superintendent with a slightly disdainful air.

Ernest Combarieu, 47 years of age, born at Marsilly, near La Rochelle (Charente-Maritime), woodcutter. Last residence Libreville, Gabon.

'He stayed six weeks with you?'

'Six weeks too many!'

'Did he not pay?'

'He paid regularly, every week...But he was crazy...He'd stay two or three days in bed with fever, sending up for rum by way of medicine and drinking whole bottles of it, then he'd come down and for several days he'd do the round of all the bistros in the neighbourhood, sometimes forgetting to come home or else waking us up at three in the morning...Sometimes we had to undress him...He used to be sick on the stair carpet or on his rug.'

'Had he any relatives in the district?'

The proprietor and his wife glanced at one another.

'He must have known somebody, but he would never tell us who. If it was a member of his family I can assure you he didn't love them, for he often used to say:

'"One day you'll hear tell of me and of a swine whom everyone thinks is a decent fellow, a phony who's the meanest thief in the world..."'

'Did you never find out whom he was talking about?'

'All that I know is that he was intolerable and that when he was drunk he used to pull out a big revolver from his pocket, aim at an imaginary target and shout: "Bang, bang!" And then he'd burst out laughing and ask for another drink.'

'You'll take a glass with us?...One more question...Do you know, somewhere in Juvisy, a gentleman of average height, stoutish without being fat, with a fine black moustache, who sometimes goes about carrying a little suitcase?'

'Does that say anything to you, love?' the *patron* asked his wife. She searched her memory.

'No...Unless...But he's rather below average height and I don't call him stout...'

'Who are you talking about?'

'About Monsieur Auger, who lives in one of the new houses on the estate.'

'Is he married?'

'Sure...Madame Auger is a pretty woman, very respectable and quiet, who practically never leaves Juvisy...I say! That reminds me...'

The three men watched her expectantly.

'That reminds me that yesterday, as I was doing my washing in the yard, I saw her going towards the station...I guessed she was taking the 4.37 train.'

'She's dark, isn't she? And carries a black leather handbag?'

'I don't know what colour her handbag was, but she was wearing a blue suit and a white blouse.'

'What is Monsieur Auger by profession?'

This time the *patronne* let her husband answer.

'He sells stamps...You'll see his name in the papers, in the small ads...*Stamps for collectors*...Packets of a thousand stamps for ten francs...packets of five hundred stamps...All sent by post, C.O.D.'

'Does he travel much?'

'He goes to Paris from time to time, about his stamps I suppose, and he always takes his little suitcase...He's stopped here two or three times, when the train's been delayed...He drinks *café-crème* or Vichy water.'

It was too easy. It was not an investigation but an outing, en-livened by the cheerful sunlight and by their ever-increasing con-sumption of white wine. And yet there was a glint in Maigret's eyes, as though he had guessed that behind this commonplace affair there lay one of the most extraordinary human mysteries that he had encountered in the whole of his career.

He had been given the Augers' address. It was a fair way off, in the plain, where alongside the river Seine some hundreds and thou-sands of little houses stood surrounded by little gardens, some of them of stone, some of red brick, some dressed with blue or yellow concrete.

He had been told that the Augers' house was called *Mon Repos*. They had to drive for a long way through streets that were too new, with rudimentary pavements along which someone had recently planted anaemic trees, as thin as skeletons, and where patches of waste ground lay between the houses.

They asked their way, and were frequently misdirected. Finally they reached their objective, and a curtain was twitched at the cor-ner window of a small pink house with a bright red roof.

Next they had to find the bell.

'Shall I stay outside, Chief?'

'Perhaps it would be wiser ... Yet I think it's going to be plain sailing ... *Since there's somebody at home* ...'

He was not mistaken. Eventually he found a tiny electric bell-push in the brand-new front door. He rang. He heard sounds, whis-pers. The door opened, and there stood before him, wearing probably the same blouse and skirt as on the previous evening, the young woman from the *Café des Ministères* and the *Escargot*.

'Superintendent Maigret from the Police Judiciaire,' he intro-duced himself.

'I guessed it was the police ... Come in.'

They went up a few steps. The staircase seemed to be just out of the carpenter's hands, and so did all the woodwork; the plaster on the walls was barely dry.

'Will you be so kind ...' She turned to a half-open door and made a sign to somebody whom Maigret could not see.

The corner room into which she ushered the Superintendent was a living room with a divan, books, ornaments and brightly coloured silk cushions. On a small table there was the midday paper with the photograph of the dead man.

'Do sit down . . . I don't know if I may offer you anything?'

'Thank you, no.'

'I should have known it's not allowed . . . My husband will be here directly . . . You needn't worry; he won't try to run away, and in any case he's done nothing wrong . . . Only he was unwell this morning . . . We came home by the first train . . . His heart's not too good . . . He had an attack when we got home . . . He's just shaving and dressing now.'

And the sound of running water could be heard from the bathroom, for the walls of the rooms were very thin.

The young woman was almost calm. She was rather pretty, with the quiet prettiness of a middle-class housewife.

'As you must have guessed, it was I who killed my brother-in-law. It was only just in time, for if I had not done so he would have killed my husband, and Raymond's life is surely worth more than his . . .'

'Raymond is your husband?'

'We've been married eight years . . . We've nothing to hide, Superintendent. Perhaps we should have gone last night to tell the police everything . . . Raymond wanted to do so, but knowing his weak heart I preferred to give him time to recover . . . I knew you'd be coming.'

'You spoke, just now, of your brother-in-law?'

'Combarieu was my sister Marthe's husband . . . I think he used to be a decent fellow, but a bit crazy . . .'

'One minute . . . Do you mind if I smoke?'

'Please do. My husband doesn't smoke because of his heart, but I don't mind tobacco smoke.'

'Where were you born?'

'At Melun . . . We were twin sisters, Marthe and I . . . My name's Isabelle . . . We were so much alike that when we were little our parents—they're dead now—used to give us different coloured hair-ribbons to tell us apart . . . And sometimes, for fun, we used to exchange ribbons . . .'

'Which of you was married first?'

'We were married on the same day...Combarieu was a clerk at the Préfecture offices at Melun...Auger was an insurance broker...They were acquaintances because, both being bachelors, they used to eat at the same restaurant...We met them together, my sister and I...After we were married we lived at Melun for several years, in the same street...'

'Combarieu still working at the Préfecture and your husband as an insurance broker?'

'Yes...But Auger was already thinking of the stamp business... He'd begun collecting himself, as a hobby...He realized there was money to be made from it.'

'And Combarieu?'

'He was ambitious and restless...He was always short of money...He got to know a man who was just back from the Colonies and who gave him the idea of going there...At first he wanted my sister to go with him, but she refused, because of what she'd heard about the climate and its effect on a woman's health...'

'So he went out there alone?'

'Yes...He stayed away two years, and came back with his pockets full of money...He spent it faster than he'd made it...He'd already begun to drink...He claimed that my husband was a weakling, that a man could do something better with his life than sell insurance policies and postage stamps.'

'Did he go back?'

'Yes, and he was less successful this time. We could sense that from his letters, although he was always inclined to boast...My sister Marthe, two winters ago, caught pneumonia and died of it... We wrote to tell her husband...Apparently he started drinking more heavily than ever...As for us, we came to settle here, for we'd been wanting for a long time to build something for ourselves and live nearer Paris. My husband had given up insurance, and the stamp business was doing well...'

She spoke slowly and calmly, weighing her words and listening to the sounds that issued from the bathroom.

'Five months ago my brother-in-law turned up without warning...He rang at our door one evening when he was drunk...He
looked at me in a funny way and the first words he uttered, with a
sneer, were: "I guessed as much!"'

'I didn't yet realize what he was thinking of. He was in a much
worse state than the first time he'd come home...His health was
poor, he was drinking far more and although he still had some
money he was no longer a rich man.

'He started saying the queerest things to us. He would look at my
husband and suddenly burst out: "Admit that you're a rotten
bastard!"

'He went off again...We don't know where to. Then he reappeared, drunk as usual. He greeted me with the remark: "Well,
Marthe my dear..."'

'"You know I'm not Marthe but Isabelle..."'

'He laughed more wildly than ever. "We'll see about that some
day, won't we? As for your swine of a husband who sells stamps..."'

'I don't know if you can understand what had happened...He
wasn't exactly out of his mind...He drank too heavily...He had
an obsession which we didn't guess for some while...We couldn't
understand at first what he meant by his threatening manner, his
sneering insinuations, or the notes that were now coming through
the post for my husband saying: "I'll get you."'

'In a word,' Maigret put in calmly, 'your brother-in-law Combarieu had got it into his head, for one reason or another, that the
woman who had died was not his own wife but Auger's.'

It was an astonishing situation. Twin sisters so alike that their
parents had to dress them differently to tell them apart. Combarieu,
abroad, learning of his wife's death...And imagining, on his return, rightly or wrongly, that there had been a substitution, that the
dead woman was Isabelle and that it was his own wife Marthe who,
in his absence, had replaced her as Auger's.

Maigret's gaze darkened, and he drew more slowly on his pipe.

'For months now our life has been impossible...Threatening
letters have come one after the other...Sometimes Combarieu

bursts in at any hour of day or night, draws out his revolver, levels it at my husband and then says with a sneer: "No, not yet, that would be too good!"

'He settled in the neighbourhood to torment us. He's as clever as a monkey. Even when he's drunk he knows perfectly well what he's doing...'

'He used to know,' Maigret corrected her.

'I'm sorry.' She blushed slightly. 'He used to know, you're quite right... And I don't imagine he wanted to get caught... That was why we weren't too frightened here, because if he had killed Auger at Juvisy everyone would have pointed to him as the murderer...

'My husband dared not leave the place... Yesterday he simply had to go to Paris on business. I wanted to go with him, but he refused. He took the earliest train on purpose, hoping that Combarieu would still be sleeping off his drink and would not notice his departure.

'He was mistaken, and he rang me up in the afternoon to ask me to come to a café in the Boulevard Saint-Germain and bring him a revolver.

'I realized that he was at the end of his tether, and wanted to have done with it... I took him his Browning... He'd told me over the phone that he would stay in the café until it closed.

'I bought a second gun for myself... You must try and understand, Superintendent.'

'In a word, you'd made up your mind to fire before he could shoot your husband...'

'I swear to you that when I pressed the trigger Combarieu had already raised his gun. That's all I have to say. I'll answer any questions you like to ask me.'

'How does it happen that your handbag still bears the letter M?'

'Because it belonged to my sister... If Combarieu had been right, if we had practised the deception that he talked so much about, I suppose I'd have taken care to change the initial.'

'So, it seems, you love a man enough to...'

'I love my husband...'

'I said: you love a man, whether or not he's your husband...'

'He is my husband.'

'You love this man, Auger, enough to bring yourself to kill in order to save him or to prevent him from killing another man himself...'

She replied simply:

'Yes.'

There was a sound outside the door.

'Come in,' she said.

At long last Maigret saw the man of whom he had been given such varying descriptions, the café customer with the blue-black moustache, who, seen in his own home, and particularly after the declaration of love which the young woman had just made, appeared hopelessly commonplace, utterly mediocre.

He was looking round him anxiously. She smiled at him, saying:

'Sit down. I've told the Superintendent everything... *Your heart?*'

He felt his chest vaguely and murmured:

'It's all right...'

The jury of the Seine department acquitted Madame Auger as having acted in legitimate self-defence.

And each time Maigret told the story, he concluded with an ironical:

'*Is that everything?*'

'Does that imply you've got a mental reservation?'

'It implies nothing... Except that a man of the utmost banality can inspire a great love, a heroic passion... Even if he sells postage-stamps and has a weak heart...'

'But Combarieu?'

'What about him?'

'Was he mad when he imagined that his wife was not the woman who'd died but the one who gave herself out to be Isabelle?'

Maigret would shrug his shoulders and repeat, on a note of parody:

'*A great love!... A grand passion!...*'

And sometimes, when he was in a good humour and had been drinking a glass of old calvados, warmed in the hollow of his hand, he would add:

'A great love!... A grand passion!... It's not always the husband who inspires it, is it?...And sisters, in most families, have a tire-some habit of falling for the same man...Combarieu was a long way off...'

He would add, drawing deeply on his pipe:

'How can one distinguish between twins whom their own parents can't tell apart, parents whom we've not been able to question because they are dead...All the same, there never was such a fine day as that...And I can't remember ever drinking so much...Janvier, if he were to be indiscreet, might tell you how we found ourselves singing in chorus in the taxi that took us back to Paris, and when I got home Madame Maigret wondered how I came to have a bunch of violets in my pocket...That blessed Marthe!...Sorry, I mean: that blessed Isabelle!'

2 May 1946

Death of a Nobody

I
Murder of a Man in his Shirt

'Nobodies don't get murdered...'

A dozen times, a score of times in the space of two hours this stupid phrase recurred to Maigret's mind, like the refrain of a song heard somewhere or other that haunts one for no reason. It was becoming an obsession, and he found himself muttering the words below his breath; occasionally he varied them:

'Men don't get murdered in their shirts...'

It was hot by nine o'clock that August morning. Paris was on holiday. Police Headquarters was almost empty, all its windows wide open over the river, and Maigret had already taken off his jacket when he got the telephone call from Judge Coméliau.

'You ought to go round to the Rue des Dames. There was a crime there last night. The local Superintendent told me a long and complicated story. He's there still, on the spot. The D.P.P. can't get there before eleven o'clock.'

That's how things are always sprung upon one. You're expecting to spend a peaceful day in the shade, and then, before you know where you are!

'Coming, Lucas?'

As usual, the Crime Squad's little car was not available and the two men had taken the métro, which smelt of disinfectant and where Maigret had to put out his pipe.

The lower end of the Rue des Dames, near the Rue des Batig-nolles, was swarming with people in the sunshine; vegetables, fruit and fish were piled high on the little barrows ranged alongside the pavement, which were being assailed by a compact mass of house-wives, while the inevitable horde of youngsters seized the opportu-nity to indulge in their rowdiest games.

A commonplace house, six floors of homes for people of very moderate means, with a laundry and a coal merchant's shop on the ground floor. A cop on duty by the door.

'The Superintendent's waiting for you upstairs, Monsieur Mai-gret... It's on the third floor... Come on, move along, folks... There's nothing to see... Clear the way, please.'

As usual, the concierge's lodge was full of gossiping women. Doors opened silently on each landing, inquiring faces peeped out. What kind of crime could have been committed in a house like this, inhabited by nobodies, who are usually decent people? A drama of love and jealousy? Even for that the setting was not right.

A door was wide open on to a kitchen, on the third floor. Three or four teenage children were making a noise, and a woman's voice called out from another room:

'Gérard, if you don't leave your sister alone...'

It was the shrill, weary voice of one of those women who spend their lives struggling against petty worries. She was the wife of the victim. A door opened, and Maigret was confronted with her and with the local Superintendent; the two men shook hands.

The woman looked at him and sighed, as if to say:

'Another of them!'

'This is Superintendent Maigret,' the local police officer ex-plained. 'He's to be in charge of the investigation.'

'So I shall have to tell him everything all over again?'

It was a living room with a sewing machine in one corner and a radio set in another. The open window let in the noise from the street. The kitchen door was open too, letting in the children's chatter, but the woman went to close it and the voices fell silent, as when one switches off the radio.

'It's the sort of thing that only happens to me...' she sighed. 'Sit down, gentlemen.'

'Tell me as simply as possible what happened.'

'How can I, when I didn't see anything? It's almost as if nothing had happened... He came back at half-past six as usual... He'd always been punctual... I even had to hustle the children, because he liked to eat as soon as he got back...'

She was speaking of her husband, an enlarged photograph of whom hung on the wall facing one of herself. And her air of desolation was not due to the tragedy. Even on the portrait she wore a weary resigned look, as though she bore all the weight of the world on her shoulders.

As for the man, moustached and stiff-collared on his photograph, he was the very image of serenity; he was so neutral, so ordinary that one could have met him a hundred times without noticing him.

'He got back at half-past six, he took off his jacket and hung it up in the wardrobe, for I have to admit that he's always been careful of his things... We had dinner... I sent the two youngest to play outside... Francine, who goes out to work, came back at eight o'clock, and I'd left her dinner on a corner of the table...'

She must have told the whole story to the local policeman, but it was obvious that she would repeat it in the same woeful voice as many times as she was asked to, with the anxious glance of someone who's afraid of forgetting something.

She might have been about forty-five, and had probably once been pretty; but she'd been battling for so many years with domestic difficulties!

'Maurice sat down in his corner by the window... Look, you're actually sitting in his armchair... He read a book, getting up from time to time to switch on the radio...'

While at the same time, in all the houses along the Rue des Dames, some hundred other men who, like him, had been working all day in shops or offices, were now relaxing beside open windows, reading an evening paper or a book.

'He never used to go out, you see. Never by himself. Once a week we all went to the pictures together, on Sunday...'

From time to time she lost the thread of her talk, because she was listening to the muffled sounds from the kitchen, worrying, wondering whether the children were fighting or something was burning on the stove.

'What was I saying? Oh, yes... Francine, who's seventeen, went out again and came home about half-past ten... The others were in bed already... I was preparing the soup for today, ahead of time because I had to go to the dressmaker's this morning... Oh Lord! and I didn't even let her know I couldn't come. She must be expecting me.'

One more disaster to worry about!

'We went to bed... That's to say we went into the bedroom and I got into bed... Maurice always took longer to undress... The window was open... We hadn't pulled the blinds on account of the heat... There was nobody opposite to look in at us... It's a hotel... People go in and go to bed straight away... They seldom hang around by the window...'

Maigret was so calm and impassive that Lucas wondered if his Chief was falling asleep. But from time to time a puff of smoke could be seen escaping from the lips that gripped the stem of his pipe.

'What else can I tell you? It *would* happen to me... He was talking... I've forgotten what he was talking about, but he'd just taken off his trousers and he was folding them. He was in his shirt... He was sitting on the edge of the bed... He'd taken off his socks and he was rubbing his feet because they were sore... I heard a noise outside... Like... like a car backfiring, or hardly as loud... It went *pshuittt*... Yes, *pshuitt*!... A bit like when the air gets into a faucet. I wondered why Maurice had stopped talking in the middle of a sentence. I must admit that I was beginning to drop off, because I'd had a tiring day... There was a silence, and then he said softly, in a funny sort of voice: "Oh, hell!"

'That surprised me, because he didn't often swear. He wasn't that sort. I asked him: "What's the matter?"

'And then I opened my eyes, because they'd been shut until then, and I saw him topple forward.

' "Maurice!" I cried.

'A man who's never fainted in his life, d'you understand?... He wasn't very tough maybe, but he was never ill...

'I got up...I kept on speaking to him...He was lying face downwards on the mat...I tried to lift him up, and I saw blood on his shirt.

'I called Francine, our eldest. And do you know what Francine said to me, when she looked at her father?

' "What have you done, maman?"

'Then she went downstairs to telephone...She had to wake up the coal merchant...'

'Where is Francine?' Maigret asked.

'In her room...She's getting dressed...Because we'd never even thought about dressing, all night long...Just look at me... The doctor came, then the police, then Monsieur...'

'Will you leave us?'

She did not understand at first, but repeated:

'Leave what?'

Then she disappeared into the kitchen, where she could be heard scolding the children in a monotonous voice.

'Another quarter of an hour of that would have driven me round the bend,' sighed Maigret, drawing a deep breath by the window.

One could not have said exactly why. She may have been a very decent woman, but she exuded a depressing atmosphere which made the very sunlight coming in through the window seem dim and almost gloomy. Everything around her became so dreary, so futile and monotonous that one began to wonder if the street was really there, practically within one's reach, teeming with life and light, with colours, sounds and smells.

'Poor beggar...'

Not because he was dead, but because he had lived!

'By the way, what was his name?'

'Tremblet...Maurice Tremblet...Forty-eight years old...According to his wife, he was cashier with a firm in the Sentier district...Let's see, I put down the address: Couvreur et Bellechasse, dealers in *passementerie*.'

Passementerie—gold lace and braid—into the bargain!

'You know,' the police officer explained, 'I thought at first that it was she who had killed him . . . I had just been woken from my first sleep . . . In the chaos that reigned here, with the children all talking at once and her shouting at them to keep quiet, and then telling me the same story over and over again—more or less what you've just heard—I thought at first that she must be crazy or half crazy . . . Particularly as my constable had just been putting her through it:

'"I don't want to hear about all that," he was saying to her. "I want to know why you killed him! . . ."

'And she was saying: "Why should I have killed him and what could I have killed him with?"

'There were some neighbours in the stairway . . . It was the local doctor, who's going to send me his report, who declared that the bullet had been fired from a distance, probably from one of the windows across the street . . . So I sent my men over to the *Hôtel Excelsior*.'

The same little phrase kept recurring to Maigret's mind:

'Nobodies don't get murdered . . .'

Particularly a nobody in his shirtsleeves, sitting on the edge of the double bed, rubbing the soles of his feet.

'Did you discover anything over there?'

Maigret scrutinized the windows of the hotel, which was more of a lodging house. A plaque of imitation black marble read: 'Rooms by the month, week or day. Running water, h. and c.'

It was pretty shabby too. But like the house, like the Tremblets' flat, its shabbiness was hardly in keeping with such dramatic events. It was decent shabbiness, respectable mediocrity.

'I began with the third floor, where my men found the lodgers in bed. There was plenty of grumbling, as you can well imagine. The proprietor was furious and threatened to lodge a complaint. Then it occurred to me to go up to the fourth floor. And there I found an empty room, just opposite the right window, if you see what I mean; a room that was supposed to be occupied; it had been taken a week ago by a certain Jules Dartoin. I questioned the night porter. He remembered having pulled the cord to let somebody out shortly before midnight, but he didn't know who it was . . .'

Maigret finally brought himself to open the door of the bedroom, where the body of the victim was still lying partly on the rug, partly on the floor, at the foot of the bed.

'Apparently he was shot through the heart, and death was practically instantaneous... I thought I'd better wait for the police surgeon to come and extract the bullet... He's expected at any time now, with the people from the D.P.P.'

'About eleven o'clock...' Maigret said absentmindedly.

It was now a quarter past ten. Down in the street the housewives were still doing their shopping around the barrows, and a pleasant smell of fruit and vegetables drifted up in the warm air.

'*Nobodies don't...*'

'Have you searched the man's pockets?'

This had obviously been done, for his clothes were lying in a heap on the table, whereas according to his wife Tremblet had folded them neatly before going to bed.

'Everything's here... A purse... Cigarettes... A lighter... Keys... A wallet containing a hundred francs and photographs of his children.'

'The neighbours?'

'My men have questioned everybody in the house... The Tremblets have lived here for twenty years... They took two extra rooms when the family increased... There seems to be nothing to say about them... Regular habits... nothing out of the way... A fortnight's holiday every year in the Cantal, where Tremblet comes from originally... They had no visitors except, occasionally, a sister of Madame Tremblet's; her maiden name was Lapointe and she came from Cantal too. Her husband always left at a regular time to go to his office, taking the métro at Villiers station... He came back at half-past twelve, left again an hour later and returned home at half-past six...'

'It's idiotic...'

Maigret spoke almost unconsciously. Because it really was idiotic. Because such a crime was inconceivable.

There are a hundred reasons for killing people, but such reasons are, as it were, catalogued. After thirty years in the police force one immediately knows what sort of crime one is dealing with.

An old woman, a shopkeeper, may be killed for the sake of the money in her till or the savings hidden in her mattress. Murders are committed out of jealousy, or because of . . .

'He wasn't mixed up in politics?'

Maigret went into the next room to look at the book the man had been reading the night before. It was a cloak-and-dagger story in a gaudy cover.

Nothing had been stolen. There had been no attempt at theft. And it was not a random crime. On the contrary, it must have been carefully prepared, since it had meant taking a room in the hotel opposite and procuring a rifle—probably an air-gun.

This could not have been done by just anybody. And it could not have been done to just anybody. Whereas Tremblet's name might well have been Mr. Just-Anybody!

'Aren't you going to wait for the men from the D.P.P.?'

'I'll probably be back here before they leave. Be kind enough to stay and put them in the picture.'

In the next room a row was going on; presumably Madame Tremblet, *née* Lapointe, was having an argument with her children.

'How many has she, by the way?'

'Five . . . Three boys and two girls . . . One of the sons, who had pleurisy last winter, is staying with his grandparents in the country . . . He's thirteen and a half.'

'Coming, Lucas?'

Maigret was not anxious to see Madame Tremblet again just yet, nor to hear her moaning, 'It's just my luck . . .'

He went downstairs, treading heavily; once again, doors opened as he passed, and people were whispering behind them. He nearly went into the coal merchant's shop to have a glass of wine, but it was full of an inquisitive crowd waiting for the arrival of the men from the D.P.P., and he chose rather to make for the Rue des Batignolles, where nothing was known about the sensational affair.

'What'll you drink?'

'Same as you, Chief.'

Maigret mopped his brow, with a mechanical glance at his reflection in the mirror.

'What do you think about it?'

'That if I'd had a wife like that . . .' Lucas fell silent.

'You go and enquire about the fellow in the *Hôtel Excelsior* . . . You probably won't find out much, because a man who goes about things the way he did . . . Hey, taxi!'

It would go down on the expense account! It was too hot to stifle in the métro or wait for a bus at the street corner.

'I'll see you again at the Rue des Dames . . . Otherwise this afternoon, at the Quai.'

Nobodies don't get themselves killed, for heaven's sake! Or if they do, it's on a large scale, in a war or a revolution. And if it should happen that nobodies kill themselves, they can hardly do it with an air-gun while they're busy rubbing their feet.

If only Tremblet had had a foreign-sounding name, instead of just being a native of Cantal! Then one might have believed that he belonged to some secret society of his compatriots.

He didn't look the sort of person to get murdered, definitely! And that was just what was so disturbing. The apartment, the wife, the kids, the husband in his shirtsleeves, and the bullet that went *pshuitt* . . .

Maigret, sitting in his open taxi, puffed at his pipe and shrugged his shoulders. For a moment he thought of Madame Maigret, who would undoubtedly say with a sigh:

'Poor woman!'

Because women are always sorry for the woman when a man dies.

'No, I don't know the number. Rue du Sentier, yes . . . Couvreur et Bellechasse . . . It must be a big firm . . . founded eighteen hundred and something . . .'

He was furious. He was furious because he could not understand and he hated not understanding. The Rue du Sentier was crowded. The driver stopped to make enquiries and just as he was hailing a passerby Maigret read the words *Couvreur et Bellechasse*, in elegant gilt script, on a housefront.

'Wait for me . . . I shan't be long.'

He couldn't be sure of that, but the heat made him lazy. Particularly when most of his colleagues and inspectors were on holiday.

Particularly when he had promised himself a nice relaxed day in the office.

First floor on the right. A suite of gloomy rooms that looked like vestries.

'Monsieur Couvreur, please.'

'On private business?'

'Extremely private.'

'I'm sorry, Monsieur Couvreur died five years ago.'

'And Monsieur Bellechasse?'

'Monsieur Bellechasse is in Normandy. If you would like to speak to Monsieur Mauvre...'

'Who is he?'

'The manager...He's at the bank at the moment, but he'll be back shortly.'

'Is Monsieur Tremblet in?' A shot in the dark.

'I beg your pardon, who did you say?'

'Monsieur Tremblet...Maurice Tremblet...'

'I don't know him...'

'Your cashier...'

'Our cashier is called Magine, Gaston Magine...'

Maigret, whose mind must have run in stock phrases that day, said to himself that you could have knocked him down with a feather.

'Will you wait for Monsieur Mauvre?'

'Yes, I'll wait for him.'

He waited amid a sickly smell of cardboard and *passementerie*. Fortunately not for too long. Monsieur Mauvre was a man of sixty, clad in decent black from head to foot.

'You wanted to speak to me?'

'Superintendent Maigret of the Police Judiciaire.'

If he had hoped to impress Monsieur Mauvre, he had miscalculated.

'And to what do I owe the honour?...'

'You have on your staff a cashier named Tremblet, I believe?'

'We had one...A long time ago...Wait a minute...It was the year our Cambrai branch was modernized...Seven years ago... Yes...Not quite seven, for he left us in the middle of the spring.'

And, adjusting his pince-nez:

'It is seven years since Monsieur Tremblet was on our staff.'

'Have you never seen him since?'

'Not personally.'

'Had you any complaint to make of him?'

'None at all. I knew him quite well, for he joined the firm only a few years after I did... He was a conscientious, reliable employee. He gave in his notice in a perfectly regular way, for family reasons, I believe... Yes, he told us he was going to settle in his native province, Auvergne or Cantal, I cannot remember exactly...'

'You never discovered any irregularities in the accounts he kept?'

Monsieur Mauvre shuddered, as though at a personal indictment.

'No, Monsieur. *Such things do not occur in our firm.*'

'Was there anything to suggest that Monsieur Tremblet had any affair, or any bad habits?'

'No, Monsieur. Never. And I am sure there was nothing of the sort.'

Curtly. And if Maigret did not understand that he was going too far, in spite of being a Police Superintendent...

He went on, nonetheless:

'It's odd, because, for the past seven years, until yesterday, Monsieur Tremblet left home every day to come to this office and, every month, handed over his pay packet to his wife...'

'I am sorry, but that's quite impossible!'

Maigret was being given the hint to remove himself.

'In short, he was an exemplary employee?'

'An excellent employee.'

'And nothing in his behaviour...'

'No, Monsieur, nothing. You'll excuse me, but two important customers from the provinces are expecting me...'

Phew! It was almost as stifling as the flat in the Rue des Dames. Maigret was glad to get back to the street and to the taxi, whose driver had had time for a glass of white wine and Vichy at the nearest bistro and was now wiping his moustache.

'Where do we go now, Monsieur Maigret?'

For all the taxi drivers knew him, and that was rather nice too. 'Rue des Dames, old man...'

And so, for the past seven years, Maurice Tremblet had left home at a specified time to go to his office, and for seven years he'd...

'Will you stop somewhere on the way for me to have a quick drink?'

Before facing Madame Tremblet and all the D.P.P. men, who must be getting in one another's way in the flat in the Rue des Dames!

'Nobodies don't...'

But was he really such a nobody as all that?

2
The Ginger-haired Murderer and the Canary-fancier

'What's the matter with you, Maigret? Can't you sleep?'

It must have been half-past two in the morning, and although both windows were wide open on to the Boulevard Richard-Lenoir, Maigret was bathed in sweat and kept tossing about in bed. He had almost dropped off to sleep. But no sooner did he hear his wife's breathing become regular, as she lay beside him, than he started thinking, involuntarily, and of course that meant thinking about the man he called his nobody.

His thoughts were vague and blurred and somewhat nightmarish. He kept going back to the beginning. Rue des Dames, half-past eight in the morning. Maurice Tremblet, finishing dressing in the flat where the mournful Madame Tremblet—he now knew that she was most unsuitably called Juliette—where Juliette, with her hair in curlers and a look of misery in her eyes, was trying to keep the children quiet in a way that only provoked storms.

'He had a horror of noise, Superintendent.'

Why was it this detail, more than anything else he had been told, that had most impressed Maigret and that kept recurring to his drowsy mind? To have a horror of noise and yet to live in the Rue des Dames, a narrow street crowded with shoppers, surrounded by five squabbling children and a wife who was incapable of keeping them quiet...

'He gets dressed, okay...He shaves every other day (according to Juliette's evidence). He drinks his *café au lait* and eats a couple of croissants...He goes down and makes his way to the Boulevard des Batignolles, to take the métro at Villiers station.'

Maigret had spent most of the afternoon in his office, dealing with unsettled business. During this time the evening papers, at the request of the police, published various photographs of Maurice Tremblet on their front pages.

As for Sergeant Lucas, he went along to the *Hôtel Excelsior* with a pile of photographs: those of all the ex-convicts and shady characters whose appearance corresponded more or less to the description of the murderer, known as Jules Dartoin.

The proprietor of the hotel, an Auvergnat, studied them all, shaking his head.

'Not that I saw a great deal of him, but he wasn't *that kind of man.*'

Lucas, listening patiently, realized what he meant: the lodger with the rifle was not a tough guy; he did not look like a suspicious character.

'You know, when he first came to rent the room by the week, I'd have thought he might be a night watchman...

'A dim sort of fellow, middle-aged. We didn't see much of him, particularly as he only went to his room to sleep and left very early in the morning.'

'Had he any luggage?'

'A little bag such as football players carry their gear in.'

And a moustache. The proprietor said it was red. The night porter said it was grey. It's true that they saw him by different lights.

'He looked shabby. Not dirty, but shabby. I made him pay a week in advance. He took some notes out of a very old wallet in which there weren't many of them...'

The chambermaid's evidence. 'I never happened to meet him, for I only did his room in the middle of the morning, after No. 42 and No. 43, but I know one thing: you could tell he was a bachelor.'

Lucas had gone over the room with meticulous care, inch by inch. On the pillow he had found three hairs, one from a moustache. On the enamel washstand a scrap of cologne-scented soap, and on the mantelpiece an old comb with several teeth missing.

That was all: not much of a harvest. And yet the laboratory experts had drawn certain conclusions: after working on the hair and the comb for several hours, they declared that the man was aged between forty-six and forty-eight, with red hair turning grey, beginning to grow bald, with a troubled lymphatic system and an unhealthy liver.

But that was not what Maigret was thinking about in his bed. He was thinking of the murdered man.

'*He gets dressed, eats, puts on his hat and goes out . . . He walks to the métro in the Boulevard des Batignolles . . .*'

Certainly not to go to the office in the Rue du Sentier, to Messrs. Couvreur and Bellechasse, where he had not set foot in seven years, but to go heaven knows where.

It occurred to Maigret that in the days when Tremblet was still cashier in the Rue du Sentier the métro was very convenient for him. The Porte de Champerret-Porte des Lilas line is a direct one. Tremblet merely had to get off at Sentier.

And then he remembered that Francine, the daughter, whom he had scarcely seen, had been working for the past year in a *Prisunic* in the Rue Réaumur. The Rue Réaumur is next to the Rue du Sentier, on the same métro line.

'Can't you sleep?' Madame Maigret asked.

And he said:

'Perhaps you can tell me something. I suppose all the *Prisunic* shops belong to the same company and follow the same rules. You've been to the République one . . .'

'What are you getting at?'

'Do you know what time those shops open?'

'Nine o'clock.'

'You're sure?' And this seemed to make him so happy that he hummed a little song before falling asleep at last.

'Her mother said nothing?'

Maigret was in his office, at a quarter past nine, and Lucas had just come in, still wearing his straw hat.

'I explained to her that you had a few enquiries to make and that, as you didn't want to bother her in her distress, you preferred to question her daughter.'

'And the young lady?'

'We came on the bus, as you'd told me. I think she's a little nervous. She tried to find out what you wanted her for.'

'Bring her in.'

'There's an old gentleman asking to see you.'

'Afterwards... Let him wait... Who is it?'

'A shopkeeper from the Quai du Louvre... He insists on speaking to you personally.'

The air was as warm as on the previous day, with a slight haze like shining steam over the Seine, where strings of boats were sailing past.

Francine came in, dressed in a neat navy-blue suit over a white linen blouse. A spruce, demure young person with curly fair hair set off by a funny little red hat, and a high round bosom. She had obviously not had time, since the previous night, to buy herself mourning clothes.

'Sit down, Mademoiselle... And if you're too warm, you're welcome to take off your jacket.'

For there were beads of sweat on her upper lip.

'Your mother told me yesterday that you worked as a saleswoman at the *Prisunic* in the Rue Réaumur... If I remember rightly, it's just before the Boulevard Sébastopol, on the left?'

'Yes, Monsieur...'

Her lip was quivering, and Maigret sensed that there was something she was reluctant to disclose.

'Since the shop opens at nine o'clock, and since it's quite close to the Rue du Sentier, where your father was supposed to go every morning, I presume you used sometimes to travel together?'

'Sometimes...'

'You're sure of that?'

'It happened occasionally...'

'And did you leave him near his office?'

'Not far... At the corner of the street...'

'So that you never suspected?'

He was puffing gently at his pipe, looking benevolent as he watched the young face clouded by anxiety.

'I'm sure a young woman like yourself would never venture to lie to the police... You realize how serious that would be, particularly now that we are trying our best to get hold of your father's murderer.'

'Yes, Monsieur.'

She had taken a handkerchief from her pocket and was dabbing her eyes, sniffing, ready to cry in real earnest.

'What pretty earrings you're wearing.'

'Oh, Monsieur...'

'Yes, they're very pretty. May I have a look? It almost seems as if you'd got a boyfriend already.'

'Oh, no, Monsieur.'

'They're made of real gold, and the two garnets are also real.'

'No, Monsieur... Mother thought so too, but...'

'But what?'

'... I told her they weren't...'

'Because you bought these earrings yourself?'

'Yes, Monsieur.'

'Didn't you give your pay-packet to your parents?'

'Yes, Monsieur. But we'd agreed that I should keep my overtime pay for myself.'

'And you bought your handbag too?'

'Yes, Monsieur.'

'Tell me, my dear...'

She looked up in surprise, and Maigret began to laugh.

'Have you finished?'

'What, Monsieur?'

'Trying to fool me.'

'I promise you...'

'One moment, do you mind?...Hello? Switchboard? Put me through to the *Prisunic* in the Rue Réaumur, will you?'

'Listen, Monsieur...'

He signed to her to be quiet and she burst into tears.

'Hello, *Prisunic*?...Will you put me through to the manager?...Is that the manager speaking?...Police Judiciaire speaking. I'd like some information, please, about one of your assistants, Mademoiselle Francine Tremblet...Yes...What's that? Three months ago? Thank you...I may call on you later in the day...'

And turning to the girl:

'So there we are, Mademoiselle!'

'I was going to have told you...'

'When?'

'I was waiting to pluck up the courage...'

'How did it happen?'

"You won't tell mother?...It's because of her that I didn't tell you right away...It's going to mean more weeping and wailing... If you knew maman!...As I told you, I sometimes travelled on the métro with father...To begin with he didn't want me to go to work, and particularly not to take that job...You understand?... But maman insisted that we weren't well off, that she found it hard enough to make ends meet, that it was an unexpected opportunity...It was she who introduced me to the manager...Then one morning, about three months ago, when I had left my father at the corner of the Rue du Sentier, I realized that I'd left without any money...Mother had asked me to buy various things in the neighbourhood...I ran after papa. I saw that he didn't stop at Couvreur and Bellechasse's, but went on through the crowd...

'I thought to myself that he was probably going to buy some cigarettes or something...I was in a hurry...I went to the shop... Then as I had a free moment during the day I went along to papa's office ... And there they told me that he'd not been working there for a long time.'

'Did you speak to him that evening?'

'No ... Next day, I followed him ... He went towards the embankment and at one point he turned round and saw me. Then he said:

'"So much the better!"'

'Why *so much the better*?'

'Because he didn't like my working in a shop. He explained to me that he'd been wanting to get me out of it for a long time ... He told me that he'd changed his job, that he'd got a much better one, where he didn't have to be shut up indoors all day. That was when he took me into a shop and bought me these earrings ...

'"If your mother asks where you got them, tell her they're fake ..."'

'And since then?'

'I'd stopped working, but I didn't tell mother. Father made up my pay. From time to time we used to meet in town and go together to the pictures or the Jardin des Plantes.'

'You don't know what your father did all day?'

'No ... But I could see why he said nothing about it to mother. If he'd given her more money it would have made no difference ... There would always have been just as much mess at home ... It's hard to explain to someone who hasn't lived with us ... Maman means very well, but ...'

'Thank you, Mademoiselle.'

'Are you going to tell?'

'I don't know yet ... Did you ever meet your father with anybody?'

'No.'

'He never gave you any sort of address?'

'We always arranged to meet on the banks of the Seine, near the Pont-Neuf or the Pont des Arts ...'

'One last question: when you met him on these occasions, was he always wearing the clothes he wore in the Rue des Dames?'

'Only once, a fortnight ago, he had on a grey suit that I'd never seen him in and that he never wore at home.'

'Thank you ... Of course you've spoken to nobody about this?'

'Nobody.'

'No boyfriend in the offing?'

'No, honestly.'

He was in a good humour, quite groundlessly, since the problem was becoming more complicated instead of simpler. Perhaps he had been glad to find that his last night's hunch had not let him down? Perhaps, too, he was beginning to take a keen interest in Tremblet, the nobody who had spent years of his life concealing things and deceiving his lugubrious Juliette.

'Send in the old gentleman, Lucas...'

'He's Théodore Jussiaume, bird-fancier and vendor, Quai du Louvre. It's about the photograph.'

'It's about the photograph...'

'You recognized the victim?'

'I certainly did, Monsieur! One of my best customers.'

And so a new aspect of Maurice Tremblet was revealed. Once a week at least he spent quite a long while in Théodore Jussiaume's shop, which was loud with birdsong. He had a passion for canaries, and bought a great many of them.

'I've sold him at least three aviaries of the largest size.'

'Did you deliver them at his home?'

'No, Monsieur. He took them away himself in a taxi.'

'Did you not know his address?'

'Not even his name. One day he happened to mention that he was Monsieur Charles, and that was what we always called him, my wife and I and the assistants. He was a connoisseur, a real one. I often wondered why he didn't enter his canaries in competitions, for he had some real prizewinners among them.'

'Did he strike you as a wealthy man?'

'No, Monsieur... Comfortably off... He wasn't closefisted, but he didn't waste his money.'

'In short, he was a good fellow?'

'An excellent fellow and a customer such as I seldom get.'

'He never brought anyone with him to your shop?'

'Never...'

'Thank you, Monsieur Jussiaume.'

But Monsieur Jussiaume was not ready to leave yet.

'There's one thing that puzzles me and worries me a bit . . . If the papers are telling the truth, there were no birds in the flat in the Rue des Dames . . . If all the canaries he had bought from me had been there it would surely have been mentioned, don't you see? Because there must have been about two hundred of them, and that's not an everyday thing . . .'

'In other words you're wondering if these birds . . .'

'Aren't somewhere or other without anyone to look after them, now that Monsieur Charles is dead . . .'

'Well, Monsieur Jussiaume, I promise you that if we find the canaries we'll let you know, so that you can attend to them if it's not too late.'

'Many thanks . . . It's my wife that's been worrying, chiefly.'

'A very good day to you, Monsieur Jussiaume.'

And, once the door was closed:

'What do you think of that, Lucas old man? Have you got the reports?'

The pathologist's report, to begin with. Dr. Paul, in his conclusions, implied that Maurice Tremblet's death had really been accidental.

Forty lines of technical details of which the Superintendent understood nothing.

'Hello! Dr. Paul? . . . Will you be kind enough to explain to me what you meant?'

That the bullet ought not to have pierced the victim's thorax, since it was not powerful, and if it had not accidentally struck a soft spot between two ribs it would never have reached the heart, but merely produced a superficial wound.

'He was unlucky, that's all!' concluded the doctor with the flowing beard. 'The shot had to be fired from a certain angle . . . and the man had to be in a certain position . . .'

'Do you think the murderer knew all this and aimed accordingly?'

'I think the murderer was an idiot . . . An idiot who's not a bad marksman, since he hit the man, but who would have been incapable of aiming so as to make sure of hitting the heart . . . To my mind, he's only got a hazy knowledge of firearms.'

And this report was confirmed by that of the ballistics expert Gastinne-Renette, according to whom the bullet—a twelve millimetre lead bullet—had been fired with an air-gun such as are used in fairgrounds.

One curious detail: the murderer had carefully filed down the tip of the bullet to make it sharper.

To a question from Maigret, the expert replied:

'Not at all! By this means he did not make it more lethal, quite the contrary! For a blunt bullet does more damage to the victim's flesh than a pointed one. The man who behaved in this way thought himself very clever, but knew nothing about firearms.'

'In short, an amateur?'

'An amateur who had misunderstood something that he'd read somewhere, maybe in some detective story.'

That was how far they had got by 11 a.m. on the day after Maurice Tremblet's death.

In the Rue des Dames, Juliette was wrestling with all her everyday problems, aggravated by those that result from the death of the head of the household, particularly when a murder is involved. To top everything, journalists assailed her from morning till night, and photographers lay in wait on the staircase.

'What did the Superintendent want to know?'

'Nothing, maman.'

'You're not telling me the truth...Nobody ever tells me the truth. Even your father used to lie to me, he lied to me for years...'

Her tears flowed; she sniffled as she spoke, as she did her housework, as she hustled her children, who had had to be dressed in black from head to foot for the funeral next day.

Somewhere, two hundred canaries were waiting to be given their daily food.

And Maigret said to Lucas with a sigh:

'All we can do is wait.'

Wait until the publication of the photographs produced some result, until somebody recognized Maurice Tremblet or Monsieur Charles!

During the past seven years, he must surely have been seen somewhere? If he changed his clothes away from home, if he bought birds and large aviaries he must have had somewhere to go, a room, a flat or a house? He may have had a landlord, a concierge, a char-woman. Friends, maybe? Perhaps even a mistress?

It was all a bit crazy, and yet Maigret's feelings were somehow stirred by the case, although he would not have liked to admit it. *Nobodies don't get murdered.*

And now he had begun to take an interest in this nobody, who had seemed so dim to begin with, this man whom he had never seen, whom he did not know from Adam and who had died in such an idiotic fashion, sitting on the edge of his bed beside dreary Juli-ette, struck by a bullet which ought never to have killed him.

A fairground rifle!... The sort of thing with which you shoot at clay pipes or at a little ball dancing on the tip of a jet of water.

And the murderer himself seemed to have been an insignificant fellow, patiently filing down the bullet in order to make it more lethal, and leaving behind him, in his bedroom at the *Hôtel Excelsior,* nothing but a dirty comb with broken teeth.

The murderer had a liver complaint. That was practically all that was known about him.

Lucas had gone off hunting again. A commonplace and unre-warding job: all the gunsmiths of Paris to be visited, then all the owners of shooting booths, for the man might have bought his gun from one of them. Inspector Janvier, meanwhile, was questioning the tradespeople of the Quai de la Mégisserie and the Quai du Louvre, and the bistros in the neighbourhood of the Pont-Neuf and the Pont des Arts, where Tremblet used to meet his daughter and where he might perhaps have had an occasional drink.

Finally Torrence, the big fellow, was questioning taxi drivers, since a fare carrying an outsize birdcage is hardly an everyday occurrence.

Maigret, meanwhile, was just sitting on the terrace of the *Brasserie Dauphine,* in the shade of the red and yellow striped awning, with a freshly drawn glass of beer in front of him. He was peacefully smoking his pipe, waiting till it was time to go home to lunch, and intermittently a brief frown clouded his forehead.

Something was worrying him, but he could not decide what it

was. What had he been told, that morning or the night before, which had struck him, which must be important and which he had forgotten?

An insignificant little remark. And yet he had noted it, he was sure of that. He had even reflected that it might hold the key to the mystery.

He pondered. Could it have been while he was questioning the young girl with the high bosom and the red hat? . . . He ran over, in his mind, all that she had said to him . . . He pictured the scene in the Rue du Sentier, when she had run after her father, who was not going to his office.

The earrings? No . . . The father and daughter used to pay clandestine visits to the cinema . . . Francine, in short, was Tremblet's favourite. He must have felt proud to go out with her and buy her expensive presents secretly . . .

But that wasn't it . . . The little remark belonged elsewhere . . . Let's see . . . He had been standing in a slanting ray of sunlight, amid that fine golden dust that lingers so long in a room where the beds have just been made.

It was in the Rue des Dames . . . The door had been open on to the kitchen . . . It was Juliette speaking . . . What could she have said that for one moment had given him the impression that he was on the verge of understanding everything?

'Joseph! What do I owe you?'

'Four francs, Superintendent.'

All the way home he was trying to remember that little sentence. He went on thinking about it while he ate, elbows on the table, in his shirtsleeves, and Madame Maigret, seeing him preoccupied, held her tongue.

She could not, however, resist murmuring as she set the fruit upon the table:

'Don't *you* think it's revolting that a man should . . .'

Of course! But Madame Maigret did not know Juliette. She did not know the flat in the Rue des Dames.

The little sentence was almost on the tip of his tongue. So his wife must have helped him involuntarily.

'Don't *you* think it's revolting...'

A tiny effort. It needed only a tiny effort, but the flash did not come, and he flung his napkin down upon the table, filled his pipe, poured himself a glass of calvados and went to lean on the windowsill until it was time to go back to the Quai des Orfèvres.

3
On the Trail of an Angler

At six o'clock the same evening, Maigret and Lucas got out of a taxi on the Quai de la Gare, beyond the Pont d'Austerlitz, accompanied by a little man with limp and shaggy hair who looked like a tramp.

And it was then, suddenly, that Maigret had an illumination, and the little sentence he had hunted for in vain recurred to his memory:

'He had a horror of noise...'

Tremblet, the nobody, the poor fellow who had been killed, in his shirt, rubbing his feet as he sat on the edge of the bed, Tremblet who lived in the Rue des Dames and who had five children, one more mischievous than the other, and a wife who spent her days moaning, Tremblet had a horror of noise.

There are people who have a horror of certain smells, others who shun heat or cold. Maigret remembered one divorce case in which the husband, after twenty-six or twenty-seven years of married life, pleaded for a separation on the grounds that he had never been able to get used to his wife's odour.

Tremblet had a horror of noise. And Tremblet, when circumstances that were still wrapped in mystery had enabled him to leave the offices of Messrs. Couvreur and Bellechasse—in the noisy Rue du Sentier—had taken refuge on this quay, one of the most deserted in all Paris.

A broad embankment, beside which several rows of barges lay idle. An embankment that had a provincial flavour about it, with one-storey houses overlooking the Seine, a few blocks of flats, and bistros into which nobody seemed to go, and courtyards where, surprisingly, hens were scratching about on dunghills.

It was the ragged cripple, old Cerise, who had discovered the place; old Cerise who, as he declared grandly, resided under the nearest bridge, and who had been the first to turn up at Police Headquarters.

While he was waiting, three others had come, of different types but all of them down-and-outs, all belonging to that species of creature only to be found nowadays on the embankments of Paris.

'I'm the first, aren't I, Superintendent? I've been waiting half an hour . . . The others hadn't got here yet . . . So about the reward . . .'

'What reward?'

'Isn't there a reward?'

That would have been too unfair. The old fellow was indignant in anticipation.

'There's always a reward, even for a stray dog . . . And I've come to tell you where that poor guy what got killed used to live . . .'

'We'll see about giving you something if the information proves worth it.'

And there had been arguments and bargaining: a hundred francs, fifty francs, twenty francs—the lowest price. They had taken him along with them. Now they were standing in front of a small one-storey house, whitewashed, with closed shutters.

'Almost every morning I used to see him fishing, just here where the tug is . . . That was how we got acquainted . . . To begin with he wasn't very good at it, but I gave him some advice . . . He used hemp-seed for bait. And thanks to me he used to catch some nice roach for frying . . . At eleven o'clock sharp he would roll up his lines and tie up his rods and go home. That was how I found out where he lived.'

Maigret rang on the off-chance, and an old-fashioned bell echoed curiously in the empty house. Lucas tried out his master keys and eventually got the lock to play.

'I'll stay around,' said old Cerise, 'in case you may need me.'

There was something uncanny about this house that reeked of emptiness and where, nonetheless, sounds could be heard. It took a moment to realize that it was caused by the fluttering of birds.

For there were aviaries in both the ground floor rooms, and these rooms were almost eerie because apart from the cages they were almost totally unfurnished.

Maigret and Lucas went to and fro, and their voices echoed; they flung open doors, creating draughts that puffed out the curtains of the front room, the only one where there were any on the windows.

The wallpaper must have been there for countless years; it had faded to an indeterminate colour and showed the marks of all the furniture that had leaned against it, of all the tenants who had ever lived there.

The first thing that Maigret did, to Lucas's surprise, was to put fresh water into the birdcages and fill the trays with little shiny yellow grains.

'You see, old man? Here, at least, he was free from noise.'

There was an old-fashioned wicker armchair beside one of the windows, a table, two or three chairs that did not match, and on the shelves a collection of cloak-and-dagger stories and historical romances.

On the first floor a bed, a brass bedstead covered with a fine red satin eiderdown, shimmering in the sunlight, that would have rejoiced the heart of a prosperous farmer's wife.

A kitchen. Plates, a frying pan; and Maigret, sniffing it, recognized a strong smell of fish. Moreover there were still fishbones and scales in the dustbin, which had not been emptied for several days. In a closet there was a whole set of fishing rods, neatly arranged.

'Don't *you* think it's a funny idea?'

Evidently, Tremblet had his own notion of happiness. The peace of a house which no one entered but himself. Fishing on the banks of the Seine. He had a couple of folding stools, one of which was of the latest model and probably very expensive. Birds in handsome cages. And books, heaps of books in gaudy covers which he could enjoy in peace.

The strangest thing was the contrast between some of these objects and the squalor of the setting. There was among other things an English fishing rod which must have cost several thousand francs. In a drawer of the sole chest of drawers in the house there was a gold lighter bearing the initials M.T. and an expensive-looking cigarette case.

'Can you understand it, Chief?'

Yes, Maigret felt he could understand it. Particularly when he discovered some perfectly useless objects, such as an elaborate electric train.

'Don't you see, he'd been longing for these things for so many years...'

'Do you suppose he used to play with the electric train?'

'I shouldn't be surprised...Did you never treat yourself to something you'd dreamed of all through your childhood?'

Presumably, Tremblet came here in the morning, as another man might go to the office. He went fishing in front of his house. He returned to the Rue des Dames for lunch, perhaps after sometimes eating the fish he had caught. He looked after his birds. He read; he must have read for hours at a time, in his wicker armchair beside the window, without anyone to disturb him, without shouts and cries going on around him.

Some days he used to go to the cinema, occasionally with his daughter. And he had bought her a pair of gold earrings.

'Do you think he'd come into a legacy, or else stolen the money he spent like this?'

Maigret made no answer. He went on roaming through the house, in front of which old Cerise mounted guard.

'Go back to the Quai des Orfèvres. Circulate all the banks in Paris to find out whether Tremblet had an account there. Enquire from solicitors...'

It seemed unlikely, however. The man had too much prudence of the old peasant sort to deposit his money where it could be traced.

'Are you going to stay here?'

'I think I'll spend the night here...Listen...Bring me some sandwiches and a few bottles of beer...Ring my wife and tell her I shall probably not be coming back...See that the papers don't publish anything about this house.'

'Wouldn't you like me to come and keep you company or send an inspector?'

'It's not worthwhile.'

He was not armed. What was the point?

The hours that followed were not unlike those that Tremblet

must have spent in the house. Maigret looked through a number of books in the strange library, and found that most of them had been read and re-read.

He spent a long time examining the fishing rods, for it had occurred to him that, for a man like Tremblet, they might prove an ideal hiding-place.

'Two thousand francs a month for seven years.'

It was quite a sum; not to mention all the further expenses that the man incurred. The hoard must be hidden somewhere.

At eight o'clock a taxi stopped at the door, while Maigret was searching the birdcages for a possible hiding-place.

It was Lucas, accompanied by a girl who looked in a very bad temper.

'As I couldn't ring you up, I didn't know what to do,' the sergeant said in some embarrassment. 'In the end I thought the best thing was to bring her along. She was his mistress.'

A tall dark girl with a pale face and hard features, who stared at the Superintendent suspiciously and remarked:

'I hope I'm not going to be accused of killing him?'

'Come in, come in,' Maigret said softly. 'You must know the house better than I do.'

'Me? I've never set foot in the filthy shack . . . I didn't even know of its existence until five minutes ago . . . Not to mention that the place doesn't smell nice . . .'

It was not her eardrums that were sensitive; it was her nose. And she began by wiping the chair on which she was invited to sit down.

4
The Fourth Life of Maurice Tremblet

Olga-Jeanne-Marie Poissonneau, twenty-nine years of age, born at Saint-Joris-sur-Isère, unemployed, residing at *Hôtel Beauséjour*, Rue Lepic, Paris XVIIIe.

And the tall, moon-faced girl hurriedly added:

'Please to observe, Superintendent, that I came forward of my own free will. As soon as I saw his picture in the papers, and in spite of the fact that it might spell trouble for me, I said to myself...'

'Did Tremblet visit you at your hotel?'

'Twice a week...'

'So that the proprietor and the staff must have seen him there?'

'Oh, they knew him very well. It's been going on for five years now...'

'And have they seen the photograph too?'

'What do you mean?'

She bit her lip, for she had finally caught on.

'Well, the landlord did ask me whether the photo wasn't of Monsieur Charles... I'd have come along all the same.'

'I'm sure you would. So you knew him under the name of Monsieur Charles?'

'I'd met him by chance outside a cinema in the Boulevard Rochechouart... I was a waitress at that time in a *prix fixe* restaurant in the Place Clichy. He followed me... He told me he only came to Paris from time to time.'

'Twice a week...'

'Yes... The second or third time I met him he took me back to the hotel, and he went upstairs with me... That's how it began... It was he who insisted on my leaving my job...'

Why had Tremblet picked her? Probably because Juliette was small and thin, a faded blonde, whereas this girl was tall, dark and soft-looking. The latter, particularly; presumably he had believed her moon-face was a sign of softness, perhaps of sentimentality.

'I soon realized that he was batty.'

'Batty?'

'A crank, anyhow... He talked of nothing but taking me into the country... That was his dream. When he came to see me we had to go into the public gardens and sit on a bench... For months he nagged at me to spend a couple of days in the country with him, and he got his way at last... I can tell you it wasn't much fun...'

'Did he keep you?'

'He gave me just enough to live on... I had to pretend I made my own dresses... He'd have liked me to spend my days sewing and mending. Talk about freaks!...Lots of times I've tried to get rid of him and told him a few home truths, but he clung on, he came back with presents and wrote me long letters...What are you laughing at?'

'Nothing...'

Poor Tremblet, seeking a change from a Juliette and landing himself with an Olga!

'So you must have spent a good part of your time together quarrelling?'

'Part of it, yes...'

'And you never had the curiosity to follow him and find out where he lived?'

'He told me it was somewhere near Orléans, and I believed him...In any case, I was going to get rid of him.'

'You had another friend, obviously.'

'I had friends, sort of...But nothing serious.'

'Did you tell them about him?'

'You don't suppose I was proud of him! He looked like the verger of a poor parish.'

'You never saw him about with anybody else?'

'Never...I tell you his idea of fun was sitting with me on park benches...Is it true he was very rich?'

'Who told you that?'

'I read in the papers that he'd probably inherited a fortune...And here I am left without a penny!... *You'll admit it's just my luck...*'

She sounded just like Juliette.

'Do you think it's going to mean trouble for me?'

'No, no. Your evidence will be checked, that's all. Is that clear, Lucas?'

And enquiries confirmed her evidence, including the rows she had with her lover each time he visited her, for she had a vicious temper.

Maigret had spent that night and part of the next day searching through every nook and cranny of the house on the Quai de la Gare, but he had found nothing.

He had felt quite sorry to leave the house, where he had, as it were, become involved in the private life of his nobody, and he had

had it discreetly watched day and night by detectives posted in the neighbourhood.

'We'll see what comes of it,' he had said to the Chief of the Police Judiciaire. 'It may take a long time, but I think it'll yield results in the end.'

Enquiries were made about Francine, who might have had a lover. Olga's movements were watched, and an eye was kept on the down-and-outs of the Quai de la Gare.

There was nothing to be got from banks or solicitors. Telegrams were sent to Tremblet's native Cantal, but it seemed certain that he had not come into any legacy.

The weather was still warm. Tremblet had been buried. His wife and children were preparing to leave for the provinces, for they could no longer afford to live in Paris.

The police now knew about Tremblet's life in the Rue des Dames, his life in the Quai de la Gare, his life with Olga... They knew him as a keen angler, a bird fancier and a reader of romantic fiction.

It was a waiter in a café who disclosed what might be described as the dead man's fourth existence. He appeared one morning at the Quai des Orfèvres and asked to speak to Maigret.

'I'm sorry not to have come sooner, but I was working at Les Sables d'Olonne for the summer season... I saw the photo in the paper, and I nearly wrote to you, then it went out of my head... I'm practically certain this was the guy who came for years to play billiards in the brasserie where I used to work, at the corner of the Boulevard Saint-Germain and the Rue de Seine.'

'He didn't play billiards all by himself?'

'Of course not... He used to come with a tall thin fellow, who had ginger hair and a moustache... The other, the man who was killed, called him Théodore, and they were on very intimate terms... They used to come in every day at the same time, about four o'clock, and leave again just before six... Théodore would have apéritifs, but the other guy never touched alcohol.'

That is how one picks up people's tracks as they come and go through a great city. Tremblet's had been discovered in the bird-fancier's shop on the Quai du Louvre and in a shady hotel in the Rue Lepic.

And now it became known that for years he had frequented a quiet brasserie on the Boulevard Saint-Germain, in the company of a tall fellow with red hair.

'Is it a long time since you saw them?'

'I left the place over a year ago.'

Torrence, Janvier, Lucas and other detectives then started visiting all the cafés and brasseries of Paris where they have billiard tables, and the trail of the two men was picked up again in one not far from the Pont-Neuf, where they had played billiards together for several months.

But nobody knew anything more about Théodore than the fact that he was a hard drinker and had the habit of brushing up his moustache with the back of his hand after every mouthful.

'He seemed to be in humble circumstances, and was poorly dressed...'

It was invariably Tremblet who paid.

For weeks, the police searched everywhere for Théodore, and Théodore remained untraceable, until one day Maigret happened to think of calling on Messrs. Couvreur et Bellechasse.

He was received by Monsieur Mauvre.

'Théodore? Why, we had an employee of that name a long time ago... Let's see... It's over twelve years since he left the firm... Of course he knew Monsieur Tremblet here... This Théodore—I could discover his surname in our books—was a messenger, and we had to get rid of him because he was always drunk and then permitted himself shocking liberties.'

His name was traced: Ballard. Théodore Ballard. But the lodging houses of Paris and the suburbs were searched in vain for any signs of a Théodore Ballard.

One fresh but inconclusive clue: five years previously a certain Théodore Ballard had worked for a few weeks at the Montmartre street fair, on a merry-go-round. He had broken his arm one night when he was drunk, and he had not been seen again.

This was obviously the man from the *Hôtel Excelsior*, the man with the air-gun.

How had he happened to renew acquaintance with the cashier of the firm where he had once been a messenger? In any case, the two men had formed the habit of meeting and playing billiards together.

Had Théodore discovered his friend's secret? Had he scented hidden treasure in the house on the Quai de la Gare? Or had there been a quarrel between the two friends?

'Keep up the watch on the embankment...'

And it was kept up. It had become a joke at Headquarters:

'What are you doing tonight?'

'Looking after the canaries...'

And yet in the long run it yielded a positive result, for one night a tall thin fellow with a reddish moustache, slouching along like a beggar, actually broke into the house.

Torrence pounced upon him, and the man begged for mercy.

If the victim had been shabby enough, so was the murderer. Théodore was a pitiful sight. He must have been several days without food, as he prowled about the streets and along the embankments. He probably suspected that the house was being watched, for he had waited a long time before venturing into it. In the end he had been unable to hold out any longer.

'Well, it can't be helped,' he sighed. 'It's better this way. I'm too hungry.'

At two in the morning he was still in Maigret's office, with beer and sandwiches before him, answering all the questions put to him.

'I'm no good, I know, but what you don't know is that he, Maurice, was a mean bastard... He'd never told me for instance, that he had a house on the quay... He didn't trust me... He was willing to play billiards with me but as far as anything else was concerned he kept himself to himself... D'you understand?... I sometimes borrowed small sums from him, but I had to pry them out of him...

'I may have gone too far... I hadn't a penny. I was in arrears with my rent and then he told me it was the last time, that he was sick of playing the sucker and that he was bored with billiards anyway...

'In short, he was giving me the sack like a servant.

'And that was when I followed him, and understood what sort of life he was leading, and I said to myself that there must be some money in the house...'

'You killed him to begin with,' growled Maigret, sucking his pipe.

'That only proves that I'm not mercenary, because it was really anger that made me do it ... Otherwise I'd have gone first to the Quai de la Gare when I knew he wasn't there.'

That wretched house was searched by the most knowing experts ten times over and it was only a year later, when it had been sold and the whole affair had been forgotten, that the hoard was discovered.

It was neither in the walls nor under the floorboards, but hidden in the depths of a disused closet on the first floor.

It was a fairly large parcel, done up in oilcloth, and containing two million and several hundred thousand franc notes.

When Maigret heard the figure mentioned, he made a rapid calculation and understood; he jumped into a taxi, and got off in front of the Pavillon de Flore.

'Have you the list of all the winners in the National Lottery?'

'Not the complete list, for certain winners prefer to remain anonymous, and they're entitled to by law. For instance, seven years ago ...'

It was Tremblet, Tremblet who had won three million and carried them off, in notes, under his arm, Tremblet who had never breathed a word of it to anyone, Tremblet who had a horror of noise and who, henceforward, had treated himself to the modest delights he had so much longed for.

'Nobodies don't get murdered ...'

And yet it had really been a nobody who had died, clad only in his shirt, sitting on the edge of his bed and rubbing his feet before slipping between the sheets.

15 August, 1946

Sale by Auction

Maigret pushed back his plate and his table, got up, grunted and shook himself, and automatically lifted the lid of the stove.

'Back to work, lads! We'll go to bed early.'

And the others, sitting round the big inn table, looked at him resignedly. Frédéric Michaux, the landlord, whose beard had grown thick in the last three days, rose first and went towards the bar.

'What will you...'

'No!' cried Maigret, 'that's enough. We've had enough wine and calvados, and another glass and another...'

They had all reached the point of weariness when one's eyelids tingle and one's whole body aches. Julia, Frédéric's wife or nearly so, carried back into the kitchen a dish containing the congealed remains of some red beans. Thérèse, the maid, was wiping her eyes, not because she had been crying but because she had a cold in the head.

'When do we begin again?' she asked. 'When I've cleared the table?'

'It's eight o'clock. We begin again at eight o'clock.'

'Then I'll bring in the tablecloth and the cards...'

It was warm, indeed too warm, in the inn, but outside the wind drove flurries of frozen rain through the night.

'Sit where you were, Père Nicolas... You, Monsieur Groux, you hadn't got here yet...'

The landlord interrupted. 'It was when I heard Groux's footsteps outside that I told Thérèse to put the cards on the table.'

'Do I have to pretend to come in again?' grumbled Groux, a peasant some six foot tall and as broad as a kitchen dresser.

They looked like actors rehearsing a scene for the twentieth time, mindlessly, with limp gestures and blank eyes. Maigret himself, the producer, sometimes could scarcely convince himself that it was all real. The place he was in, for instance! Imagine spending three days in an inn miles from the nearest village, in the middle of the marshes of La Vendée!

Its name was Le Pont du Grau, and there was in fact a bridge, a long wooden bridge over a sort of canal whose muddy waters rose twice a day with the tide. But you could not see the sea. You could only see marshy meadows intersected by ditches, and far off against the horizon the flat roofs of farms, which here they called *cabanes*.

Why was there an inn by the roadside? To attract duck and plover shooters? There was a red-painted petrol pump, and on the gable-end a big blue advertisement for a brand of chocolate.

On the other side of the bridge was a shack, a regular rabbit hutch, the home of old Nicolas, who fished eels. Three hundred yards farther on, a largish farm with long low buildings: Groux's property.

... On January 15 ... at 1 p.m. precisely ... at La Mulatière ... the sale by public auction of a farm ... 30 hectares of marshland meadow ... livestock and farm implements ... agricultural material ... furniture, crockery ... To be sold for cash down.

Everything had started from there. For years life had gone on just the same at the inn each evening. Old Nicolas would arrive, invariably half drunk, and before sitting down to his *chopine* he would drink a tot at the bar. Then Groux would come along from his *cabane*. Thérèse spread a red cloth on the table and brought in the cards and the dice. They had to wait for the exciseman to make the fourth, or, failing him, Julia would make up the party.

Now on January 14, the day before the sale, there had been two extra guests in the inn, peasants who had come from some distance for the auction, one, Borchain, from near Angoulême, the other, Canut, from Saint-Jean-d'Angély.

'One minute,' said Maigret as the landlord was starting to shuffle the cards. 'Borchain went to bed before eight o'clock, as soon as he'd finished eating. Who showed him to his room?'

'I did,' replied Frédéric.

'Had he been drinking?'

'Not that much. He wanted to know who the gloomy-looking fellow was, and I told him it was Groux, whose property was going to be sold. Then he asked me how Groux had managed to go broke with such good marsh-meadows as he'd got, and I...'

'That'll do!' growled Groux.

The big fellow was in a black mood. He did not want to admit that he had never taken much care of his land or his cattle, and he blamed heaven for his ruin.

'All right. At that point, how many people had seen Borchain's wallet?'

'Everybody had. He'd taken it out of his pocket while he was eating to show us a picture of his wife... So we could see it was full of notes... Even if we hadn't seen it we'd have known, since he'd come to buy and knew he'd have to pay cash.'

'So you, Canut, also had more than a hundred thousand francs on you?'

'A hundred and fifty thousand... I didn't want to go higher.'

On his arrival at the place, Maigret, who was then at the head of the crime squad in Nantes, had frowned as he looked Frédéric Michaux up and down. Michaux, who was about forty-five, with a broken nose and a sports pullover, looked most unlike a country innkeeper.

'Look here... Haven't you the feeling we've already met somewhere?'

'No point in wasting your time... You're quite right, Superintendent... But I've gone straight since then.'

Procuring in the Ternes district, assault and battery, illegal betting and slot machines... In short Frédéric Michaux, innkeeper at Pont du Grau in the remotest corner of La Vendée, was better known to the police as Fred the Boxer.

'You'll probably recognize Julia too...You jugged us together, ten years ago...But you'll see how respectable she's become.'

It was true. Julia, who had become fat and flabby, sluttish and greasy-haired, shuffling about in slippers between the kitchen and the bar parlour, in no wise resembled the Julia of the Place des Ternes; and the most unexpected thing was that her cooking was quite first rate.

'We took Thérèse along with us...She's an orphan from a home.'

Eighteen years old, tall and slender with a pointed nose, a comical mouth and a cheeky look.

'Are we to play in earnest?' queried the exciseman, whose name was Gentil.

'Play as you did the other night. You, Canut, why didn't you go to bed?'

'I was watching the game...' muttered the peasant.

'That's to say he kept after me,' Thérèse corrected him crossly, 'trying to make me promise to come up to his room.'

Maigret observed that Fred cast a hostile glance at the other man, while Julia was watching Fred.

Good...they were in their right places...And the other evening, too, it had been raining...Borchain's room was on the ground floor, at the end of the passage...In that passage there were three other doors: one leading into the kitchen, one on to the stairway down to the cellar, and the third bearing the number 100.

Maigret heaved a sigh and passed a weary hand over his forehead. He had been here three days, and he felt steeped in the smell of the house; its atmosphere clung to his skin till he felt quite sick.

And yet what other course could he pursue? On the 14th, shortly before midnight, while the game of cards was proceeding somewhat half-heartedly, Fred had sniffed repeatedly. He had called Julia, who was in the kitchen.

'Isn't there something burning in the oven?'

He had got up and opened the door into the passage.

'God almighty, there's an awful smell of burning here!'

Groux had followed him, and Thérèse. It came from the guest's bedroom. He had knocked at the door, then opened it, since there was no lock.

The mattress was slowly burning, a mattress that gave out an acrid smell of scorched wool grease. On the mattress lay Borchain, in his shirt and underpants, with his skull fractured.

The inn had a telephone. Maigret was roused at one in the morning. At four o'clock he turned up in the pouring rain, red-nosed and frozen-fingered.

Borchain's wallet had disappeared. The bedroom window was closed. Nobody could have got in from outside, for Michaux had a fierce Alsatian dog.

It was impossible to arrest everyone. But all of them were suspect except Canut, the only one who had not left the inn parlour all evening.

'Come on, fellows!... I'm here to listen and watch you... Do exactly what you did on the 14th at the same time...'

The sale had been postponed to a future date. All day on the 15th people had been filing past the house, which had been locked up on Maigret's orders.

Now it was the 16th. Maigret had practically never left the room, except to snatch a few hours' sleep. Nor had any of the others. They were sick of seeing one another from morning till night, of hearing the same questions asked and of repeating the same gestures.

Julia did the cooking. The outside world was forgotten. It took an effort to realize that there were people living elsewhere, in towns, who were not endlessly repeating:

'Let's see... I had just played hearts, which was trumps... Groux put down his hand saying: "I give up... I've not got a single card... Just my rotten luck!"'

'Then he got up...'

'Get up, Groux!' ordered Maigret. 'Do what you did the other day.'

The big man shrugged his shoulders.

'How many more times are you going to send me to the lavatory?' he growled. 'Ask Frédéric... Ask Nicolas... Don't I go at least twice every evening? What d'you expect me to do with the four or five bottles of wine I drink in a day?'

He spat, then made for the door, walked down the passage and pushed open the door marked 100.

'Well, have I got to stay there now?'

'As long as is necessary, yes . . . The rest of you, what did you do while he was gone?'

The exciseman was laughing nervously at Groux's anger, and there was something hysterical about his laughter. He was the least tough of them all, and was obviously on edge.

'I told Gentil and Nicolas that it was going to mean trouble,' Fred admitted.

'What was going to mean trouble?'

'Groux and his farm . . . He had always believed the sale would not take place, that he'd be able to borrow some money. When they came to stick up the poster he threatened the bailiff with his gun . . . At his age, when you've always owned your own land, it's not easy to begin again as somebody else's farmhand . . .'

Groux had returned and was staring at them fiercely.

'So what?' he shouted. 'Have you finished or not? Was it me that killed the man and set fire to the mattress? Why not say so at once and stick me in jail . . . The way things are now . . .'

'Where were you, Julia? . . . I don't think you're in the right place . . .'

'I was peeling vegetables in the kitchen . . . We were expecting a crowd for lunch because of the sale . . . I'd ordered two legs of mutton, and we've only finished one of them . . .'

'Thérèse?'

'I'd gone up into my room.'

'When was that?'

'Soon after Monsieur Groux came back.'

'Well, let's go up there together . . . The rest of you carry on . . . You started playing again?'

'Not right away . . . Groux didn't want to . . . We talked . . . I went to fetch a packet of cigarettes from the bar . . .'

'Come along, Thérèse.'

The room where Borchain had died was strategically placed. The staircase was only three steps away. So Thérèse could have...

The girl's room was a narrow one, with an iron bedstead and a chair on which clothes were lying.

'What did you come up here for?'

'To write...'

'To write what?'

'That we shouldn't have a moment alone together next day...' She was looking him in the eyes, defiantly.

'You know very well what I'm talking about... I've understood from your questions and the way you looked at me... The old woman suspects... She's always after us... I begged Fred to take me away, and we'd decided to make a bolt for it in the spring.'

'Why in the spring?'

'I don't know... Fred fixed the date... We were going to Panama, where he once lived, and we were going to set up a bistro there together...'

'How long did you stay in your room?'

'Not long... I heard the old woman coming upstairs... She asked me what I was doing... I said *nothing*... She hates me and I hate her... I could swear she guessed what we were planning...'

Thérèse returned Maigret's gaze without flinching. She was one of those girls who knows what they want and are determined to get it.

'You don't think that Julia would rather see Fred in prison than have him go off with you?'

'That's quite likely!'

'What was she going to her bedroom for?'

'To take off her girdle... She needs a rubber girdle to hold what's left of her together...'

Thérèse had the pointed teeth and the unconscious cruelty of some small animal. As she spoke of the woman whom she had replaced in Fred's affection her lips curled.

'In the evening, specially when she's had too much to eat... and it's disgusting the way she stuffs herself!... she feels uncomfortable in her girdle and she goes upstairs to take it off.'

'How long did she stay upstairs?'

'About ten minutes . . . When she came down again I helped her do the vegetables. The others were still playing cards.'

'Was the door open between the kitchen and the parlour?'

'It's always open . . .'

Maigret looked at her again, then walked heavily down the creaking stairs. In the courtyard the dog could be heard tugging at its chain.

A heap of coal was lying just behind the door of the cellar, and it was from this that the murder weapon had been taken: a heavy coal hammer.

There were no fingerprints. The murderer must have wrapped a rag round the handle. Elsewhere in the house, including on the handle of the bedroom door, there were a great many blurred prints, those of all the people who had been present on the evening of the 14th.

As for the wallet, they had all set to work looking for it in the most unlikely places, with the thoroughness of men used to that sort of search, and the previous day they had had the cesspool professionally emptied.

Poor Borchain had come from his distant home to buy Groux's farm. He had been only a tenant farmer, and he wanted to become a landowner. He was married, with three daughters. He had dined at one of the tables. He had chatted with Canut, who was also a potential purchaser, and had shown him the photograph of his wife.

He had eaten and drunk rather too copiously, and had staggered sleepily to bed. Probably he had slipped the wallet under his pillow.

In the inn parlour, four men were playing *belote*, as they did every evening, and drinking white wine: Fred, Groux, old Nicolas—who turned purple when he'd had a skinful of liquor—and Gentil the exciseman, who would have done better to carry out his round.

Behind them, astride a chair, Canut was watching the game and intermittently glancing at Thérèse, in the hope that this night away from home might end in some adventure.

In the kitchen, two women, Julia and the girl from the orphanage, were busy over a basin of vegetables.

One of these people, at a given moment, had gone into the passage on some pretext, and had first opened the cellar door to pick up the coal hammer and then the door of Borchain's room.

Nothing had been heard. The murderer's absence could not have been a long one, since it had aroused no surprise. And yet he must have had time to put the wallet away in a safe place.

For since the mattress had been set on fire the alarm would quickly be given. The police would be sent for and everyone would be searched.

'To think that you don't even have any decent beer!' Maigret complained as he went back into the bar parlour. He longed for a glass of cool, foaming draught beer instead of this filthy bottled stuff!

'What about this game?'

Fred looked at the time on the clock in its sky-blue china frame (a bargain offer). He was used to the police. He was as tired as the rest, but rather less edgy.

'Twenty to ten...not quite...We were still talking...Was it you, Nicolas, who asked for another bottle of wine?'

'Maybe...'

'I shouted to Thérèse: "Go and draw some wine..." Then I got up and went down to the cellar myself.'

'What for?'

He shrugged. 'Well, it can't be helped now, she may as well hear it. When all this is over, life won't start up again just as it was...I'd heard Thérèse go up into her room...I guessed she'd written me a note...It would have been put into the keyhole of the cellar door...You hear, Julia? I can't help it, old girl!...You've given me enough rows to make up for our occasional bits of fun...'

Canut reddened. Nicolas sniggered to himself behind his ginger whiskers. Monsieur Gentil averted his eyes, for he, too, had made advances to Thérèse.

'Was there a note there?'

'Yes...I read it down there while the wine was running into the bottle. Thérèse simply said that we should probably not get a moment alone together next day...'

Strangely enough, Fred's voice betrayed genuine passion and indeed an unexpectedly emotional note. In the kitchen, Thérèse suddenly rose, and she came up to the cardplayers' table.

'Aren't you through yet?' she asked with quivering lips. 'Why don't you get it over with and have us all arrested. Then we'd see... But this roundabout way of doing things, as though... as though...'

She burst into tears, and went to lean against the wall with her head buried in her hands.

'So you stayed several minutes in the cellar,' went on Maigret quite imperturbably.

'Three or four minutes, yes...'

'What did you do with the note?'

'I burnt it in the candle-flame.'

'Are you afraid of Julia?'

This remark aroused Fred's indignation.

'You don't understand, do you? And you arrested us both ten years ago!... Don't you understand that, when one's been through certain things together... Well, have it your own way!... Don't get upset, Julia old girl...'

And a calm voice came from the kitchen:

'I'm not upset.'

As for the motive, that essential factor according to all textbooks on criminology—why, everybody here had a motive! Groux more than the rest, since he was broke and expected to be turned out of his home next day, without even his furniture or belongings, everything sold, with no alternative left him but to work as a farmhand!

He knew the place, the way to the cellar, the coal heap and the hammer...

And Nicolas? An old soak, granted. He lived in squalor. But he had a daughter at Niort; she was in service, and all that she earned went to pay for the fostering of her child. Might he not...

Not to mention that, as Fred had said earlier, it was Nicolas who came every week to chop wood and break up coal for them.

And about ten o'clock Nicolas had made his way towards the lavatory, staggering drunkenly. Gentil had commented:

'Let's hope he doesn't open the wrong door!'

Chance plays strange tricks! Why had Gentil said that, while mechanically fingering his cards? And could not the thought of the crime have occurred to Gentil himself when, a few minutes later, he had gone the same way as old Nicolas?

He was an exciseman, to be sure, but everyone knew that he didn't take his job seriously, that he spent most of his time in cafés and that one could always make a deal with him.

'Look here, Superintendent...' began Fred.

'Sorry... It's five past ten... Where had we got to the other night?'

Then Thérèse, sniffling, came to sit down behind her employer, with her shoulder rubbing against his back.

'Is that where you were?'

'Yes... I'd done the vegetables... I picked up the jersey I'm knitting, but I didn't work at it.'

Julia was still in the kitchen, but remained unseen.

'What were you going to say, Fred?'

'One thing has struck me... It seems to me there's one detail that proves it wasn't one of the household that killed the fellow... Because... Suppose... No, that's not what I meant to say... If I were to kill someone in my own house d'you think I'd go and set fire to the place?... Whatever for?... To attract attention?...'

Maigret had just filled himself a fresh pipe and was slowly lighting it.

'I'll have a small calvados after all, Thérèse... Now, Fred, why wouldn't you have set the place on fire?'

'Why, because...' He was speechless.

'If it hadn't been for the fire, nobody would have worried about the fellow... The others would have gone home and...'

Maigret was smiling, his lips twisted in an odd grin round the stem of his pipe.

'Pity you're proving exactly the opposite of what you intended to prove, Fred... That fire starting is the only significant piece of evidence, and it struck me as soon as I got here... Suppose you had killed the old fellow, as you said... Everybody knew he was in your house... so you couldn't hope to get rid of the body... Next morning you'd have had to open the bedroom door and give the alarm . . . By the way, what time had he asked to be woken?'

'At six o'clock . . . He wanted to visit the farm and the land before the sale . . .'

'So then if the body had been discovered at six o'clock there would have been nobody in the house but you, Julia and Thérèse, for I don't count Monsieur Canut, whom nobody could have suspected . . . Nobody would have imagined that the crime might have been committed during the game of cards . . .'

Fred was following the Superintendent's argument closely, and it seemed to Maigret that he had turned paler. He was even mechanically tearing up a card and letting the pieces drop on to the floor.

'Careful, if you want to play presently you'll have to do without the ace of spades . . . I was saying, then . . . Ah, yes . . . How could the murder be discovered before the departure of Groux, Nicolas and Monsieur Gentil, so that they might also be suspect? There was no pretext for going into the bedroom . . . Yes! There was one . . . fire . . .'

This time Fred sprang up, his fists clenched, a fierce glint in his eye, and he shouted:

'God Almighty!'

Nobody spoke. They had all received a sudden shock. Hitherto, through sheer weariness, they had scarcely believed in the existence of the criminal. They had ceased to realize that he was there in the house, that they were speaking to him, eating at the same table, playing cards maybe and clinking glasses with him.

Fred was striding up and down the inn parlour while Maigret sat huddled, peering through half-closed eyes. Was he on the verge of success? For the past three days he had kept them all in suspense, minute by minute, making them repeat the same movements and words ten times over, in the hope, of course, that some forgotten detail might suddenly emerge, but above all with the aim of wearing down their resistance, of driving the murderer to breaking-point.

He spoke in a quiet voice, the syllables interspersed with little puffs as he drew on his pipe.

'The crucial question is this: who had available a hiding-place secure enough for the wallet not to be discovered?'

Everyone had been searched. The first night they had all been stripped naked. The heap of coal near the cellar door had been turned over. The walls had been sounded and so had the barrels. Nevertheless a fat wallet containing over a hundred thousand-franc notes...

'Don't be so restless, Fred. You're making me seasick.'

'But for God's sake, don't you understand that...'

'That what?'

'That I didn't kill him! That I'm not crazy enough for that! That I've a bad enough record without...'

'It was next spring, wasn't it, that you were planning to leave for South America with Thérèse and to set up a bistro there?'

Fred turned to glance at the kitchen door, then asked through clenched teeth:

'So what?'

'With what money?'

He glared back at Maigret.

'So that's what you were getting at? You're on the wrong track, Superintendent. I shall have plenty of money on 15 May. It was a thrifty notion that occurred to me while I was making a nice living organizing boxing matches. I took out an insurance policy for a hundred thousand francs to be drawn when I'm fifty. And I'm going to be fifty on 15 May... Why yes, Thérèse, I'm a bit longer in the tooth than I usually admit...'

'Did Julia know about this insurance?'

'That's no concern of women's!'

'So then, Julia, you didn't know that Fred was going to draw a hundred thousand francs?'

'I did know.'

'What?' exclaimed Fred with a start.

'And I knew he wanted to go off with that bit of trash.'

'And you'd have let them go?'

Julia stood motionless, her eyes fixed on her lover, and a strange quietness about her.

'You haven't answered me!' Maigret insisted.

She looked at him in her turn. Her lips moved. Perhaps she was about to say something important. But she just shrugged her shoulders.

'Can one tell what a man'll do?'

Fred was not listening. He seemed to be thinking about something else. He was frowning reflectively, and Maigret had the impression that their thoughts were running along the same lines.

'Look, Fred!'

'What?'

It was as though he had been roused from a dream.

'About that insurance policy . . . that policy that Julia saw without your knowing . . . I'd like to have a glance at it myself . . .'

What a devious route truth was taking to come to light! Maigret had believed he had thought of everything. Thérèse, in her room, had spoken of going away, and that meant money . . . Fred had admitted the existence of his insurance policy . . .

But . . . it was so obvious, so simple that one couldn't help laughing; they had searched the house ten times over and yet had found no insurance policy, no identity papers, no military registration!

'All right, Superintendent,' sighed Fred resignedly. 'You'll be able to check up on my savings at the same time . . .'

He went towards the kitchen.

'You can come in . . . When one lives in a hole like this . . . Not to mention that I've got a few bits of paper that some of my old pals wouldn't be sorry to get from me . . .'

Thérèse followed them, astonished. Groux's heavy step was heard, and Canut had risen too.

'Don't imagine it's anything very clever . . . It just so happens that I was a tinsmith in my younger days . . .'

To the right of the stove there was a huge refuse-bin of galvanized iron. Fred overturned it in the middle of the room and prised open a double bottom. He took the first look. Slowly, he frowned; slowly, his jaw dropped, and he raised his head . . .

A heavy, well-worn wallet, grey with age, fastened by a piece of red rubber cut from a tyre, lay there among various papers.

'Well, Julia?' asked Maigret quietly.

Then he had the impression that something of the old Julia came to life again, visible through the heavy features of the woman she had become. She looked at them all. Her upper lip curled contemptuously. There was a hint of a suppressed sob; but it did not break forth. It was a dull, toneless voice that replied:

'So what? I'm finished...'

The most surprising thing was that it was Thérèse who suddenly burst into tears, like a dog howling, while the woman who had killed asked:

'I suppose you're going to take me away at once, since you've got a car? Can I get my things together?'

He let her pack her bag. He was depressed—a reaction after so much nervous tension.

How long had Julia known about Fred's hiding-place? Had she guessed, on discovering that insurance policy—which he had never mentioned to her—that as soon as he could draw his money he would go away with Thérèse?

An opportunity had occurred: an even greater sum of money than Fred was to get! And it was she who would bring it to him, in a few days or weeks, when the case had been shelved!

'Do you see, Fred... I knew all about it... You wanted to run off with her, didn't you?... You thought I was no use any more... Now have a look in your hiding-place... It was I, the old girl as you called me, who...'

Maigret kept an eye on her, just in case, while she moved to and fro in the bedroom where the photograph of Fred as a boxer hung above the big mahogany bed.

'I've got to put my girdle on...' she said. 'You'd better not look... It's not a very pretty sight.'

It was only in the car that she collapsed, while Maigret stared at the raindrops on the windows. What were the others doing now, in the inn parlour? And to whom would Groux's *cabane* be knocked down when the auctioneer's candle went out for the third time?

The Man in the Street

The four men were packed close together in the taxi. Paris was in the grip of frost. At half-past seven in the morning, the city looked leaden, and the wind drove powdery rime across the ground.

The thinnest of the four men, on a folding seat, had a cigarette stuck to his lower lip and handcuffs on his wrists. The biggest of them, a heavy-jawed man in a thick overcoat and a bowler hat, was smoking a pipe and watching the railings of the Bois de Boulogne race past.

'Would you like me to put up a lovely fight?' the handcuffed man proposed amiably. 'With writhing, cursing, foaming at the mouth, the lot?'

And Maigret growled, as he took the cigarette from the man's lips and opened the car door, since they had now reached the Porte de Bagatelle:

'Don't you try and be too clever!'

The avenues in the Bois were deserted, as white as limestone and as hard. A dozen people were kicking their heels at the corner of a woodland ride, and a photographer attempted to take a picture of the group as they approached. But Louis the Kid, as he had been instructed, held his arms in front of his face.

Maigret looked slowly round like a sulky bear, noticing everything, the new blocks of flats in the Boulevard Richard-Wallace, with their shuttered windows, a few workmen on bicycles coming in from Puteaux, a tram with its lights on, a couple of concierges approaching, their hands purple with cold.

'All set?' he asked.

The day before, he had had the following paragraph inserted in the newspapers:

THE CRIME AT BAGATELLE

This time the police have not been slow in clearing up a case that appeared to present insuperable difficulties. As has already been stated, on Monday morning a park-keeper in the Bois de Boulogne discovered on one of the walks, some hundred metres from the Porte de Bagatelle, a body which was identified on the spot as that of Ernest Borms, a well-known Viennese doctor, who had been living in Neuilly for some years.

Borms was in evening dress. He must have been attacked during the Sunday night as he was returning to his flat in the Boulevard Richard-Wallace.

He was shot point-blank through the heart with a small calibre revolver.

Borms was a youngish man, handsome and very well-dressed, who moved in fashionable society.

Scarcely forty-eight hours after this murder, the Criminal Investigation Department have made an arrest. Tomorrow morning, between seven and eight, a reconstitution of the crime will take place on the spot.

Later on, at Police Headquarters, this case was to be cited as particularly characteristic of Maigret's method; but when it was spoken of in his presence, he had a peculiar habit of averting his head with a growl.

Well! Everything was ready. Almost no loiterers, as he had foreseen. It was not without good reason that he had chosen such an early hour. In fact, among the ten or fifteen people who were kicking their heels were a number of detectives wearing their most innocent air; one of them, Torrence, who adored dressing up, had disguised himself as a milkman, which caused Maigret to shrug his shoulders.

Provided Louis the Kid didn't overdo things!...He was an old acquaintance of the police and had been arrested the day before for picking pockets in the métro...

'You can lend us a hand tomorrow morning and we'll see to it that you get off lightly this time...'

He had been taken out of the cells.

'Let's go!' growled Maigret. 'When you heard footsteps you were hiding in this corner, weren't you?'

'Just as you say, Superintendent...I was staring, you see...Absolutely broke!...So I said to myself that a big shot in a dinner jacket on his way home must have plenty of dough on him... "Your money or your life," I breathe in his ear...And I give you my word it wasn't my fault if the gun went off. I think it was the cold that made my finger press the trigger...'

11 a.m. Maigret was prowling about his room in the Quai des Orfèvres, smoking his pipe and fiddling endlessly with the telephone.

'Hello! Is that you, Chief? It's Lucas...I followed the old boy who seemed to be interested in the reconstruction...Nothing doing there...He's a crank who goes for a walk in the Bois every morning...'

'All right! You can come back.'

11.15 a.m. 'Hello, Chief? This is Torrence. I shadowed the young man you tipped me the wink about...He's a salesman in a Champs-Elysées shop, who's hoping to become a private enquiry agent...Shall I come back?'

Not until 11.55 was there a call from Janvier.

'I'm working fast, Chief...I'm afraid the bird may get away... I'm watching him in the little mirror set in the door of the phone box. I'm at the *Nain Faune* bar in the Boulevard Rochechouart... Yes...He spotted me...He's not got a clear conscience...As we crossed the Seine he threw something into the river. He's tried to lose me about ten times...Shall I wait for you here?'

And thus began a chase which was to go on for five days and five nights, through a city that was unaware of it, among hurrying pedestrians, from bar to bar, from bistro to bistro, Maigret and his detectives taking it in turns to pursue a solitary man and becoming, in the end, as exhausted as their quarry.

Maigret alighted from his taxi in front of the *Nain Faune*, at apéritif time, and found Janvier leaning against the counter. He made no effort to assume an innocent air; quite the reverse!

'Which is he?'

With a jerk of his chin the detective indicated a man sitting at a small table in a corner. The man was watching them with pale blue-grey eyes that gave his face a foreign look. A Scandinavian or a Slav? Probably the latter. He wore a grey overcoat, a well-cut suit, a soft felt hat.

'What'll you drink, Chief? A hot *picon*?'

'Hot *picon* be it... What's he drinking?'

'A brandy... the fifth since this morning... You mustn't mind if my speech is a bit slurred, but I've had to follow him into every bistro... He's tough, you know. Look at him... he's been like that all morning. He wouldn't drop his eyes for the world.'

It was quite true. And it was odd. One could not call it arrogance or defiance. The man was simply looking at them. If he was feeling anxious, he did not show it. His face expressed sadness, rather; but a calm, thoughtful sadness.

'At Bagatelle, when he noticed that you were watching him, he immediately moved away and I followed suit. He turned round before he'd gone a hundred metres. Then instead of leaving the Bois as he had apparently meant to, he strode off down the first walk he came to. He turned round again. He recognized me. He sat down on a bench, in spite of the cold, and I stopped... On several occasions I had the feeling that he wanted to speak to me, but he always ended by shrugging his shoulders and moving off again...

'At the Porte Dauphine I nearly lost him, for he jumped into a taxi, and it was only by sheer luck that I found another almost immediately. He got out in the Place de l'Opéra and rushed into the métro. One behind the other, we changed lines five times, and he began to understand that he wouldn't get rid of me that way...

'We came up above ground again. We were in the Place Clichy. Since then we've been going from bar to bar... I was waiting for a convenient place with a telephone booth from which I could keep an eye on him. When he saw me telephoning he gave a sort of bitter little laugh ... And afterwards one would have sworn he was expecting you ...'

'Ring them up at the "office" ... Tell Lucas and Torrence to be ready to join me at short notice ... And a photographer from the Records Department with a very small camera ...'

'Waiter!' the stranger called out. 'How much?'

'Three francs fifty.'

'I'm willing to bet he's a Pole,' Maigret whispered to Janvier. 'Let's go ...'

They did not get far. In the Place Blanche they followed the man into a small restaurant and sat down at the table next to his. It was an Italian restaurant, and they ate pasta.

At three o'clock Lucas came to take over from Janvier, who was sitting with Maigret in a brasserie opposite the Gare du Nord.

'The photographer?' Maigret enquired.

'He's waiting to catch the man when he comes out.'

And when the Pole left the place, after reading the newspapers, a detective stepped up briskly towards him. When he was less than a yard away the click of a camera was heard. The man swiftly covered his face with his hand, but it was too late, and then, showing that he had understood, he cast a reproachful glance at the Superintendent.

'It's clear, my friend,' Maigret soliloquized, 'that you've some good reasons for not taking us to your home. But however much patience you have, mine's at least equal to yours ...'

By evening a few snowflakes were drifting in the streets, while the stranger walked about, his hands in his pockets, waiting for bedtime.

'Shall I relieve you for the night, Chief?' Lucas proposed.

'No! I'd rather you saw to the photograph. Consult the files first of all. Then ask around in foreigners' circles. He's no recent arrival; somebody must know him.'

'Suppose we published his picture in the papers?'

Maigret gave his subordinate a contemptuous glance. So Lucas, who had worked with him for so many years, didn't understand? Had the police got a single piece of evidence? Not one! A man had been killed at night in the Bois de Boulogne; no weapon had been found, no fingerprints; Dr. Borms lived alone, and his one servant did not know where he had been the night before.

'Do as I tell you. Off with you . . .'

Finally, at midnight, the man brought himself to enter a hotel. Maigret followed. It was a second-rate, indeed a third-rate hotel.

'I want a room . . .'

'Will you fill in the form?'

He did so, hesitantly, his fingers numb with cold.

He looked Maigret up and down, as if to say:

'If you think this worries me! . . . I can write whatever I fancy.'

And he put down a name at random: Nicolas Slaatkovitch, arrived in Paris the previous day.

It was obviously false. Maigret rang the Police Judiciaire. The records of lodging houses and registers of foreigners were searched; enquiries were made to frontier police. There was no sign of any Nicolas Slaatkovitch.

'A room for you too?' asked the proprietor somewhat resentfully, for he had recognized a policeman.

'No, thanks. I shall spend the night on the stairs.'

It seemed safer. He sat down on a step in front of the door of room number seven. Twice the door opened. The man peered into the darkness, caught sight of Maigret's figure and eventually went back to bed. In the morning his beard had grown and his cheeks were rough. He had not been able to change his shirt. He had not even a comb with him, and his hair was dishevelled.

Lucas appeared.

'Shall I take over, Chief?'

But Maigret could not bring himself to leave the stranger. He watched him pay for his room. He saw him turn pale, and he guessed.

A little later, in fact, in a bar where, practically side by side, they drank *café crème* and ate croissants, the man openly counted his store of wealth. One hundred-franc note, two twenty-franc pieces and one piece of ten, plus some small change. His lips twisted in a bitter grin.

Well, he wouldn't get far with that. When he came to the Bois de

Boulogne he must just have left home, for he had freshly shaven cheeks and clothes without a speck of dust or a crease. He had probably expected to be back shortly afterwards; he hadn't even looked to see what money he had in his pockets.

What he had thrown into the Seine, Maigret guessed, must have been identity papers and possibly visiting cards.

At all costs, he wanted to prevent anyone finding out where he lived.

And he set off again on the long, weary ramble of the homeless, lingering in front of shops and stalls, entering bars from time to time for somewhere to sit and take refuge from the cold, reading newspapers in brasseries.

A hundred and fifty francs! No restaurant for him at midday; he had to content himself with hard-boiled eggs, which he ate standing up at a bar counter, washed down with a glass of beer, while Maigret devoured sandwiches.

The man hesitated for a long time in front of a cinema, wondering whether to go in. He fingered the coins in his pocket. Better try and last out... He went on walking, walking...

In fact, one detail struck Maigret: this exhausting ramble always followed the same course, through the same districts: between the Trinité and Place Clichy, between Place Clichy and Barbès by way of the Rue Caulaincourt, then from Barbès to the Gare du Nord and the Rue La Fayette...

Was the man afraid of being recognized elsewhere? Surely he had chosen the districts farthest from his home or his hotel, those which he did not habitually visit...

Did he, like so many foreigners, frequent the Montparnasse district? The neighbourhood of the Panthéon?

To judge by his clothes, he was moderately well-off; they were comfortable, quiet and well-cut. A professional man, no doubt. Maigret noticed that he wore a wedding ring.

Maigret had had to resign himself to handing over his place to Torrence. He had hurried home. Madame Maigret was disappointed, because her sister had come on a visit from Orléans and she had prepared a special dinner, and now her husband, after shaving and changing, was off again, announcing that he didn't know when he would be back.

He made straight for the Quai des Orfèvres.

'Anything for me from Lucas?'

Yes. There was a message from the inspector. He had passed round the photograph in a number of Polish and Russian circles. Nobody knew the man. Nor was there anything to be learnt from the various political groups. As a last resort he had had a great many copies of the photograph printed; in every part of Paris policemen went from door to door, enquiring from concierges, and showing the document to the landlords of bars and the waiters in cafés.

'Hello! Superintendent Maigret? I'm an usherette at the news-cinema in the Boulevard de Strasbourg... There's a gentleman here, Monsieur Torrence... He told me to call you to say that he's here, but daren't leave the hall...'

It was cunning of the man; he had reckoned that this was the warmest place to spend a number of hours at little expense... Two francs entry... and you could stay on for several performances!

A curious intimacy had sprung up between the hunter and the hunted, between the man with the unshaven chin and rumpled clothes and Maigret, who kept stubbornly on his trail. There was even one comical detail: they had both caught colds. Their noses were red. Almost rhythmically, they pulled out their handkerchiefs, and once the man gave an involuntary smile on seeing Maigret give a whole series of sneezes.

After sitting through five consecutive programmes at the news-cinema, they moved on to a squalid hotel in the Boulevard de la Chapelle. The man signed the same name on the register. And Maigret, once again, settled down on the staircase. But since this was a hotel frequented by prostitutes, he was disturbed every ten minutes by couples who stared at him with curiosity, and the women felt uneasy.

Would the man make up his mind to go home once his money was spent or when he was at the end of his tether? In a brasserie

where he stayed for some length of time and took off his grey overcoat, Maigret seized hold of this without hesitation and examined
the inside of the collar. It bore the label of the 'Old England' shop
in the Boulevard des Italiens. It was a ready-made garment, and the
shop must have sold dozens like it. Maigret noticed one significant
piece of evidence: it was a year old. So the stranger must have been
in Paris for a year at least. And during that year he must have stayed
somewhere...

Maigret had begun drinking toddies to get rid of his cold. The
stranger was becoming close-fisted; he drank only coffee, not even
laced with spirits, and ate hard-boiled eggs and croissants.

The news from the 'office' was still the same: nothing to report!
Nobody had recognized the photograph of the Pole, and no missing
person had been reported.

Nor was there any further information about the dead man. He
had earned a good income, took no interest in politics, led a busy social life, and since he specialized in nervous diseases his patients
were chiefly women.

Maigret had never yet had occasion to study the question of how
long it takes for a well-bred, well-dressed, well-groomed man to
lose his gloss once he is turned out into the streets.

He knew, now, that it took four days. The beard, for one thing.
The first morning the man looked like a lawyer, a doctor, an architect
or an industrialist, and one could imagine him living in a comfortable flat. A four-day beard had transformed him so much that if his
picture had been published in connection with the Bois de Boulogne
affair people would have declared: 'He's obviously a murderer!'

The cold air and the lack of sleep had reddened his eyelids, and
there was a hectic flush on his cheekbones. His shoes were unpol-
ished and shapeless, his overcoat looked shabby and his trousers
bagged at the knees.

Even his gait...He no longer walked in the same way...He
slunk along by the wall...he lowered his eyes when people looked
at him as they passed...One further point: he averted his head
when he went past a restaurant where customers were sitting in
front of well-filled plates...

'Your last twenty francs, poor fellow!' Maigret reckoned. 'And what next?'

Lucas, Torrence and Janvier relieved him from time to time, but he gave up his post to them as seldom as possible. He would burst into his chief's office at Police Headquarters.

'You ought to take a rest, Maigret...'

Peevish and prickly, Maigret seemed torn by conflicting feelings.

'Is it or isn't it my job to catch the murderer?'

'Obviously...'

'Then I'm off!' he sighed with a touch of resentment in his voice. 'I wonder where we shall go to bed tonight?'

Only twenty francs left, not even that! When he rejoined Torrence, the latter informed him that the man had eaten three hard-boiled eggs and drunk two coffees, laced with brandy, in a bar at the corner of the Rue Montmartre.

'Eight francs fifty... He's got eleven fifty left...'

He admired the man. Far from trying to conceal himself he walked level with him, sometimes right beside him, and had to control an impulse to speak to him.

'Come on, old chap! Don't you think it's time for a meal?... Somewhere or other there's a warm home waiting for you, a bed, slippers, a razor... eh? And a good dinner...'

The man, however, went on prowling aimlessly under the arc lamps of the Halles, among the heaps of cabbages and carrots, stepping aside when he heard the whistle of a train, avoiding market gardeners' trucks.

'You won't be able to afford a room!'

The Meteorological Office that evening registered eight degrees below zero. The man treated himself to hot sausages from an open-air stall. He would reek of garlic and burnt fat all night!

At one point he tried to slip into a shed and lie down in one corner. A policeman, to whom Maigret had not had time to give instructions, sent him packing. Now he was limping. The Quais. The Pont des Arts—provided he didn't take it into his head to throw himself into the Seine! Maigret felt he would not have the courage to jump in after him into the black water, where ice was beginning to drift.

He walked along the tow-path. Some tramps were grumbling; under the bridges, the best places were already taken.

In a little street near the Place Maubert, through the windows of a strange tavern, old men could be seen asleep, their heads on the table. For twenty sous, a glass of red wine included! The man looked at Maigret through the darkness. Then, with a fatalistic shrug, he pushed open the door. Before it had closed, Maigret caught a nauseating whiff; he decided to remain outside. Summoning a constable on the beat, he posted him as sentry on the pavement while he went off to ring Lucas, who was on duty that night.

'We've been hunting for you for the past hour, Chief! We've found out who the man is, thanks to a concierge... His name's Stephan Strevzki, thirty-four years old, born in Warsaw; he's been living in France for the past three years... He's married to a fine-looking Hungarian girl called Dora... They rent a twelve thousand franc flat in Passy, in the Rue de la Pompe... Nothing to do with politics... The concierge has never seen the murdered man... Stephan went out on Monday morning earlier than usual... She was surprised not to see him come back, but she didn't worry because...'

'What's the time now?'

'Half-past three... I'm alone at Headquarters... I've had some beer brought up, but it's very cold!'

'Listen, Lucas... You're to... Yes, I know! Too late for the morning ones, but in the evening ones... Understood?'

That morning an indefinable odour of poverty seemed to cling to the man's very clothes. His eyes were more sunken. The glance he threw at Maigret, in the pale dawn, was one of pathetic reproachfulness.

Had he not been brought, gradually but yet at a dizzying speed, to the lowest rung of the ladder? He pulled up the collar of his overcoat. He did not leave the district. He dived into a bistro which had just opened, and there drank four brandies in quick succession, as though to drive away the appalling aftertaste that the night had left in his throat and his breast.

Now there was nothing left for him but to keep on walking along streets slippery with frost. He must be aching in every limb; he was limping with the left leg. From time to time he halted and looked around despairingly.

Since he no longer went into cafés where there was a telephone, Maigret could not be relieved. Back to the quais! And there the man almost automatically fingered the secondhand books, turning their pages, occasionally checking the authenticity of a print or an engraving. An icy wind swept the Seine. As the barges moved forward, the water made a clinking sound due to the clashing of tiny fragments of ice.

From afar off, Maigret could see the Police Judiciaire building and the window of his office. His sister-in-law must have gone back to Orléans. If only Lucas...

He did not know, as yet, that this appalling case was going to become a classic, and that generations of detectives would relate it in every detail to their juniors. Absurdly, what disturbed him most was a trivial detail: the man had a spot on his forehead, which, looked at closely, would probably prove to be a boil, and which was turning from red to purple.

If only Lucas...

At midday, the man, who unquestionably knew his Paris well, made his way towards the paupers' soup kitchen at the far end of the Boulevard Saint-Germain. He joined the queue of down-and-outs. An old man spoke to him, but he pretended not to understand. Then another, whose face was pitted with smallpox, addressed him in Russian.

Maigret crossed over to the pavement on the other side of the street, and after a moment's hesitation yielded to the irresistible urge to enter a bistro and eat sandwiches; he turned away so that the man, if he looked through the window, should not see him eating.

The poor fellows moved on slowly, and were let in four or five at a time into the hall where they were given bowls of hot soup. The queue grew longer. From time to time someone would push at the back, and the others protested.

1 p.m.... The newsboy came running from the far end of the street, leaning forward eagerly.

'Paper! Paper *L'Intransigeant... L'Intran...*'

He, too, was trying to forestall his rivals. He could spot likely purchasers from afar. He paid no attention to the line of paupers.

'Paper...'

Humbly the man raised his hand, saying: 'Pssstt!'

People in the queue looked at him. So he still had a few sous for a paper?

Maigret, too, hailed the newsboy, unfolded the paper, and found to his relief, on the front page, what he was looking for: the photograph of a young woman, smiling and beautiful.

MISSING WOMAN

A young Polish woman, Mme Dora Strevzki, is said to have disappeared four days ago from her home in Passy, 17 Rue de la Pompe. A disturbing factor in the case is that the husband of the missing woman, M. Stephan Strevzki, also disappeared from his home the day before, Monday, and the concierge, who informed the police... stated...

The man, borne forward by the moving queue, had only five or six paces more to go to get his bowl of steaming soup. At that very moment he stepped out of line, crossed the street, nearly got knocked over by a bus, but reached the pavement just as Maigret stood in front of him.

'I'm all yours,' he declared quite simply. 'Take me off... I'll answer all your questions.'

Everyone was waiting in the passage at Police Headquarters, Lucas, Janvier, Torrence, and others who had not been working on the case but knew about it. As they passed, Lucas gave Maigret a sign that meant: 'It's all right!'

A door opened and then shut. Beer and sandwiches were on the table.

'Have something to eat first...'

Embarrassed, the man could scarcely swallow. Then at last he said:

'Since she's gone away and is safe somewhere...'

Maigret felt impelled to turn and poke the stove.

'When I read about the murder in the paper ... I'd suspected for quite some time that Dora was having an affair with that man ... I knew she was not his only mistress ... I knew Dora with her impulsive character ... D'you understand? If he had tried to get rid of her, I knew she was capable of ... And she had a pearl-handled revolver, she always carried it in her bag ... When the papers announced the capture of the murderer and the reconstruction of the crime, I wanted to watch ...'

Maigret would have liked to say, like an English policeman: 'I warn you that anything you say may be taken down and used in evidence ...'

The man had kept on his hat and overcoat.

'Now that she's safe ... For I suppose ...' He cast an anxious look around, as a sudden suspicion crossed his mind. 'She must have understood, when she saw that I'd not come back ... I knew it would end like that, I knew Borms was not the man for her and that she'd come back to me ... She went out alone on Sunday evening, as she had taken to doing recently ... She must have killed him when ...'

Maigret blew his nose; he took a long time blowing it. A ray of sunlight, that bleak winter sunlight that goes with icy weather, came in through the window. The boil was gleaming on the man's forehead; Maigret could only think of him as 'the man'.

'Yes, your wife killed him ... When she realized that he was not serious about her ... And *you* realized that she had killed him ... And you didn't want ...'

He suddenly went up close to the Pole.

'I'm sorry, old fellow,' he muttered as though he was speaking to an old friend, 'I had to get at the truth, hadn't I? It was my duty to ...'

He opened the door.

'Bring in Madame Dora Strevzki ... Lucas, you carry on, I'm going to ...'

And nobody saw him again at Headquarters for two days. The director rang him up at home.

'Look here, Maigret ... You know that she's confessed everything and that ... By the way, how's your cold? I gather ...'

'It's nothing at all. It's all right...In twenty-four hours...And how is he?'

'What?...Who?...'

'The man!'

'Ah, I follow...He's engaged the best lawyer in Paris...He hopes...You know, crimes of passion...'

Maigret went back to bed and doped himself with aspirin and hot toddies. Later on, when anyone asked him about the investigation, he would growl discouragingly:

'What investigation?'

And the man came to see him once or twice a week to keep him informed about the lawyer's hopes.

The result was not outright acquittal: a year with remission of sentence.

And it was from this man that Maigret learnt to play chess.

1939

Maigret in Retirement

I
The Old Lady in the Garden

Madame Maigret, who sat shelling peas in a glowing shade where the blue of her apron and the green of the pea pods made rich patches of colour, Madame Maigret, whose hands were never idle, even at two in the afternoon on the hottest day of a sultry August, Madame Maigret, who watched over her husband as though he were a babe in arms, had begun to worry:

'I bet you're going to get up already . . .'

And yet the deck chair in which Maigret was lying had not creaked. The retired Chief Superintendent had not heaved the slightest sigh.

Probably, with the knowledge born of long familiarity, she had noticed an imperceptible quiver flit across his face, which was gleaming with sweat. For it was quite true; he had been on the point of getting up. But by a sort of personal pride he forced himself to remain supine.

This was the second summer they had spent in their house at Meung-sur-Loire since his retirement. Barely a quarter of an hour ago, he had stretched himself out with satisfaction in the comfortable deck chair, and the smoke was rising gently from his pipe. The air around him felt all the cooler because barely two yards away, beyond the borderline of shade and sunshine, there was a blazing furnace loud with flies.

The peas dropped at an even rhythm into the enamel bowl. Madame Maigret, sitting with her lap spread wide, had an apron full of them, and there were two big baskets full, picked that morning, ready for preserving.

What Maigret liked best about his house was the place they were now sitting in, a place which had no name, a sort of courtyard between the kitchen and the garden which was partially roofed over, and into which they had gradually introduced furniture, a cooking stove, a sideboard, and where they ate most of their meals. It was something like a Spanish patio, and the red tiles on the floor gave the shade a very special quality.

Maigret held out for five minutes or a little longer, looking through half-closed lids at the kitchen garden, which seemed to be steaming under the oppressive sun. Then, abandoning all pride, he stood up.

'What are you going to do now?'

In the privacy of his home he often looked like a sulky boy caught in the act of wrongdoing.

'I'm sure the Colorado beetles have got at the aubergines again,' he grumbled. 'All because of *your* lettuces...'

The minor war over the lettuces had been going on for a month: As there had been room between the aubergine plants Madame Maigret, one evening, had planted out some lettuce seedlings there.

'We don't want to waste the space,' she had observed.

At the time he had not protested, because it had not yet struck him that Colorado beetles relish aubergine leaves even more than potatoes, and that because of the lettuces it was now impossible to spray them with pesticide.

And so ten times a day Maigret would go, as he went now, wearing his huge straw hat, to bend over the pale green leaves and turn them over carefully, removing the little striped creatures. He held the beetles in his left hand till he had filled it and then came, looking cross, to throw them into the fire with a defiant glance at his wife.

'If you hadn't planted out those lettuces...'

The real truth was that since his retirement she had not yet seen him spend one full hour in the precious deck chair that he had brought back in triumph from the *Bazar de l'Hôtel de Ville*, vowing to enjoy many a peaceful siesta in it.

There he was in the blazing sun, his feet bare in wooden sabots, wearing baggy denim trousers that made him look like an elephant from the rear and a peasant's shirt, with a complicated little pattern on it, open on his hairy chest.

He heard the sound of the door-knocker echo through the empty, shadowy rooms of the house, like a bell in a convent. Someone was knocking at the front door, and Madame Maigret, as usually happened when any unforeseen visitor arrived, was seized with panic. She looked at him imploringly for advice, from a distance.

Then she lifted up her apron, which formed a huge pocket, wondered where to tip her peas, and finally undid her apron strings, for she would never have gone to open the door carelessly dressed.

The knocker struck again, twice, three times, imperiously and almost angrily. Behind its vibrations Maigret thought he noticed the faint purr of a car engine. He went on bending over the aubergines, while his wife tidied her grey hair in front of a small mirror.

No sooner had she disappeared into the darkness of the house than a small door opened in the garden wall, the little green door that gave on to the lane and which only their close acquaintances used. An old lady in mourning stood framed in the doorway, looking so stiff and severe and at the same time so comical that he was to remember the picture for a long time.

She stood motionless only for one moment, and then with a firm, lively step hardly in keeping with her great age, she marched straight up to Maigret.

'Tell me, my man...It's no good pretending your master isn't here...I've already made enquiries...'

She was tall and thin, with a wrinkled face on which a thick coat of powder was clogged with sweat. Her most striking feature was a pair of intensely black and extraordinarily bright eyes.

'Go and tell him immediately that Bernadette Amorelle has travelled a hundred kilometres to speak to him...'

Of course she had not had the patience to wait before a closed
door. She would never have stood for that! As she said, she had enquired from the neighbours and had not been put off by the closed
shutters of the house.

Had anyone shown her the little garden door? That would have
been unnecessary; she was quite equal to finding it by herself. And
now she walked up to the shady patio on to which Madame Maigret
had just re-emerged.

'Will you go and tell Superintendent Maigret...'

Madame Maigret could not understand. Her husband came up
slowly behind the old lady, and there was an amused glint in his eye.
He was saying:

'Please be so good as to come in...'

'I'm willing to bet he's having a sleep. Is he still as fat?'

'Do you know him well?'

'What business is that of yours? Go and tell him Bernadette
Amorelle is here, and don't interfere...'

She changed her mind and rummaged in her old-fashioned
handbag, a black velvet reticule with a silver clasp such as were
fashionable at the turn of the century.

'Here you are,' she said, offering him a few francs.

'Forgive me for not accepting, Madame Amorelle, but I am ex-
Superintendent Maigret...'

Then she made a superb remark, which was to remain a household word for the Maigrets. Looking him over, from sabots to dishevelled hair—for he had removed his enormous straw hat—she
replied:

'If you say so...'

Poor Madame Maigret! She kept making signs to her husband,
which he disregarded; she was trying to insinuate discreetly that he
must take the visitor into the drawing room. 'You can't entertain
people in a courtyard which is also used as a kitchen!'

But Madame Amorelle had settled down in a small wicker armchair and seemed quite at home. It was she who, noticing Madame Maigret's nervousness, exclaimed impatiently:

'Stop bothering the Superintendent!'

She practically asked Madame Maigret to leave the room, which the latter in fact did, feeling unable to go on working in the visitor's presence and at a loss what to do with herself.

'You know my name, don't you, Superintendent?'

'Amorelle of the gravel-pits and tugboats?'

'Amorelle and Campois, yes...'

He had once conducted an enquiry in the Upper Seine region and there, all day long, he had seen strings of boats pass by, all bearing the green triangle of the firm of Amorelle and Campois. In the Ile Saint-Louis, while he was still working at the Quai des Orfèvres, he had often noticed the offices of Amorelle and Campois, who were both shipbuilders and quarry owners.

'I've no time to waste and you've got to understand me. This morning I took advantage of my daughter and son-in-law's being out at the Maliks' place to make François get the old Renault going... They suspect nothing... They'll probably not be back before this evening... Do you understand?'

'No... Yes...'

He understood, at any rate, that the old lady had given her family the slip.

'On my word of honour, if they knew I was here...'

'Excuse me, but where were you?'

'At Orsenne, of course...'

Just as a queen of France might have said: 'At Versailles!'

Of course everybody knew, everybody was bound to know that Bernadette Amorelle, of Amorelle and Campois, lived at Orsenne, a small village on the bank of the Seine between Corbeil and the forest of Fontainebleau.

'You needn't look at me as though you thought I was mad. They'll certainly try to make you believe I am. I swear it's not true.'

'Excuse me, Madame, but may I ask how old you are?'

'You may, young man. I shall be eighty-two on 7th September... But all my teeth are my own, if that's what you're looking at...

And it's more than likely I shall bury some of the rest of them...
I'd be particularly glad to bury my son-in-law...'

'Wouldn't you like something to drink?'

'A glass of cold water, if you have some...'

He poured her some himself.

'What time did you leave Orsenne?'

'Half-past eleven...As soon as they had gone...I'd warned
François...François is the gardener's boy, a good little lad...I
helped his mother at his birth...Nobody in the house suspects that
he can drive a car...One night when I couldn't sleep—for I must
tell you, Superintendent, that I never sleep—I discovered that he
was experimenting on the old Renault in the moonlight...Are you
interested?'

'Very much so.'

'You're easily interested...The old Renault, which wasn't even
kept in the garage, but in the stables, is a limousine which used to
belong to my late husband...As he's been dead twenty years, you
can reckon for yourself...Well, the boy, I can't think how, managed
to get it going and at night he took it out for little jaunts on the
road...'

'Was it he who brought you here?'

'He's waiting for me outside...'

'Have you had no lunch?'

'I eat when I have time to...I detest people who are always having to eat...'

And involuntarily she cast a censorious glance at the Superintendent's bulging waistline.

'Just see how you're sweating. None of my business...My husband was just the same, he always wanted to have his own way, and
now he's been dead and gone a long time...You retired two years
ago, didn't you?'

'Nearly two years, yes...'

'Then you must be getting bored...So you're going to accept
my suggestion...There's a train that leaves Orléans at five o'clock
and I can drop you there on my way home...Of course it would be
simpler to take you to Orsenne in the car, but you'd be noticed and
that would ruin everything.'

'Excuse me, Madame, but...'

'I know you're going to make a fuss. But I've got to have you at Orsenne for a few days. Fifty thousand if you're successful. And if you don't find out anything, let's say ten thousand, plus your expenses...'

She had opened her bag and was fingering the notes she had got ready.

'There's an inn. You can't make a mistake, for there's only one. It's called the Angel. You'll be most uncomfortable there, because poor Jeanne is half crazy. Someone else that I knew as a child. Perhaps she won't want to take you in, but you'll manage to get round her, I don't doubt. Provided you talk to her about illnesses she'll be satisfied. She's convinced she's riddled with them.'

Madame Maigret brought in a tray with coffee and the old lady, far from appreciating such attention, berated her:

'What's all this for? Who told you to bring us coffee? Take it away...'

She mistook her for the maid, just as she had mistaken Maigret for the gardener.

'I could tell you a lot of stories, but I know your reputation and I'm sure you're clever enough to find it all out for yourself. Don't let yourself be taken in by my son-in-law, that's my only advice. He gets round everybody. He's polite. There's never been anyone so polite. It's positively sickening. But the day they cut off his head...'

'Excuse me, Madame...'

'Not so many apologies, Superintendent. I had a granddaughter, my only one, the daughter of that wretched Malik. That's my son-in-law's name, Charles Malik. You must know that too. My granddaughter, Monita, would have been eighteen next week...'

'Are you telling me that she is dead?'

'She died exactly seven days ago. We buried her the day before yesterday. They found her, drowned, by the downstream weir... And when Bernadette Amorelle tells you that it was no accident, you can believe her. Monita could swim like a fish. They'll try and make you believe that she was rash, that she used to go and bathe by herself at six in the morning and sometimes at night. She'd not have drowned on that account. And if they insinuate that she may have committed suicide, you can tell them they're lying.'

Suddenly, without any transition, the atmosphere had shifted from comedy to drama, but the curious thing was that the tone was still that of comedy. The old lady shed no tears. There was no trace of moisture in her astonishing black eyes. Her lean, wiry figure, her whole being was still animated by the same vitality which, in spite of everything, was somehow rather comical.

She went straight ahead, following out her idea without regard for customary formalities. She looked at Maigret as though she did not for one moment doubt that he was entirely at her disposal, simply because that was how she wanted it to be.

She had left secretly, in a fantastic car, with a lad who scarcely knew how to drive. She had travelled all across Beauce in this fashion, without stopping to eat, in the heat of the day. Now she was consulting a watch which she wore dangling from an old-fashioned chain.

'If you've anything to ask me, do so quickly,' she announced, preparing to leave.

'You don't like your son-in-law, I gather.'

'I hate him.'

'Does your daughter hate him too? Is she unhappy with him?'

'I don't know and I don't care.'

'Don't you get on with your daughter?'

'I prefer to ignore her. She has no character, no blood in her veins.'

'You said that seven days ago, that's to say Tuesday of last week, your granddaughter was drowned in the Seine.'

'Nothing of the sort. You ought to pay more attention to what I say. Monita's body was found in the Seine, just above the downstream weir.'

'But the body was uninjured and the doctor issued a death certificate?'

She merely glanced at him with an air of supreme contempt, tinged with pity.

'As I understand it, you are the only person to suspect that the death may not have been accidental?'

This time she stood up.

'Listen, Superintendent. You have the reputation of being the cleverest detective in France. At any rate, the most successful one. Get dressed and pack your suitcase. In half an hour I shall drop you at Les Aubrais station. By seven o'clock this evening you'll be at the Angel Inn. We'd better not appear to be acquainted. Every day about noon François will go to the Angel for an apéritif. Usually he doesn't drink but I shall order him to do so. Thus we shall be able to communicate without arousing their suspicions.'

She took a few steps towards the garden, as though she had decided to take a turn there, in spite of the heat, while waiting for him.

'Hurry up!'

Then, turning round: 'Please be kind enough to give François something to drink. Wine diluted with water. Not neat wine, since he's got to drive me home, and he isn't used to it.'

Madame Maigret, who must have overheard everything, was standing behind the hall door.

'What are you doing, Maigret?' she asked, seeing him make for the staircase with its brass-knobbed handrail.

It was cool inside the house, with a pleasant smell of polish, dried hay, ripening fruit and something gently cooking on the stove. It was the smell of Maigret's childhood, of his parents' home, and it had taken him fifty years to rediscover it.

'You're not going to follow that crazy old woman?'

He had left his sabots on the doorstep. He walked barefoot on the cool tiles and then on the polished oak steps of the stair.

'Give the driver something to drink and then come and help me pack.'

There was a little gleam in his eyes, a gleam that he recognized when he looked at himself in the bathroom mirror after a wash in cold water.

'I don't understand you!' his wife sighed. 'And such a short while ago you were worrying about Colorado beetles!'

He felt hot in the train. He sat smoking in his corner. The grass on the embankment was yellow, the little flower-decked stations came past one after the other, and in the sun-haze a man looked ridiculous waving his little red flag and blowing a whistle like a small boy.

Maigret's temples were greyer, he was somewhat calmer and heavier than he used to be, but he did not feel that he had grown any older since leaving the Police Judiciaire.

It was rather out of vanity, or a sort of discretion, that for the past two years he had systematically refused to take up any of the cases about which he had been approached, particularly when bankers, insurance agents and jewellers came to him with difficult problems.

They'd have said, back in the Quai des Orfèvres: 'Poor old Maigret's back on the job. He's fed up already with his garden and his fishing-rod!'

And now he had let himself be inveigled by an old woman who had suddenly turned up in the doorway.

He could picture her sitting, stiff and dignified, in the ancient limousine which was being driven with perilous unconcern by a gardener's boy who had not even had time to exchange his sabots for shoes.

He could hear her remark, after watching Madame Maigret wave to him from the front door as they drove off: 'That's your wife, isn't it? I must have annoyed her by taking her for the maid. I'd taken you for the gardener ...'

And the car had started off again on its more than adventurous course, after dropping him at Les Aubrais station, where François, muddling up his gears, had almost crashed backwards into a bunch of cyclists.

It was the holiday season. There were Parisians everywhere, about the countryside and in the woods, there were fast cars on the roads and canoes on the rivers, and straw-hatted anglers at the foot of every willow tree.

Orsenne was not a station, merely a halt where a few trains deigned to stop. Through parkland trees one could glimpse the roofs of a few large villas and beyond them the Seine, broad and majestic at this point.

Maigret would have found it very hard to say why he had obeyed the orders of Bernadette Amorelle. Maybe because of those Colorado beetles?

Suddenly, like the people he had rubbed shoulders with in the train, like those he met as he walked down the steep, narrow path, indeed like those he had seen all around since leaving Meung, he felt in holiday mood. He was breathing a different air from that of his garden, he was walking lightheartedly in an unfamiliar setting, and at the foot of the slope he found the Seine with a broad highway running alongside it.

Notice boards with arrows on them had, ever since the station, been directing him towards the Angel Inn, and he followed the arrows till he came to a garden with dilapidated arbours and finally pushed open the glass door of a verandah where the air was stiflingly hot because of the sunlight trapped between glass panes.

'Anybody there?' he called.

There was only a cat on a cushion on the ground and some fishing rods in one corner.

'Anybody there?'

He went down one step and found himself in the dining room, where the brass pendulum of an ancient clock was lazily swinging with a click at the end of each stroke.

'There's nobody in this shack!' he grumbled.

At that very moment somebody moved beside him. He gave a start, and then discovered in the half-darkness a figure swathed in bedclothes. It was a woman, doubtless the Jeanne of whom Madame Amorelle had spoken. Her black greasy hair hung down on either side of her face, and she had a thick white compress round her neck.

'We're closed,' she said in a hoarse voice.

'I know, Madame. I heard you were unwell...'

Surely the term was so inadequate as to be insulting!

'You mean I'm nearly dead? Nobody will believe it... They persecute me...'

However, she finally flung off the blanket that covered her legs and got up, showing swollen ankles above felt slippers.

'Who sent you here?'

'Would you believe it? I came here once, over twenty years ago, and so it's a kind of pilgrimage...'

'So then you knew Marius?'

'Of course!'

'Poor Marius . . . You know he's dead?'

'They told me so. I refused to believe it.'

'Why? His health was always rotten too . . . He died three years ago and I'm still dragging on . . . Did you expect to stay here?'

She had caught sight of the suitcase which he had set down on the threshold.

'I hoped to spend a few days here, provided it was no bother to you. In your state of health . . .'

'Have you come a long way?'

'From the neighbourhood of Orléans.'

'You've not got a car?'

'No. I came by train.'

'And you haven't got a train to go back on today. Good heavens! Good heavens! Raymonde! . . . Raymonde! . . . I bet she's on the loose again. Here she is at last! I'll go and have a look with her, if she's willing . . . Because she's a queer customer. She's the maid, but she takes advantage of my being ill to do whatever suits her and you'd think she's the one that gives the orders. Hello, what's *he* doing round here?'

She was looking through the window at a man whose step could be heard on the gravel. Maigret looked too, and then knit his brows, for the newcomer reminded him vaguely of somebody.

He was dressed in casual country clothes, white flannel trousers and a white jacket and shoes. What struck Maigret was the black mourning band he wore on his arm.

He walked in like a familiar visitor.

'Good evening, Jeanne . . .'

'What d'you want, Monsieur Malik?'

'I came to ask you if . . .'

He broke off, looked straight at Maigret and then with a sudden smile exclaimed:

'Jules! For goodness' sake! What are *you* doing here?'

'I'm sorry . . .'

For one thing, not for years and years had anybody addressed him as Jules, so that he had almost forgotten his own Christian name. His wife herself had, somewhat to his amusement, taken to calling him Maigret.

'Don't you remember?'

'No...'

And yet that face with its high colour and clear-cut features, that prominent nose and those pale, over-pale eyes were not unfamiliar. Nor was the name Malik, which had already stirred some obscure memory when Madame Amorelle had first uttered it.

'Ernest...'

'Ernest who?'

It was of Charles Malik, surely, that Bernadette Amorelle had spoken.

'The lycée at Moulins!'

Maigret had indeed spent three years at school at Moulins when his father was farm manager of an estate in that region. And yet...

The strange thing was that although his recollections were hazy he felt sure that he was reminded of something unpleasant by this well-groomed, self-confident man. Moreover, he disliked being addressed as *tu*. He had always detested overfamiliarity.

'The Tax Collector...'

'Yes, now I remember...I shouldn't have recognized you.'

'What are you doing here?'

'Me? Why, I...'

The other burst out laughing.

'We'll talk about that presently. Of course I knew that Superintendent Maigret was none other than my old friend Jules. Do you remember the English teacher?...You needn't prepare a room, Jeanne. My friend will sleep at the villa...'

'No!' declared Maigret sullenly.

'What did you say?'

'I said I shall sleep here. I've settled that with Jeanne.'

'You insist?'

'I insist.'

'Because of the old woman?'

'What old woman?'

A malicious smile flitted over Malik's thin lips, and that, too, re-called the smile of the schoolboy he had once been.

They used to call him the Tax Collector because his father held that post at Moulins. He'd been very thin, with a hatchet face and pale eyes of an unattractive grey.

'Don't worry, Jules. You'll understand it all by and by... Look here, Jeanne, don't be afraid to answer me frankly. Is my mother-in-law mad or isn't she?'

And Jeanne, gliding noiselessly in slippered feet, muttered sullenly:

'I'd as soon not get mixed up in your family affairs.'

She was looking at Maigret, now, with a more hostile, almost suspicious eye.

'Well, are you staying or are you going with him?'

'I'm staying.'

Malik was still gazing at his former schoolfellow with a mocking air, as though it was all part of a practical joke of which Maigret was the victim.

'You'll have a jolly time, I promise you... I can't think of a more cheerful place than the Angel Inn. You've seen the angel, you've been had!'

Did he suddenly remember that he was in mourning? At any rate he assumed a more serious look as he added: 'If it wasn't all so sad, we could have a good laugh over it together... Come up to the house, in any case. Yes, you've got to!... I'll explain... By the time we've had a drink together you'll have understood.'

Maigret was still hesitant. He stood there, looking huge by the side of his companion, who was as tall as himself but uncommonly slender.

'I'll come,' he said at last, almost reluctantly.

'You'll consent to have dinner with us, I hope? I don't say the house is very cheerful at the moment, since the death of my niece, but...'

Just as they were leaving, Maigret noticed Jeanne watching them from a dark corner. And he got the impression that there was hatred in her gaze, as it lingered on the elegant figure of Ernest Malik.

2
The Tax Collector's Younger Son

As the two men were walking along the river bank, it must have looked as though one was holding the other on a leash, and Maigret, as sullen and clumsy as a big shaggy dog, was letting himself be pulled along.

The fact was that he was ill at ease. Already at school he had felt little fondness for the 'Tax Collector'. Moreover he hated people who suddenly spring up out of your past to pat you on the shoulder and address you familiarly.

Ernest Malik, in short, represented a type of humanity that had always aroused his aversion.

The fellow strode along with the utmost unconcern, free and easy in his beautifully cut white flannel suit, physically fit, with glossy hair and no hint of sweat on his skin despite the heat. He was already playing the great nobleman showing off his estates to a yokel.

There was—there had always been even when he was a boy—a glint of irony in his pale eyes, a furtive gleam that seemed to say:

'I've got the better of you and I'll do so again... I'm so much cleverer than you!'

The Seine flowed by in a gentle curve to their left: a wide expanse of water fringed with rushes. On their right, low walls, some very old and others almost new, divided the road from the villas.

There were not many of these, four or five as far as the Superintendent could judge: handsome houses hidden in great well-kept grounds, the paths of which could be seen through garden gates as one passed.

'That's the home of my mother-in-law, whom you had the pleasure of meeting today,' announced Malik as they came to a wide gate with pilasters surmounted by stone lions. 'Old Amorelle bought it some forty years ago from a financial baron of the Second Empire.'

Amid shady trees, Maigret could make out an enormous building which was not particularly beautiful, but which gave an impression of wealth and solidity. Tiny whirling sprays were watering the lawns, while an old gardener, who seemed to have come straight from the pages of a seedsman's catalogue, was raking the gravel paths.

'What do you think of Bernadette Amorelle?' asked Malik, fixing his keen, mischievous gaze on his former schoolfellow.

Maigret mopped his brow, and his companion was obviously thinking:

'Poor old fellow *You*'ve not changed. You're still the loutish son of a country house bailiff. A crude, naive peasant with a certain common sense!'

Aloud, he said:

'Let's go on . . . I live a little further on, past the turning. Do you remember my brother? Of course you didn't know him at school, because he's three years younger than we are. My brother Charles married one of the Amorelle girls about the same time that I married the other . . . He spends the summer in this villa with his wife and our mother-in-law. It was his daughter who died last week.'

Some hundred yards further on they came upon a floating landing-stage by the river bank, painted white and as luxurious as that of any big sailing club.

'This is where my domain begins . . . I've a few small boats, since one's got to amuse oneself somehow in this Godforsaken place . . . Do you like sailing?'

What irony there was in his voice as he asked the heavily-built Superintendent if he liked sailing in one of the slender skiffs visible between the buoys!

'This way . . .'

An iron gate topped with gilt spikes. A glittering gravel path. The garden sloped gently down and soon disclosed a modern building, far larger than the Amorelles' house. Tennis courts on the left, dark red in the sunlight. A swimming pool on the right.

And Malik, with an ever more casual air, like a pretty woman toying carelessly with a jewel worth millions, seemed to be saying:

'Take a good look, you great lout. This place belongs to Malik, to little Malik whom all of you contemptuously called the Tax Collector because his father spent his days in a dark office, behind a grating.'

Some Great Danes came up to lick his hands and he accepted their humble homage with indifference.

'If you like we'll take an apéritif on the terrace while we wait for the dinner bell... My sons are probably out boating on the Seine.'

Behind the villa, a chauffeur in shirtsleeves was hosing down a powerful American car with gleaming nickel-plated fittings.

They went up the steps and sat down under a red parasol in enormous cane chairs. A footman in a white jacket came forward promptly, and Maigret felt as though he were in a grand hotel in some watering-place rather than in a private house.

'A Martini? A Manhattan? What d'you prefer, Jules? According to your legend, which like everyone else I know through the news-papers, you'd rather have a pint of beer at the bar counter... Un-fortunately I've not yet had a bar counter installed here... That'll come, maybe... It would be rather amusing... Two Martinis, Jean! Go ahead, smoke your pipe. What were we saying? Oh yes... My brother and my sister-in-law have been pretty well knocked out by this business, as you can imagine... They only had that one daugh-ter, you see. My sister-in-law's health has never been good...'

Was Maigret listening? If so, it was half unconsciously, and yet the words being spoken were automatically engraved on his memory.

Sunk in his armchair, his eyes half closed, his pipe between pursed lips, he was staring vaguely at the landscape, which was very fine. The sun was sinking and beginning to redden. The terrace where they sat overlooked the whole bend of the Seine and the wooded hills behind it, scarred by the harsh white of a quarry.

A few white sails were moving about on the dark, silken surface of the river, a few gleaming canoes were gliding slowly past, the hum of a motor boat could be heard, and even after it had disappeared into the distance the air still throbbed with the rhythm of its engine.

The manservant had brought them crystal glasses, faintly misted.

'This morning I'd invited them both to spend the day at my house. No point in asking my mother-in-law. She loathes her family, she's liable to spend weeks at a time without leaving her room ...'

His smile seemed to assert:

'You can't understand, poor old Maigret. You're used to humble folk who lead a commonplace life and can't afford the slightest touch of eccentricity.'

And in fact Maigret was ill at ease in this setting. Even the surroundings, too smooth and harmonious, irritated him. He felt no petty jealousy but an actual loathing of that immaculate tennis court, of the well-fed chauffeur whom he had seen polishing the sumptuous car. The landing-stage with its diving boards, its small boats moored all round, the swimming pool, the trimmed trees, the smooth unblemished gravel paths were all part of a world into which he entered reluctantly and in which he felt terribly clumsy.

'I'm telling you all this to explain why I turned up just now at good old Jeanne's. I call her that but actually she's the most treacherous creature on this earth. She was never faithful to her husband Marius in his lifetime but since his death she laments his loss from morning till night.

'So then, my brother and sister-in-law were here. As we were about to sit down to lunch my sister-in-law noticed that she had forgotten her pills. She has a passion for drugs. It's her nerves, she says. I offered to go and fetch them. Instead of taking the road I went through the gardens, for the two estates are contiguous.

'I happened to look down, and on passing the old stables I noticed wheel tracks. I opened the door and I was surprised not to see my father-in-law's old limousine in its place ...

'And that, old man, is how I came to encounter you. I questioned the gardener, who confessed that his boy had gone off an hour previously with the car and that he'd taken Bernadette.

'When they got back I sent for the lad and questioned him. I learned that he had gone to Meung-sur-Loire and that he'd deposited a big fat man with a suitcase at Les Aubrais station. Sorry, old chap. It was he who said a big fat man.

'I immediately thought that my delightful mother-in-law must have been to confide in some private detective, for she's got persecution mania and she's convinced there's Lord knows what mystery about her granddaughter's death.

'I must confess I never thought of you...I knew there was a Maigret in the police force, but I wasn't sure it was my old schoolfellow Jules. What d'you say about it?'

And Maigret merely replied:

'Nothing.'

He said nothing. He was thinking of his house, which was so different, of his garden, of the aubergines, of the peas dropping into the enamel bowl; and he was wondering why he had unquestioningly followed the authoritarian old lady who had literally abducted him.

He was thinking of the hot, noisy train, and of his former office in the Quai des Orfèvres, of all the scoundrels he had examined, of all the little bars, the sordid hotels, the incredible places into which his enquiries had taken him.

Thinking of all this only increased his fury and resentment at being here, in an unfriendly atmosphere, under the sardonic eye of the Tax Collector.

'By and by, if it amuses you, I'll show you round the house. I drew up the plans of it myself with the architect. Of course we don't live here all the year, only in the summer. I've a flat in Paris, in the Avenue Hoche. I've also bought a country house three kilometres from Deauville, and we went there in July. In August the seaside's impossible, because of the people. Now, if you feel like it, you're very welcome to spend a few days with us. Do you play tennis? Do you ride?'

Why not ask him if he went in for golf or water-skiing?

'Note that if you attach the slightest importance to my mother-in-law's story, I'm not stopping you from conducting your little enquiry. I'm entirely at your disposal, and if you need a car and a chauffeur...Hello, here's my wife.'

She emerged from the house on to the terrace, and she, too, was dressed in white.

'My dear, this is Maigret, an old school friend...Maigret, my wife...'

She held out a limp white hand at the end of a white arm, and everything about her was white, her face, her excessively blonde hair.

'Please sit down, Monsieur ...'

What was it about her that gave one a sense of unease? Perhaps it was that her thoughts seemed to be far away? Her voice was neutral, so impersonal that one couldn't be sure whether it was she who had spoken. She sat down in a huge armchair, and one felt that she might just as well have been somewhere else. Nevertheless she kept making slight signs to her husband, which he did not understand. She cast a meaningful glance at the upper floor of the villa, and explained:

'It's Georges-Henry ...'

Then Malik got up, frowning, and said to Maigret:

'Will you excuse me for a moment?'

The other two, his wife and the Superintendent, sat there still and silent. Then suddenly a noise broke out on the upper floor. A door was flung open. Rapid footsteps sounded, a window was banged, and there were muffled voices suggesting a quarrel, or at any rate a sharp argument.

All that Madame Malik could find to say was:

'Had you never been to Orsenne before?'

'No, Madame.'

'It's quite a pretty place if you're fond of the country. And it's so restful, isn't it?'

The word restful took on a particular significance on her lips. She was so limp, maybe so weary, or so lacking in vitality, her body slumped so inertly in the garden chair that she seemed the personification of rest, of perpetual rest.

Yet she was listening attentively to the now diminishing noises from the upper floor, and when these had ceased she spoke again:

'I understand you're having dinner with us?'

For all her good breeding, she was incapable of expressing ordinary polite pleasure. She merely stated a fact, reluctantly. Malik came back, and as Maigret looked up at him he put on his narrow smile again.

'I do apologize ... One always has problems with servants.'

They waited for the dinner bell with a certain embarrassment. Malik, in his wife's presence, seemed to lose some of his carefree manner.

'Jean-Claude's not back yet?'

'I think I can see him on the landing-stage.'

A young man in shorts had, in fact, just landed from a light sailing-boat which he then moored, and, carrying his sweater over his arm, he made his way slowly towards the house. At that moment the dinner bell rang and they moved into the dining room, where they were presently joined by Jean-Claude, Ernest Malik's elder son, now spruced up and dressed in grey flannel.

'If I'd known earlier that you were coming I'd have asked my brother and sister-in-law, so that you could make the acquaintance of the whole family. Tomorrow, if you like, I'll invite them, and our few neighbours. This is where everybody forgathers...There is nearly always a crowd of people, coming and going, making themselves at home.'

The dining room was large and sumptuous. The table was of pink-veined marble and places were laid on tiny individual place mats.

'On the whole, if I'm to believe what the papers say about you, you've not done badly in the police force? Funny job, that. I've often wondered why one becomes a policeman, how and at what point one discovers a vocation for it. For after all...'

His wife was more absentminded than ever. Maigret was watching Jean-Claude, who, as soon as he thought himself unobserved, was himself scrutinizing the Superintendent.

This young man was clearly as cold as the marble table. At nineteen or twenty, he was quite as self-assured as his father. The latter seemed fairly imperturbable, and yet there was a sense of unease in the atmosphere.

Nobody spoke of Monita, who had died the week before. Perhaps they did not like to mention her in the presence of the butler.

'You see, Maigret,' Malik was saying, 'you were all of you blind at school, and you had no idea what you were saying when you called me the Tax Collector. There were some of us, you may remember, who were not well off, who were more or less cold-shouldered by the sons of country gentry and rich bourgeois. Some of us minded, others, like yourself, didn't care.

'They called me the Tax Collector as a term of contempt, and yet that was where my strength lay...

'If you only knew all that a tax collector gets to see! I've discovered the sordid secrets of the most apparently respectable families...the crooked deals by which people get rich. I've watched some go up in the world and others go down, even tumble down, and I began to study the mechanism of it all. The mechanism of society, if you like. Why some go up and others go down.'

He was speaking with contemptuous arrogance, in his luxurious dining room through whose windows could be glimpsed a setting which was itself a further assertion of his success.

'I've gone up, myself...'

The fare was undoubtedly choice, but the ex-Superintendent had no liking for these complicated little dishes with their sauces invariably studded with bits of truffles or crayfish tails. The butler was constantly bending to fill one or other of the glasses set out before him.

The sky was turning green on one side, a cold and seemingly unalterable green, and red on the other, with purplish streaks and a few innocently white clouds. Some canoes still lingered on the Seine, where at intervals the leap of a fish set a series of rings slowly spreading.

Malik's hearing must have been acute, as acute as that of Maigret, who heard the sound too. And yet it was barely perceptible; it was only because of the stillness of the evening that the slightest sound was amplified.

A scraping sound first, coming from a window on the upper floor, from the direction where earlier, before dinner, voices had been raised in anger. Then a soft thud in the garden.

Malik and his son had exchanged glances. Madame Malik had not flinched, but had gone on raising her fork to her mouth.

In a flash, Malik had laid his napkin on the table and a minute later had leapt outside, supple and noiseless in his crepe-soled shoes.

The manservant had seemed as unmoved by the incident as the mistress of the house. But Jean-Claude had flushed slightly. And now he was hunting for something to say, opening his mouth and stammering out a few words.

'My father's still pretty nimble for his age, isn't he?'

He smiled, as he spoke, in just his father's way. And his words implied:

'Something is obviously happening, but it's no concern of yours. Just go on eating and pay no more attention.'

'He beats me at tennis regularly, although I'm not too bad a player myself. He's a remarkable man . . .'

Why did Maigret echo, staring at his plate:

'Remarkable . . .'

Somebody must have been shut up in a room overhead, that was clear. And that somebody must have resented being imprisoned thus, since, before dinner, Malik had been obliged to go up and reprimand him.

The same somebody had sought to take advantage of the meal, during which the whole family was assembled in the dining room, to escape. He had jumped into the soft earth, planted with hydrangeas, which surrounded the house.

It was the sound of his fall on to the flowerbed which Malik had heard at the same time as Maigret.

And he had rushed outside. It must be something serious, serious enough to make him behave in a way that was, to say the least, peculiar.

'Does your brother play tennis too?' asked Maigret, raising his head and looking the young man in the eyes.

'Why do you ask that? No, my brother doesn't care for sport.'

'How old is he?'

'Sixteen. He's just failed his *bachot,* and Father is furious.'

'Is that why he shut him up in his bedroom?'

'Probably. Father and Georges-Henry don't always get on very well together.'

'On the other hand, you get on very well with your father, don't you?'

'Pretty well.'

Maigret happened to glance at his hostess's hand and noticed with astonishment that it was clenched so tightly on her knife that the knuckles wore a bluish tinge.

They all three waited while the butler changed their plates yet again. The air was stiller than ever, so that the slightest rustle of leaves in the trees could be heard.

Georges-Henry, on landing in the garden, had started running. In which direction? Not towards the Seine, for they would have seen him. Behind the house, at the end of the park, ran the railway line. On the right were the grounds of the Amorelles' house.

The father must be running after his son. And Maigret could not resist a smile at the thought of Malik's rage at being forced to undertake this humiliating chase.

They had had time to eat cheese and then dessert. By now they should have left the table and moved to the drawing room or on to the terrace, where darkness had not yet fallen. Looking at his watch, Maigret noticed that twelve minutes had passed since his host had rushed outside.

Madame Malik did not rise. Her son was trying to remind her discreetly of her duty, when at last steps were heard in the hall next door.

The Tax Collector was back again, with the same smile, somewhat strained however, and the first thing that Maigret noticed was that he had changed into a fresh pair of white flannel trousers, whose intact crease showed that they had just come out of the wardrobe.

Had he got caught in some brambles in his chase, or fallen into a stream? He had not had time to go far. His reappearance was none the less something of a record, for he was not out of breath, his iron-grey hair was carefully smoothed, and there was no sign of disarray about his dress or bearing.

'I've got a good-for-nothing for a ...'

The elder son was worthy of his father, for he interrupted him in the most natural way in the world:

'Georges-Henry again, I bet? I was just telling the Superintendent that he'd failed his *bachot* and that you'd shut him up in his room to force him to work.'

Malik remained impassive, betraying no relief, no admiration for this swift rescue. And yet it had been a brilliant stroke, like a precise volley in a tennis match.

'No, thank you, Jean,' Malik said to the butler who was offering to serve him. 'If Madame is willing, we'll go on to the terrace.' Then, to his wife:

'Unless you're feeling tired? ... In that case my friend Maigret will excuse you if you retire. You don't mind, Jules? These last few days have been very hard for her. She was so fond of her niece.'

Something rang false. The words were commonplace enough, the man's tone of voice ordinary enough. Yet Maigret was conscious of discovering, or rather of sensing, under every remark something disturbing or threatening.

Madame Malik sat quite straight in her white dress, looking at them, and Maigret, although he could not have said why, would not have been surprised to see her collapse on to the black and white marble floor.

'If you'll excuse me,' she stammered.

She held out her hand once more; he touched it and found it cold. The three men moved through the french window on to the terrace.

'Cigars and brandy, Jean,' ordered the host.

And then he asked Maigret point-blank:

'Are you married?'

'Yes.'

'Any children?'

'I've not been so lucky.'

A curl of his father's lips did not escape Jean-Claude's notice, but caused him no surprise.

'Sit down, take a cigar!'

Several boxes of these had been brought, Havanas and Manilas, several bottles of liqueurs of various shapes.

'The kid's like his grandmother, you see. There's no trace of Malik about him.'

One of the difficulties about this conversation, the thing that worried Maigret was that he could not bring himself to *tutoyer* his former schoolfellow.

'Did you catch up with him?' he asked hesitantly.

The other inevitably misunderstood Maigret's formality. A glint of satisfaction showed in his eyes. He obviously believed that the ex-Superintendent was impressed by his splendour and did not dare assume a more familiar tone.

'You can say *tu* to me,' he remarked condescendingly, unwrapping a cigar with his long, well-tended fingers. 'When one's sat side by side on a school bench ... No, I didn't catch up with him and I never intended to.'

He was lying. That was clear from the way he had rushed out of the room.

'Only I wanted to know where he was going ... He's a neurotic, as hypersensitive as a girl.

'When I left the room for a moment just now, I'd gone up to give him a talking-to. I was rather harsh with him and I'm always afraid ...'

Did he read in Maigret's eyes that the latter, by analogy, was thinking of Monita, who had drowned herself and who had also been a neurotic? It was highly probable, for he promptly added:

'Oh, it's not what you imagine. He's too fond of himself for that! But he's liable to go on the loose. On one occasion he disappeared for a whole week and he was found by chance on a work site where he'd got himself a job.'

The elder son was listening with an air of indifference. He was on his father's side, clearly. He profoundly despised the brother of whom they were speaking, who bore such a resemblance to their grandmother.

'As I knew he had no pocket money I followed him, and I'm not worrying ... He simply went to see old Bernadette, and at this moment he's probably weeping on her bosom.'

The darkness was gathering, and Maigret had the impression that his interlocutor was being less careful to control his facial expression. His features seemed harder, his eyes even more piercing, without the irony that sometimes tempered their fierceness.

'Do you really want to go back to sleep at Jeanne's? I could send a servant to pick up your luggage.'

This insistence annoyed Maigret, who read a kind of threat in it. Was he making a mistake, perhaps? Was he being influenced by his own ill-humour?

'I shall go and sleep at the Angel,' he said.

'You'll accept my invitation for tomorrow? You'll meet a few interesting characters here. There aren't many of us; just six villas, including the old chateau on the other side of the water. But that's enough to provide a few freaks!'

At that moment a shot rang out in the direction of the river. As Maigret gave a start, his companion explained:

'That's old Groux shooting woodpigeon. He's an eccentric whom you'll meet tomorrow. He owns the whole of the hill that you can see, or rather that the darkness prevents you from seeing, on the far bank. He knows I'm anxious to buy, and for the past twenty years he's stubbornly refused to sell, although he hasn't a penny.'

Why had he almost imperceptibly lowered his voice, as though a fresh idea had struck him in the middle of his remark?

'Can you find your own way back? Jean-Claude will go with you as far as the gate. You'll lock up, Jean-Claude? Follow the tow-path, and two hundred metres on you take the path that leads directly to the Angel . . . If you like listening to stories you'll be well provided for, for old Jeanne, who suffers from insomnia, is bound to be waiting up for you and will give you your money's worth, particularly if you sympathize with her misfortunes and express pity for her many ailments.'

He finished his glass and remained standing, implying that the meeting was at an end.

'Well, I look forward to seeing you about noon tomorrow.'

He held out a hard, muscular hand.

'It's fun meeting again after so long . . . Goodnight, old fellow.'

There was a somewhat patronizing, superior note about the last words.

And while Maigret, accompanied by the elder son, walked down the steps of the terrace, Malik disappeared into the house.

There was no moon, and the night was getting very dark. Maigret, as he walked along the towpath, heard the slow monotonous splash of oars. A voice said softly:

'Stop!'

The noise ceased and was replaced by another, that of a sweep-net being flung from the river bank. Poachers, presumably.

He went on his way, smoking his pipe, thrusting his hands into his pockets, dissatisfied with himself and everyone else, and wondering, actually, what he was doing there instead of being at home.

He went past the wall which enclosed the grounds of the Amorelles' house. As he passed the gate he noticed a light in one of the windows. Now, on his left, there were dark thickets among which, a little further on, he was to find the path that would take him to old Jeanne's.

Suddenly there was a sharp report, followed by a slight rustle on the ground a few yards ahead of him. He stopped short, somewhat disturbed, although it was very like the shot he had heard previously, when Malik had spoken of the old eccentric who spent his evenings shooting woodpigeon.

All was silent. And yet there was somebody there, not far away, probably on the Amorelles' wall, somebody who had fired with a rifle and who had not aimed into the air at some woodpigeon perched on a branch but towards the ground, at Maigret as he went past.

He gave a frown of mingled annoyance and satisfaction. He clenched his fists angrily, and yet he felt relief. He liked it better this way.

'Bastard!' he muttered half aloud.

There was no point in looking for his attacker, in rushing forward as Malik had done a short while previously. In the darkness he would see nothing, and ran the risk of tumbling into a ditch.

His hands still in his pockets, his pipe between his teeth, square-shouldered and deliberately slow-moving, he went on his way and demonstrated his contempt by not for one moment interrupting the rhythm of his step.

He reached the Angel Inn a few minutes later without having been anyone's target again.

3
Family Group in a Drawing Room

At half-past nine, he was not yet up. The wide open window had long since let in the noises from outside, the clucking of hens as they scratched about in the poultry-yard dunghill, the clank of a dog's chain, the persistent hooting of tugs and that, more muted, of motorized barges.

Maigret had a hangover, indeed what he might have described as a filthy hangover. He now knew his old landlady's secret. She had still been there in the dining room when he got back the night before, sitting beside the clock with the brass pendulum. Malik had rightly foreseen that she would be waiting up for him. But it was probably not so much in order to talk as in order to drink.

'She's a regular soak!' he said to himself now, half asleep and reluctant to wake up too abruptly for fear of the headache that he knew awaited him.

He should have realized it from the start. He had known other such ageing women who, having lost all personal vanity, slouched about like this one, moaning and groaning, with shiny faces and greasy hair, complaining of every ailment under the sun.

'I wouldn't mind a glass of something,' he had said, sitting down or rather straddling a chair beside her. 'What about you, Madame Jeanne? What will you take?'

'Nothing, Monsieur. I'd better not drink. Everything upsets me.'

'A tiny drop of liqueur?'

'Well, just to keep you company... Some kümmel, then. Will you help yourself? The bottles are on the shelf. My legs are so terribly swollen this evening.'

Kümmel was her tipple, then. And he, too, had drunk kümmel out of politeness. It had left him still feeling queasy. He vowed never to touch a drop of kümmel again in his life.

How many glasses had she put away on the sly? She had gone on talking, at first in her whining voice and then more excitedly. From time to time, looking the other way, she would grab the bottle and help herself. Until the point when Maigret understood, and filled up her glass every ten minutes.

It was a queer evening. The maid had gone to bed long ago. The cat lay curled up in a ball on Madame Jeanne's lap, the pendulum of the clock swung to and fro in its glass case, and the woman went on talking—about her late husband Marius first,

then about herself, a lady by birth, who for Marius's sake had
given up the chance of marriage with an officer who had since
risen to the rank of general.

'He came here with his wife and children three years ago, a few
days before Marius died. He did not recognize me.'

About Bernadette Amorelle she commented:

'They say she's crazy, but that's not true. Only she's a queer
character. Her husband was a big brute. It was he and Campois who
together started the big quarries on the Seine.'

She was no fool, Madame Jeanne.

'I know by now what you're here for . . . Everybody knows. I believe you're wasting your time.'

She talked about the Maliks, Ernest and Charles.

'You haven't met Charles yet? You will . . . and his wife, the
younger of the Amorelle girls, Mademoiselle Aimée that was. You'll
see them. This is a tiny place, isn't it? Barely a hamlet. And yet
some funny things happen here. Yes, they found Mademoiselle
Monita by the weir.'

No, she—Madame Jeanne—knew nothing. Can one ever tell
what's going on in a girl's head?

She went on drinking, Maigret went on drinking, listening to
her, filling their glasses; he sat there as though under a spell, remarking from time to time:

'I'm stopping you from going to bed.'

'You don't need to worry about me. I sleep so little, with all my
aches and pains! But if you're sleepy . . .'

He had stayed there a little longer. And when they had each gone
up by a different staircase, he had heard a din which implied that
Madame Jeanne had fallen down on the stairs.

She must still be in bed. Maigret got up at last and went to the
bathroom to have a long drink of cold water and then to wash away
the unpleasant sticky sweat, redolent of alcohol, of kümmel. No,
never again would he touch a glass of kümmel!

Hello! Somebody had just come to the inn. He heard the maid's
voice saying:

'I tell you he's still asleep . . .'

He leaned out of the window and saw a lady's maid, dressed in black with a white apron, in conversation with Raymonde.

'Is it for me?' he asked.

And the lady's maid, looking up, remarked:

'You see he's not asleep!'

She was holding a letter in her hand, a black-edged envelope, and she declared:

'I'm to wait for an answer.'

Raymonde brought up the letter. He had put on his trousers and his braces were hanging loosely over his thighs. It was hot already, and a light haze was rising from the river.

Please come and see me as soon as possible. You had better follow my maid, who will bring you to my room, otherwise they might perhaps stop you coming up. I know that you are to meet them all at lunch.

Bernadette Amorelle.

He followed the lady's maid, who was fortyish and very ugly, with the same boot-button eyes as her mistress. She did not utter a single word and her whole attitude seemed to say:

'It's no use trying to make me talk. I've got my orders and you won't make me budge.'

They skirted the wall, passed through the gateway, and followed the walk that led to the huge Amorelle residence. Birds were singing in every tree in the park. The gardener was pushing a wheelbarrow full of manure.

The house was less modern than that of Ernest Malik, less sumptuous, as though the mists of time had already dimmed its splendour.

'This way...'

They did not go in through the main door, which stood at the top of a flight of steps, but by a small door in the right wing, and they went up a staircase whose walls were hung with nineteenth-century prints. They had not even reached the landing when a door opened and Madame Amorelle appeared, as upright and categorical as on the previous day.

'You've taken a long time,' she declared.

'The gentleman wasn't ready . . . I had to wait while he got dressed.'

'Come in this way, Superintendent. I should have expected a man like yourself to be an early riser.'

Her bedroom was huge, with three windows. The four-poster bed was already made. There were things lying about on various pieces of furniture, and one felt that the old lady spent almost her entire life in this room, that it was her exclusive domain, the door of which she opened only reluctantly.

'Sit down. Yes, sit down. I hate talking to people who are standing up. You may smoke your pipe, if that's what you want to do. My husband smoked a pipe from morning till night. It smells less revolting than cigars . . . So you've already dined with my son-in-law?'

It might have been amusing to find oneself thus treated like a small boy, but Maigret's sense of humour was lacking that morning.

'Yes, I dined with Ernest Malik,' he said sullenly.

'What did he tell you?'

'That you were a crazy old woman and that his son Georges-Henry was nearly as mad as yourself.'

'Did you believe him?'

'Later, as I was on my way back to the Angel, somebody, presumably considering that my career had gone on long enough, fired a shot in my direction. I suppose the young man was here?'

'What young man? . . . Do you mean Georges-Henry? I didn't see him all evening.'

'But his father declared that he had taken refuge with you.'

'If you take all that he says as gospel truth . . .'

'Have you no news of the boy?'

'None, and I'd be very glad to have some. In short, what have you learnt?'

He looked at her then and wondered, he didn't know why, whether she was really anxious for him to have learnt anything.

'Apparently,' she went on, 'you're on very good terms with my son-in-law Ernest.'

'We were in the same class in school at Moulins, and he insists on addressing me as *tu*, as though we were still twelve years old.'

He was in a bad mood. His head was aching, his pipe tasted

nasty, and he had had to leave the inn without a cup of coffee, since there had been none ready there.

'I'm worried about Georges-Henry,' she was muttering now. 'He was very fond of his cousin. I'm not sure that there wasn't something going on between them.'

'He's sixteen years old!'

She looked him up and down.

'And what difference does that make? I was never so much in love as when I was sixteen, and if I'd ever done something crazy, that's when I would have done it. You'd better find Georges-Henry.'

Coldly, almost sarcastically, he asked:

'Where do you advise me to look?'

'That's your job and not mine. I wonder why his father pretended he'd seen him come here? Malik knows very well that's not true.'

Her voice betrayed real anxiety. She was pacing to and fro about the room, but each time Maigret made as though to rise she repeated the order:

'Sit down.'

She seemed to be speaking to herself.

'They've organized a big lunch for today. Charles Malik and his wife will be there. And they've invited old Campois and that old dodderer Groux. I got a card, too, first thing this morning. I wonder if Georges-Henry will be back.'

'You've nothing else to say to me, Madame?'

'What do you mean by that?'

'Nothing. When you came to Meung yesterday you implied that you refused to believe that your granddaughter's death was a natural one.'

She was staring intensely at him, without betraying her thoughts.

'And since you've been in this place,' she retorted with some vehemence, 'are you going to tell me that you find the goings-on here natural?'

'I never said that.'

'Well, carry on. Go to that lunch.'

'Will you be there?'

'I don't know. Keep your eyes and ears open. And if you're as clever as they say . . .'

She was not pleased with him, obviously. Had he not been sufficiently docile, sufficiently respectful of her whims? Was she disappointed that he had as yet discovered nothing?

She was uneasy and on edge, in spite of her self-control. She went to the door, thus dismissing him.

'I'm very much afraid those scoundrels are too clever for you!' she remarked by way of farewell. 'We shall see. In the meantime I'm willing to bet whatever you like that the others are waiting for you downstairs.'

It was quite true. As he reached the passage a door opened noiselessly. A lady's maid, not the one who had brought him, addressed him deferentially:

'Monsieur and Madame Malik are expecting you in the small drawing room. If you'll be so kind as to follow me . . .'

The house was cool, with the walls painted in faded colours, carved doors, pier-glasses, paintings and prints everywhere. Soft carpets muffled footsteps, and the Venetian blinds let in just the right amount of light.

One last door. He took a couple of steps forward and found himself in the presence of Monsieur and Madame Malik, in deep mourning, waiting for him.

For some reason, he had an impression not of real life but of a cunningly composed picture, a family group. Charles Malik, whom he now met for the first time, had very different features from his brother, although there was a family likeness. He was somewhat younger, and stouter; his florid face was rosier and his eyes were not grey like Ernest's but of an almost candid blue.

He lacked his brother's self-confidence, and he had pouches under his eyes, a weak mouth and an uneasy glance.

He stood very upright in front of the white marble chimney piece, and his wife sat beside him in a Louis XVI armchair, with her hands folded on her knee, as though posing for a photograph.

There was an air of unhappiness, almost of despondency, about them both. Charles Malik spoke in a hesitant voice:

'Come in, Superintendent, and forgive us for asking you to spare us a moment.'

Madame Malik was a more delicate version of her sister, with something of her mother's vivacity. Just now that vivacity was dimmed, but her recent bereavement was enough to explain that. In her right hand she clutched a small handkerchief rolled into a ball, and she kept pressing it throughout their interview.

'Do sit down, please. I know that we are to meet at my brother's presently. I shall be there, at any rate, although I doubt whether my wife will feel strong enough to join the party at lunch. I am aware of the circumstances under which you have come here, and I would like...'

He glanced at his wife, who merely returned his look with great simplicity and firmness.

'We have been going through a very distressing time, Superintendent, and my mother-in-law's obstinacy seems likely to involve us in even more painful ordeals. You have seen her. I don't know what you think of her.'

Maigret, in any case, was careful not to tell him, for he sensed that his interlocutor was beginning to flounder and was once more appealing to his wife for help.

'My mother,' she said, 'is eighty-two years old, one mustn't forget that. One forgets it too readily because she has such exceptional vitality. Unfortunately her reasoning powers are not always equal to her energy. The death of my daughter, who was her favourite, has been a terrible shock to her.'

'I realized that, Madame.'

'You can see now in what sort of atmosphere we've been living since the catastrophe. Mother has got it into her head that there's some mystery underlying it.'

'The Superintendent has certainly understood,' Charles Malik put in. 'Don't get so het-up, dearest... My wife is in a highly nervous state, Superintendent. We all are, just now. It's only our affection for my mother-in-law that prevents us from taking certain necessary steps. That is why we are asking you...'

Maigret was all ears.

'...We are asking you... to weigh the pros and cons carefully before...'

In fact, might not this fat, diffident man have been his last night's assailant? The idea struck Maigret suddenly, and it was by no means implausible.

Ernest Malik was a cool character, and undoubtedly if he had fired he would have aimed more accurately. This man, on the other hand...

'I understand your position,' Charles Malik went on, leaning against the mantelpiece in an attitude more than ever suggestive of a family portrait. 'It is an exceedingly delicate one. On the whole...'

'On the whole,' Maigret cut him short, assuming his demurest manner, 'I wonder what I'm doing here at all.'

He cast a surreptitious glance at the other man and did not fail to note his quiver of relief.

That was exactly what they had wanted to make him say. What was he doing there, after all? Nobody had sent for him, except an old woman of eighty-two who was not in her perfect mind.

'I wouldn't go so far as to say that,' Charles Malik rectified, like a perfect gentleman, 'seeing that you're a friend of Ernest's. But I think it would be better...'

'Please go on.'

'Yes...I think it would be proper, shall we say desirable, not to encourage my mother-in-law in ideas which...that...'

'You are convinced, Monsieur Malik, that your daughter's death was completely natural?'

'I think it was an accident.'

He had reddened, but his voice was quite firm.

'And you, Madame?'

By now the handkerchief was a tiny ball in her hand.

'I think the same as my husband.'

'In that case, obviously...'

He was giving them hope. He could feel them exulting in the hope of being rid forever of his oppressive presence.

'...I am of course obliged to accept your brother's invitation. After that, if nothing happens, if no fresh fact should emerge requiring my presence...'

He rose, feeling almost as uncomfortable as they were. He couldn't wait to be outside, so as to breathe freely.

'We shall meet presently, then,' said Charles Malik. 'I apologize for not seeing you out, but there's still so much I have to do.'

'Of course. My respects, Madame.'

He was still in the grounds making his way towards the Seine when he heard a noise that struck him. It was the click of a rural telephone, followed by the brief ringing note that meant the call was being answered.

'He's calling his brother to put him in the picture,' he thought. And he could imagine the words:

'It's all right! He's going away. He's promised to. Provided nothing happens at lunchtime.'

A tug was dragging eight barges upstream, a tug bearing the green triangle of the Amorelle and Campois company; the barges, too, belonged to the same firm.

It was only half-past eleven. He could not face a visit to the Angel, where indeed there was nothing for him to do. He walked along the river bank, ruminating vaguely. He paused, with his back to Ernest Malik's house, to contemplate the latter's luxurious diving board.

'Hello, Maigret!'

It was Ernest Malik, now wearing a grey tweed suit, white suede shoes and a panama hat.

'My brother has just rung me up.'

'I know.'

'I gather you're already fed up with my mother-in-law's romances.'

There was a certain pent-up feeling in his voice, a certain insistence in his gaze.

'If I understand correctly, you're anxious to get back to your wife and your vegetable patch?'

Then, without knowing why (perhaps that is what they call inspiration), Maigret deliberately assumed an even greater stolidity and inertia:

'No,' he said.

Malik was clearly taken aback. All his presence of mind could not prevent him from betraying it. For a moment he seemed to have difficulty in swallowing, and his Adam's apple rose and fell two or three times.

'Ah!...'

He glanced round briefly, but it was not with the intention of pushing Maigret into the Seine.

'We've plenty of time before the guests arrive. We usually lunch late. Come into my study for a moment.'

Not a word was uttered while they crossed the park. Maigret caught sight of Madame Malik arranging flowers in the drawing room.

They went round the villa, and Malik led his guest into a large study with deep leather armchairs, its walls adorned with models of boats.

'You can smoke...'

He closed the door carefully, and drew down the Venetian blinds part way, for the sunlight was pouring into the room. Finally he sat down at his desk and started playing with a crystal paper knife.

Maigret had perched on the arm of a chair and was slowly filling his pipe, apparently thinking of nothing. When the silence had lasted a fair while, he asked gently:

'Where is your son?'

'Which one?'

Then, correcting himself:

'We're not concerned with my son.'

'We're concerned with me.'

'What do you mean.'

'Nothing.'

'Well, yes! We're concerned with you.'

By the side of the well-dressed, well-groomed man with his lean elegant figure and his finely cut features, Maigret really looked like a yokel.

'How much are you offering me?'

'Who says I'm planning to offer you anything?'

'I assume you are.'

'Why not, after all? The administration's not very generous. I don't know what your pension amounts to.'

Maigret, still meek and gentle, replied:

'Three thousand two hundred.'

He added, with disarming candour:

'Of course we've saved a little.'

This time Ernest Malik was really disturbed. It all seemed to him too easy. He had the impression that his old schoolfellow was making fun of him. And yet...

'Listen to me...'

'I'm all ears.'

'I know what you're going to think.'

'I think so little!'

'You're going to imagine that you embarrass me, that I've got something to hide. And even if that were so?'

'Yes, even if that were so? It's none of my business, is it?'

'Are you being sarcastic?'

'By no means.'

'You'd be wasting your time with me, you see. You probably think yourself very clever. You've made a success of an honourable career by hunting down thieves and murderers. Well, my poor Jules, you'll find neither thieves nor murderers here. Do you understand? By sheer chance you've landed in a social set that you don't know and in which you're likely to do a good deal of harm. That's why I'm telling you...'

'How much?'

'A hundred thousand.' He did not falter, but after a certain hesitation, nodded:

'A hundred and fifty. I'd go up to two hundred thousand.'

He had stood up, tense and edgy, still playing with the paper-knife, which suddenly snapped between his fingers. A drop of blood oozed on his forefinger, and Maigret commented:

'You've hurt yourself.'

'Shut up. Or rather answer my question. I'll write you a cheque for two hundred thousand francs. Not a cheque? It doesn't matter... We'll drive up to Paris presently and I'll get the cash from my bank. Then I'll take you back to Meung.'

Maigret sighed.

'What's your answer?'

'Where's your son?'

This time Malik could not restrain his anger.

'That's none of your business. It's nobody's business, d'you hear? I'm not in your office at the Quai des Orfèvres, and you're not there yourself now. I'm asking you to go away because your presence here is inopportune, to say the least. People have started wondering...'

'What are they wondering, exactly?'

'For the last time, I'm asking you to go away quietly. I'm ready to offer you ample compensation to that end. Is it yes or no?'

'It's no, of course.'

'Very well. In that case, I shall have to adopt another tone.'

'By all means.'

'I'm no choirboy, and I never have been. Otherwise I'd not have become what I am now. But by your obstinacy, your stupidity—yes, stupidity—you're liable to trigger off tragedies of which you've not even dreamt. And you're pleased with yourself, aren't you? You think you're still at Police Headquarters, grilling some little thug or some young hooligan who's strangled an old woman.

'I tell you I've strangled nobody and I've robbed nobody.'

'In that case...'

'Silence! You want to stay, so you shall stay. You'll go on sticking your clumsy nose into things. Only it'll be at your own risk.

'I tell you, Maigret, I'm much stronger than you are and I've proved it. If I'd been made of the same stuff as you I'd have become a worthy little tax collector like my father.

'Meddle in other people's business if you like. It'll be at your own risk.'

He had recovered his outward calm, and his lips once again curled sarcastically.

Maigret had risen and was looking about him for his hat.

'Where are you going?'

'Out.'

'Aren't you having lunch with us?'

'I'd sooner lunch elsewhere.'

'Just as you please. This again shows you to be mean-minded and petty.'

'Is that all?'

'For the time being, yes.'

Hat in hand, Maigret walked calmly to the door; he opened it and went out without turning back. Outside, a figure moved swiftly away, and he had time to recognize Jean-Claude, the elder son, who must have been hidden under the open window during the whole conversation and heard it all.

Maigret now went back round the villa, and in the main walk he met two men he had never seen before.

One of them was short and squat, with a very thick neck and large coarse hands: Monsieur Campois, undoubtedly, for he fitted the description Jeanne had given Maigret the night before. The other, who must have been his grandson, was a tall open-faced lad.

Both stared at him in some surprise as he walked calmly towards the garden gate, then both turned round and stopped to watch him.

'That was a good job done,' Maigret said to himself as he walked off along the river bank.

A boat was crossing the river, piloted by an old man wearing a suit of unbleached holland with a bright red tie. It was Monsieur Groux, on his way to join the party. They would all be there except himself, for whose sake actually the lunch had been organized.

And Georges-Henry? Maigret stepped out faster. He was not hungry, but terribly thirsty. In any case he vowed to himself that under no circumstances would he drink any more glasses of kümmel with old Jeanne.

When he entered the inn, he did not see the landlady in her usual place beside the old clock. He looked into the kitchen, and Raymonde exclaimed:

'I thought you weren't coming back to lunch here!'

Then, raising her sturdy arms to heaven:

'I've nothing ready. As it happens, Madame is ill and won't come down.'

There was not even any beer in the house.

4
The Kennel in the Upper Park

It would have been hard to say how it had happened; the fact was
that Maigret and Raymonde had become firm friends. Only an
hour before, she had practically denied him entry into her kitchen.

'Haven't I told you there's nothing to eat?'

Moreover, she disliked men. They were all brutes, and they
smelt. Most of those who came to the Angel, even married men,
had tried to fondle her, and this disgusted her.

She would have liked to become a Sister of Charity. She was a
big girl, rather limp in spite of her apparent robustness.

'What are you looking for?' she asked impatiently on seeing the
Superintendent standing squarely in front of the open cupboard.

'A bit of something to eat. Any leftovers. It's so hot that I haven't
the courage to go off to the lock to eat.'

'If you think there are any leftovers here, you're wrong! For one
thing, the place is supposed to be closed. Or rather it's for sale. Has
been for the last three years. And each time it's on the point of
being sold the *patronne* changes her mind, makes some objection
and in the end says no. She doesn't need to make her living by it,
you can be sure!'

'What are you going to eat yourself?'

'Some bread and cheese.'

'And do you think there won't be enough for both of us?'

He looked gentle enough, with his somewhat flushed face and his
big round eyes. He had settled down in the kitchen, making himself
at home. And Raymonde had protested in vain:

'You can't stay there, I haven't even done the housework. I'll set
your place in the dining room.'

He had stubbornly persisted.

'I'll see if there's a tin of sardines left, but it's not very likely.
There are no shops hereabouts. The butcher, the pork-butcher and
even the grocer from Corbeil deliver at the big houses, at the Maliks' and the Campois'. They used to stop here once, and we could
stock up. But now the *patronne* eats nothing and she thinks other

people can just do like her. Wait till I see if there are any eggs in the henhouse.'

There were three. Maigret insisted on making an omelette, and she was amused to see him beat the egg yolks and whites separately.

'Why didn't you go to lunch at the Maliks' since you were invited? It seems they've got a cook who's been chef to the King of Norway or the King of Sweden, I've forgotten which.'

'I'd sooner stay here and have a snack with you.'

'In the kitchen! On a table without a cloth!'

It was quite true, however. And Raymonde, without realizing it, was being a great help to him. Here he felt at his ease. He had taken off his jacket and rolled up his shirtsleeves. From time to time he got up to pour boiling water on to the coffee.

'I wonder what keeps her here,' Raymonde had said about old Jeanne, among other things. 'She has more money than she'll ever spend, no children, and no heirs, for she quarrelled with her nephews a long time ago.'

Such comments, combined with his recollections of the previous night and with various trifling details, gave real solidity to Maigret's picture of the landlady.

She had been goodlooking, Raymonde had said. And it was true. One could sense it, even though at fifty she was a sloven with greasy hair and a drab skin.

A woman who had once been goodlooking, who was intelligent, and who all of a sudden had let herself go, who had taken to drink and lived in unsociable seclusion, moaning and groaning, sometimes so tipsy that she took to her bed for days on end.

'She'll never bring herself to leave Orsenne.'

Well! When all the people concerned had assumed the same human solidity, when he could 'feel' them as he felt the landlady of the Angel, he'd have come close to solving the mystery.

There was Bernadette Amorelle, whom he had almost understood.

'Old Monsieur Amorelle, who died, wasn't at all the same sort of man as his sons-in-law. More like Monsieur Campois. I don't know if you can understand. He was hard, but fair-minded. He'd sometimes go to the lock to have a chat with his bargees and he never minded having a drink with them.'

The first generation, in short, the rising men. The big solid house, without excessive ostentation.

Then the second generation, the two daughters who had married the Malik brothers: the modern villa, the landing-stage, the luxury motorcars.

'Tell me, Raymonde, did you know Monita well?'

'Of course I knew her. I used to see her when she was quite a little girl, for I've been seven years at the Angel, and seven years ago she wasn't more than ten years old. A real tomboy... She was always running away from her governess and they had to hunt for her everywhere. Sometimes all the servants had to be sent out along the river calling Monita. Most of the time she was up to some mischief or other with her cousin Georges-Henry.'

Another character whom Maigret had never met. Raymonde described him.

'He wasn't always spick and span like his brother, you bet! Almost always wearing shorts, grubby shorts too, with bare legs and untidy hair. He was scared stiff of his father!'

'Were Monita and Georges-Henry in love?'

'I don't know if Monita was in love. A woman's always better at hiding her feelings. But he certainly was.'

It was quiet in the kitchen, lit only by a slanting sunbeam. Maigret was smoking his pipe and sipping his coffee, elbows on the shiny wooden table.

'Have you seen him since his cousin's death?'

'I saw him at the funeral. He was very pale and his eyes were red. In the middle of the service he began to sob. In the churchyard, when we were all walking past the open grave, he suddenly seized armfuls of flowers and flung them on to the coffin.'

'And since then?'

'I believe they haven't allowed him out.'

She was looking at Maigret with curiosity. She had heard say that he was an important policeman, that during the course of his career he had arrested hundreds of criminals and had solved the most complicated cases. And here he was in her kitchen, in his shirtsleeves, smoking his pipe and talking familiarly to her, asking her the most ordinary sort of question.

What could he be hoping for? She almost felt a little sorry for him. He was probably getting old, since he had retired.

'Now I've got to do my dishes, then I must wash the floor.'

He went on sitting there with the same placid expression, as though he hadn't a thought in his head.

Then he suddenly muttered under his breath:

'So Monita is dead and Georges-Henry has disappeared.'

She looked up quickly.

'Are you sure he's disappeared?'

He stood up then, his whole attitude changed and hardened, as though he had suddenly come to a decision.

'Listen to me a moment, Raymonde. Wait. Give me a pencil and paper.'

She tore a page from a greasy notebook in which she kept her accounts. She could not make out what he was getting at.

'Yesterday ... Let's see ... We'd reached the cheese course. So it was about nine o'clock. Georges-Henry jumped out of his bedroom window and ran off.'

'Which way?'

'Towards the right. If he had gone towards the Seine I'd have seen him cross the grounds. If he had gone to the left I'd have seen him too, for the dining room has windows on both sides. Wait a minute ... His father went after him. Ernest Malik was away for twelve minutes. It's true that he took some of the time to change his trousers and tidy his hair: for that, he must have gone up to his room, say three or four minutes at least. Think carefully before answering, you who know the neighbourhood. Which way could Georges-Henry have gone if he'd wanted to get away from Orsenne?'

'To the right there's his grandmother's and his uncle's house,' she said at first, looking at the rudimentary map he had drawn as he spoke. 'Between the grounds of the two houses there's no wall, but a quickset hedge that you can get through in two or three places.'

'And then?'

'From the next-door park he could have reached the tow-path. If you follow that, you come to the station.'

'It's not possible to leave the path before the station?'

'No . . . unless you take a boat and cross the Seine.'

'Is it possible to get out at the far end of the park?'

'Only if you've got a ladder. The railway line runs past at the end of the two parks. Both the Amorelles' estate and the Maliks' have a wall that's too high to be climbed.'

'One more piece of information. When I was coming back an hour later, there was a boat on the river. I heard a sweep-net being thrown.'

'That's Alphonse, the lockkeeper's son.'

'Thank you, Raymonde. If you don't mind, let's have dinner together.'

'But there's nothing to eat.'

'There's a grocer's next to the lock. I'll buy whatever we need.'

He was pleased with himself. He felt he was on terra firma again, and Raymonde watched him tramp off towards the weir, which was about five hundred metres distant. There were no boats in the lock, and the lockkeeper, sitting on his slate doorstep, was cutting a piece of wood for one of his small sons, while in the dark kitchen a woman could be seen moving to and fro with a baby in her arms.

'Tell me . . .' the ex-Superintendent began.

The other man had already stood up and touched his cap.

'You've come about the young lady, haven't you?'

He was well known in the neighbourhood already. Everybody had heard of his presence.

'Why, yes and no . . . I suppose you know nothing about her?'

'Except that I found her there, just by the third bar of the weir. It gave me quite a turn, because we knew her very well. She often came through the lock on her way down to Corbeil in her canoe.'

'Was your son on the river last night?'

The man showed some embarrassment.

'You needn't worry. I'm not after poachers. I noticed him about ten o'clock, but I'd like to know if he'd already been out an hour earlier.'

'He'll tell you himself. You'll find him in his workshop, a hundred metres lower down. He's the boatbuilder.'

The workshop was a wooden shed where two men were busy finishing a flat-bottomed fishing boat.

'I was on the water with Albert, yes... he's my apprentice. We laid the nets first, then on the way back...'

'If anyone had crossed the Seine in a boat, about nine o'clock, between the Maliks' house and the lock, would you have seen him?'

'Certainly. For one thing it wouldn't have been really dark. And then, even if we hadn't seen him we'd have heard him. When you do our sort of fishing you need to have sharp ears and...'

In the little store where the bargees got their provisions, Maigret bought tinned food, eggs, cheese and sausage.

'It's obvious you're staying at the Angel,' commented the woman who kept the shop. 'There's never anything to eat in that place. They'd do better to close it down completely.'

He went on to the station. It was merely a halt, with a little house for the gatekeeper.

'No, Monsieur, nobody passed at that time of the evening, no one passed until half-past ten. I was sitting on a chair in front of the house with my wife. Monsieur Georges-Henry? Certainly not him. We know him well and in any case he'd have stopped for a chat, for he knows us too and he's not proud.'

Maigret persisted nonetheless. He peered over hedges, hailed the good people, mostly retired folk, who were working in their gardens.

'Monsieur Georges-Henry? No, we haven't seen him. Has he disappeared like his cousin?'

A big car passed. It was Ernest Malik's car, carrying not Ernest but his brother Charles towards the Paris road.

It was seven o'clock when Maigret got back to the Angel Inn. Raymonde burst out laughing to see him empty his pockets, which were loaded with provisions.

'With all that,' she said, 'we can have a proper snack!'

'Is the *patronne* still in bed? Has anyone called to see her?'

Raymonde had a moment's hesitation.

'Monsieur Malik came just now. When I told him you'd gone to the lock, he went upstairs. They spent about a quarter of an hour whispering together, but I couldn't hear what they said.'

'Does he often come to visit Jeanne?'

'Sometimes, when he happens to be passing. Have you any news of Georges-Henry?'

He went to smoke a pipe in the garden while waiting for dinner. Bernadette Amorelle had seemed to be speaking the truth when she said she had not seen her grandson. That proved nothing, of course. Maigret was almost inclined to believe that they were every one of them liars.

And yet he had the impression that what she had said was true.

There was something at Orsenne, in the Malik circle, that had to be hidden at all costs. Was this something connected with the death of Monita? Possibly, though not inevitably.

The fact remained that one person had already run away; old Madame Amorelle had taken advantage of the absence of her daughter and son-in-law to travel to Meung in the ancient limousine and summon Maigret to her rescue.

And that same day, while the ex-Superintendent was actually in Ernest Malik's house, somebody else had tried to escape. This time it was Georges-Henry.

Why had his father asserted that the boy was at his grandmother's? Why, in that case, had he not brought him back? And why had Georges-Henry not been seen again next day?

Undoubtedly, it was all very puzzling. Ernest Malik had every right to look at Maigret with a sarcastic and contemptuous smile. This was no job for him. He felt ill at ease in it. This was a world with which he was unfamiliar and which he found it hard to reconstruct.

Even the setting offended him by what struck him as its artificiality. These big country houses with their empty parks, their drawn blinds, the gardeners going to and fro along the paths, the landing-stage with its miniature, over-glossy boats, the sleek cars waiting in the garages...

And the inhabitants who stuck together, brothers and sisters-in-law who may well have detested one another but who warned each other of possible dangers and united against him.

They were in deep mourning, into the bargain. They had in their favour the dignity of mourning and grief. On what pretext, by what right had he come prowling around them and thrusting his nose into their affairs?

He had almost given it all up a short while ago, at the moment when he had gone back to the Angel for lunch. And it was the atmosphere of that kitchen, with its homely untidiness, it was the amenable Raymonde and the remarks she had let fall casually, unintentionally, sitting with elbows on the table, which had detained him, and which he had retained.

She had spoken about Monita who was a tomboy and who loved to run wild with her cousin; and about Georges-Henry in his grubby shorts, with his tangled hair.

Now Monita was dead and Georges-Henry had disappeared.

Maigret would look for him. He would find him. That, at any rate, was his job. He had been all round Orsenne; he was practically certain, now, that the lad had not left the place. Unless he had gone to earth somewhere pending nightfall, and had then slipped away without being seen.

Back in the kitchen with Raymonde, Maigret enjoyed his meal.

'If the *patronne* were to see us, she'd be annoyed,' the maid commented. 'She asked me just now what you'd had to eat. I told her I'd given you a couple of fried eggs in the dining room. Then she asked me if you'd spoken of leaving.'

'Before or after Malik's visit?'

'After . . .'

'In that case I'm prepared to bet she won't come downstairs tomorrow either.'

'She came down a short while ago. I didn't see her, I was at the far end of the garden. But I noticed that she'd been down.'

He smiled. He had understood. He could picture Jeanne creeping down noiselessly, after waiting till her servant had gone out, and removing a bottle from the shelf.

'I may be back late,' he announced.

'Have they invited you again?'

'No, I haven't been invited. But want to go for a stroll.'

He first walked along the tow-path till nightfall. Then he went towards the level crossing, where he saw the gatekeeper, in the dark, sitting by his door smoking a long-stemmed pipe.

'Do you mind if I take a little walk along the line?'

'Why, it's not strictly speaking allowed, but since you're police, why not? Watch out for the train that passes at 10.17.'

Some three hundred metres brought him in sight of the wall that enclosed the first estate, that of Madame Amorelle and Charles Malik. Night had not completely fallen, but the lights had long since gone out in most houses.

There was a light on the ground floor of the Amorelle house. One of the first floor windows, in the old lady's bedroom, was wide open, and it was a strange sensation to peer from afar, through the bluish air of the quiet park, into the privacy of an interior where objects and furniture seemed held fast in a yellow glow.

He lingered a few minutes to watch. A figure passed within his field of vision, and it was not Bernadette's but that of her daughter, Charles's wife, walking to and fro excitedly and apparently speaking with some vehemence.

The old lady must have been in her armchair or in bed, or in some corner of the room out of his sight.

He walked on along the railway line and reached the second park, that of Ernest Malik, which was more open and less thickly wooded, with broad, carefully kept walks. In that house, too, lights were on, but they percolated faintly through the slats of the Venetian blinds and nothing could be seen within.

Hidden behind some young hazel bushes that grew alongside the line, Maigret could overlook the park itself, where he now caught sight of two big white silent figures, and he recalled the Great Danes which, on the previous evening, had come to lick their master's hands.

Presumably they were let out every night, and they must be fierce watchdogs.

To the right, at the far end of the park, there stood a cottage which Maigret had not seen before and which must house the gardeners and the chauffeur.

Here too there was a light, a single light, which went out half an hour later.

The moon had not yet risen, but it was less dark than on the previous night. Maigret sat quietly on the embankment, hidden by the nut bushes which he could push aside with his hand like a curtain.

The 10.17 train passed, less than three metres away from him, and he watched its red light disappear round the bend of the line.

The sparse lights of Orsenne went out one after the other. Old Groux could not have been shooting woodpigeon this evening, for no shot disturbed the stillness of the night.

At last, at about eleven o'clock, the two dogs, which had been lying side by side at the edge of a lawn, rose simultaneously and moved towards the house.

They vanished for a moment behind it, and when they reappeared they were prancing beside the figure of a man who was walking hurriedly and, it seemed, directly towards him.

It was Ernest Malik, without a doubt. The figure was too slender and wiry to be one of the servants. He wore rubber-soled shoes and was walking over the lawns, carrying some object which it was impossible to make out but which was fairly voluminous.

At first Maigret wondered where Malik could possibly be going. He saw him suddenly bear right and come so close to the wall that he could hear the two dogs breathing.

'Down, Satan...Down, Lionne...'

There, between the trees, was a small brick building which was obviously older than the house itself, a low building roofed with old tiles, possibly a former stable or kennel.

'It's a kennel,' Maigret said to himself. 'He's simply coming to feed the dogs.'

But Malik now turned away the dogs, drew a key from his pocket and entered the building. Maigret could distinctly hear the key turning in the lock. Then there was a long silence, during which Maigret let his pipe go out without daring to light it again.

Half an hour went by thus, and at last Malik emerged from the hut, closed the door carefully behind him and, after casting a look all round, went rapidly back towards the house.

At half-past eleven all was still and seemingly asleep, and when Maigret went back past the Amorelle estate there was only a night-light dimly shining in old Bernadette's bedroom.

The Angel Inn, too, was in darkness. He wondered how he was going to get in; then the door opened noiselessly. He saw, or rather guessed at, the figure of Raymonde, in her nightgown, her bare feet in slippers; laying a finger on her lips she whispered:

'Go upstairs quickly. Don't make a noise. She wouldn't let me leave the door open.'

He would have liked to linger, put a few questions to her and have something to drink, but a creaking sound from Jeanne's bedroom scared the girl and she rushed upstairs.

Then Maigret stood still for some little while. The air smelt of fried eggs, with a whiff of alcohol. Why not? He struck a match, took a bottle from the shelf and tucked it under his arm to go up to bed.

Old Jeanne was stirring in her room. She must have realized that he was back. But he had no desire to go and keep her company.

He took off his jacket, his collar and tie, let his braces hang down loosely and mixed himself a brandy and water in his tooth glass. Then a final pipe, leaning on the windowsill, gazing out over the faintly rustling foliage.

He did not wake up until seven o'clock, when he heard Raymonde moving about in the kitchen. With his pipe between his lips—the first pipe, always the best—he went down and greeted her cheerfully.

'Tell me, Raymonde, as you know all the houses in the neighbourhood...'

'I know them without really knowing them.'

'All right. At the far end of Ernest Malik's park there is the gardeners' house on one side.'

'Yes. The chauffeur and the menservants sleep there too. Not the maids, who sleep in the villa.'

'But on the other side, close to the railway embankment?'

'There's nothing there.'

'There's a very low, long building, a sort of hut.'

'That's the upper kennel,' she said.

'What d'you mean by that?'

'In the old days, long before I came here, there was just the one park. It belonged to the Amorelles. Old Amorelle liked shooting. He had two kennels, one at the lower end of the park for the watch-dogs, one at the upper end for the game-dogs.'

'Does Ernest Malik not go in for shooting?'

'Not here, where there's not enough game for his liking. He's got a shooting lodge and some dogs in Sologne.'

Something still worried Maigret.

'What sort of state is the building in?'

'I don't remember. It's a long time since I went into the park. There used to be a cellar where ...'

'You're sure there's a cellar?'

'There used to be, at any rate. I know, because people used to say there was a treasure hidden in the park. I must tell you that before Monsieur Amorelle had his place built, forty years ago or more, there was a sort of little ruined castle there. It was said that during the Revolution the people of the chateau had hidden their treasure in the park. At one point Monsieur Amorelle took up the question and sent for some metal-diviners. They all declared that the treasure must be in the upper kennel and that he'd have to do some digging.'

'All that's of no importance,' Maigret muttered. 'The point is that there's a cellar there. And it's in that cellar, Raymonde my girl, that poor Georges-Henry must be shut up.'

He looked at her suddenly with a different expression in his eyes.

'When is there a train for Paris?'

'In twenty minutes. After that you've not got one till 12.39. Some others go by but they don't stop at Orsenne.'

He was half way up the stairs already. He dressed without taking time for a shave, and shortly afterwards was striding towards the station.

As her employer was knocking on the floor of her bedroom, Raymonde went upstairs herself.

'Has he gone?' asked old Jeanne, still lying in her clammy sheets.

'He's just run off in a great hurry.'

'Did he say anything?'

'No, Madame.'

'Has he paid? Help me to get up.'

'He hasn't paid, Madame. But he's left his suitcase and all his things behind.'

'Oh!' said old Jeanne, disappointed and perhaps somewhat uneasy.

5
Maigret's Accomplice

Paris was magnificently huge and empty. In the cafés around the Gare de Lyon there was a delicious smell of beer and croissants dipped in coffee. And during the quarter of an hour he spent in a barber's shop on the Boulevard de la Bastille Maigret felt supremely lighthearted, for no special reason, just because it was Paris in August, because it was morning, and perhaps, too, because he was soon going to say hello to his old friends.

'You're obviously just back from your holidays. You've got a splendid tan!'

It was true; he must have got it the day before when he was scouring the countryside round Orsenne to make sure that Georges-Henry had not left the village.

The whole affair seemed to have become strangely insubstantial, seen from a distance. Meanwhile, however, after a shave and a haircut, with a speck of powder still behind his ear, Maigret climbed on to the platform of a bus, and a few minutes later was crossing the threshold of Police Headquarters.

Here, too, there was a sense that people were on holiday, and in the empty corridors where all the windows were wide open he recognized a familiar atmosphere. Many offices were deserted. In his own, in his old room, he found Lucas, who seemed too small for the vacant space and who jumped up as though he felt guilty at sitting in his former Chief's place.

'You're in Paris, Chief? . . . Sit down.'

Lucas immediately commented on Maigret's tan. Everybody was to notice that tan today and nine people out of ten would not fail to comment with satisfaction:

'You've obviously been in the country!'

As if he hadn't been living in the country for the past two years!

'Tell me, Lucas, do you remember Mimile?'

'Mimile from the circus?'

'That's right. I'd like to get hold of him straight away.'

'It looks as if you are on a case, Chief . . .'

'It looks rather as if I were making a bloody fool of myself. Well . . . I'll tell you all about it some other time. Will you see about finding Mimile?'

Lucas opened the door of the inspectors' room and said something in a low voice. He was no doubt telling them that their former Chief was there and that he needed to get hold of Mimile. During the next half hour almost all those who had been Maigret's men contrived to come into Lucas's office under some pretext or other to shake him by the hand.

'You're splendidly sunburnt, Chief! You've obviously been . . .'

'Something else, Lucas. I could do this myself but it bores me. I'd like some information about the firm of Amorelle and Campois on the Quai Bourbon. Gravel pits along the Seine, tugboats etcetera.'

'I'll put Janvier on to it, Chief. Is it urgent?'

'I'd like to have done with it by midday.'

He prowled about the building, and went to pay a brief call in the Finance department. They knew the firm of Amorelle and Campois, but had no special tips about it.

'A big firm, with lots of branches. It's a sound concern, and we've never had any dealings with it.'

It was good to be breathing the air of the place, shaking his friends' hands and reading the pleasure in their eyes.

'How's your garden, Chief? And your fishing?'

He went up to the Records room. Nothing on the Maliks. Only at the last minute, when he was about to leave, did he think of looking under the letter C.

Campois...Roger Campois...Well, well! So there was a file on Campois: Roger Campois, son of Désiré Campois, industrialist. He had shot himself in the head in a hotel bedroom in the Boulevard Saint-Michel.

He checked the dates, addresses, christian names. Désiré Campois was indeed old Amorelle's former partner, the man of whom Maigret had caught a glimpse at Orsenne. He had married one Armande Tenissier, daughter of a public works contractor, who was now deceased and by whom he had had two children, a son and a daughter.

It was Désiré's son Roger who had committed suicide at the age of twenty-two.

Had been frequenting the gambling dens of the Latin Quarter for some months past and had recently incurred large gaming losses.

As for the daughter, she had married and had a child, presumably the young man who had been with his grandfather at Orsenne.

There was nothing in the dossier to say whether she was still alive, or what had become of her husband, a man named Lorigan.

'Shall we go out for a pint, Lucas?'

To the *Brasserie Dauphine,* needless to say, behind the Palais de Justice, where he had put away so many pints in the past. The air was as delicious as a fruit, with puffs of cool air against a background of warmth. And it was delightful to see a municipal water-cart sprinkling broad bands of wetness on the asphalt.

'I don't mean to be inquisitive, Chief, but I must confess I wonder...'

'What I'm up to, eh? I wonder the same thing. And it's quite possible that I may be letting myself in for unpleasant developments tonight. Hello, here's Torrence!'

Torrence, the big fellow, who had been sent after Mimile, had known where to find him, and had already completed his mission.

'Unless he's changed his job again in the last couple of days, Chief, you'll find him working at the Luna Park menagerie. A pint, please!'

Then Janvier, good fellow—what good fellows they all were that day, and how good it was to be with them again, to be at work just as in the old days!—Janvier came to join them at the round table where saucers were piling up in impressive fashion.

'What exactly did you want to know about the firm of Amorelle and Campois, Chief?'

'Everything...'

'Wait a sec...'

He pulled a scrap of paper from his pocket.

'Old Campois, for a start. Came to Paris from his native Dauphiné at the age of eighteen. A sort of shrewd and stubborn peasant. Worked first for a building contractor in the Vaugirard district, then for an architect, finally for a contractor at Villeneuve-Saint-Georges. That was where he met Amorelle.

'Amorelle came from Berry. He married his boss's daughter. He formed a partnership with Campois and the pair of them bought land by the Seine, upstream from Paris, and made their first gravel pit there. That was forty-five years ago...'

Lucas and Torrence watched their former Chief with an amused smile, as he listened calmly to all this. As Janvier spoke, Maigret seemed to become his old self again.

'I learnt all this through a former employee of theirs, who's vaguely related to a relative of my wife's. I knew him by sight and a few little drinks soon got him talking.'

'Go on.'

'It's the usual story of these big concerns. After a few years Amorelle and Campois owned half a dozen gravel pits in the Upper Seine. Then, instead of having their gravel carried by barges they bought boats, and finally tugs. Apparently it made quite a sensation at the time, because it meant the end of the 'stable-boats'. There were demonstrations in front of their offices on the Ile Saint-Louis... The offices are still there, but they were on a smaller scale in those days. Amorelle even received threatening letters. He stood firm, and things settled down.

'At the present moment it's a huge concern. You can't conceive of the scale of the business, and I was quite dumbfounded by it.

After the gravel pits came the quarries. Then Amorelle and Campois took shares in the building sites at Rouen where they had their tugboats built. At present they're the biggest shareholders in a dozen concerns at least, shipping companies, quarries, naval constructions, and also in public works undertakings and a concrete-mixer business.'

'And the Maliks?'

'I'm coming to them. My chap talked about them. Apparently the first of the Maliks...'

'Who d'you call the first of them?'

'The one who first entered the firm. Wait till I look at my paper. Ernest Malik of Moulins.'

'That's him.'

'He hadn't been in the business at all, he'd been secretary to a leading local councillor. That was how he got acquainted with Amorelle and Campois. On account of the contracts. Bribery and corruption and so forth. And he married the daughter. It was soon after the suicide of young Campois, who had been in the firm and had killed himself.'

Maigret seemed to have withdrawn into himself and his eyes were half closed. Lucas and Torrence exchanged glances again, amused to find their Chief just as they had known him in his heyday, with his lips pursed around the stem of his pipe, his big thumb stroking the bowl of it and his shoulders hunched up.

'That's about all, Chief... Once in the firm, Ernest Malik sent for his brother from somewhere or other. He knew even less about the business than Ernest. Some people say he was only a petty insurance agent from near Lyons. All the same he married the second Amorelle girl and since then the Maliks have been on all the boards of directors. For there are a whole string of different firms, all interconnected. Apparently old Campois has practically no authority. He seems to have been fool enough, moreover, to sell a whole lot of shares when he thought they were at their peak.

'The Maliks still have one enemy, though, and that's old Madame Amorelle, who can't stand them. And she's believed to be still the major shareholder in the various companies. They say, in the firm's offices, that she's quite capable of disinheriting her sons-in-law out of spite, in so far as the law will allow it.

'That's all I've discovered.'

A few more pints all round.

'Have lunch with me, Lucas?'

They lunched together, as in the good old days. Then a bus took Maigret to Luna Park, where he was at first disappointed not to find Mimile at the menagerie.

'He's sure to be in some bistro in the neighbourhood! You might find him in the *Cadran* or at *Léon's*, unless he's at the *café-tabac* at the corner of the street.'

Mimile was in the *tabac*, and Maigret began by standing him a marc. Mimile was a man of indeterminate age, with hair of an indeterminate colour, one of those men whom life has worn down like coins, so that they have, so to speak, no clear outline. You never knew if he was drunk or sober, since from morning till night he had the same misty gaze and the same nonchalant walk.

'What can I do for you, Chief?'

He had a police record, indeed quite a bad one, but for many years now he had gone straight and he did an occasional good turn to his former adversaries at the Quai des Orfèvres.

'Can you leave Paris for twenty-four hours?'

'Provided I get hold of the Pole.'

'What Pole?'

'A chap I know, whose name's too complicated for me to remember. He knows the ropes and he could look after my animals. Wait while I ring him up. A quick one first, eh, Chief?'

Two or three quick ones, a little time spent in the call box, and at last Mimile announced:

'I'm all yours!'

While Maigret explained to him what he was to do, Mimile wore the astonished look of a clown being bashed on the head, and he kept mumbling with his thick lips:

'Well, for heaven's sake! For heaven's sake!... If it wasn't you yourself asking me to do this I'd have reported you to Headquarters... It's a funny job and no mistake.'

'You've really understood?'

'I'll say I've understood!'

'You'll have whatever's needed?'

'The works! Leave it to me.'

Out of prudence the Superintendent drew him a map of the locality, consulted the railway timetable and repeated his meticulous instructions twice over.

'Everything'll be ready at ten o'clock, okay. You can depend on me. So long as you'll undertake to do the explaining if we run into trouble.'

They boarded the same train shortly after four o'clock, giving no sign of knowing one another, and Mimile, who had put into the luggage van an old bicycle belonging to the owner of the menagerie, got off one station before the Orsenne halt.

Maigret, a few minutes later, left the train quite calmly, as though he were a regular passenger, and lingered to talk to the gatekeeper who acted as stationmaster.

He began by observing that it was warmer in the country than in Paris, which was quite true; the heat in the valley that day was overpowering.

'Don't you think they might have a decent white wine in the bistro over there?'

For there was a bistro some fifty metres from the station, and presently the two men were sitting at a table with a bottle of white wine before them, to be followed in increasingly rapid succession by glasses of spirits.

An hour later it was obvious that the gatekeeper would sleep soundly that night, and that was all that Maigret required of him.

He himself had been careful to pour away most of the alcohol that had been provided for them, and so he was not excessively drowsy as he walked down towards the Seine and, a little later, entered the small garden of the Angel Inn.

Raymonde looked surprised to see him back so soon.

'What about the *patronne*?' he asked.

'She's still in her bedroom. By the way, a letter came for you. It was brought soon after you'd left. The train may not even have gone past. If I hadn't been all on my own I'd have taken it to the station.'

It was, appropriately, in a black-edged envelope.

Monsieur,

 I shall be obliged if you will close the investigation I had asked you to make in a moment of depression which can surely be accounted for by my age and the shock I have just undergone.

 Under the circumstances I interpreted certain distressing events in a manner incompatible with the facts, and I am sorry now that I troubled you in your retirement.

 Your presence at Orsenne can only complicate an already painful situation, and I venture to add that the indiscretion with which you have carried out the task I had entrusted to you, the clumsiness you have displayed hitherto make me extremely anxious that you should leave as soon as possible.

 I hope that you will understand this and not persist in disturbing a family which has already suffered so greatly.

 During my ill-considered visit to Meung-sur-Loire I left on your table a wad of notes to the sum of ten thousand francs, intended to cover your initial expenses. I enclose herewith a cheque for the same amount and I hope you will now consider this business at an end.

Sincerely yours,
Bernadette Amorelle

It was undoubtedly her big spiky writing, but it was not her style, and Maigret, with a peculiar grin, put the letter and the cheque away in his pocket, convinced that the sentences he had just read emanated from Ernest Malik rather than from the old lady.

'I must also tell you that the *patronne* asked me just now when you were going to leave.'

'Is she turning me out?'

Raymonde, whose big sturdy figure had a certain flabbiness about it, became very red.

'That's not what I meant to say. Only she thinks she's going to be unwell for some time. When her attacks come on ...'

He cast a sideways glance at the bottles which were the chief source of those attacks.

'And what else?'

'The house is going to be sold any day now.'

'Again!' Maigret commented ironically. 'And what else, Raymonde my dear?'

'Don't bother about me. I'd rather she had told you herself. She says it's not proper that I should be alone with a man in the house. She heard that we were eating together in the kitchen. She ticked me off about it.'

'When does she want me to leave?'

'Tonight, tomorrow morning at latest.'

'And there's no other inn in the neighbourhood, is there?'

'There's one five kilometres away.'

'Well, Raymonde, we'll see about it tomorrow morning.'

'But I've got nothing to eat for tonight and I've been forbidden...'

'I shall eat at the lock.'

This he did. There was beside the lock the usual small store where bargees could buy provisions and get a drink. A train of boats was at this moment in the lock and the women, with their children about them, had taken the opportunity to do their shopping, while the men came in for a quick drink.

They were all employed by Amorelle and Campois.

'I'd like a bottle of white wine, a piece of sausage and half a pound of bread,' he ordered.

There was no restaurant service. He sat down at the corner of a table, watching the water foaming above the sluice-gates. Formerly barges had travelled slowly alongside the banks, drawn by stout horses, which some small girl, often walking barefoot along the tow-path, guided with a stick.

These were the 'stable-boats' which were still to be seen on some canals, but which Amorelle and Campois, with their steaming tug-boats and their motorized barges, had driven from the Upper Seine.

The sausage was good, the wine light, with a slightly acid taste. The shop smelt of cinnamon and petrol. The upstream gates were open and the tugboat led its train of barges, like so many chicks, towards the upper reach of the river. The lockkeeper came to Maigret's table for a drink.

'I thought you were going away tonight.'

'Who told you so?'

The lockkeeper seemed somewhat embarrassed.

'You know, if one listened to everything people say!'

Malik had been setting up his defences. He had wasted no time. Had he come in person to the lock?

From afar Maigret could see, amidst their surrounding greenery, the proud homes of the Amorelle and Campois partners—that of old Madame Amorelle and her son-in-law, that of Ernest Malik, the most sumptuous of them all, and that of Campois, half way up the hill, which for all its bourgeois solidity had a countrified look, with its pink-washed walls. On the other side of the water was the old-fashioned, dilapidated manor house belonging to old Monsieur Groux, who chose to mortgage his properties sooner than see his woods transformed into quarries.

Monsieur Groux himself was not far away. He could be seen, his bald head shining in the sun, clad as always in brown holland, sitting in a green rowing boat moored between two posts and fishing with rod and line.

The air was still and the water unwrinkled.

'Tell me, since you know about such things, will there be a moon tonight?'

'It depends what time. It'll rise a little before midnight behind the wood you can see there upstream. It's in its first quarter.'

Maigret was fairly pleased with himself, and yet he could not dispel a gnawing sense of anxiety that increased instead of diminishing as time passed.

A certain nostalgia, too. He had spent an hour at the Quai des Orfèvres with men whom he knew so well, who still called him *patron*, but who...

What had they said to one another after he had left? That he missed his work, of course! That he wasn't as happy as he made out in his country retreat! That he jumped at the first opportunity of enjoying the old excitement again!

In short, an amateur! That was what he must seem to them, an amateur!

'Another drink?'

The lockkeeper did not say no. He had a habit of wiping his mouth on his sleeve after each mouthful.

'I'm sure the Malik boy, Georges-Henry, must often have gone fishing with your son.'

'Oh yes, Monsieur.'

'He must have enjoyed that, musn't he?'

'He loved the water, he loved the woods, he loved animals!'

'A good lad!'

'Yes, a good lad. Not proud at all. If you could have seen the two of them, him and the little lady... They often took their canoe downstream. I would offer to take them through the lock, although usually we don't do that for small boats. But it was they who didn't want to. They preferred to carry their canoe over to the other side of the weir. I used to see them come back at nightfall.'

And at nightfall, or rather after night had fallen, he, Maigret, would have an unpleasant task to perform. Afterwards, they would see whether he had been mistaken, whether he was only an old fool who'd deservedly been pensioned off or whether he was still capable of doing something.

He paid his bill. Then he walked slowly along the river bank, smoking his pipe. It was a long wait; it was as if the sun could not bring itself to set that evening. The shimmering water flowed gently, noiselessly, with a barely perceptible murmur, and tiny flies skimmed it daringly, provoking fishes to leap.

He saw nobody, neither the Malik brothers nor their servants. A state of utter stillness prevailed. Shortly before ten o'clock, leaving behind him the light shining in Jeanne's room at the inn, and in the kitchen where Raymonde was sitting, he walked, as on the previous night, towards the station.

The glasses of white wine had doubtless had their effect, for the gate-keeper was not at his post on the threshold of his house. Maigret was able to pass without being seen and he walked on along the railway track.

Behind the screen of hazel bushes, at approximately the same spot where he had been hidden the night before, he found Mimile at his post, sitting peacefully with his legs spread wide apart, a cigarette stump in his mouth, as though he was enjoying the cool of the evening.

'He hasn't come yet?'

'No.'

They waited thus in silence. From time to time they exchanged a few whispered words. As on the previous night, Bernadette Amorelle's window was open and they could occasionally see the old lady going past in the faint light.

Not until half-past ten did a figure emerge in the park, and then things happened exactly as on the previous night. The man, who was carrying a parcel, was greeted by the dogs, which followed him as far as the door of the kennel. He went in, stayed there far longer than on the night before, and finally returned to the house, where a light went on in an upper window which opened for a moment while the shutters were being closed.

The dogs wandered about the park before going to sleep, and they came to sniff the air close to the wall, presumably smelling the presence of the two men.

'Shall I go now, *patron*?' whispered Mimile.

One of the Great Danes curled its lips as though to utter a growl, but the man from the menagerie had already flung towards it an object that fell to the ground with a soft thud.

'Unless they're better trained than I expect,' muttered Mimile. 'But I'm not afraid of that. The gentry don't know how to train dogs, and even when they're given a well-trained animal they soon spoil him.'

He was quite right. The two dogs prowled round the object that had been thrown to them, sniffing it. Maigret, in his anxiety, had let his pipe go out. Finally one of the dogs seized the meat between his teeth and shook it, while the other, jealous, growled threateningly.

'There's enough for everyone!' sniggered Mimile, flinging down a second piece. 'Don't quarrel, my lambs!'

It lasted barely five minutes. They saw the animals' white figures wandering about for a moment, turning uneasily round and round, then collapsing, and at that point Maigret was not proud of himself.

'That's done, *patron*. Shall we go in?'

It seemed wiser to wait a little longer until darkness had completely fallen and all the lights were out. Mimile was growing impatient.

'By and by the moon will have risen and it'll be too late.'

Mimile had brought a rope which he had already fastened to the trunk of a young ash tree by the side of the road, close to the wall.

'Wait till I go down first.'

The wall was over three metres high, but it was in good condition and there were no projecting ledges.

'It's going to be more difficult to get back up. Unless we can find a ladder in their blasted garden. Look, there's a wheelbarrow down that path. If we stand it against the wall it'll be a help.'

Mimile was excited and in high spirits, like a man who's once more in his element.

'If anyone had told me I'd be doing a job like this with you...'

They went up to the low brick building which had once been a kennel or a stable, in front of which there was a yard paved with concrete and surrounded by a railing.

'We don't need the torch,' whispered Mimile, fiddling with the lock.

The door opened and a reek of musty straw met them.

'Shut the door! Say, it seems to me there's nobody in here!'

Maigret switched on his torch, and they saw nothing around them except an old broken stall-wall, a mouldering harness hanging on a hook, a whip lying on the ground, and a dusty mixture of straw and hay.

'What are you waiting for?' whispered Mimile.

For nothing. And yet it was years since he had felt such tense excitement.

'D'you want me to open it?'

No. Maigret raised the trap door himself. There was no sound to be heard in the cellar, and yet they both felt simultaneously that there was a living creature there.

The electric torch suddenly lit up the black space beneath

them, and its white beam swept over a face, a figure that suddenly sprang up.

'Keep still,' said Maigret in a low voice.

He was trying to follow with his torch the figure that was running from one wall to the other like a cornered animal. He kept saying mechanically:

'I'm a friend.'

Mimile suggested:

'Shall I go down?'

Below, a voice said:

'Nobody's to touch me.'

'No, no; nobody's going to touch you.'

Maigret kept on talking as though in a dream, or rather as one might talk to quieten a child in the throes of a nightmare. And indeed there was something nightmarish about the scene.

'Keep quiet. Wait till we get you out of here.'

'And suppose I don't want to get out?'

It was the hectic, savage voice of a crazed child.

'Shall I go down?' repeated Mimile, who was anxious to get it over.

'Listen, Georges-Henry! I'm a friend. I know everything.'

And suddenly it was as though he had spoken the magic word of a fairy story. The boy's agitation was instantly quelled. There was silence for a few seconds, then an altered voice queried mistrustfully:

'What do you know?'

'You've got to get out of here first, young fellow. I give you my word you've nothing to fear.'

'Where's my father? What have you done to him?'

'Your father is at home in bed, I expect.'

'That's not true!'

There was deep bitterness in his tone. They were deceiving him. He was convinced he was being deceived, as he had always been deceived. This obsession was what his voice revealed to the Superintendent, who was beginning to grow impatient.

'Your grandmother has told me everything.'

'That's not true!'

'She came to fetch me and she . . .'

And the lad almost screamed:

'She knows nothing! I'm the only person who . . .'

'Hush! You've got to trust me, Georges-Henry. Come on. When you're out of here we can talk quietly.'

Was he going to let himself be persuaded? Otherwise they would have to go down into the hole and take brutal action, grapple with him and overpower him, and perhaps he would struggle, scratching and biting like a terrified young animal.

'Shall I go down?' Mimile kept saying, for he was beginning to feel uneasy and kept glancing anxiously towards the door.

'Listen, Georges-Henry. I'm from the police.'

'It's nothing to do with the police! I hate the police! I hate the police!'

He broke off. An idea had just struck him and he went on in a different tone:

'Besides, if it was the police, you'd have . . .'

He yelled:

'Leave me alone! Leave me alone! Go away! You're telling lies. You know you're telling lies! Go and tell my father . . .'

At that moment a hard voice rapped out, as the door opened noiselessly:

'Sorry to interrupt you, gentlemen.'

Maigret's torch lit up the figure of Ernest Malik, who stood there, very calm, with a big revolver in his hand.

'I believe, my poor Jules, that I would be within my rights if I were to shoot you and your companion down.'

Below them, they could hear the boy's teeth chattering.

6
Mimile and His Prisoner

Without showing the least surprise, Maigret turned slowly towards the newcomer and appeared unaware of the gun that was levelled at him.

'Get the boy out of here,' he said in his most ordinary voice, like a man who, having failed to accomplish a certain task, asks someone else to attempt it for him.

'Listen to me, Maigret . . .' began Malik.

'Not now. Not here. Presently, I'll listen to anything you like.'

'You realize you've broken the law?'

'I tell you to see to the boy. You're still unwilling? Mimile, down with you into the hole.'

Only then did Ernest Malik call out in a sharp voice:

'You can come out, Georges-Henry.'

The boy did not stir.

'Do you hear what I say? Come out! The punishment's gone on long enough.'

Maigret gave a start. So that was what he was supposed to believe? That the boy was being punished?

'You're not so clever, Malik.'

And leaning over the hole he said in a quiet, gentle voice:

'You can come now, Georges-Henry. You've nothing to be afraid of. Not from your father nor from anybody else.'

Mimile reached down and helped the lad to hoist himself up. Georges-Henry remained withdrawn, averting his eyes from his father and awaiting an opportunity to escape.

And this Maigret had foreseen. For he had foreseen everything, including, even, Malik's surprise arrival. So much so that Mimile had been given the necessary instructions and now these merely had to be carried out.

The four of them could not remain there indefinitely standing in the disused kennel, and Maigret led the way to the door, ignoring Malik's attempts to bar his way.

'We can talk better in the house,' he said softly.

'Do you really want to talk?'

The Superintendent shrugged his shoulders. As he went past Mimile he had time to give him a warning glance that meant:

'Careful of the next step.'

For the next step was a tricky one, and a mistake might jeopardize everything. They went out one after the other; Georges-Henry came out last, crept out rather, keeping far away from his father. All

four of them walked along the path and now it was Malik who displayed a certain anxiety. The night was pitch dark. The moon had
not yet risen. Maigret had switched off his torch.

They had barely a hundred metres to go. What was the boy waiting for? Could Maigret have made a mistake?

It looked now as if nobody wanted to talk, nobody wanted to take
the responsibility for what was going to happen.

Sixty metres more. In a minute it would be too late, and Maigret
wanted to nudge Georges-Henry to bring him back to reality.

Twenty metres...Ten metres...There was nothing for it.
What would they do, the four of them together, in one of the rooms
of that house, whose white walls were already visible?

Five metres. Too late! But it was not too late. Georges-Henry
showed himself more cunning than Maigret himself, for he had
thought of one thing: that when they reached the house his father
would have to go ahead of the others to open the door.

At that precise moment he gave a leap, and the minute after
there was a rustle of grass and branches amidst the thickets of the
park. Mimile had not bungled the manoeuvre, but was running at
his heels.

Malik was just one second off the mark. His reflex action was to
aim his gun at the figure of the man from the circus. But before he
had time to press the trigger, Maigret brought his fist down on
Malik's forearm and the weapon dropped to the ground.

'That's that!' Maigret said with satisfaction. He did not bother
to pick up the gun, but kicked it into the middle of the path. A sort
of pride prevented Ernest Malik from picking it up. What would
have been the point?

The match that was now being played between them could in no
way be decided by a gun.

For Maigret this was an exciting moment, precisely because he
had foreseen it. The night was so quiet that the running footsteps
could be heard in the distance. Malik and Maigret were both listening
attentively. It was easy to realize that Mimile was losing no ground.

They must have gone into the neighbouring park, where they
were still running and from whence, no doubt, they would make for
the towpath.

'That's that,' Maigret repeated as the sound decreased until it was barely perceptible. 'Shall we go in?'

Malik turned the key he had already inserted in the lock and slipped in. Then he switched on the electric light, and revealed his wife, clad in a white dressing gown, standing at the bend of the staircase.

She looked at them both with wide astonished eyes, unable to say a word. Her husband called out irritably:

'Go to bed!'

The two of them stood in Malik's study and Maigret began to fill his pipe, glancing at his adversary from time to time with some satisfaction. Malik was walking up and down, his hands behind his back.

'You've no intention of bringing an action?' Maigret asked gently. 'Yet now or never is your opportunity. Your two dogs have been poisoned and your property broken into. You might even argue that there's been an attempted abduction. After dark, into the bargain. It's obviously a case for hard labour. Come on, Malik... the telephone's there, within your reach. A call to the police station at Corbeil and they'll have to arrest me...

'What's wrong? What prevents you from doing what you're longing to do?'

Now he no longer felt embarrassed about using the familiar *tu*, quite the reverse, but the familiarity was no longer that which Malik had initiated at their first meeting. It was the professional *tu-toiement* which, as Superintendent, Maigret generally used towards his 'clients'.

'Will you mind having to tell everybody that you kept your son shut up in a cellar? For one thing, your paternal authority gave you the right to punish him. How many times, when I was small, was I threatened with being shut up in the cellar!'

'Be quiet, will you?'

He was standing in front of Maigret and looking at him intently, trying to read what lay behind the other man's words.

'What do you know exactly?'

'At last that's the question I was waiting for.'

'What do you know?' Malik repeated impatiently.

'And what are you afraid of my knowing?'

'I've asked you once before not to meddle in my affairs.'

'And I refused.'

'For the second and last time I tell you ...'

But Maigret shook his head.

'No ... You see, it's impossible now.'

'You don't know anything ...'

'In that case, what are you afraid of?'

'You won't learn anything ...'

'So why are you worrying?'

'As for the kid, he won't talk. I know you're banking on him.'

'Is that all you have to say to me, Malik?'

'I ask you to think it over. Just now I could have shot you down and I'm beginning to be sorry I didn't do so.'

'You may indeed have been mistaken. In a few minutes, when I go out, there'll still be time for you to shoot me in the back. It's true that by now the boy is far away, and there's somebody with him. Well, I want to go to bed. So, no telephone calls? No complaint? No police station? Agreed and understood?'

He went to the door.

'Goodnight, Malik.'

Just as he was about to disappear into the entrance hall he changed his mind, retraced his steps and said, with a grave face and an insistent gaze:

'You see, I feel that what I'm about to discover is so revolting, so foul that I wonder whether I can bear to go on with it.'

He went off without turning back, slammed the door violently behind him and made his way towards the park gate. It was closed. He was in an absurd position, at large in the grounds of the estate without anyone being aware of his presence.

The light was still on in the study, but Malik was not interested in showing his adversary out.

Should he climb over the wall at the end? Alone and unaided, Maigret had no faith in his own agility. Should he look for the path which led into the Amorelle estate, the gate of which might perhaps be unlocked?

He shrugged his shoulders, went up to the gardener's lodge and knocked gently at the door.

'Who's there?' said a sleepy voice from inside.

'A friend of Monsieur Malik's who would like to have the gate opened.'

He heard the old servant pulling on his trousers and hunting for his sabots. The door opened a crack.

'How d'you come to be in the park? Where are the dogs?'

'I believe they're asleep,' murmured Maigret. 'Unless they're dead.'

'And Monsieur Malik?'

'He's in his study.'

'He has the key to the gate.'

'Maybe. But he's so preoccupied that he never even thought about it.'

The gardener went ahead of him grumbling, turning back from time to time with an anxious glance at his nocturnal visitor. Whenever Maigret altered the rhythm of his step the man gave a start, as though he expected to be struck from behind.

'Thank you, my man.'

He went back quietly to the Angel. He had to fling pebbles at Raymonde's window to waken her and get the door opened.

'What's the time? I didn't expect you'd be coming back. Just now I heard some one running along the path. It wasn't you?'

He helped himself to a drink and went to bed. At eight next morning, freshly shaven, carrying his suitcase, he caught the train for Paris. At nine-thirty, after drinking his coffee and eating croissants in a small bar, he entered the Quai des Orfèvres.

Lucas was in his Chief's room, dealing with reports. Maigret sat down in his old place, beside the open window, and one of Amorelle and Campois's tugboats happened to be passing down the Seine, giving two loud blasts on its hooter before going under the Pont de la Cité.

At ten o'clock Lucas came in, carrying a bundle of papers which he laid on the edge of the desk.

'So you're here, Chief? I thought you'd gone back to Orsenne.'

'Has there been a phone call for me this morning?'

'Not yet. Are you expecting one?'

'Tell the switchboard to put the call through to me at once and if I'm not there, let somebody take the message.'

He did not want to betray his nervous tension, but he lit one pipe after another with exceptional rapidity.

'Carry on with your work as if I wasn't there.'

'Nothing thrilling this morning. A knifing in the Rue Delambre.'

The usual run of the mill with which he was so familiar. He had taken off his jacket, just as he used to when he was at home here. He went into the various rooms, shook his colleagues' hands, heard people being questioned, listened to scraps of telephone conversations.

'Don't let me disturb you, boys.'

At half-past eleven he went down for a drink with Torrence.

'Actually there's a piece of information I'd like you to hunt out for me. It's still about Ernest Malik. I'd like to know if he goes in for gambling, or if he did when he was young. It must be possible to find somebody who knew him twenty or twenty-five years ago.'

'I'll find somebody, Chief.'

At quarter to twelve there was still no news, and Maigret showed his dejection by his drooping shoulders and hesitant movements.

'I think I've been a bloody fool,' he remarked to Lucas, who was dealing with current business.

Each time the telephone bell rang in the room he unhooked the receiver himself. Finally, a few minutes before twelve, he heard his own name.

'Maigret here . . . Where are you? . . . Where is he?'

'At Ivry, Chief. I must be quick, for I'm afraid he may give me the slip. I don't know the name of the street. I hadn't time to see it. A little hotel. The house has three storeys and the ground floor is painted brown. It's called *À ma Bourgogne*. Just opposite there's a gas works.'

'What's he doing?'

'I don't know. I think he's asleep. I'd better run now, to make sure.'

Maigret went to stare at a map of Paris and the suburbs.

'Do you know of a gas works at Ivry, Lucas?'

'I think I can visualize it, a little way beyond the station.'

A few minutes later Maigret was being driven in an open taxi towards the smoking chimneys of Ivry. He had to spend some time searching the streets around the gas works, and eventually discovered a shabby hotel, the ground floor of which was painted a dingy brown.

'Shall I wait?' asked the taxi driver.

'I think you'd better.'

Maigret went into the restaurant, where workmen, nearly all foreigners, were eating on bare marble tables. There was a heavy, stifling smell of stew and coarse red wine. A buxom girl in black and white was threading her way between the tables, carrying incredible numbers of little dishes made of thick greyish earthenware.

'You're looking for the chap who came down and telephoned a short while ago? He said you were to go up to the third floor. You can come this way.'

A narrow passage with graffiti scrawled on the walls. The staircase was dark, lit only by a skylight on the second floor. When he had passed this landing Maigret caught sight of a pair of feet and legs.

They belonged to Mimile, who was sitting on the lowest step of the staircase, with an unlit cigarette between his lips.

'Give us a light first, Chief. I didn't even take time to ask for matches when I went to ring up. I haven't had a smoke since last night.'

There was a joyful, mocking glint in his pale eyes.

'Shall I make room for you?'

'Where is he?'

Along the passage could be seen four doors painted in the same gloomy brown as the front of the house. They bore numbers, clumsily inscribed: 21, 22, 23, 24.

'He's in number 21. Mine's 22; that's a joke, you'd think it was done on purpose. *Vingt-deux, v'làles flics*—watch out, here come the cops!'

He inhaled the smoke greedily, then stood up and stretched.

'If you'd like to come into my pad—but I warn you it doesn't

smell good and the ceiling's not high. While I was on my own I
thought I'd sooner block the way, you see.'

'How did you manage to telephone?'

'Well, I'd been waiting all day for the chance. Because we've been
here quite a while. Since six o'clock this morning.'

He opened the door of No. 22 and Maigret saw an iron bedstead,
painted black and covered with a sordid red blanket, a straw-
bottomed chair and a basin without a jug on a small table. The
third-floor bedrooms were attics, and past the middle of the room
one had to bend down.

'Don't let's stay here, for he's as slippery as an eel. He's tried to
get away twice this morning already. I wondered for a moment if he
mightn't be capable of escaping over the rooftops, but I realized
that couldn't be done.'

Opposite was the gas works with its coal-grimed yards. Mimile
had the haggard look of people who haven't slept and haven't
washed.

'It's more comfortable on the staircase and it doesn't smell so
bad. There's a sick reek about this place, don't you think? Like old
swabs.'

Georges-Henry was asleep or pretending to sleep, for, when one listened at the door, one could hear no sound in his room. The two
men stood in the stairway and Mimile told his story, smoking one
cigarette after another to make up for lost time.

'First of all, how I managed to phone you. I didn't want to leave
the hideout, but on the other hand I had to keep you informed as
we'd arranged. At one point, about nine o'clock, a woman came
down from room 24. I thought of asking her to give you a ring or to
take a message to the Quai des Orfèvres. Only here it might not
have been wise to mention the police, and I might have got myself
thrown out.

'Better wait for another chance, Mimile, I said to myself. This
isn't the moment to have a fight.

'When I saw the chap from 23 coming out of his room I knew at
once that he was a Pole. I know all about Poles and I can jabber their
language pretty well.

'I began talking to him and he was ever so pleased to hear his lingo. I made up a story about a bird, I told him she was in the room and wanted to chuck me. Well, he agreed to keep guard for a few minutes while I went down to telephone.'

'You're sure the kid's still there?'

Mimile gave him a sly wink, and took from his pocket a pair of pincers with which he grasped the end of the key which was inside the room, but which protruded a little.

He signalled to Maigret to come up noiselessly, and with incredibly gentle movements he turned the key and half opened the door.

The Superintendent leaned forward and, in a room exactly like the one next door, with an open window, he saw the boy lying fully dressed across the bed.

He was asleep, there could be no doubt of that. He was sleeping as boys of his age sleep, his features relaxed, his mouth half open like a child's. He had not taken off his shoes, and one of his feet was hanging down over the edge of the bed.

With equal caution, Mimile closed the door.

'Let me tell you now how things happened. That was a swell idea of yours to make me take a bike. And an even better one of mine to hide it by the level crossing.

'You remember how he went tearing off. He ran like a rabbit. He dodged about in the park and dashed into the bushes in the hopes of shaking me off.

'At one moment we went through a hedge, one behind the other, and I lost sight of him. It was from the sound that I knew which way he'd gone, towards a house, or rather not exactly towards the house but towards a sort of shed, from which I saw him bring out a bike.'

'His grandmother's house,' Maigret specified. 'And it must have been a woman's bike, his cousin Monita's.'

'Yes, it was a woman's bike. He jumped on to it, but he couldn't go fast down the paths and I was behind him all the time. I dared not speak to him yet because I didn't know what was happening your end.'

'Malik tried to shoot you.'

'I thought as much. It's funny, but I had a sort of feeling that would happen, so much so that at one point I stood quite still for a moment as though I was waiting for the shot. Well, we set off again, blundering about in the darkness, and by now he'd got off his bike and was pushing it. He lifted it over another hedge. Now we were on a path going down to the river and here, too, he couldn't ride fast. On the towpath it was different, and I lost a bit of ground, but I caught up with him on the way to the station, because it was uphill.

'He must have been quite pleased with himself, because he couldn't have guessed that I had my own bike a little further on.

'Poor kid! He was riding his fastest, with all his might. He was sure he'd get away from me, see?

'What a hope! I picked up my bike at the level crossing. I put my back into it and just as he least expected it I was spinning alongside of him just as if nothing had happened.

'"Don't be afraid, kid," I says to him.

'I wanted to put him at his ease. He was sort of crazy. He was racing along fit to burst.

'"Aren't I telling you not to be afraid? You know Superintendent Maigret, surely? He doesn't want to do you any harm, just the contrary."

'From time to time he turned to me and shouted in a rage: "Leave me alone!" Then with a sort of sob in his voice he'd say: "I shan't tell them anything, in any case."

'I was sorry for him, I can tell you. It's no sort of a job, what you'd given me to do. Not to mention that going downhill somewhere, on some highway, he skidded and went sprawling on the tarmac, banging his head so that you could literally hear the noise.

'I got off my bike. I tried to help him get up. He was back in the saddle in no time, crazier and angrier than ever.

'"Stop, kid. I bet you've hurt yourself. It can't do you any harm to stop and talk for a moment, can it? I'm not against you."

'I'd been wondering for a moment or two what he'd been doing leaning over the handlebars, because I couldn't see his hand. I must tell you the moon had risen and it was pretty light.

'I rode up closer. I wasn't a yard away from him when he raised his arm. I bent down. Lucky for me! The little bastard had flung a spanner at my head; he'd taken it out of his tool-bag. It missed my forehead by inches.

'Then he got the wind up even more. He imagined I had it in for him and that I wanted to have my revenge. And I kept on talking. It would be quite a joke to tell you all I said to him that night.

' "You've got to realize," I told him, "that you're not going to get rid of me. Besides, I've got my orders. Wherever you go you'll find me behind you . . . It's on account of the Super; when he comes, my job'll be over."

'At a crossroads he must have mistaken the way, for we went off in the opposite direction to Paris, and after riding through I don't know how many villages, all white in the moonlight, we found ourselves on the road to Orléans. Just imagine what a way we'd come, from the Fontainebleau road!

'He had to slow down in the end, but he still wouldn't speak to me or even turn in my direction.

'Then by daybreak we were on the outskirts of Paris. I got the wind up again, because now he tried dashing down every little byway in the hopes of shedding me.

'He must have been worn out . . . I could see he was pale and his eyes were red. He only stuck to his saddle by force of habit.

' "We'd do better to go to bed, kid. You'll make yourself ill."

'And then he spoke to me after all. He must have done so automatically, without being aware. Yes, I'm convinced he was so done in he didn't know what he was doing. You've seen what a cross-country runner looks like when he reaches the finishing post and they have to hold him up, and he stares at the ciné camera with wild eyes?

' "I've got no money," he says to me.

' "Doesn't matter. I've got some. We'll go wherever you like, but you've got to rest."

'We were hereabouts. I didn't expect he'd obey me so soon. He saw the word hotel over the door; it was open and some workmen were coming out. He got off his bike and he could hardly walk, he was so stiff. If the bistro had been open I'd have stood him a drink, but I doubt if he'd have accepted. He's proud, you know. He's a queer sort of boy. I don't know what's going on in his head, but he's sticking to his idea and you haven't finished with him yet.

'We put the two bikes under the stairs. If they've not been pinched they must still be there.

'He went up the stairs ahead of me. When we got to the first floor he didn't know what to do because there was nobody to be seen.

'"*Patron!*" I shouted.

'The *patron* turned out to be a *patronne,* tougher than a man, and pretty grim.

'"What d'you want?" And she looked at us as if we were dirt.

'"We want two rooms, one next to the other."

'In the end she gave us two keys, for room 21 and room 22. That's all, Chief. Now, if you don't mind stopping here a moment, I'd like to go and have a drink or two and maybe something to eat . . . Ever since this morning I've been smelling things cooking . . .'

'Open the door for me,' Maigret said when Mimile came upstairs again, reeking of marc.

'D'you want to wake him up?' the other protested, for he had begun to consider the boy as his protégé. 'You'd better let him sleep his fill.'

Maigret nodded reassuringly and went into the room without making a sound. He tiptoed up to the attic window and looked out. The furnaces of the gas works were being stoked and the flames glowed bright yellow in the sunlight, while workers, stripped to the waist, wiped the sweat from their bodies with grimy arms.

The wait was a long one. The Superintendent had ample time for thought. At intervals he turned to look at his young companion, who was beginning to emerge from the realm of deep and peaceful sleep into the more restless slumber that precedes awakening. From time to time he frowned. His mouth opened wider as though to speak. He was probably dreaming that he was speaking. He grew angrier; he seemed to be saying *no* with all his might.

Then his look of distress became more acute and tears seemed imminent. But he did not weep. He turned round heavily on the bumpy mattress, which creaked. He brushed away a fly that had settled on his nose. His eyelids fluttered, surprised by sunlight.

At last he opened his eyes wide and stared up at the sloping ceiling with an expression of naive surprise, then at the big dark figure of the Superintendent, looming up against the light.

At that point he recovered his wits. Instead of showing signs of agitation he remained motionless, and his whole face expressed a cold determination that hardened his features and brought out a certain likeness to his father.

'I shan't tell you anything, all the same,' he declared.

'I'm not asking you to tell me anything,' Maigret replied, with scarcely a trace of harshness in his voice. 'And in any case what could you tell me?'

'Why did that man run after me? What are you doing in my room? Where is my father?'

'He's stayed at home.'

'You're sure?'

It seemed as if he dared not stir, as if the slightest movement might bring down unknown dangers on him. He lay on his back, his nerves tense, his eyes staring wildly.

'You've no right to pursue me like this. I've done nothing.'

'Would you sooner I took you back to your father?'

Terror showed in the grey eyes.

'That's what the police would do immediately if they laid hands on you. You're only a minor, a child.'

He sat up suddenly, seized with a fit of despair.

'But I don't want to!...I don't want to!...' he howled.

Maigret heard Mimile moving about on the landing, evidently convinced of his brutality.

'I want to be left alone. I want...'

The Superintendent noticed the frantic glances the boy was casting at the attic window and he understood. Surely, if he had not stood between the boy and the window, Georges-Henry would have been capable of jumping out into the void.

'Like your cousin?' he said slowly.

'Who told you that my cousin...'

'Listen to me, Georges-Henry.'

'No...'

'You'll have to listen to me. I know the situation you're in.'

'It's not true.'

'Shall I mention details?'

'I forbid you. D'you hear?'

'Hush!... You can't go back to your father and you don't want to.'

'I shall never go back to him.'

'On the other hand, in your present frame of mind you might do something foolish.'

'That's my own business.'

'No. It's other people's business too.'

'There's no one who cares about me.'

'Nonetheless, for a few days you need to be looked after.'

The youth gave a bitter, sneering laugh.

'And that's what I've decided to do,' finished Maigret, calmly lighting his pipe. 'Whether you want to or not... that's up to you.'

'Where d'you want to take me?'

And it was quite clear that he was already envisaging a possible escape.

'I don't know yet. I admit that the question is a tricky one, but you certainly can't stay in this slum.'

'It's no worse than the cellar.'

There was some slight improvement, since he had become capable of irony about his own fate.

'To begin with we'll have breakfast peacefully together. You're hungry. But if...'

'I'm not going to eat anything, all the same.'

How young he was, God bless him!

'But *I* am; I'm as hungry as a hunter,' asserted Maigret. 'You'll behave quietly. The friend you know, who has followed you so far, is nimbler than I am, and he'll keep an eye on you. Don't you agree, Georges-Henry? A bath would have been welcome, but I see no possibility of having one here. Wash your face.'

He obeyed sulkily. Maigret opened the door.

'Come in, Mimile. I suppose the taxi is still down below? We'll all three go out for lunch somewhere in a quiet restaurant. Or rather we two will, since you've already eaten.'

'I can eat again, don't you worry.'

It seemed as though Georges-Henry was recovering his sense of reality, for once downstairs he raised an objection:

'What about the bikes?'

'They'll be collected or sent for.'

And to the driver:

'*Brasserie Dauphine.*'

It was almost 3 p.m. when they sat down at table in the cool shady brasserie, and an imposing array of hors d'oeuvres was set before them.

7
Madame Maigret Takes Charge

'Hello . . . Is that you, Madame Maigret? What did you say? Where am I?'

The question reminded him of the time when, as a member of the Police Judiciaire, he used to stay away from home four or five days at a time, sometimes unable even to communicate with his wife, and would eventually ring her up from the most unexpected places.

'I'm right here in Paris. And I need you. I give you half an hour to get dressed. I know . . . it's impossible . . . that doesn't matter. In half an hour, you'll take Joseph's car, or rather Joseph will pick you up. What? Suppose he's not free? . . . Don't worry, I've rung him up already. He'll take you to Les Aubrais and at six o'clock you'll arrive at the Gare d'Orsay. Take a taxi and in ten minutes you can be at the Place des Vosges.'

This was their former Paris home, which they had kept on. Without waiting for his wife's arrival, Maigret took Georges-Henry and Mimile there. The windows were covered with brown paper,

there were dust sheets and newspapers on all the furniture and in-
secticide powder on the carpets.

'Give us a hand, boys.'

Georges-Henry could scarcely be said to have become more
human during their meal. But although he had not uttered a word
but had gone on glaring savagely at Maigret, he had at least eaten
heartily.

'I still consider myself a prisoner,' he declared emphatically
when they entered the flat, 'and I warn you I shall escape as soon as
I get the chance. You've no right to keep me here.'

'Quite true! In the meantime, lend a hand, please!'

And Georges-Henry set to work like the other two, folding papers, removing dust sheets, working the vacuum cleaner. They had
just finished, and the Superintendent was pouring brandy into
three small glasses belonging to the precious set they had not taken
to the country for fear of breaking it, when Madame Maigret
appeared.

'Is that bath meant for me?' she asked on hearing the water running in the bathroom.

'No, darling. It's for this young man, a charming boy who's going
to stay here with you. His name is Georges-Henry. He's promised to
run away at the first opportunity, but I rely on Mimile—let me in-
troduce Mimile—and on yourself to prevent him from leaving. Is it
long enough after your meal, Georges-Henry? Then please go into
the bathroom.'

'Are you leaving?... Will you be back for dinner?... You don't
know, as usual! And there's nothing to eat here!'

'You've plenty of time to do your shopping while Mimile keeps
an eye on the lad.'

He spoke a few words to her in an undertone and she glanced,
with sudden gentleness, towards the bathroom door.

'All right, I'll try. How old is he? Seventeen?'

Half an hour later, Maigret was back in the familiar atmosphere
of the Police Judiciaire and asked for Torrence.

'He's back, Chief. He must be in his room, unless he's gone
down for a pint. I've left a message for you on your old desk.'

The message referred to a telephone call received about three o'clock:

Please inform Superintendent Mongrel that on Monday of last week Bernadette Amorelle sent for her solicitor to draw up her will. He is Maître Ballu, presumably living in Paris.

The switchboard girl did not know exactly where the call had come from. She had only heard an operator on the line saying: 'Are you there, Corbeil? I'm putting you through to Paris.'

It must therefore have come from Orsenne or thereabouts.

'It was a woman's voice. I may be wrong, but I got the impression that it was somebody who wasn't used to telephoning.'

'Find out from the Corbeil exchange where the call came from.'

He went in to see Torrence, who was busy writing a report.

'I made the enquiries you asked for, Chief. I tried a dozen clubs, but found no trace of Ernest Malik except in a couple of them, the Haussmann and the Sporting. Malik still goes there from time to time, but far less regularly than he used to. Apparently he's a first class poker player. He never goes near the baccarat table. Just poker and écarté. He seldom loses. At the Sporting Club I was lucky enough to come across an old attendant who knew him some thirty years ago.

'While he was still a student Malik was one of the best poker players in the Latin quarter. The old fellow, who'd been a waiter at *La Source* in those days, declares that he made all his money from cards.

'He'd settle on a figure beyond which he would never go. As soon as he'd won a certain sum he had enough self-control to step out, which made him unpopular with other players.'

'Do you know a lawyer called Ballu?'

'I seem to have heard the name. Wait a moment.'

He leafed through a directory.

'Batin ... Babert ... Bailly ... Ballu ... 75 Quai Voltaire. Just across the way!'

Oddly enough, this lawyer business annoyed the Superintendent. He did not like being diverted by the sudden introduction of a fresh trail, and he felt inclined to disregard it.

The switchboard informed him that the call had come from the call box of Seine-Port, five kilometres from Orsenne. The post-mistress at Seine-Port, questioned by telephone, said that the caller had been a woman of between twenty-five and thirty, but knew nothing more about her.

'I didn't look at her closely, because the mailbags were just being collected. What? More like a working-class woman ... Yes! Possibly a servant.'

Might not Malik have been capable of getting one of the maids to telephone for him?

Maigret went to call on Maître Ballu, whose office was closed but who agreed to see him. He was very old, almost as old as Bernadette Amorelle herself. His lips were stained yellow with nicotine, he spoke in a weak hoarse voice, and then held out a tortoise-shell ear-trumpet to his interlocutor.

'Amorelle! Yes, I hear you. She's an old friend, indeed! Dating back from ... wait a minute ... It was before the Exhibition of 1900 that her husband came to see me about some property deal. A strange man! I remember asking him whether he was connected with the Amorelles of Geneva, an old Protestant family ...'

He readily admitted that he had, in fact, visited Orsenne on Monday of the previous week. Yes, indeed, he had helped Berna-dette Amorelle draw up a fresh will. About that will itself he could obviously say nothing. It was there, in his old-fashioned safe.

Had there been other wills before this one? Maybe ten, maybe more? Yes, his old friend had a passion for making wills, a very in-nocent passion, surely?

Was Monita Malik mentioned in this latest will? The solicitor was very sorry, but he could say nothing about that. Professional secrecy!

'She's sound in mind and limb, mark my word! I'm sure that this isn't her final will and that I shall have the pleasure of going to see her again.'

So Monita had died twenty-four hours after the solicitor's visit to Orsenne. Was there any connection between the two events?

Why on earth had anyone taken the trouble to complicate things for him with this new story?

He walked along the quayside. He was on his way home to dine in the company of his wife, Georges-Henry and Mimile. From the Pont de la Cité he saw a tugboat sailing upstream with its five or six barges. One of Amorelle and Campois's tugboats. At the same moment there passed a big yellow taxi of an up-to-date model, almost new, and these unimportant details probably influenced Maigret's decision.

Without pausing to think, he raised his arm. The taxi drew up beside the curb.

'Have you enough petrol for a long drive?'

Possibly if the taxi's tank had not been full...

'The Fontainebleau road. After Corbeil I'll direct you.'

He had not dined, but he'd had a rather late lunch. He stopped the taxi in front of a tobacconist's and bought a packet of shag and some matches.

It was a mild evening and the taxi was an open car. He had sat beside the driver, possibly with the intention of making conversation. But he scarcely opened his mouth.

'Left, now.'

'You're going to Orsenne?'

'You know the place?'

'Years ago I drove some customers to the Angel.'

'We're going farther. Keep on along the towpath. It's not this villa nor the next. Just keep on.'

They had to take a little lane on the right to reach Campois's house, which was invisible from outside, being completely surrounded by walls and, instead of an iron gate, there was a solid door painted pale green.

'Wait for me!'

'I've plenty of time. I'd just had my dinner when you hailed me.'

Maigret pulled the bell and heard a pleasant tinkle in the garden, sounding like the bell of a priest's house. Two old stone posts stood on either side of the gateway, and a small door had been inserted on one side.

It was not late, just after eight o'clock. Maigret rang again and this time steps were heard approaching on the gravel; an old servant woman in a blue apron turned a heavy key in the lock, opened the small door a crack and looked at Maigret suspiciously.

'What do you want?'

He caught a glimpse of a sort of cottage garden, densely planted with humble flowers, and full of surprising nooks and corners and of weeds.

'I'd like to speak to Monsieur Campois.'

'He's gone away.'

She was about to close the door, but he had thrust his foot forward to prevent her.

'Can you tell me where I can get hold of him?'

Did she know who Maigret was through having seen him at Orsenne?

'You won't be able to get hold of him. Monsieur Campois is travelling abroad.'

'For a long time?'

'For six weeks at least.'

'Forgive me for insisting, but it's about something very important. Can I write to him, at any rate?'

'You can write to him if you like, but I doubt whether he'll get your letters before he comes back. Monsieur is going for a cruise to Norway on the *Stella Polaris*.'

Just at that moment Maigret heard in the garden, behind the house, the sound of a car engine sputtering as it was started up.

'You're sure he's left already?'

'Didn't I tell you...'

'And his grandson?'

'He's taking Monsieur Jean with him.'

Maigret pushed open the door, not without difficulty, since the maid was pushing it hard the other way.

'What's the matter with you? What a way to behave!'

'The matter with me is that I'm sure Monsieur Campois hasn't left yet.'

'That's his own business. He doesn't want to see anyone.'

'He'll see me, though.'

'Will you please get out, you ill-mannered creature!'

Having shaken her off and left her to close the door carefully behind him, he went through the garden and found an unpretentious pink house, with rose trees clambering all round the green-shuttered windows.

As he looked up he saw an open window from which a man was looking down at him with an air of great alarm.

It was Monsieur Campois, partner of the late Amorelle.

Luggage was standing in the wide entrance hall, whose coolness was pervaded by a pleasant smell of ripening fruit, and where the old servant now joined him.

'Since Monsieur has told you to come in,' she grumbled. And she reluctantly opened the door of a drawing room which resembled the waiting room of a convent; in one corner, beside a window with half-closed shutters, there stood one of those old black desks that recall old-fashioned business premises of the sort where, amid green filing cabinets, clerks used to sit perched on high stools, with leather pads under their backsides and eyeshades on their foreheads.

'You can just wait! Too bad if he misses his boat.'

The walls were lined with faded paper against which photographs in black or gilt frames stood out. There was the inevitable wedding portrait of a plump-faced Campois with crew-cut hair, and, leaning against his shoulder, the head of a woman with full lips and a gentle, sheepish look in her eyes.

Immediately on the right was that of a young man of about twenty, whose face was a longer oval than that of his parents but who had his mother's gentle eyes and an equal timidity in his pose. And under that frame was a bow of black crepe.

Maigret was just going up to a piano loaded with photographs when the door opened. Campois stood in the doorway, and Maigret thought he looked smaller and older than the first time he had seen him.

He was a very old man already, in spite of his square shoulders and his peasant sturdiness.

'I know who you are,' he said without preamble. 'I could not refuse to receive you, but I have nothing to say to you. I'm setting off in a few moments for a long voyage.'

'Where do you embark from, Monsieur Campois?'

'The cruise starts from Le Havre.'

'You're probably taking the 10.22 train to Paris? You shall catch it.'

'You must excuse me, but my packing is not finished, and besides I have not had dinner. I tell you I have absolutely nothing to say to you.'

What was he frightened of? For he was visibly frightened. He was dressed in black, with a black tie, and his pale face stood out sharply in the semi-darkness of the room. He had left the door open, as though to show that the conversation was to be a brief one, and he did not invite his visitor to sit down.

'Have you been on many such cruises?'

'Well...'

Was he going to lie? He obviously wanted to. He gave the impression of needing somebody beside him to prompt his reply. His innate honesty got the upper hand. He did not know how to lie. He admitted:

'This is the first time.'

'And you're seventy-five years old?'

'Seventy-seven!'

Maigret felt he must stake everything. The poor man was not strong enough to defend himself very long, and his timid glance showed that he anticipated defeat and perhaps was already resigned to it.

'I'm sure, Monsieur Campois, that three months ago you knew nothing whatever about this trip. I'm willing to bet, indeed, that you're a bit scared of it. The Norwegian fjords, at your age!'

He stammered, as though repeating a lesson:

'I've always wanted to visit Norway.'

'But you hadn't thought of doing so this month! Somebody thought of that for you, didn't they?'

'I don't know what you mean. My grandson and I...'

'Your grandson must have been as surprised as yourself. It doesn't matter, for the moment, who organized this cruise for you. By the way, do you know where the tickets were taken?'

He knew nothing about it, as his bewildered look proclaimed. His role had been laid down for him. But there were incidents that had not been foreseen, such as Maigret's untimely intrusion, and the poor man did not know which way to turn.

'Listen, Superintendent, I must repeat that I've nothing to say. I'm in my own home. I'm going off on a journey presently. You'll admit that I have a right to ask you to leave me alone.'

'I have come to talk to you about your son.'

As he had foreseen, old Campois became agitated, turned pale, and cast a look of distress at his son's portrait.

'I've nothing to say to you,' he repeated, clinging to the phrase which no longer had any meaning.

Maigret listened attentively, for he had caught a slight sound in the passage. Campois must have heard it too, and he went to the door to say:

'You can leave us, Eugénie. The luggage can be put into the car. I'm coming very soon.'

This time he closed the door and went mechanically to sit down at the desk which must have accompanied him throughout his long career. Maigret, unasked, took a seat in front of him.

'Monsieur Campois, I've given a great deal of thought to the death of your son.'

'Why have you come to speak to me about that?'

'You know very well. Last week a young girl whom you know died in similar circumstances. And a short while ago I left behind me a boy who came very close to suffering the same fate. It was your fault, wasn't it?'

'My fault?' he protested vehemently.

'Yes, Monsieur Campois! And you're well aware of that, too. Perhaps you're unwilling to admit it, but in your innermost heart...'

'You've no right to come into my house and say such monstrous things. All my life I've been an honest man.'

But Maigret did not leave him time to indulge in protestations.

'Where did Ernest Malik make your son's acquaintance?'

The old man passed his hand over his brow.

'I don't know.'

'Were you already living at Orsenne?'

'No. At that time I was living in Paris, on the Ile Saint-Louis. We had a big apartment above the firm's offices, which were smaller then than they are now.'

'Did your son work in the office?'

'Yes. He had just got his degree in law.'

'Were the Amorelles already living at Orsenne?'

'Yes, they were the first to come here. Bernadette was a very restless woman, and she loved entertaining. There were always young people around her. On Sundays she invited a great many friends to their country place. My son used to go there too.'

'Was he in love with the elder Amorelle girl?'

'They were engaged.'

'And did Mademoiselle Laurence love him?'

'I don't know. I suppose so. Why do you ask me that? After all these years...'

He would have liked to escape from the sort of spell under which the Superintendent held him. The room was growing darker now and the photographs were staring at them with dead eyes. Mechanically, the old man had picked up a meerschaum pipe with a long cherrywood stem, but he made no effort to fill it.

'How old was Mademoiselle Laurence at this time?'

'I don't know. I'd have to reckon. Wait a minute...'

He mumbled some dates half-heartedly, as though telling his beads. He wore a worried frown. Perhaps he was still hoping that someone would come and deliver him?

'She must have been seventeen.'

'So her younger sister, Mademoiselle Aimée, would have been barely fifteen?'

'That must be right, yes. I've forgotten.'

'And your son made the acquaintance of Ernest Malik, who, if I'm not mistaken, was then private secretary to a local councillor. It was through that councillor that he himself had got to know the Amorelles. He was a brilliant young man.'

'Very likely...'

'He became your son's friend and, under his influence, your son's character altered?'

'He was a good, gentle lad,' the father protested.

'He took up gambling and ran into debt...'

'I didn't know.'

'His debts became ever larger and more pressing, so that one day he was driven to shady expedients...'

'He'd have been wiser to tell me everything.'

'Are you sure you'd have understood?'

The old man hung his head, admitting:

'Perhaps, at that time, I'd...'

'Perhaps you would not have understood, you would have thrown him out. If he'd told you for instance that he'd taken money from your partner's till, or forged entries, or...'

'Be quiet!'

'He chose rather to disappear. Perhaps because someone had advised him to disappear? Perhaps...'

Campois hid his anguished face in his hands.

'But why have you come to tell me all this today? What are you hoping for? What are you aiming at?'

'Admit, Monsieur Campois, that at that time you thought what I am thinking today.'

'I don't know what you are thinking... I don't want to know!'

'Even if at the time of your son's death you did not immediately become suspicious, you must have begun to wonder when a few months later you saw Ernest Malik marrying Mademoiselle Amorelle. You see what I mean, don't you?'

'I could do nothing about it.'

'And you were present at the wedding?'

'I had to be. I was Amorelle's friend and partner. He had taken a fancy to Ernest Malik and nobody else counted.'

'So you held your tongue.'

'I had an unmarried daughter for whom I had to find a husband.'

Maigret stood up, a heavy, menacing figure, and cast a look of concentrated anger on the dejected old man.

'And for years and years you...'

His voice, which had grown louder, softened again as he looked at the face of the old man whose eyes were brimming with tears.

'But after all,' he went on in an almost anguished tone, 'you always knew what sort of fellow Malik was, and how he'd caused the death of your son.

'And you said nothing! You went on shaking him by the hand, and you bought this house close to his! And even today, you're ready to do what he tells you!'

'What else could I have done?'

'Because he'd practically reduced you to poverty. Because, by heaven knows how many cunning contrivances, he'd succeeded in robbing you of most of your shares. Because you're nothing but a name now in the firm of Amorelle and Campois. Because...'

And his fist crashed down on the desk.

'But damn it! Don't you realize that you're a coward, that it's because of you that Monita died in the same way as your son and that a boy, Georges-Henry, came close to following their example?'

'I've got my daughter and my grandson. I'm an old man.'

'You weren't old when your son killed himself. But even then you were fond enough of your money, though you were incapable of safeguarding it from a man like Malik!'

It was almost dark now, in the long room, but neither of the two men thought of putting on the light.

The old man, obviously in the grip of fear, asked in a low, muffled voice:

'What are you going to do?'

'And you?'

Campois seemed to cower.

'Are you still planning to leave for this cruise against your will? Haven't you understood that you're being got rid of post-haste, as weak people are got rid of at crucial moments? When was this cruise planned?'

'Malik came to see me yesterday morning. I didn't want to go, but I had to give in at last.'

'What pretext did he choose?'

'That you were trying to make trouble for us over business matters. That it would be better if I was out of the way.'

'And you believed him?'

The old man did not reply, but presently went on wearily:

'He's been here three times already today. He upset the whole household making sure I should get off. Half an hour before you came he rang up again to remind me it was time.'

'Are you still anxious to go?'

'I think it would be better, considering what may be going to happen. But I might stop at Le Havre. It depends on my grandson. He was very fond of Monita. I think he had some secret hopes in that direction. He was very much upset by her death.'

The old man suddenly got up and rushed to the telephone, an old-fashioned instrument fastened to the wall. The bell had rung out sharply, calling him to order.

'Hello! Yes... The luggage is in the car. I'm leaving in five minutes... Yes... Yes... No... No... It wasn't for me... Probably...'

He hung up, and cast a somewhat shamefaced glance at Maigret.

'That was him! I'd better go.'

'What did he want to know?'

'Whether anyone had come to see me. He'd seen a taxi go past. I told him...'

'I heard.'

'Can I go?'

What was the point of keeping him back? He had worked hard, once. He had pulled himself up by his own efforts. He had acquired an enviable position.

And then he had been scared, scared of losing his money, scared of the poverty he had known as a child. He was still scared now, at the close of his life.

'Eugénie, is the luggage in the car?'

'But you've had no dinner!'

'I'll eat something on the way. Where is Jean?'

'He's by the car.'

'Goodbye, Superintendent. Don't tell anyone you've seen me. If you keep on down the lane and turn left when you see a stone cross, you'll come to the main road three kilometres from here. There's a tunnel underneath the railway line.'

Maigret walked slowly through the peaceful garden, while the old cook stalked grimly behind him. The taxi driver was sitting in the grass, playing with wild flowers. Before getting back into the car he stuck one behind his ear, as gangsters do with their cigarettes.

'Back the same way?'

'Straight on,' growled Maigret, lighting his pipe. 'Then left when you come to a cross.'

Soon they heard, in the darkness, the engine of another car going in the opposite direction, taking old Campois out of harm's way.

8
The Skeleton in the Cupboard

As though to foster his ill-humour, he made the taxi stop in front of a poorly-lit bistro in Corbeil and ordered two glasses of marc, one for the driver and the other for himself.

The harsh taste of the brandy burnt the back of his throat, and he reflected that marc had been the presiding influence over this whole enquiry. Why? Pure chance. It was probably his least favourite drink. But there had also been old Jeanne's revolting kümmel, and the recollection of his tête à tête with the blowsy old alcoholic still made him feel queasy.

And yet she had once been goodlooking. She had loved Malik, who had made use of her as he made use of anyone who came near him. And now she felt a strange mixture of love and hatred, resentment and animal devotion for this man, who had only to appear and give her orders.

There are some people like that in the world. There are others, like the two other customers in the little bar, the only two at this late hour, one fat man who was a pork butcher, and one thin man, sly, pontifical, proud of being a clerk in some office, possibly in the town hall—the pair of them playing draughts together, at ten o'clock at night, beside a big stove against which the pork butcher leaned back from time to time.

The pork butcher was self-confident because he had money and he didn't mind losing the game. The thin man felt that the world was out of joint because an educated intellectual ought to have an easier life than someone who slaughters pigs.

'Another marc...sorry, two marcs!'

Campois was now on his way to the Gare Saint-Lazare with his grandson. He must be feeling pretty sick, too. He was probably recalling Maigret's harsh words, as well as certain bygone memories.

He was off to Le Havre. He was being dispatched to the Norwegian fjords very nearly against his will, like a parcel, because Malik...And he was already a very old man. It was distressing to have to tell anyone as old as that the sort of truths that Maigret had told him.

They drove off again. The Superintendent, in his corner of the car, was sullen and gloomy.

Bernadette Amorelle was an even older woman. And what Maigret did not know, could not know because he was not God Almighty, was that she had seen old Campois go past in his car with all his luggage.

She, too, had understood. Perhaps she was even shrewder than Maigret. There are some women, old women in particular, who have a real gift of second sight.

If Maigret had been there, on the railway line for instance, as on the two previous evenings, he would have seen her three windows wide open, with the light on, and in that rosy glow he would have seen the old woman summoning her lady's maid.

'He's sent old Campois away, Mathilde.'

He would not have heard, but he might have seen the two women talking at great length, a sharp-tongued pair, then he would have seen Mathilde disappear and Madame Amorelle moving about her bedroom, until finally her daughter Aimée, Charles Malik's wife, came in with a guilty look.

The drama was about to break out. It had been brewing for over twenty years. For the last few days, since Monita's death, it had been on the verge of exploding at any moment.

'Stop here!'

Right in the middle of the Pont d'Austerlitz. He did not want to go home right away. The Seine was black. There were little lights shining on the sleeping barges, and shadowy figures prowling about the quays.

Maigret walked along slowly, smoking, hands in pockets, along the deserted streets with their strings of lamps.

In the Place de la Bastille, at the corner of the Rue de la Roquette, there were sharper, more dazzling lights, with that livid brightness which is the luxury of the poorer districts—like certain fairground booths where you play for such prizes as packets of sugar or bottles of pop—the lights that are probably necessary to make people leave their dark, close little streets.

He, too, went towards those lights, towards the huge half empty café where an accordeon was playing and where a few men and a few women were drinking while they waited for something or other.

He knew them. He had spent so many years probing people's affairs that he knew them all, even people like Malik who thought themselves stronger or more cunning than the rest.

With such men, one had a difficult moment to go through, the moment when in spite of oneself one is impressed by their fine houses, their cars, their servants, their manners.

One must come to see them like the rest, naked and unadorned...

Now Ernest Malik was frightened, as frightened as some petty pimp from the Rue de la Roquette picked up in a police raid at two in the morning and taken away in a Black Maria...

Maigret did not witness the touching scene between the two women in Bernadette's room. He did not see Charles's wife Aimée fall on her knees and crawl across the floor to her mother's feet.

Not that it mattered. Every family has, as the English say, its skeleton in the cupboard.

Two fine houses over there beside the river, at a bend which made it seem wider and more delightful, two fine gracious houses amid greenery, between gently sloping hills, the sort of house you look at through the windows of your train with a sigh of envy. How happy their inhabitants ought to be!

He thought of the long lives of people like Campois, who had worked so hard and was now being shunted off into a siding. And of Bernadette Amorelle who had displayed so much frenzied energy.

He walked on, angrily. The Place des Vosges was deserted. There was a light in his own windows. He rang, growled out his name as he passed the concierge's lodge. His wife, recognizing his step, came to open the door.

'Hush! He's asleep. He's only just dropped off.'

And what then? Couldn't he wake him up, take him by the shoulders and shake him?

'Come on, young man, we can't have you making a fuss now.'

He wanted to have done, once and for all, with that skeleton in the cupboard, that revolting business in which, from beginning to end, money was the only motive.

For that's what lay behind those fine houses with their well-kept parks: filthy lucre!

'You seem in a bad temper. Have you had dinner?'

'Yes . . . No.'

In fact he had had no dinner, and so he ate while Mimile stood at the window enjoying the fresh air and smoking cigarettes. When he went towards the room where Georges-Henry lay sleeping, Madame Maigret protested:

'You oughtn't to wake him up.'

He shrugged his shoulders. A few hours more or less . . . Let him sleep! Not to mention the fact that he, too, was sleepy.

He did not know what dramatic events were to take place that night.

He could not guess that Bernadette Amorelle would go out into the darkness all alone and that her younger daughter, Aimée, wild-eyed, would try in vain to telephone, while Charles, at her back, kept saying:

'But what's come over you? What has your mother been telling you?'

Maigret did not wake until eight next morning.

'He's still asleep,' his wife told him.

Maigret shaved and dressed, had his breakfast at a corner of the table and filled his first pipe. When he entered the boy's room, the sleeper was beginning to stir.

'Get up,' Maigret said to him in that quiet, rather weary voice that he assumed when he had decided to have done with something.

It took him a few moments to understand why the boy dared not get out of bed. It was because he was naked under the sheets and felt ashamed to show himself.

'Stay in bed if you like. You can get dressed by and by. How did you discover what your father had done? Was it Monita who told you?'

Georges-Henry was staring at him with genuine terror.

'You may as well talk, now that I know . . .'

'What do you know? Who told you?'

'Old Campois knew too.'

'Are you sure? That's not possible. If he'd known . . .'

'That your father had killed his son. Only he did not kill him with a knife or a gun. And that sort of crime . . .'

'What else have you been told? What have you done?'

'Why, there are so many beastly things about this business that one more or less . . .'

He felt nauseated. This was often the case when he came to the end of an investigation, perhaps because of the nervous tension, perhaps because when you uncover human nature it's liable to be ugly and depressing.

A pleasant smell of coffee pervaded the flat. Birdsong and the splash of fountains sounded from the Place des Vosges. People were going off to their jobs in the fresh, sparkling morning sunlight.

In front of him lay a pale boy cowering under a sheet and staring fixedly at him.

What could Maigret do for him or for the rest of them? Nothing! You cannot stop a Malik. Justice does not deal with that sort of crime. There would only have been one solution . . .

It was odd that he should have thought of that just before the telephone call. He was standing there, sucking his pipe, embarrassed by the presence of the bewildered boy, and he had for a moment the vision of Ernest Malik being presented with a gun and calmly ordered to shoot himself.

But Malik would not shoot! He would not consent to kill himself! He would have to be helped to do so.

The telephone bell rang insistently through the flat. Madame Maigret answered the call and knocked at the door.

'It's for you, Maigret.'

He went into the dining room and picked up the receiver.

'Maigret here . . .'

'That you, Chief? This is Lucas. When I reached Headquarters I found an important message for you from Orsenne, yes . . . Last night Madame Amorelle . . .'

Probably nobody would have believed him if he had claimed that, from that moment, he knew. And yet it was true.

She had taken roughly the same route as himself and had reached the same conclusions, almost at the same time. Only she had carried the thing through to the end.

And since she knew that Malik would not fire, she had quite calmly fired herself.

'. . . Madame Amorelle shot Ernest Malik with a revolver, in his own house . . . in his study. He was in pyjamas and dressing gown. The local *gendarmerie* rang us up at the first opportunity and wanted us to inform you, for she's asked to see you . . .'

'I'll go,' he said.

He went back into the bedroom. The lad was now wearing his trousers, but his thin torso was bare.

'Your father is dead,' he announced, averting his eyes.

There was a silence. He turned round. Georges-Henry was not crying, but standing motionless, looking at him.

'Did he kill himself?'

So there were not just two but three of them who had thought of the same solution. Who knows whether the boy had not at some point been tempted to use the weapon himself?

There was nevertheless a vestige of incredulity in his voice as he asked:

'Did he kill himself?'

'No. It was your grandmother.'

'Who told her?'

He bit his lip.

'Who told her what?'

'What you know . . . Campois?'

'No, my boy. That's not what you were thinking of . . .'

And he knew that he was right, because the boy was blushing.

'There's something else, isn't there? It was not because your father once drove young Campois to commit suicide that Bernadette Amorelle shot him down.'

He walked to and fro. He could have persisted. He would have got the better of an adversary who was so much weaker than himself.

'Stay here,' he said finally.

He fetched his hat from the dining room.

'Keep an eye on him still,' he said to his wife and to Mimile, who was now having his breakfast.

The weather was radiant, the air so fragrant in its morning freshness that one wanted to bite it like a fruit.

'Taxi . . . The Fontainebleau road. I'll direct you.'

There were three or four cars on the towpath, probably from the Public Prosecutor's department. A few inquisitive onlookers in front of the gate, now guarded by an apathetic gendarme. He saluted Maigret, who went up along the path and presently climbed up the terrace steps.

The Superintendent of the Security Police of Melun was already there, his hat on his head and a cigar between his lips.

'Glad to see you again, Maigret . . . I didn't know you were back at work. Curious business this, eh? She's expecting you. She refuses to speak until she's seen you. It was she herself who rang up the gendarmerie about 1 a.m. to say that she'd just killed her son-in-law.

'You'll see her. She's as calm as if she had just been making jam or tidying cupboards. In fact she spent the night putting her things in order and when I arrived her suitcase was packed.'

'Where are the others?'

'Her second son-in-law, Charles, is in the drawing room with his wife. The Deputy Public Prosecutor and the examining magistrate are questioning them. They declare they know nothing about it, that the old lady had been acting strangely for some time past.'

Maigret stumped up the staircase and, uncharacteristically, he emptied his pipe and put it into his pocket before knocking at the door, which was guarded by a second gendarme. It was a very simple gesture, and yet it seemed a sort of tribute paid to Bernadette Amorelle.

'Who's there?'

'Superintendent Maigret.'

'Let him come in.'

She had been left alone there with her maid, and when Maigret entered she was sitting at a pretty little desk writing a letter.

'It's for my solicitor,' she said by way of apology. 'Would you leave us, Mathilde.'

The sunlight was pouring in through the three windows, into the room where the old woman had spent so many years. There was a joyful gleam in her eyes and even—very incongruously—a sort of childish mischievousness.

She was pleased with herself. She was proud of what she had done. She assumed a somewhat mocking attitude towards this clumsy Superintendent who could never have seen the thing through as she had done.

'There was no other solution, was there?' she said. 'Sit down. You know I detest talking to people when they're standing up.'

Then, standing up herself, blinking slightly because of the dazzling sunlight:

'Yesterday evening, when I finally got Aimée to confess everything...'

On hearing the name of Aimée, Charles Malik's wife, Maigret unfortunately gave a slight start. The old lady was as shrewd as himself and she understood.

'I might have guessed you didn't know that. Where is Georges-Henry?'

'At my place, with my wife.'

'In your house at Meung?'

She smiled as she remembered the Maigret whom she had taken for a servant when she had gone through the little green door to find him in his garden.

'In Paris, in my flat in the Place des Vosges.'

'Does he know?'

'I told him before I came here.'

'What did he say?'

'Nothing, he's quite calm.'

'Poor child! I wonder how he found the courage not to speak. Don't you think it's funny to be going to prison at my age? Anyhow, these gentlemen have been very kind. To begin with they didn't want to believe me. They thought I was accusing myself to shield somebody else. They almost required me to prove my guilt.

'It all went off very well. I don't know exactly what time it was. I had my revolver in my handbag. I went over there. There was a light on, up on the first floor. I rang. Malik looked out of the window and asked me what I wanted...

'"To speak to you," I said.

'I'm certain he was frightened. He asked me to come back next day, declared that he was unwell, that he was suffering from neuralgia.

'"If you don't come down at once," I shouted to him, "I shall have you arrested."

'He came down eventually, in pyjamas and dressing gown. Have you seen him?'

'Not yet.'

'I insisted: "Let's go into your study. Where's your wife?"

'"In bed. I think she's asleep."

'"So much the better."

'"Don't you think, maman, that this conversation had better be put off till tomorrow?"

'And do you know what I replied? "That won't do you much good. A few hours more or less..."

'He was trying to understand. He was as cold as a fish. I've always said he reminded me of a fish—of a pike—but they only laughed at me.

'He opened the door of his study.

'"Sit down," he told me.

'"There's no point."

'Did he guess what I was going to do? I'm convinced he did. The proof is that he automatically glanced at the drawer of his desk where he keeps his revolver. If I'd given him time he'd surely have defended himself and he'd probably have fired first.

'"Listen to me, Malik," I went on. "I know about all your filthy doings. Roger is dead (Roger was Campois's son), your daughter is dead, your son..."'

At the words *your daughter* Maigret's eyes widened. He had understood at last, and he stared at the old woman with an astonishment that he no longer sought to conceal.

'"Since there's no other way out and nobody has the courage to do the job, it may as well be left to an old grandmother. Goodbye, Malik."

'And as I said that I fired. He was three yards away from me. He put his hands to his stomach, for I'd fired too low. I pressed the trigger again, twice.

'He fell, and Laurence rushed in like a madwoman.

'"That's done," I said. "Now we shall be able to breathe freely."

'Poor Laurence, I believe it was a relief for her too. Aimée was the only person who wept for him.

'"Call a doctor if you like, but I don't think there's much point," I went on. "He's well and truly dead. And if he weren't I'd finish him off with a bullet through the head. Now I'd advise you to come and spend the night in our house. No point in waking the servants."

'We went off together. Aimée rushed out to meet us, while Charles stood in the doorway, looking shifty.

'"What have you done, maman? Why is Laurence...?"

'I told Aimée what I had done. She had almost expected it after the conversation we had had in my room. Charles dared not open his lips. He followed us about like a great dog.

'I came back here and I rang up the police. They behaved very decently.'

'So,' murmured Maigret after a pause, 'it was Aimée.'

'I'm just an old fool, for I ought to have guessed. About Roger

Campois, for instance, I'd always suspected something. At any rate that it was Malik who had made a gambler of him.

'To think that I was glad, at the time, to have him as a son-in-law! He was more brilliant than the others. He had the art of amusing me. My husband's tastes were those of a petty bourgeois, even of a peasant, and it was Malik who showed us how to live. He took us to Deauville, for instance; before I met him I'd never set foot in a casino, and I remember it was he who gave me the first counters for roulette.

'He married Laurence...'

'Because Aimée was too young, wasn't she? Because she was only fifteen at that time? If Aimée had been two years older, Roger Campois might not have died. He would have married the elder sister and Malik the younger.'

People could be heard coming and going down below. Through the windows they could see a group moving towards Malik's villa, where his body still lay.

'Aimée really loved him,' sighed Madame Amorelle. 'She still loves him, in spite of everything. She hates me now because of what I did last night.'

The skeleton in the cupboard! If Roger's body had been the only skeleton in that symbolic cupboard!

'When did he think of sending for his brother to marry your younger daughter?'

'About two years after his own marriage. How naive I was! I could see that Aimée was interested only in her brother-in-law, that she was far more in love than her sister. Strangers misunderstood the position and when we were all together she was the one, in spite of her youth, whom they called *Madame*.

'Laurence was not jealous. She noticed nothing, she was content to live in her husband's shadow; his personality overshadowed her.'

'So Monita was Ernest Malik's daughter?'

'I learnt that yesterday. But there are other things that, old as I am, I would rather not know.'

The brother who had been fetched from Lyon, where he was earning a pittance, to marry a rich heiress—did he know, at the time?

He probably did; he was a humble, spineless fellow. He got married because he was told to get married. He provided a screen! In return for playing the role of husband he would share the Malik fortune with his brother.

And so Ernest had two wives, and a child in each of the two houses.

This was what Monita had discovered. This was what had overwhelmed her with disgust and led her to drown herself.

'I don't know exactly how she discovered the truth, but I've had my suspicions since yesterday evening. Last week I sent for the lawyer to change my will.'

'Maître Ballu, I know...'

'I'd been on bad terms with the Maliks for some time, and oddly enough, Charles was the one I hated most. I don't know why... He seemed to me shifty. I was inclined to think him worse than his brother.

'I wanted to disinherit them both and leave all my fortune to Monita.

'That same evening, as Aimée admitted to me during the scene that took place between us, Ernest came to see Charles to discuss the matter.

'They were alarmed about this new will, the terms of which they did not know. They remained a long time together in Charles's study on the ground floor. Aimée had gone up to bed. It was not until much later, when her husband finally came upstairs, that she observed:

'"Hasn't Monita come in?"

'"What makes you say that?"

'"She didn't come to say goodnight to me as usual."

'Charles went into the girl's bedroom. There was nobody there and the bed had not been disturbed. He came down again and found Monita in the boudoir, pale and ice-cold in the darkness.

'"What are you doing here?"'

She looked as if she hadn't heard him, apparently. She agreed to go upstairs, however.

'I am convinced now that she had overheard everything. She

knew. And next morning, before anyone was up, she went out as
though for a swim, which she often did.

'Only she did not swim.'

'And she'd found time to speak to her cousin...that cousin
whom she loved and who is in fact her brother.'

There came a timid knock at the door. Bernadette Amorelle went
to open it and found herself confronted by the Superintendent
from Melun.

'The car's downstairs,' he announced, somewhat ill at ease, since
this was the first time in his career that he had had to arrest a
woman of eighty-two.

'In five minutes,' she replied, as though addressing one of her
manservants. 'We've still got something to say to one another, my
friend Maigret and I.'

Then she came back and said to Maigret, displaying amazing
self-control:

'Why haven't you been smoking your pipe? You know you may. I
went to fetch you. I didn't know what was being plotted. I wondered at first whether Monita hadn't perhaps been killed because
I'd made her my heir. I confess to you—but that doesn't concern
the police, there are things that don't concern them—that I wasn't
sure they didn't intend to poison me. There you are, Superintendent. There remains the boy. I'm glad you're looking after him, for
I'm firmly convinced he would have come to the same end as
Monita.

'Put yourself in their shoes...At that age, to discover all of a
sudden...

'For the boy, it was even worse. He tried to find out. Boys are
more enterprising than girls. He knew his father kept his private
papers in a little desk in his bedroom, the key of which he always
carried about with him.

'He forced it open the day after Monita's death. I learnt that
from Aimée. Ernest Malik kept her informed of everything; he
knew that he could depend on her, that she was his slave or worse.

'Malik noticed that his desk had been forced and he immediately
suspected his son.'

'What documents can he have discovered?' asked Maigret with a sigh.

'I burned them during the night. I told Laurence to go and fetch them, but she dared not go back into the house where her husband's body lay.

'Aimée went.

'There were letters from her, and little notes they used to send one another in this very house to arrange meetings.

'There were receipts signed by Roger Campois. Not only did Malik lend him money so as to corrupt him more thoroughly, but he arranged for usurers to do so and then bought back the bills himself.

'He kept everything.'

With a contemptuous curl of the lip:

'After all, he had a bookkeeper's spirit!'

She did not understand why Maigret corrected her, as he rose with an effort:

'A tax collector's!'

He himself saw her into the car, and she put out her arm through the window to grasp his hand.

'You're not too angry with me?' she asked as the police car started up to take her to prison.

And he never knew whether she was referring to the fact of having snatched him, for a few days, from his peaceful retreat at Meung-sur-Loire, or to the revolver shot.

There had been a skeleton in the cupboard for many years, and it was the old lady who had undertaken to clean things up, like one of those grandmothers who cannot bear having any dirt about the house.

4 August 1945